TWILIGHT

Condemned for a [...]
MacGreggor approac[...]
ened yet unbowed. But with a word, her
young life will be spared—if she agrees to
wed the despised enemy who destroyed her
stepfather on the field of battle.

SHAWNEE MOON

When his Shawnee mother died, handsome
half-breed Sterling Gray left the noble tribe
that raised him—and crossed an ocean to become a British soldier and a gentleman. Now
he is returning to his homeland with a
breathtaking new bride—a Scottish hellion
wearing an ancient Celtic necklace, whom he
rescued from the hangman's noose. And
though his very presence inflames Cailin's
heart with vengeful fire, Sterling knows the
dangerous beauty is his destiny—a love foretold in mystic visions that he must risk his
passion, his pride, and his future to win.

Praise for THIS FIERCE LOVING
★★★★★
"Judith French has penned a wonderful novel
that will hold you captive
from first word to last . . .
should be on everyone's
want list this fall."
Affaire de Coeur

JUDITH E. FRENCH

SHAWNEE MOON

An Avon Romantic Treasure

AVON BOOKS ◆ NEW YORK

SHAWNEE MOON is an original publication of Avon Books. This work has never before appeared in book form. This work is a novel. Any similarity to actual persons or events is purely coincidental.

AVON BOOKS
A division of
The Hearst Corporation
1350 Avenue of the Americas
New York, New York 10019

Copyright © 1995 by Judith E. French
Inside cover author photo by Jeff Fasano
Published by arrangement with the author
Library of Congress Catalog Card Number: 94-96557
ISBN: 0-380-77705-3

First Avon Books Printing: June 1995

AVON TRADEMARK REG. U.S. PAT. OFF. AND IN OTHER COUNTRIES, MARCA REGISTRADA, HECHO EN U.S.A.

Printed in the U.S.A.

RA   10   9   8   7   6   5   4   3   2   1

For Joyce A. Flaherty, my dear friend and very special agent. Thank you for believing in me and for helping to fulfill a lifetime dream.

... whosoever possesses the Eye of Mist shall be cursed and blessed. The curse is that you will be taken from your family and friends to a far-off land. The blessing is that you will be granted one wish. Whatever you ask you shall have—even unto the power of life and death.

—Cameron Stewart

Chapter 1

Culloden Moor, Scotland
April 16, 1746

Cailin MacGreggor clung to the gray mare's mane as cannon roared and the trembling animal reared and pawed the sky with her muddy front hooves. "Mother of God," Cailin cried. She was lost in the murky depths of hell, while all around her shot flew and steel clashed against steel.

Bagpipes shrilled above the cadence of drums. Wild clan war cries mingled with the shrieks of dying men and the crack of musket fire. Clouds of smoke swirled around her, adding to the confusion of mist and falling rain. The stench of black powder and blood filled her nose; she could taste death in the air. But Cailin's eyes shed no tears—she was shocked past the point of weeping. Not even the realization of her beloved cousin's death could pierce the terror that gripped her.

Cailin wasn't sure how long ago she'd come across Father Tomas kneeling beside a wounded Highlander. The priest had railed at her and had bidden her flee. But flee where? The fog made her uncertain of direction, and she lost sense of time. She thought it must be somewhere near noon, but without the sun or a timepiece, it was impossible to tell.

1

Alasdair was dead. The words echoed in her head, but it was hard to believe. Alasdair's homely freckled face bending down as he seized her by the waist and lifted her high over his head. Alasdair setting her on the back of a fat Shetland pony. Alasdair gripping her hand silently as dirt fell onto the grave of her dead husband.

Alasdair was too full of life to die here on this damp, foggy moor. But Father Tomas had told her that it was so . . . that Alasdair had been killed in the first minutes of the fighting, and that he'd been given the last rites and his sightless eyes had been closed.

Her mare came down hard on her front legs and lowered her head, blowing red-tinged foam from her nostrils. "Steady, Lady! Steady!" Cailin soothed, tightening her hands on the reins. She wanted to dismount and try to lead Lady, but she was afraid that if she got off the horse, she'd lose control of her altogether.

An angry swarm of bees whined over Cailin's head, and the hair rose on the back of her neck. Instinctively, she flung herself forward onto Lady's neck and dug her heels into the gray mare's side. The gallant little horse plunged forward, sinking to her knees in the churned bog.

A man in a red coat staggered into Cailin's line of vision, his mud-smeared face contorted with fear. "Help me!" he cried. But before she could react, a huge kilted warrior struck the British soldier a mighty blow with his claymore, nearly cleaving his head from his body.

Blood splashed across Cailin's gray cloak, and she stifled a scream. The Scot turned slowly and stared at her with glazed eyes. For a second, she believed that he might turn the ghastly weapon on her, and a queer fluttering in the pit of her belly made her light-headed. "For God and Charlie," she whispered.

"Peggie?" the giant Highlander rasped. He swayed on his big feet and shifted the claymore restlessly. He was nearly naked; his hairy bare chest and MacDonnel plaid were streaked with blood. "Peggie?"

"Nay, laddie," she murmured. "I'm nay your Peg." The battle sickness was on him; she could see madness flickering behind his pale blue eyes. "Just Cailin MacGreggor looking for my menfolk," she said softly. Fear made her normally rich voice quaver. "Have ye seen Duncan MacKinnon or Johnnie MacLeod this day?"

He didn't seem to hear her question. Instead, he shook his head like one demented and mumbled woodenly, "Nay the moor. Nay the moor. Lord Murray said it. He warned Culloden Moor be no fit place for Highlanders to stand and fight. The hilly ground across the Nairn—that's for us, he said. But Charlie wouldna listen. Not him, God rot his greedy bowels."

Cannons thundered, nearly drowning the man's anguished words. "Have ye seen my kin?" Cailin begged. "Johnnie MacLeod?"

"No. No." He shook his massive head. His yellow hair hung halfway to his waist; it was matted with blood. His broad smashed nose was black with smears of gunpowder. His eyes narrowed dangerously. "You're nay my Peggie?"

"Nay. I'm Johnnie MacLeod's lass," she stammered.

"Get ye gone, woman!" he bellowed. Swinging the claymore, he slammed the flat blade against her horse's rump. The mare squealed and leaped ahead, nearly unseating Cailin, but she hung on with every ounce of strength and finally righted herself in the saddle.

The terrified horse's lunge carried them over the fallen Englishman's body and into the ever-thickening mist. Cailin heard the thud as Lady's hind hoof struck something soft. She clenched her eyes shut and clung to her mount as she tried to reason why she had ever left the safety of Inverness to be caught in the thick of a battle between the Hanoverian army and that of Prince Charlie.

There had been no fog or rain at dawn when she'd ridden out of the town in a desperate attempt to find her sister Jeanne's young bridegroom. Jeanne had been in labor for two long days and nights with Duncan MacKinnon's babe. Jeanne was only fifteen and slight of frame, scarce more than a child herself. The bairn was wedged sideways; it could not be born, and the midwife had shaken her head in despair. Jeanne had squeezed Cailin's hands until she thought her bones would snap. And when Jeanne had begged to see Duncan's face, Cailin could not deny her sister her last wish.

Now, even Jeanne's suffering seemed far away. Could it be only a few hours since she'd left her dying sister's bedside? Lady slowed to a trot, and Cailin opened her eyes and tried to ignore the gunfire and cries of agony all around her. "Ah, Lady, I'm naught but a fool," she murmured more to herself than to the trembling animal. "Had I had sense enough to keep to the road this morning, I might have realized that a clash of armies was imminent."

Instead, she had left the town of Inverness by a little-used country lane and followed a line of straggling trees and dirt dikes along the shore of the firth. The bleak moorland of Drummossie, the land that some called Culloden, stretched gray and barren to the east, but across the water, she could see magnificent towering mountains. After so many days in the narrow streets and shuttered house, it felt good to breathe fresh air again. Under different circumstances—if she wasn't so worried about her sister and the rest of her family—she would have been glad for the outing.

After an hour's ride, she had met three wild-eyed Highlanders in the blue, green and red Murray *breacan-feile*, bone-weary and half-starved. Pity for their plight caused her to give them most of the oatcakes she'd brought for her kin. While none of the Murrays could tell her where the Earl of Cromartie's men were camped, all warned her against going farther when Cumberland's army was abroad.

But Cailin had stubbornly continued on, determined to seek out her brother-in-law, and if possible find either her cousin Alasdair or her stepfather, Johnnie MacLeod. Both had chosen to ignore the orders of their chief and were marching for Prince Charlie under the banner of MacLeod of Raasay.

Not long after she'd left the Murrays, Cailin had thought her luck had changed for the better. A lad herding two shaggy cows to pasture had directed her to a wooded spot in a hollow near the ruins of an old crofter's cottage. There she'd found the still-warm ashes of campfires from a large body of Highlanders. She had known that the men were her own and not English because of the signs of haphazard sleeping arrangements. These soldiers had erected no tents; those who had spent the night here had wrapped themselves in all-encompassing wool plaids and slept on the damp, bare ground. And the only scraps of food that remained were the tail, hooves, and bones of a requisitioned calf.

She'd been following the trail the men had left, south toward the River Nairn, when she'd nearly been run down by two enemy messengers. Fleeing from them had taken her deeper onto the moor, and before she'd known what was happening, the first volley of shots had echoed across the plain, and she had realized that she was really in trouble.

She was nearly paralyzed with fear. Men were fighting and dying around her. Common sense told her that if she wasn't shot, someone would drag her off her horse and steal it. Cailin had given up all hope of finding her stepfather or Duncan. All she wanted was to get away from the killing, but she didn't know how.

Never had she ever felt so helpless—so panicked. The stench of the dying was the worst. She was no dainty English wench; she'd grown up around men and horses. She'd shot game and skinned and gutted it as well, and she'd sewn up wounds when her men-folk were injured in sport or battle. She'd tended the sick and helped to bury some, but she'd never been in a place that reeked of mindless death. Every breath she drew filled her head with the scent of sulphur and human agony. Dark Drummossie Moor was a nightmare—all the more terrifying because it was one from which she knew she'd not awaken.

"Get off that horse!" snarled a rough voice.

Cailin twisted in the saddle to see a Hanoverian soldier step into her path and aim a flintlock pistol at her head. His red coat was torn: one sleeve hung loose and empty. A great gash in the man's face ended in an ear hanging by a rope of skin.

"Down I say, afore I blow you to hell!" he shouted.

She didn't stop to think. Instead, she flung herself sideways and brought the trailing leather reins down across Lady's rump and yanked the right one hard. The mare snorted and wheeled, lashing out with her hind feet. Cailin heard a scream, and then the soldier's pain was lost in the confusion as she gave Lady her head and the little horse bolted away into the mist.

Cailin concentrated on keeping her seat, certain that at any second the pistol would fire and she'd feel the blow of a lead ball piercing her back. But no bullet found her, and they galloped madly on, leaping over fallen bodies and dodging armed men of both sides. The hood of her cape flew back, and her hairpins tumbled out. Soon her carefully braided hair streamed around her like a tavern strumpet's. But now was no time to worry about the state of her appearance, not when her very life was in jeopardy.

Finally, Lady's strength began to wane. Her breath came in great tearing gulps, and her legs trembled. "Easy, easy," Cailin soothed. "Whoa, girl. Whoa, my sweet." She slowed the weary animal to a walk and looked around her.

Either they had moved away from the scene of the worst fighting, or the battle was coming to a close. She could see two men struggling to her left, hand to hand, but neither took notice of her or the horse. To her right, a British soldier too young to shave was on his knees crying next to the body of a dying comrade. And just ahead, two opponents faced each other with drawn swords.

The British dragoon—a broad-shouldered officer in a cocked hat, knee-high black boots, and a red coat with silver lace—was on foot. His wounded horse lay on its side behind him, struggling to rise. The animal's shrill cries of pain brought tears to Cailin's eyes.

Facing the enemy dragoon was a stocky Highlander in a brown leather waistcoat and Scots bonnet, wielding a blood-streaked broadsword. His back was to Cailin and his clothing was too filthy to be identifiable, but the outline of his brawny figure seemed familiar.

The Scot attacked, weapon in his left hand, his right lifting his targe, the small round Highland shield that protected his body against the Englishman's lighter basket-hilted sword. The enemy officer sidestepped and blocked the blow. His hat flew off, and Cailin saw that he wore his own hair, black as the devil's cauldron, pulled into a queue at the back of his olive-skinned neck. His eyes were as black as his hair, fierce heathen eyes that might have belonged to some Turkish warlord.

Cailin's heart rose in her throat. Faintness threatened to overpower her. She couldn't be sure but ... Mother of God! It was! The Scot facing the British spawn of Satan was her stepfather, Johnnie MacLeod. She covered her mouth with her hand and forced back the cry that rose in her throat.

For an instant, they stood knee to knee, muscles locked, swords joined as one. Then they pushed back away from each other. This time it was the Englishman who lunged forward, moving so fast that Cailin almost missed the thrust. Steel rang as Johnnie met the stroke with his own sword. Then he flung aside his targe, drew his dirk with his right hand, and stabbed upward at the Englishman's belly.

Time seemed to slow as Cailin stared in silent horror. From nowhere, a thin dagger appeared in the redcoat's left hand. He twisted and sliced down across Johnnie's sword wrist, then followed with a powerful riposte, driving the point of his steel knife deep into Johnnie's chest.

Johnnie staggered backward, his falling weight wrenching him free from the fatal thrust. He dropped to one knee as a river of blood spouted from his breast. He turned his head as if to look one last time into Cailin's face, and then his dear, sweet features went slack, and he slid slowly to the ground.

"Johnnie!" Cailin screamed.

Sterling's gaze snapped from the dying Highlander to the source of the sound. Instinct told him that he'd heard a woman's cry of anguish, but he didn't believe it. No female would be here in the remains of the bloodiest battleground he'd ever endured.

Fog and cannon smoke obscured his line of vision; he could see no more than a dozen yards. Yet ... There. Unconsciously, he tightened his grip on his sword hilt and strained to see. Yes! There on a pale horse sat a woman with long red-gold hair. So still and motionless was she that she didn't seem real. Her face was white, her hand frozen in midair like some haunting specter.

Sterling blinked, half-expecting this disembodied spirit to vanish. But when he looked again, she was still there, staring at him across the blood-soaked earth.

His heart began to pound; his breathing quickened. Spots appeared before his eyes as his mind struggled to rise above the confusion. "You," he whispered. "It's you."

And then the rolling mist swallowed horse and rider, enveloping her with a white nothingness.

"Come back," he entreated. "Come back." He ran

toward the spot where he'd seen her, but when he reached it, there was only standing water . . . not even the mark of a single hoofprint to prove that she was not a vision of his strained imagination.

Chapter 2

Inverness
April 23, 1746

Captain Sterling Gray was exceedingly drunk for the second time in his life. His first experience with strong drink at seventeen had produced such horrendous results that he'd vowed never to repeat the incident. He had held fast to that rule for nineteen years; tonight he'd broken it with a vengeance.

He was not alone in his excessive consumption of potent Scots whiskey. Half the king's soldiers in this Inverness public house had imbibed beyond the dictates of reason. Sterling's best friend, Lieutenant George Whithall, was so intoxicated that he'd been attempting to relate the same story for the better part of an hour and couldn't get past his opening sentence.

"And ... and ..." Whithall slid forward onto the table and dissolved into laughter. "What the hell was that ... that wench's name, St ... St ... Sterlin'? The one ... the one ... with the ... nose?"

Sterling mumbled an incoherent reply and drained the last of the whiskey from his pewter cup. Someone opened the outer door, and a blast of cold guttered the candle on the table in front of him. A scowling tavern girl relit the taper as Whithall stiffened in his chair and demanded another drink.

The air in the room was thick with the stench of too many unwashed men, spilled ale, and wet wool uniforms. A leg of stringy mutton sizzled on the spit in the open hearth, and the smell made Sterling's stomach turn over. He'd never acquired a taste for mutton. Absently, he broke an oatcake in two as he stared at Whithall. From where he sat, it seemed as though there were two Georges. Either that or Whithall had a twin brother. "Have you a brother?" he asked, his sentence broken crudely by a loud hiccup.

Whithall laughed in reply and pinched the maid's bottom. "Drink up, Sterlin'," he urged. "Tomorrow we'll be back in the saddle."

They would that, Sterling mused. And he'd do his duty for king and country as befitted a son of Lord Oxley—even a half-breed son born on the wrong side of the blanket. For a few more days or weeks, he'd do his duty ... Sterling signaled for another cup of whiskey. There'd be hell to pay when Baron Oxley learned what he'd done. Sterling smiled for the first time in over a week. His father would fly into a rage when he found out he had resigned his commission in the dragoons, the honor that had cost the old man two years' income from his estates.

There'd be few men who'd not think Sterling a fool. Even Whithall would roast him royally.

The thought that he might be making the biggest mistake of his life crossed Sterling's mind, but he shrugged it off. A man had to do what it took to maintain his self-respect ... and he couldn't live with himself if he continued to follow commanders like Butcher Cumberland.

He was as drunk as a dragoon could be and still stand on two feet, but he hadn't lost all sense of reason. He'd made his decision regarding the army, and he'd stick to it. What troubled him beyond the breaking point was the vision of the woman he'd seen in the heat of battle on Culloden Moor.

Sterling prided himself on his intelligence, on his ability to overcome the obstacles of his unorthodox birth and carve a place for himself among gentlemen. He had been decorated for bravery on the field of battle, and he'd earned the respect of his fellow soldiers as well as his superiors.

But tonight he was afraid.

He'd not been able to get her out of his mind since she'd vanished into the mist. Every time he closed his eyes, he saw her—as real as if she sat in Whithall's chair across from him. More real than Whithall—he'd sprung a second head. The red-haired woman was flesh and blood.

She was also a ghost from his past . . . A past he'd believed he'd put behind him twenty-two years ago.

A pistol went off and Sterling stiffened, his hand on his own flintlock. When the loud crack was followed by a chorus of ribald laughter, he allowed himself the indulgence of sinking back into his own reverie.

No matter how many times he mentally attacked the problem of the woman's appearance, he came to the same conclusion. She could only be a figment of his imagination, an illusion.

But she had been there. And she'd been as solid as the Scotsman's broadsword that had nearly cleaved him from neck to cod.

His head ceased to spin, and the dizziness was gradually replaced by a deep, throbbing ache.

Maybe he'd been injured worse than he'd thought at Culloden, he reasoned. Or perhaps some tumor was growing in his head. A few more months and they could carry him home to Oxley Hall and lock him in the tower room until his beard hung to his knees and the village children shrieked taunts at the wild-eyed madman.

Except that he'd never been able to summon much of a beard, and his esteemed father would be as likely to have him committed to Bedlam as to trouble his nightly sleep or to bring shame on his true-born brothers by sheltering a madman. His light-skinned brothers. Henry and Hugh would be delighted if he went crazy. They'd made his home life a mockery, and if he obliged them by going quietly out of his mind, they'd whoop for joy.

Or give their version of Indian war whoops.

Sterling folded his hands, closed his eyes against the dancing candlelight, and leaned forward on the scarred table. Whithall seemed not to have noticed that anything was amiss. He was still trying to remember his story about Nora, the willing dairymaid they had both tumbled one night in Yorkshire, the girl with a nose the size and shape of his horse's saddle.

Whithall was as drunk as a sow, but he was a stout comrade, as good a man as any dragoon needed at his back. Born illegitimate himself, Whithall had never held Sterling's Indian blood against him. In fact, he'd shown little curiosity about his captain's former life as a savage running half-naked in the forests of the American Colonies.

Few people had asked questions, and those who had were usually seeking to make Sterling the butt of their jokes. It was not a mistake often repeated by the same man.

Sterling himself had pushed that part of his existence so far back in memory that at times it seemed like a dream. Tonight, his former life returned to sit on his shoulders with a heavy weight.

She had brought back his past.

So strong were his recollections that the man he'd once been threatened to suck the soul from the British Sterling Gray he was now. He'd fought the tide for days and nights.

With a groan of relief, he surrendered to his fears and let the familiar scents and sights of the wilderness sweep over him.

He was no longer Captain Sterling Gray, son of Lord Oxley and an officer in his Majesty's dragoons. That man no longer existed.

He was Snow Ghost, a son of the Shawnee, born to the Wolf Clan, and about to endure his last trial of manhood—his vision quest.

For a Shawnee male, this ordeal was the most important spiritual search of his life. He was fourteen, and he had already proved his courage six months earlier by facing a Mohawk in full war paint in the midst of an attack on the Shawnee village. He'd killed the enemy brave in hand-to-hand combat and earned the right to wear a single eagle feather. But none of that mattered if he did not survive his vision quest or if Wishemenetoo showed His disapproval by failing to grant him a spirit guide.

Snow Ghost didn't feel especially courageous as he began the ritual. For days, he had fasted and prayed; he'd endured the sweat lodge and danced for the brotherhood of warriors along with the two other boys who were candidates for manhood. He had chanted the poems that told of the creation of the world by the Creator, and he'd sung the sacred songs of his people. Now he was alone and must find his spiritual awakening or perish in the attempt.

The shaman had instructed him to go naked into the forest and seek a high place. There he must wait and search his heart until a vision came or he died of hunger and thirst. He was forbidden to run from danger or to cry for help. He was forbidden to utter a sound that was not a prayer or a hymn. The holy man told him to think of himself as an empty vessel and wait patiently for the spirit of the Almighty to fill it.

Snow Ghost had been determined to return to his village under the protection of a powerful guide. Since he had been a small child, he had waited for this time. He'd wondered if his personal guardian would be the spirit of the wolf, or a great humpbacked bear, or perhaps a soaring eagle.

Men rarely talked about their own experience, but when they did, it was to relate tales of fiery beasts or wise owls. Black Otter's totem was a river catfish; Morning Sky looked to the Elk Spirit for wisdom. Old Two Toes claimed that his guide was a spotted frog. Snow Ghost had spent many nights lying awake and hoping that the Frog Spirit would pass him by. Two Toes was a poor hunter and as lazy as his slovenly wife. Morning Sky said that Two Toes wasn't to blame, because a man protected by a lowly frog had poor luck to begin with and little hope that his life would ever improve.

Worse than having a frog or an insect for a spirit guide would be to have no vision at all. A man without a visitation by a protector was doomed to be a luckless outcast. No woman would choose to become his wife, and few war chiefs would ever include such a worthless individual in a scouting party or raid.

And so Snow Ghost had waited and prayed, watching the sun rise over the trees, cross the sky, and fade slowly into orange and purple before vanishing at twilight. Two days passed without the slightest sign, the longest days of Snow Ghost's life. On the third day, he doubled his efforts, using every ounce of his strength to dance and chant, hoping to attract some passing spirit. At this point, he would have joyfully welcomed Rabbit . . . even Anequoi the silly squirrel.

The thought that he might lie and make up a story never crossed his mind. Such action would be unthinkable. The punishment for such treachery was swift and terrible—banishment from family and tribe. A boy without morals was not fit to call himself a Shawnee.

In the soft light of that third day, Snow Ghost's vision came. So clear, so real, was the sight that he could hardly believe his eyes. One moment he was alone on the rocky hilltop, and the next—his greatest wish was fulfilled.

Except that nothing was as he had expected. There was no snarling wolf, no noble eagle landing gracefully at his feet. Instead, he saw a white woman, fair of skin and freckled, with hair as red as an English fox.

This was no heavenly angel such as the French priests spoke of—this was a living, breathing woman. She was not tall, and not nearly as plump as the white women Snow Ghost had seen at the Dutch trader's post. Her mouth was wide and full, her chin too firm for a sweet disposition, her eyes large . . .

not deep brown as those of his people, but golden-brown.

She wore a long skirt and leather shoes. Her upper body and part of her hair were covered by a single gray hooded garment. And she was staring at him as though she was every bit as astonished as he was.

He was so shocked that he forgot he wasn't supposed to speak. "Who are you?" he demanded in Algonquian, then immediately repeated his question in English. "What are you doing here? Don't you know that this is a sacred place?"

Her lips parted, and her eyes narrowed. For a second, he thought she was going to give him a piece of her mind. Mentally, he winced, preparing for the flood of abuse he knew she was going to heap on him. Then, suddenly, her mood changed. A look of comprehension came over her face, and she broke into a smile so intense, so endearing, that his heart began to pound and his breath caught in his throat.

"Who are you?" he repeated.

Her smile became teasing laughter.

Incensed, he rushed toward her and threw out his arms to capture her. He had no plan; he didn't have the slightest idea what he would do once he had her, but he had to make certain she was solid and not a dream woman. She didn't move. His hands closed around her, and he felt the warmth of her living body. He smelled the scent of a strange herb in her hair and felt the silken springiness as a lock brushed against his cheek.

She looked directly into his eyes, and the shock of recognition gladdened his heart.

Then she vanished.

Sterling Gray had carried the image, the scent, the memory of her warm body with him ever since. He kept it close to his heart when his mother died and his white father came to claim him. He held the memory of his vision when Oxley took him across the ocean and placed him in an English boarding school. He remembered her the day he'd received his commission in the dragoons, and he remembered her now.

All those years had not dimmed her image, and he'd never ceased to search for her. He'd looked into a thousand women's faces without seeing the one face that haunted him. Until the Battle of Culloden . . .

Until he'd found her again, and once more she had disappeared as quickly and as mysteriously as she had on that long ago forest mountaintop.

And that enigma was why he was drunk tonight. That was what troubled his heart and soul until he could think of nothing else. Cumberland and the dragoons be damned. He had to find that woman again.

Whether she was real or a delusion, he had to know the truth.

Sixty miles to the north, Cailin stood by the bed and looked down at the sleeping faces of her sister Jeanne and Jeanne's infant son. Firelight played across their features, hiding Jeanne's pallor and the babe's exhaustion. Offering a silent prayer for their continued recovery, she pulled another coverlet over them and backed slowly out of the master bedchamber.

Jeanne had protested weakly when Cailin directed the servants to carry her to the great carved bed, but Cailin had insisted. "Our father will need it no longer, and his room has the largest fireplace of any sleeping chamber in the house. He would want you to lie there."

"Our stepfather," Jeanne had corrected her.

"Our father," Cailin insisted. It cut her sore that she'd been unable to recover his body from Culloden field. She had returned the following day, but English soldiers had turned her away, saying that the traitors were being buried in mass graves.

Jeanne and the baby were both alive, and that was something to be thankful for. When Cailin had reached Inverness, she'd found that the ten-pound boy had righted himself and popped out into the midwife's hands, seemingly none the worse for his mother's long, difficult labor.

As soon as Cailin heard that Cumberland's men were murdering the wounded Jacobites, she'd known that she had to get Jeanne and young Jamie away from Inverness and safely home to Glen Garth. It had taken five cold, wet days of traveling, and Jeanne had wept most of the way. She cried for their father and for Alasdair, but most of all, she wept for her husband, Duncan. He was either fleeing for his life, dead on the field, or a prisoner. No one could tell them.

Cailin hoped that Duncan MacKinnon was still alive. With Johnnie and Alasdair dead, they needed him desperately. She had opposed her sister's marriage on the grounds that both Jeanne and Duncan were too young, but no one had listened to her. Not counting their grandsire, Duncan MacKinnon was their closest living male kin.

Cailin walked down the dark corridor of the old house without a candle. She didn't need one. This had been her home since she was six and her mother had wed Johnnie MacLeod. Many called the old house at Glen Garth haunted, but if it was, Cailin believed the ghosts must be happy ones. She had loved this rambling gray pile of stone since she'd first laid eyes on it.

From somewhere, perhaps the kitchens, she could hear a woman keening. If Cailin let herself think too long on Johnnie, she'd be bawling as well. It would be hard to imagine Glen Garth without her stepfather's booming laughter. She folded her arms over her chest and hugged herself hard to ease the pain. Johnnie and Alasdair both lost on the same day. It was enough to shatter her if she didn't steel herself against the hurt.

She couldn't afford the luxury of mourning her men; too many in the household depended on her. She swallowed the lump in her throat. In the morning, she'd have to take her little brother, Corey, aside and tell him that his daddy wouldn't be coming home.

Cailin entered the shadowy great hall. Beside the hearth, an old hound raised its head and thumped a greeting against the stone floor with its tail. Cailin scanned the room, half-expecting to see British troops charging through the far door, but all was still except for the dog's whining. Antlers of long-dead stags, faded tapestries, and ancient weapons lined the walls. The ridgepole was lost in darkness overhead. Nothing seemed the least bit out of place.

Then she stopped short, and goose bumps rose on her arms. She smelled tobacco ... her stepfather's special blend. She stiffened as she became aware of the hunched figure sitting in the high-backed chair near the fireplace. Cailin's mouth went dry. "Johnnie?" she called.

"Hist, lass. 'Tis only me." Her grandfather's deep voice rumbled through the chamber.

"Grandda." Relieved, she hurried to him.

As she drew near, he raised his wrinkled face and smiled at her. His sightless eyes shone white in the firelight. "Cailin."

She threw her arms around his neck and hugged him. "Ye gave me such a start," she confided. "I thought—"

"Ye thought I was a ghost," he finished. "Nay, hinney." He squeezed her hand as she sat on the arm of his chair. "Nay. I wish I was. Even a ghost would be more help to ye than a sightless old man."

Tears rose in Cailin's eyes. Never once before had she ever heard Grandda mention his affliction. Even now, there was no self-pity in his tone. "You're of more use to me than a dozen young men," she insisted. "You're the only one left with any sense around here. Glynis told me you'd already ordered the servants to bury the silver plate and drive the cows into the hills."

"Aye, that I did. We'll have Sassenach crawling over this house as thick as fleas on a dog's back."

"Most of the MacLeods didn't rise for Prince Charlie. I hoped the British would pass us—"

"Johnnie's kin will tell them soon enough. We Scots have a weakness for English gold. We'd nay be where we are today with our necks in George's yoke if our own people hadn't sold us out."

"I hope not." She patted her grandfather's bald head affectionately. "I thought you were abed and sleepin'. I saw no need to wake ye for bad news."

"How is Jeanne?"

"Weak but not feverish. And the babe is strong. With a warm bed and something to eat, I'm sure they'll be all right." Her hand tightened on his again. "Have you heard that Alasdair . . ."

"Aye. Glynis told me. God takes the good ones early."

"That says a lot for what you think of me," she teased with black humor.

He tapped the thornwood cane that leaned against his knee. "You're strong, lass, as strong as this old cane I had from my da. And you've lived long enough to know that good men and bad die in war."

"I was there. I saw Johnnie fall. I saw the dragoon put a sword through his chest."

"Ach. I dinna ken that, sweeting. 'Tis sorry I be for ye. You've had a broth of sorrow in your years. First your father—dead afore you saw the light of day— and then your mother, my own girl Elspeth, and then your husband. 'Tis a wonder you're not as mad as Angus's cow."

"Prince Charles has done me little good, and that's for certain," she said softly. Her husband, Iain, had caught an ague on the way to join the prince's party in September of '41 and died without ever seeing his sovereign. She and Iain had had another terrible fight about his leaving; she'd not even kissed him good-bye. It had been a sorry ending to a sorry marriage. "I always regretted that we didn't make a child before he died. Now, I suppose it's for the best. I'll have Corey."

"You've always been more mother to Corey than a stepsister."

"He's as dear to me as Jeanne, but God knows that she's as much a child as my mother was."

"Haven't I always said your good sense came from your father? I loved Elspeth well. She was the only babe of mine that lived past weaning, but I always knew her faults."

"Grandda, promise me you'll live forever."

"I wasn't thinkin' of goin' any time soon."

"Good." She slid to the floor and leaned her head against his legs. "I'm tired, Grandda. I'm tired and hungry, and I hurt too much to cry."

"It's bed ye need, lass."

"I can't sleep. It will be light soon, and there's too much to do. I've got to count our food stores and gather up whatever valuables the servants have missed. I have to—"

"Ye ha' to sleep," he said firmly. "And that's an order. Whatever comes tomorrow will be none the worse for a good night's rest."

"I keep thinking about the battlefield. I keep seeing that dragoon's face. Every time I close my eyes, I—"

"A cup of whiskey will cure that. Dead's dead. One Englishman is like another. 'Twill do ye no good to hate. You'll never see him again, as surely as you'll never see Johnnie MacLeod this side of paradise."

"He had black devil eyes, Grandda ... the dragoon who killed Johnnie. He was an officer, but he didn't wear a wig. His hair was his own, and it was as black as coal. If I'd had a pistol, I'd have shot him myself, the murdering spawn of Satan."

"And like been shot yourself. Ye did what was right, lass. Ye brought your sister and her babe home safe. Now we must prepare ourselves for the worst, for German George's fist will fall hard on the Highlands. And it may be that those who fell at Drummossie Moor will be the lucky ones."

Chapter 3

Three days passed and then four. Cailin's daylight hours were filled with work and anxiety. She dismissed the servants—sending all those who had family in the hills away for their own safety—and cared for her sister and the child herself. Of the women, only Glynis stayed. She was an orphan, and Glen Garth had been her home since she was ten.

Old Angus and the twins remained. Angus's bad knee and advanced years would not allow him to walk far or to ride without pain. Long ago, pretty girls had sung songs about his daring cattle raids and wenching along the English borders. Now, he sat beside the hearth and contented himself with porridge and memories of companions long dead. Cailin could no more have ordered Angus to leave than she could Fergus and Finley. The brothers were handsome red-haired men in their prime, standing over six feet tall, with shoulders like oxen and hands like shovels. But the twins' minds had never developed, and they were apt to wander off and play like children.

Cailin's sister, Jeanne, still lay abed, showing little physical or emotional improvement. She refused to eat and was so weak that she produced scant breast milk. Her wee son, Jamie, screamed with hunger for hours at a time, but Cailin was afraid to supplement his diet for fear that Jeanne's milk would dry up altogether.

Despite Jeanne's wailing and constant prayers, her husband, Duncan, did not come. No rider arrived with news of him, although refugees streamed through Glen Garth spilling tales of horror. The stories were so awful and so wild that Cailin wasn't sure what was true and what was distorted rumor. She fed them and tried not to listen.

"Cumberland's troops slaughtered the wounded Jacobites and left their bodies to lie like carrion on the battlefield."

"The English burned our men's corpses in great pyres. They threw living prisoners on the fires as well."

"Inverness has been put to the torch and lies in smoking ashes."

"Prince Charlie has been killed."

"The prince has escaped and raised a larger army."

"The Hanoverian troops are laying a swath of blood and flames across the Highlands, murdering fleeing Jacobite soldiers and civilians with equal bloodlust."

"The scent of smoke and rotting cattle drifts across the hills."

"The Duke of Cumberland is Old Scat incarnate. They fashion special boots to hide his cloven hooves."

"Butcher Cumberland, they call him. He feasts each night on the flesh of Highlanders."

Take each tale with a grain of salt, Cailin's grandfather had counseled. She tried to remember that, while every instinct warned her that the coming of enemy troops would mean disaster.

If Jeanne had been fit to travel and the babe older, Cailin would have taken her family south to her mother's birthplace and begged shelter from the Stewarts. Instead, she salvaged what she could of her family. She sat Johnnie MacLeod's only living son, Corey, on a stout Highland pony and gave the seven-year-old boy a dagger and a leather pouch of coins.

"Keep the sun on your left in the morning and your right at the end of the day," she told him. "You must go south to Fort William and then beyond to the nearest Stewart farmstead. If anyone asks you, your father died fighting for King George."

"No!" Corey replied hotly. "I won't leave you, and I won't tell such a lie! Charlie is our rightful prince, and our daddy—"

She slapped the child's face so hard that the imprint of her hand rose white on his cheek. For a second, Corey stared at her in disbelief, and then his big brown eyes filled with tears.

Cailin wanted to weep as well. Her little half-brother Corey was the son she'd never had. She'd cared for him since his own mother had died in childbirth. Cailin had never struck him before in his life, but this was no time to show compassion. She had to make the boy obey her. His life was at stake. "Listen to me," she said harshly. "Ye be a MacLeod and a soldier. You will do as I say. And you will live as your father would want you to do. You will kiss German George's feet if you have to. Do ye ken?"

Corey bit his lower lip and nodded, his eyes huge and filled with fear.

"I will come for you, Corey. As soon as it's safe, I'll bring you home. I promise." She put her arms around him and hugged him tightly.

He could no longer contain his tears. "Dinna send me away," he pleaded. "I'll be good. I will."

"You are the MacLeod of Glen Garth now," she admonished him. "But you aren't a man grown yet. You have much to learn."

"I love you, Cailin," he sobbed. "I want to stay with you and Grandda."

"As your father wanted to stay with you, but he couldn't," Cailin said sternly. "We will be together again. I swear it."

"Glynis said I'm an orphan now, just like her. She said ye were nay my real sister, just a stepsister, an' ye'd not have me here. She said you'd send me off forever to be a shepherd or apprentice me to a weaver."

"Glynis is a foolish girl," she replied. "Glynis has the sense of a broody hen. You are my father's son and my brother. Stepbrother means nothing between us, Corey. Besides, I couldn't send you away forever. You own Glen Garth now. You will be the MacLeod here when I'm an old woman toasting my toes by the fire."

He flashed a wan smile—his father's smile—and pain knifed through Cailin. So long as Corey lived, Johnnie lived as well. She hoped that she was making the right decision for them both.

She called to her serving man, Big Fergus. "I'm entrusting Corey to ye," she told Fergus intently. "Go with him and protect him. More than God, I count on you. Do not fail your little chief, Fergus. For if you do, the ghost hounds of Glen Garth will hunt you down and eat you, skin, bones, and tallow."

She gave Corey a final hug, then sent him off on the shaggy brown pony with Fergus striding through the cold rain beside him. Finley wept loudly at his twin's departure, but Fergus was so proud of the old-fashioned claymore strapped over his shoulder that he grinned from ear to ear. Fergus might be slow of wit, but there was nothing wrong with his strength. As faithful as the black and white sheepdog that trailed behind them, Fergus would guard Corey with his life.

They'd not been gone an hour when the first patrol of English dragoons arrived at Glen Garth. Cailin was changing baby Jamie's nappie when she heard the first musket shot. Thrusting the infant into Jeanne's arms, she threw an old plaid over her shoulders and ran out of the house.

By the time she reached the courtyard, soldiers were smashing windows and shouting orders. Finley ran from the dairy with a pet goose in his arms. A dragoon bore down on him and and seized the squawking bird by the head. Finley's eyes dilated with anger as the soldier proceeded to wring the goose's neck.

"Don't—" Cailin began, but before she could get the words out, Finley grabbed the dragoon's horse by the bridle with his left hand and drove his right fist into the soldier's belly. Another dragoon drew his sword and galloped toward them on a fiery roan. Cailin screamed. She dashed forward, trying to block the charge, but the horse's shoulder knocked her aside, and she fell heavily to her knees.

Finley groaned as the dragoon's sword slashed across his back. The man struck again amid a flurry of goose feathers, and Finley fell beneath the hooves of the two animals. Blood splashed to the roan's fetlock.

"No!" Cailin cried.

A third rider brandished a flaming torch and hurled it through a broken window into the house as still more mounted dragoons cantered into the courtyard.

Cailin whirled to face the leader, a bewigged major in a bright red coat and gold buttons. "What are you doing?" she demanded. "There's a sick woman and a babe in the house."

"This house and land are the property of King George," he replied coldly. "Confiscated for treason against the Crown. You are trespassing."

Realizing that further conversation with this English tyrant was useless, Cailin turned and ran back into the house. Acrid smoke drifted from the scattering of ashes on the stone floor. "Grandda!" she called. "Get out of the house!"

A dog's insistent bark became a high-pitched howl as the sound of shattering glass and tramping boots came from the kitchen wing. Waves of icy sensation washed over Cailin as she rushed toward her sister's bedchamber. "Jeanne! Jeanne!" she cried. But when she flung open the door, Johnnie's great poster bed stood empty, the covers flung carelessly on the floor.

Cailin glanced into the cradle; the baby wasn't there. Bundling up a blanket in her arms, she retraced her steps down the stone corridor and nearly tripped over the sprawled body of old Angus. He lay, eyes staring blankly, gnarled hands outstretched. She paused long enough to kneel and touch his twisted lips. When she felt no breath of life, she leaped up and ran on. "Grandda! Grandda, where are you?" She raced down a flight of twisting stairs to his bedchamber. Soldiers were already there, overturning furniture and setting fire to the bed hangings. The hall passage was quickly filling with smoke.

"Halt!" a man cried, but she paid him no heed. She dropped the blanket, darted around a corner, and slipped behind a heavy tapestry, taking the ancient hidden staircase to the rear of the house. More shots sounded from the courtyard, but to her relief, when she reached the postern door, she saw Jeanne and her grandfather huddled together in the rain. Jeanne was clutching a squirming bundle to her breast.

"Cailin!" Jeanne shouted. "A soldier dragged Glynis away! There!" She pointed toward the stable yard.

Cailin shook her head. Her knees were weak. She was breathing hard, and her heart felt as though it would burst through her chest. She didn't care about Glynis. All she wanted was to throw herself into her grandfather's arms and let him protect her from this madness.

Then Glynis shrieked, and the plaintive cry for help sent shivers down Cailin's spine. Glynis belonged to Glen Garth, and Johnnie would expect Cailin to protect her as much as he would expect her to look after Corey and Jeanne. Swallowing her own fear, Cailin glanced back once more at her grandfather and ran through the downpour to the old barn.

Glynis was on her back in a pile of hay, skirts and petticoats awry, with a yellow-haired dragoon on top of her. She was kicking and screaming, fighting desperately, but it was plain to Cailin that the soldier was too strong for her. Glynis's green bodice was ripped to her waist, and Cailin glimpsed a flash of bare flesh as the maid bucked and struggled against her attacker.

"Shut your trap, slut!" the soldier growled. He backhanded her and rose to his knees, fumbling with the front of his breeches. Glynis sobbed in pain and helpless fright.

Cailin drew herself up to her full five feet. "Let her go!" she ordered in her most regal voice. "You've no right to abuse my servant. Have you no sense of decency?"

The dragoon twisted around, grimaced, and then got to his feet. "Let her go?" He braced his fists on his hips and devoured Cailin with hungry eyes. "You've a mind to have some of me for yerself, do you?"

Behind him, Glynis scrambled to her feet and fled down the center passageway, disappearing through a door at the far end of the stable.

"I am a respectable woman," Cailin answered, taking a step backward. She'd not be bullied by this English vermin, but she was no fool. "Touch me and you shall be court-martialed."

He laughed again and lunged for her.

She dodged him, but the stall wall loomed solid in front of her. He threw his arms wide to catch her, and she ducked into the only place she could go—a box stall.

"Nice." His thick bulk blocked the doorway. "Nice and private."

Heart pounding, Cailin backed up until she felt the barn wall behind her. He smelled of unwashed wool and sour sweat. One front tooth was crooked, and his thin British nose bore a scar across the bridge.

Cailin's mouth went as dry as oat flour. Unconsciously, her trembling fingers rose to clasp the amulet she'd worn since she was a babe. The smooth gold felt warm to the touch, and the sensation gave her strength. "You will regret this," she warned.

The dragoon leered, showing an empty space where a tooth used to be and mouthing something so foul that her fright drained away, leaving only white-hot rage.

"Sassenach bastard," she flared.

He came toward her, step by step, backing her into the shadowy corner of the stall.

She shook her head. "Don't do this."

"Relax. You may love the taste of English cod."

Frantically, Cailin reached behind her, her finger-nails scraping across the splintery wood. She'd not beg him, she vowed. Not if it meant her life.

Then her searching fingers brushed an oak handle, and her eyes narrowed. "Let me go," she whispered softly.

"If you're real good, maybe I'll keep you all to my-self. If not . . ." he scoffed, "I've got a lot of friends." His laughter ceased abruptly when she whipped the iron-tipped pitchfork from behind her back and bran-dished it in both hands.

Captain Sterling Gray halted his bay gelding at the crest of the hill and gazed down on Glen Garth. His gut twisted as he smelled the smoke pouring from the broken windows of the stone house and heard the jeers and scattered gunshots.

His lieutenant, Whithall, brought his own horse up beside him and surveyed the scene below. "Looks like Major Ripton's troops beat us to this one, Ster-ling. No need for us to interfere in their fun." He raised a hand, and the weary-faced patrol behind him reined in their horses.

Sterling's scowl darkened as he watched the spiral-ing column of black smoke. Another farmstead, he mused. More weeping women and pitiful old men. How much blood and misery would it take to satisfy Cumberland? Or would the duke keep on burning and looting until the Highlands were a charred wasteland?

Whithall swore under his breath. "I know that look. Why don't we just ride around this one?"

Sterling's eyes narrowed. "You know our orders as well as I do. Reinforce Major Ripton and give whatever aid he requires."

Whithall grimaced. "Don't turn your foul temper on me." He swore again, with great imagination. "Our lads have been in the saddle since an hour before dawn. We're all wet and tired, and our arses feel like raw liver. Bloody hell! We've chased hostiles from Inverness to the sea and back. We both know what you think of Jacob Ripton. Let him subdue his own dairymaids this time. What difference does it make if we *reinforce* him today or tomorrow? It's not as though he's under fire from a superior force. Hell, there's nothing down there but sheep and a few women."

Sterling shook his head. "This business sickens me, but orders are orders."

"Then why do it? You know you don't have the belly for this mopping up."

Sterling fixed his friend with a frosty gaze. "Are you questioning my—"

"Damn your courage, man! This has nothing to do with nerve. Bloody Christ! I've ridden beside you for ten years. Who knows better than me what you're made of? You're no coward. You've saved my life more times than I can count, but fact is, Sterling, you always were too squeamish for your own good. What do you think Charlie's Scots would be doing to English farms and decent Englishwomen if they'd won at Culloden?"

"Aye, I'll grant you that. But I'm a soldier, not a butcher. As soon as my discharge comes through, I'm putting all this behind me."

"Exactly. So why push yourself into Ripton's pudding when there's no need?"

"As long as I wear this uniform—"

"Spare me from an honorable man," Whithall replied. He turned in the saddle and signaled to the troops. "Ready when you are, sir," he said sarcastically.

Sterling's insides felt as if he'd swallowed ground glass as he set his heels into the gelding's sides and led the way down the twisting, stone-strewn sheep path toward the farmstead. He was several hundred yards from the house when he heard the blast of a musket and shouting.

"There she goes! Stop her!"

A red-haired woman ran from the cluster of outbuildings and dashed directly in his path. Behind her, two dragoons on horseback bore down upon her.

"Stop her!" came the cry.

The lead soldier drew his pistol and took aim at the fleeing figure. Sterling heard the crack of the flintlock and saw smoke and fire come from the muzzle of the weapon. The bullet obviously missed its target, because the woman glanced back over her shoulder and put on a burst of speed.

Sterling's heart rose in his throat. There was something familiar about the girl . . . something . . . A peculiar buzzing rang in his ears as he stared at her.

The second dragoon leveled his pistol, and Sterling broke from his trance, spurring his bay forward. "Hold your fire!" he yelled. Whithall and the patrol were right on his heels; hoofbeats thundered behind him. "Hold your fire!"

He was only a horse length away from her when she turned her head and saw him. Her eyes dilated with fear, and she darted left. Sterling reined the gelding to intercept her. The horse spun in midair and its front hooves missed her by inches. Sterling leaned in the saddle and seized her by the waist, lifting her free of the ground and swinging her up in front of him.

She was all teeth and nails and flying fists. For a moment, he thought he'd laid hands on a bee-stung badger. His horse reared up and pawed the sky, the woman landed a blow to his chin, and they both slid out of the saddle and landed on the ground in a heap of arms and legs.

He heard the wind go out of her with a whoosh. Her body stiffened and then went limp. Her eyelids closed as he scrambled up and put himself between her and the dragoon who leaped from his saddle and ran toward her, pistol in hand.

"Stop there," Sterling warned.

"She's a murderer."

The newcomer threw up a hand to push Sterling aside, and Sterling caught the dragoon's right wrist in an iron grip. "Not so fast," he said.

The soldier drove a booted knee up toward Sterling's groin. He sidestepped the attack and sliced an open palm across the man's windpipe. The dragoon toppled like a sack of grain, groaned once, and lay still.

More dragoons galloped from the house. Whithall rode up and dispersed his men to form a shield around Sterling as he turned back to the unconscious woman.

Kneeling beside her, Sterling saw the steady rise of her breast as she drew in breath. Her eyelids fluttered, and he became aware of a sweet scent of heather that surrounded her. Hair rose on his neck as he stared down at the face he'd sought for so long.

It was she. This was the woman of his vision . . . the same one he'd seen at Culloden Field. She was here, and she was as real and as alive as he was.

He slipped an arm under her neck and raised her to a half-sitting position. His hand brushed her skin, and the touch sent a jolt of electricity down his spine. *"Mesawmi,"* he murmured reverently, unconsciously using the language of his childhood. Roughly, it translated as "gift of sacred power bestowed by the Creator." But he was long past the point of rational thought.

She opened her eyes. They were large and golden-brown . . . the color of peach honey. And they scorched him with resentful fire.

"Take your hands off me!" she said. Then she blinked again, and her face paled from ashen to alabaster. "You!" she accused. "It's you, isn't it?"

"What's the meaning of this?" Major Ripton's precise speech knifed through Sterling's concentration. "Seize the prisoner."

Sterling looked up at Ripton. "This woman—" he began.

"Murdered one of my dragoons," Ripton finished.

"Did you?" Sterling turned back to peer into the woman's face. "Did you do what they say you did?"

"Killed him in cold blood," Ripton said. "Drove a pitchfork through his chest."

"Did you?" Sterling repeated, helping her to her feet. This was all wrong. It wasn't supposed to be this way. He'd found her . . . but now . . .

She stiffened under his touch and recoiled as though he were a leper. Chin up, eyes sparkling with tears of rage, she glared at him. "Aye, I killed him right enough," she replied. "He was trying to rape me."

The major scoffed. "A likely story." He motioned to a soldier behind him. "Bring a rope. We'll show her king's justice for murder."

"Even an accused murderess has the right to a trial," Sterling said. "We have a code of law, and we are bound to follow it."

Ripton looked at him with disgust. "Very well, Captain. Have it your way. We will send this murdering bitch back to Edinburgh for trial. And then we'll hang her."

Chapter 4

Edinburgh Castle
July 1746

Cailin cupped her hands and dipped water from the bucket near the cell door. The smell of the slimy wooden pail sickened her worse than the stench of urine and human misery that surrounded her in this prison, but she knew she would die without liquid. She drank, thinking of the clear, sparkling water that sprang from the hill behind Glen Garth . . . water so cold and pure that it stung your tongue. But no amount of wishing could change the taste or remove the minute worms swimming at the bottom of the container.

My father would have thrashed any servant careless enough to give this stagnant horse piss to the pigs, she thought.

She forced herself to swallow as the image of Johnnie's face materialized in her mind. Tears sprang to her eyes.

When would the pain of his violent death lose its sting?

She had been roughly abused by King George's soldiers, but her bruises and the aches had faded. Here in the bowels of Edinburgh Castle, the guards had starved and beaten her, denying her even a breath of fresh air. Nothing hurt as badly as the loss of her father.

Her throat constricted with emotion.

Damn the blackhearted dragoon who had killed Johnnie! Damn him to an unhallowed grave! Twice he'd wronged her, once when he'd driven that sword into her father and again when he'd stopped her from escaping pursuit at Glen Garth. If she lived, she'd find him and take a MacGreggor's revenge. Woman or not, she'd never rest until he'd paid the price of a blood feud.

Ignoring the protests of her fellow inmates, Cailin gritted her teeth and took a second handful of the stagnant water, splashing it on her face.

"Look at her!" Janey Shaw cried. "Making herself all fine."

"Aye, she's a fancy one. Mistress Cailin MacGreggor—too good for the likes of common whores," called a painted slattern.

A toothless old woman with stringy gray hair cackled and tapped her temple with a dirty finger. "Mad as May butter, she is. Thinks she's taking supper with the Duke of Cumberland."

Cailin retreated to the corner where her gray wool cloak lay stretched out on the floor. This was her space, a section of cell that she'd fought for and defended with pluck and sinew. She cared not a tinker's damn for what the other women in the cell said about her. She was the smallest in size and weight but one. Fat Janey Shaw still bore the black eye that came of thinking Cailin's lack of height meant anything.

High up in the prison wall, a small shaft let in the only light that shone into this underground dungeon. Hardly sunlight at all, she decided. What filtered down to them was more a weak reflection of the midday July sun. By four o'clock, the gray stone chamber would begin to darken, and with the night came rats and mice and all manner of nasty vermin.

Rats terrified Cailin. One night, she had awakened to find one of the creatures nipping at her knee. She'd screamed loud enough to wake the dead in potter's field, but at daylight Janey found the dead rat against the far wall. Even in her fear, Cailin had seized the rodent and thrown it against the stones hard enough to kill it.

She shivered inwardly as she remembered that particular rat and rubbed her cramping belly. It was her woman's cycle and not the water that gave her this misery. Her back had ached since yesterday, and her head throbbed. She longed for a hot bath and clean clothes. Keeping decent in this place was near impossible. She had only a few cloths to bind herself with. When they were soiled, she didn't know what she'd do. She had traded her last earbob to the jailer's wife for food, a scrap of soap, and the menstrual rags.

Not that she regretted her bleeding time. It gave her a way to keep track of the endless days and proved again that the soldiers who had raped her so brutally on the journey to Edinburgh Castle had not left her carrying a child.

Absently, she rubbed the amulet known as the Eye of Mist that hung around her neck. Even through the coat of ugly blue paint Cailin had hastily dabbed on it before she'd fled from Inverness with her sister, the oddly shaped pendant gave her comfort.

According to her grandfather, the necklace was solid Pictish gold, so ancient that the history of the piece was lost in time. All that remained was the curse ... *whosoever possesses the Eye of Mist shall be cursed and blessed. The curse is that you will be taken from your family and friends to a far-off land. The blessing is that you will be granted one wish. Whatever you ask you shall have—even unto the power of life and death.*

Well, the curse still works, Cailin thought wryly. I killed a man to keep from being sexually assaulted, but ended up raped anyway. So the curse is active— why not the blessing?

When she was a child, she had loved the story of the necklace and had demanded that her mother and grandfather tell it over and over. All too soon, she had learned that the Eye of Mist was nothing more than a fairy tale. It was why she continued to wear it, even though she knew that the magic was a lie. Whenever she touched it, she was reminded that all she had in life was what she could take and hold for herself.

So strong was her belief that she wouldn't part with the amulet . . . not for food or drink . . . not for anything. Besides, she reminded herself, possession of anything so valuable as a piece of gold would mean her death. Someone, guard or fellow inmate, would kill her for it.

She sighed and continued to rub the token between her fingers. Soon it would be dark again, and she would while away the hours by thinking up original ways to murder the English dragoon. Her count to date was forty-three. Sometimes it took her several days to decide on a new punishment to add to her collection. To top what she had, she must be brilliant and inventive. Nothing but the most painful end would do for her greatest enemy—anything less would add insult to Johnnie's death.

Yesterday, she had decided to bury the devil up to his neck at the shore of the North Sea and wait for the tide to come in. That had been one of her favorites. Today, she must come up with something even better.

Cailin's stomach hurt. It was more than just her monthly bleeding; she was desperately hungry. Last night, the guards had brought a mess of meat and vegetables. She'd taken one whiff of her bowl and dumped the lot back into the common pail. She'd not eat worms, and she'd not eat rotten meat, no matter how ravenous she was. She'd suffered hunger before. She'd do it again rather than risk dying with a running of the bowels and the agony of food poisoning.

A young whore had died like that the first week Cailin was here in prison. The woman's cries still haunted her in the night. No, there were easier ways to die than eating tainted meat, she reasoned. But she had no intention of dying. She meant to live, to find her family and make sure that they were well, and she meant to kill—

The sudden tramp of heavy boots broke through her reverie. Puzzled, Cailin glanced toward the cell door. There was no reason for guards to come at this time, not unless they were bringing another prisoner ... or coming to take one away.

An iron key grated in the lock, and the door banged open. "Cailin MacGreggor!" the bearded warder called. "You are summoned. Can ye walk, or maun ye be carried?"

She scrambled to her feet and snatched up her cloak. "Who wants me?"

"Hold your tongue, woman," he snapped. "Ye be summoned to answer for the murder of Lloyd Hedger, private, late of His Majesty's service." He hawked up a great gob of phlegm and spat on the floor. "God rest his soul."

"May he rot in hell," Cailin retorted.

"No talking." He motioned with his head. "This way."

She ignored the flurry of whispers as she left the cell. A guard slammed and locked the door, then took a lit torch from a socket on the wall and led the way.

"Go on," the warder ordered.

"Am I to go before a judge and jury?" she asked. Her mouth went dry, and she felt faint. At times during her long confinement, she had wondered if she would die without ever facing charges. Now, she knew that she would only die. No daughter of a dead rebel would find justice in Edinburgh Castle—not today . . . perhaps not ever. She only hoped that she would meet her end with the pluck and dignity of a Highlander.

The bearded man gave her a rough shove. "Shut your mouth, or I'll have ye gagged." By his accent, she knew that he was a Lowlander. She'd find no compassion here.

Trying not to show her fear, Cailin wrapped her cloak around her shoulders and followed the guard down the damp, narrow passage and up a flight of steep stone stairs. The warder strode hard on her heels.

They traversed another corridor, another flight of steps leading up from the bowels of the castle. When they reached the top, the warder grabbed her arm. "Stop here," he said. He pointed to a low doorway. "In there."

"What are you—" she began.

"Hold your tongue, woman," he snarled. The guard took a position beside the entrance, and the warder followed Cailin into the room.

The outer chamber seemed to be some sort of office. There was no window; the only light came from a whale-oil lantern hanging over the table and a small fire on the hearth. As Cailin scanned the room, a stout woman appeared in the doorway on the far side of the chamber.

The warder sat heavily in a straight-backed chair. "Be quick about it, Hattie. It's late."

"This way," the woman said, motioning to Cailin.

She stepped into the second room, obviously a sleeping chamber, and the woman closed the door behind them. "What do ye mean to do with me?" Cailin demanded. "I whore for no man. If ye—"

"Shhh. I'm Hattie." She made a quick move with her head toward the first room. "I'm wife to that sour biscuit out there. I can tell you he will put up with no nonsense from you, girl. Off with them filthy clothes."

Cailin took a step back. "Why?"

"A *gentleman* has paid for clean garments, and soap and water. You've a quarter-hour to make yourself ready for your trial."

Cailin exhaled sharply in relief as she noticed the basin of water and the towel on a stool beside the fireplace. "What gentleman?" she asked, flinging off her cloak. What should she wash first? she wondered. Her head itched so badly that she was afraid she had lice, but she'd not had an all-over wash since her arrest. The container of water was small, and the saucer of soft lye soap looked as though it had been shared by many bathers. "Who paid for this?" She stripped off her bodice and skirt, and dropped her ragged petticoat to the floor.

"There's decent things for you. We can burn these," Hattie said, not unkindly.

"Have you a comb?"

"Aye, but it's not paid for. You can't keep it. I'm only loanin' it from the goodness of me heart."

Cailin shed her undergarments, wet her hands, and scooped up a little of the strong, yellow soap. She worked it into a lather and washed her face and neck, then rubbed the stinging mixture over her bare breasts.

"Have the decency to turn your back," Hattie admonished. "God save us," she sputtered. "Do you mean to wash your titties too?"

Cailin shut her eyes and gave herself over to the luxury of soap and water. A quarter of an hour, Hattie had said. She didn't know how much dirt she could wash away in that time, but she meant to do the best she could. Bless the gentleman, whoever he was. It would be a hell of a lot easier to be brave before the judge if she didn't smell like a pigsty.

"Saints preserve us!" Hattie gasped. "You shameless hussy."

Cailin only smiled and continued rubbing the clean, soapy water over her naked body with slow, sensual movements.

Sterling Gray sat on a bench at the back of the court, feeling oddly uncomfortable in his new civilian garments. His stock was damnably tight on his neck, and the seams of his blue satin coat strained at his shoulders. Worse, he was the only person of quality in the large chamber who was not wearing a wig.

Face it, old boy, he thought wryly. You're sadly out of fashion. When he got back to Oxley, he'd have his father's tailor sew— The reality of his situation brought his idle musing up short.

Oxley. He'd receive short shift at Oxley once his father received his letter explaining that he'd resigned his commission. He doubted very much that he'd be welcome at home ever again.

Not that he'd ever felt particularly comfortable in his father's house ... His half-brothers had despised him for his illegitimacy and dark skin, his three stepmothers had ignored him, and his father had made it abundantly clear that he was a disappointment.

He'd have to give serious consideration to what he was going to do with the rest of his life, now that his military career had come to an abrupt end. So far, he hadn't thought of anything more than getting out of Scotland and away from the stench of spilled blood and smoking ashes. Other than this damnable woman ...

She had plagued him day and night.

Reason told him that this Highland rebel couldn't be the woman of his youthful vision. She had appeared suddenly out of the mist on Culloden Field when he was weary and heartsick from battle. She'd surprised him, and his mind had played tricks on him.

He was an educated man, not a superstitious savage. He'd put feathers and war paint and heathen drums behind him. The only similarity between this woman and the one he'd carried in his dreams was the color of her hair.

That had to be the truth, because if it wasn't, he was in far worse trouble than the difficulty he'd have in trying to explain away his resignation from the army.

He should have left Scotland the day his release papers had come through. There had been no reason to come to Edinburgh and inquire into the status of her criminal case. He'd gone as far as saddling his horse and packing his few belongings, but in the end, he'd headed the animal toward this Scottish city rather than home.

Paying for her bath and a change of clothing had been simple Christian charity. Once he'd learned her name and been told the conditions of prisoners in Edinburgh Castle, he'd felt obligated to assist her in some small way. In all honesty, he had to admit he'd been relieved that her name hadn't struck a chord. Cailin MacGreggor. It meant nothing to him. She meant nothing . . . as long as he avoided reliving the memory of holding her in his arms . . . as long as he denied the sorcery that had drawn him unwillingly to Edinburgh and to this courtroom.

A bewigged judge pronounced sentence on the prisoner before the bar, and the doomed man was dragged away cursing and struggling against his captors. Someone called for order, a door opened to the left of the chamber, and a bearded warder led in a woman in manacles.

Gooseflesh prickled on Sterling's arms and torso. His hands closed on the back of the bench in front of him, gripping the wood so tightly that his fingernails bit into the worn surface. His chest felt tight, and it was hard to breathe.

He couldn't take his gaze off the slender feminine figure in rough homespun. He knew that this was Cailin MacGreggor before the bailiff called out her name. There could not be two women with such glorious hair. Damp red-gold curls escaped the plain linen cap to frame her face and catch the last rays of afternoon sun that streamed in a sooty barred window.

Sterling's heart hammered against his chest as an

unnatural weakness washed over him. The thought that whatever happened to Cailin MacGreggor in the next few moments would affect the rest of his life echoed through in his mind.

He strained to hear the judge's words, but the whispers of the crowd drowned them out. Sterling continued to grasp the bench back as colors and sounds swirled around him. It seemed that all his senses were enhanced tenfold. He could hear the loud buzz of flies, smell the unwashed wool clothing of the waiting prisoners, see the faint stain on the wide-board floor that might have been old blood. And deep in the recesses of his soul, he could swear he heard the throb of an incessant drum.

He lost track of time. Witnesses were called, barristers argued, and the judge slammed his gavel against a polished wood table. And all the while, Cailin MacGreggor stood, back straight, chin high, and faced her accusers.

As shadows lengthened, servants came to light the candles. Suddenly, Sterling felt a gust of cold wind. Startled, he glanced around the room, wondering who had opened an outer door, and then remembered that it was summer. He could feel the wind straining against his skin and clothing, but when he looked at the candles, their flames had not even flickered. Unable to stand the tension, he leaped to his feet and started forward. Then the judge's voice came as clear and loud as thunder.

". . . you, Cailin MacGreggor, be taken at first light to Edinburgh gallows and there be hanged by the neck until you are dead for the heinous crime of murder. And may God have mercy on your soul."

Chapter 5

Purple ribbons of dawn flowed across the gray eastern sky. It would be a clear day, Cailin decided, one of those jewel-box mornings of brilliant light and sweet sparkling air that gave the inhabitants of Edinburgh a taste of Highland glory. Somehow, she felt it would have been easier to die on a cold, cloudy day with a promise of rain. It was hard to keep her head high and the tremor from her step as she neared the gallows, knowing that she'd never see another morning ... that she'd never smell the blooming heather again ... that she'd never hear the deep voice of her grandfather this side of hell.

The warder had offered her a priest and a chance to make confession for her sins. She'd refused. She'd not make a lie of her death by saying she was sorry she'd killed that dragoon in her father's barn. She only wished she'd killed the three soldiers who had made sport of her on the way to prison. Now she would die with blood on her hands and hatred in her heart. There would be no heavenly gates opening for Cailin MacGreggor. Her stubborn will would see her serve an eternity in Satan's kitchen.

At least I'll have company, she thought wryly. Johnnie had always said that heaven would be hard-put for saints and hell have standing room only. Truth was truth, and the MacGreggors were no better

50

than the MacLeods. "A wee bit rough around the edges," Johnnie had admitted, "cattle thieves and rebels all—but loyal to their families until the last stroke of eternity."

Loyalty meant taking revenge on those who wronged them, man or lass. And loyalty to Johnnie's memory meant sending his murderer to his grave. "Mayhap I'll come face to face with that accursed English blackguard in hell," she murmured. Leaving him alive to walk free and boast of Johnnie's death would be a duty unfulfilled. And she had always been a woman who liked to finish what she'd started.

"No talking!" the warder snarled. He gave her a shove, and she whirled on him with such a black look that his Lowland curses died on his tongue and his pocked face paled.

An oversized raven fluttered down to peck at scraps on the cobblestones directly in the path of the execution party. The bird's black feathers gleamed ebony in the early light as it cocked its head and stared round-eyed at Cailin. One of the guards muttered "Witch" in English.

The second crossed himself furtively. " 'Tis her familiar," he said in the same harsh language.

Cailin smiled at their ignorance. It gave her some comfort to know that the guards were afraid of her. "Were I a witch, I'd show ye a trick or two," she replied in perfect English. "Brave men ye be to fear a chained woman and a poor bird."

They'd not expected her to understand their words. Gaelic was the native tongue of most Highlanders, but she'd had the benefit of a formal education; Johnnie had seen to that. "Ye never know when your blood sire may call you to London," he'd said with a wink. "It never hurts a lass to be smarter than the men around her."

Her blood sire. She almost laughed aloud. He'd showed little concern for her, once when he'd sent a silver christening cup and again when he'd sent her the amulet, and a final time when she'd received a sum of money from Edinburgh bankers on her wedding day. Cameron Stewart had never laid eyes on her since she'd been born. He'd not have known her if they'd shared a pew at Sunday Mass. If caring and love mattered, Johnnie MacLeod was her blood sire.

She glanced back at the raven, wishing she had a scrap of bread to throw the bold creature. Or a scrap of bread for herself, she corrected silently. They'd not fed her that morning. She was going to her grave with an empty belly and cold stones under her feet.

Others better than I have died this way, she thought. Maybe it was preferable to be one mourned over than one who must live out a life forever in mourning. Still, there was much left undone, and she bitterly regretted being unable to care for Jeanne and the others who depended on her. Her sister was too gentle, too sweet to survive in a Scotland ravaged by the likes of Cumberland's army. Her pretty face and soft voice would only bring her to sorrow. And brave little Corey ... How long would he wait and watch the road for her to come for him as she'd promised? He was so young to be cast adrift in a hard world with none but Fergus to guide him.

God in heaven! Why had she fought the soldier in the barn? If she'd lain back and let him have his way with her, she might have still been free to help her family.

The self-pitying notion passed as quickly as it came. What she had done would make the English think twice about cornering a Scottish lass in a dark stable. She'd do the same thing again, given the chance. She was no sheep to go meekly to the slaughter. She was a Highlander, by God, and they'd best remember it.

Suddenly, she heard an outburst of cheers and shouting. Startled, Cailin looked up to see the gallows platform looming black and ominous before her. A single tartan-clad body dangled from a rope. The condemned man—a Mackintosh by the weave of his kilt—no longer lived; his twitching corpse swung slowly to and fro to the delight of the gathering crowd.

"So die all traitors to the Crown!" shouted a man in an old-fashioned Scots bonnet.

"The Mackintosh danced good, didn't he?" crowed an old woman beside him. "They all dance, but some dance higher than others."

A peddler with a tray of gingerbread skeletons suspended from a cord around his shoulders held up his wares and cried, "Death cakes! Who'll buy my death cakes!"

A painted whore laughed and tossed him a coin. "Bring on the next!" she demanded as she reached for a sugar-coated treat and bit off the skeleton's head.

"Aye!" echoed a drunken baker. "We want to see another! Where's the lass?"

"Bring on the woman!"

"Hang her! Hang the murderer!"

Cailin shuddered. She caught her lower lip between her teeth and bit down hard, trying to fight the faintness that had come over her. Her hands were fastened behind her back, and she was afraid she'd lose her balance and have to be carried like a sack of grain up the thirteen steps to the noose.

Tears filled her eyes, and she blinked them away. She'd give no show to these ghouls. She took a deep breath and kept walking. Under her bodice next to her skin, she wore her amulet. The ancient necklace was an empty token, as powerless to aid her as it had been the night her mother died. But still the familiar weight of the gold necklace gave her comfort, and she could imagine that the metal emitted a warm pulsing.

If only the legend were true, she thought; if only the Eye of Mist did carry a blessing. But then she heard Johnnie's voice in the far corner of her mind. *If wishes were horses, beggars would ride.* And she knew that desperation had made her foolish. There would be no miraculous rescue. She had been sentenced to die this day, and die she would. Her only choice was to remember who she was and to go with dignity.

At the foot of the platform, a brown-robed priest waited patiently. "Will you make last confession?" he asked. His breath smelled of strong cheese.

Cailin shook her head. She could not trust her voice to keep from breaking.

"Have thought for your immortal soul," he cautioned sternly. "Will you go to your grave unrepentant?"

Cailin put her foot on the bottom step. At the top, a tall figure in a black hood waited. Only his eyes were visible through slits in his mask. They gleamed as cold as glass . . . as pitiless as the raven's eyes.

"Repent," the priest intoned.

Pulse racing, Cailin forced herself to climb the narrow wooden stairs. When she reached the platform, the executioner raised a dirty blindfold.

"Nay!" she said. "Do not bind my eyes. I've a mind to see the sunrise."

"As ye wish."

His voice grated on her ears like a rusty hinge. As he settled the rough hemp around her neck, she caught a strong odor of whiskey. Ah, she thought, so even death's accomplice needs some added courage to fulfill this job.

She heard a squawk, and a raven flew up and landed on the wooden railing that surrounded the platform. "Come to see the performance firsthand, did you?" she murmured to the bird.

The mob surged forward.

"Get on with it!" someone cried.

"Hang her! Hang the murderess!" shouted a man at the foot of the steps.

The priest appeared at Cailin's shoulder and began a prayer in Latin. She stared at the blossoming sunrise, marveling at the streamers of coral and mauve and crimson that tinted the clouds with gold. Her head bade her heed the cleric, but her stubborn heart held firm. I'll find Johnnie's killer and make him pay, she thought, if I have to come back from hell to do it.

The priest stepped back. Cailin stared into the executioner's eyes and knew that her moment had come. Time seemed to stand still for her, and a calm acceptance replaced the fear and anger that had filled her body and mind. The MacLeod clan motto echoed in her brain. "Hold fast," she said clearly in Gaelic.

"Hold!" shouted a stranger in English. "Executioner! Hold your place! I have a decree from . . ."

The rest of his words were lost to her in the angry roar of the crowd. Why did the executioner hesitate? she wondered. One motion of his hand, and the trap door beneath her feet would fall away. Seconds passed, and sweat beaded on her forehead.

"For the love of God," she cried. "If you're goin' to hang me, do and be done with!"

Then gloved hands were lifting the noose off her head. Her cap fell off, and one braid came undone, but she stood like a statue, unable to comprehend. She was prepared to die like a Highlander. What was happening?

Hands closed on her shoulders and spun her around. The din of the mob was so loud that she couldn't hear what was being said to her. Something hard struck her in the center of the back. Vaguely, she was aware that people were throwing eggs, turnips, and—A stone slammed into her elbow, and the sudden pain jerked her from her stupor.

Half-dazed, Cailin looked up into the face of the man who had killed Johnnie MacLeod. "Sweet Jesus," she exclaimed in Gaelic. "I'm already dead and in hell."

"Listen to me!" he shouted in English. "I have a writ for your release."

She began to laugh. This was hell for certain.

"Your sentence has been commuted to exile for life," he said. "Provided that you marry me immediately. I—"

A musket shot from the foot of the steps sent the surging onlookers into a scramble away from the gallows. A woman screamed, a horse reared up, and a second gun fired. Soldiers rushed from the castle toward the mob.

"Do you understand?" the priest demanded, pushing his seamed face into Cailin's. "If you would save your life, you must join in marriage with this man. Will you?"

She shook her head.

"You choose death over marriage?" the cleric asked in disbelief.

"I canna," she said.

"Are you now married to another?" her English enemy demanded.

She shook her head again.

The priest tugged at her arm. "Are you bound by vows to the church? Are you a nun?"

She laughed at that thought. "No."

"Then you must wed me or die."

"There is no time," the priest insisted. "Now, will you—"

"I'd sooner wed Old Scat himself," she replied hotly.

The priest gasped. "Blasphemy!"

An egg hit his right cheekbone, smashed, and spattered over the three of them. A volley of shots rang out, and the remaining rioters scattered. Hoofbeats thundered on the cobblestones as a company of dragoons galloped down the street.

Johnnie's killer shook her. "You'll be the devil's bride soon enough if you don't agree to—"

"Enough of this." The bearded warder pushed forward. "She has made her decision. She hangs. Executioner! Do your duty."

"She agrees," the dark-eyed Englishman declared. He pushed her toward the steps.

"Nay!" she protested. "I dinna—"

He slapped her across the face with the flat of his hand so hard that her ears rang. "Think, woman!" he snapped. "Are you daft?" He pointed to the body of the Mackintosh still hanging from the rope. A raven had landed on the dead man's shoulder and was beginning to peck at his face. "Will you end like that with your eyes—"

"Nay," she said. Tears betrayed her. "Nay, I will wed," she said in broken sobs. "If only to have the chance to send you to hell first."

"Fair enough," he answered. "Priest, you have the woman's agreement. Read the marriage lines."

"Here? Without banns or—"

"Here and now, priest, before those eggs and rocks turn to musket balls. For you'll not descend those stairs until you've made us man and wife."

"How dare you?" the cleric sputtered. "I'll protest to—"

"Little protesting you'll do with a broken neck, Father. The words! This platform makes too easy a target."

"I warn ye," Cailin said softly, "I know not what madness possesses ye, but ken this, Englishman—I mean to take your life."

"And I mean to save yours. Will ye, nill ye, woman, you shall not stir from this spot until you are my legal wife."

"You'll regret it," she retorted.

"We'll chance that, won't we?"

"Aye, we will."

And then the priest began to mutter the ceremony, and Cailin shut her eyes and made the correct responses with a heart as cold and dead as those that lay in Culloden Field.

Chapter 6

"You arrogant Sassenach bastard," Cailin reviled him. "You murder my father. You hit me when my hands are chained, and then ye force me to go through the mockery of a marriage ceremony. And now ye expect gratitude?"

Sterling glanced over his shoulder at his newly acquired wife and decided that marrying her was the stupidest thing he'd ever done in his life. The four days since he'd rescued her from the gallows had been a complete and utter disaster. After reason and patience had failed, he'd resorted to tying her wrists together in front of her and securing her ankles by a leather strap that ran under her horse's belly. She was still far from subdued, and only the threat of gagging her with his stock had put an end to her calling out to every Scot that they passed to save her from an English kidnapper.

They'd not been in the saddle an hour this morning when he'd had to come to blows with a scowling Border lout who weighed twenty stone at the least. It wasn't until he'd unhorsed the crude fellow and produced their marriage papers that the giant had let them cross his farm in peace.

The terms of Cailin MacGreggor's release from the death penalty had been clear. He had to take her out of Scotland at once. If she ever returned, she was subject to arrest and hanging. She'd insisted on reading the writ herself, and she seemed to understand the English. Still, she had pleaded with him to let her go. When he'd refused, she'd turned the full force of her anger against him, and they'd remained at odds with each other since they'd ridden out of Edinburgh.

"Whatever ye plan on doin' with me, you'll regret it, I vow," she flung at him.

He reined in his horse. "Woman, I warn you. I've heard enough of your foul tongue. I saved your life. Can you get that through your thick Scots head? I slapped you, I admit it. It's not an act I'm proud of, but it was the only way I could keep you from committing suicide. You were hysterical, and if I hadn't brought you to your senses, you'd be food for the ravens."

"Aye," she retorted. " 'Twas all a favor you were doing me. And now ye will try to convince me that your running a sword through Johnnie MacLeod was for my own good too."

His hand ached to slap her again. Not even the sound of her husky whiskey-voice, which made him go shaky inside every time she opened her mouth, took the edge off his temper. He was not a man for using violence against women. It went against his grain, and he'd suffered many a bruise in his lifetime for coming to the defense of some soiled tavern flower. But this woman ... He gritted his teeth in frustration.

"You murdered a better man than you'll ever have the fortune to know," she continued with obvious relish in English. At first, she'd contented herself with mumbling under her breath in Gaelic. Then, when she realized that he didn't understand a word

she said, she'd switched to his father's tongue—
liberally laced with a lilting Scots burr and an occasional sprinkling of colorful local expressions.

"You prove yourself to be more of a fool with
every word that tumbles from your lips," he replied
with exasperation. "Your Johnnie MacLeod was trying mightily to kill me. And damned near succeeded.
Was I to stop every Scot I met on Culloden Moor and
say, 'Pardon me, are you my future father-in-law?'"

His barb struck home. For an instant, his gaze
locked with hers, and Sterling read the surprise in
her large, liquid eyes. Her lips twitched and almost
curved into a smile.

"Aye, he nearly did catch you with that parry,
didn't he?" The smile took hold and lit her face with
a glow that was almost supernatural. "He was a caution with a sword, was our Johnnie."

Sterling sucked in his breath and turned away.
What was this hold she had over him? Was it witchcraft, as the guard taking her to the gallows had muttered? One minute, he wanted nothing more than to
choke the life from her—and the next ... He stiffened
in the saddle and took the weight off his swelling
groin.

He desired her ... this Scottish prize of war. He
wanted to peel the clothes from her and lay her
down in a bed of heather. He wanted to see for himself what was hidden beneath the rough homespun.
Small she might be, but she was all woman. Her
breasts were high and firm, her waist tiny enough to
span with both hands. Her rounded bottom ...
Heart's wounds! Her backside was as sweet and
curving as that of any bold wench who plied her
trade on London's stage.

He could think of nothing else but seeing Cailin

proud and naked, all that red-gold hair tumbled around her bare shoulders, arms upraised to welcome him.

He swallowed at the thickness in his throat.

He wanted her, but she had taken pains to tell him what she thought of him. He had never forced a woman—never had to. Wife or not, he was too old to change his habits. She must come to him, this little russet bird, of her own free will, lips parted, eyes heavy-lidded with sensual abandon ...

"Luck. 'Twas luck alone, not skill, Englishman," she said. "On a good day, Johnnie MacLeod would have carved you stem from stern."

"Then I'm fortunate to have met him on a bad day."

"It was a bigger mistake than you know. Untie me, Sassenach. You can keep your horse. Just let me return to my home and family. I've a blood feud to settle with you, but if you—"

"Enough." His composure was fast slipping away. Most women liked him as he liked them. He'd met angry ones before, but a smile and reasonable words usually brought them around. With Cailin, everything he said to her seemed to be a spur in her side. "There is nothing for you to return to," he explained with more patience than he felt. "Your home has been confiscated by the Crown. The Highlands lie under Cumberland's boot. Everything you had before the rebellion is gone forever. Accept it."

"I have a sister, a grandfather, and a young brother. He's only a child, and I promised him—"

"You can do nothing for him. If you were caught on Scottish soil and he was with you, he would suffer for your acts. Any who give aid to proscribed outlaws will receive the same punishment."

"My family—"

"Your grandfather and sister were well when last I saw them."

"Liar! Ye dinna—"

"They were at the farm, were they not?" He turned and glared at her. "Your sister was the girl with the new baby?"

Cailin stared back at him with eyes as cold as frost-glazed flint. "Aye, still weak from childbed and turned out into the rain like a stray cur."

"I ordered them sheltered from the weather and provided escort to a loyal household the next morning." He glanced back at the narrow road ahead, remembering the tears running down the old man's face as he'd asked Sterling what would happen to Cailin.

"Ye expect me to believe—"

"Believe what you want, woman. But never call me a liar again. I have many vices, but lying isn't one of them."

"My sister's bairn? Was it a lad or a lassie?"

He swore mightily. "It was a babe. A crying, red-faced infant. How the hell would I know whether it was a boy or a girl?"

She pursed her lips and looked at him shrewdly. "A good answer, but one that proves nothing. What of my brother, Corey? He's seven years old. He's safe with my sister, is he?"

Sterling shook his head. "I didn't see a child. Just the baby. I'm sorry, but—"

" 'Tis all right," she replied. "I sent him away before the soldiers came."

"Then why in hell did you ask me—"

"I was but testing you, Sassenach."

He felt the heat of blood rising in his neck and cheeks. "I told you I wasn't a liar."

She nodded. "So ye did. So ye did."

She fell silent then, and Sterling rode in peace for the better part of an hour. The rugged Border land was becoming more settled now. Dwellings were closer together, and from time to time they passed herds of cattle and sheep. They were on English soil—had been for some time—but he knew better than to relax. This country had seen too much blood spilled. Scots and Brits had fought over every inch of this land, and before that, Saxons had clashed with Normans. Hell, he supposed Roman legions had battled the pagan tribes across these hills and wooded valleys.

It wasn't Romans or Scots that he was worried about today; it was outlaws. Not that the barons in the vicinity would trouble their consciences over a little mayhem and robbery. A man and woman traveling alone on good horses were always a target on the back roads of England, and if he didn't keep alert, he might wind up in a ditch with his pockets empty and his throat cut.

The lack of sleep was telling on him, and his head was splitting. He was getting old, he supposed. Ten years ago, he'd thought nothing of going without proper rest for days and then spending the night carousing with his comrades. He was tired and hungry. Another outburst of vile temper from his bride, and he swore he'd drown her in the next farm pond they came to.

Cailin broke the silence between them when the sun was sinking in the west and the trees cast long shadows across the faint, rutted trail. "If ye did as ye said—if ye helped my sister, grandsire, and the bairn—I will let ye live, Englishman."

Her audacity made him laugh. "That's magnanimous of you."

"Ye did murder my father, but 'twas fair. It was battle, as you stated. And any man would do the same. I was a fool to blame ye."

"It took you long enough to come to that conclusion."

"Aye." She nodded solemnly. " 'Tis hard to reason when dealing with a Sassenach. You be the lowest form of human scum."

Just ahead, a covey of grouse broke from cover and exploded into the air. Both horses shied, and Cailin's horse reared up. Sterling pulled hard on his mount's reins to check the animal's excited plunging and then reached out to tighten the lead line that held her mare. "Whoa, whoa, girl," he soothed.

Cailin sat her saddle as erect and calm as if she were tied into it—as she was—without showing the slightest expression of fear. The hood of her cloak had fallen back, revealing her glorious hair, and he was struck again by her likeness to the girl in his long-ago vision.

"Are you all right?" he asked. She should have been in tears. But she wasn't. She was still watching him with the ferocity of a hunting hawk. "Would you think me worse if I told you that my mother was a savage—a red Indian from America?"

Her brow wrinkled as she considered that notion for a moment. "Nay," she said finally. "That might be why ye show some intelligence. For an Englishman." She smiled. "In truth, I must tell ye that my father's spilled blood still lies between us. I will hate ye to your grave, but I won't try to kill you—not unless you force me to it."

"That's comforting to know."

"What can you expect?" She shrugged. "Ye come unasked to my country, murder those I love, and—"

"And saved your neck. Don't you feel the slightest bit indebted to me?"

"Nay. What ye did, ye did for reasons of your own, not for my sake."

"You can't know that."

She grimaced. "All men act on their own desires. Since Adam was driven from the Garden of Eden, men have done as they pleased. 'Tis only when a thing goes wrong that they seek out a woman to blame."

"I am not your enemy, Cailin. I am your husband in the eyes of God, of church, and in law. As hard as it is for you to understand, I mean you no harm."

"So ye say."

"We have far to go. If we can't have peace, can we make a truce between us?" he asked.

Her eyes narrowed so that her thick, dark lashes hid her expression. "Can ye turn back time? Change what happened at Drummossie Moor?"

"Can you?"

"Nay," she admitted. "But I would if I could. I would trade my immortal soul to do so." She looked away so that he'd not see the tears rising in her eyes, and swallowed the lump in her throat.

The thing about death was that it was so final, she thought. All else could be altered, softened, done again to make a wrong into right. So many of hers were dead . . . her mother . . . her laughing cousin Alasdair . . . poor dumb Finley . . . Johnnie . . . Why was it that they were dead and she was spared from the gallows by her greatest foe?

If only her necklace held truth. Or magic. One wish, the legend promised, one wish for the bearer, even unto the power of life and death. But what to wish for? Her mother's life? Her first husband's? For Prince Charlie's victory, or for his death before he led so many good Scotsmen to their unhallowed graves? Or would she abandon them all to their fates and wish her little Corey safe in her arms?

She let the breeze dry the tears from her cheeks, then looked again at the man who held her future in his hands. His back was rigidly straight. He rode with the grace of a true horseman, his hands firm on the reins.

She drew in a deep breath and tried not to think of his hands. She had always been a woman to notice the hands of men. Sterling's hands were clean but scarred and calloused from years of holding leathers and steel. His nails were unusual for a man, trimmed short and neat. His palms were wide, his fingers lean and powerful. His thumbs were broad and squared off at the tip.

A man's hands told a lot about his character, she mused. Iain's hands had been cool and dry, but Sterling's radiated heat. She moistened her lips with her tongue and tried not to wonder what those sinewy fingers would feel like against her naked skin.

Better not to permit herself such wanton images. Sterling Gray was a soldier, an Englishman, and her enemy. She shouldn't think about him at all.

Still . . . She suppressed a shiver. There was something more, something that eluded her. Then she remembered the way he handled a weapon, deft and precise. Yes, if she touched Sterling's hands with her eyes blindfolded, she would know from the rough feel that he was a horseman and a swordsman.

From the moment he'd first laid hands on her at the farm, she'd been aware of his strength. The soldiers who had held her down and forced their will upon her had been strong and brutal, but Sterling Gray was not a brutal man. As much as she wanted to hate him, she had to be honest about that.

Were he a Scot instead of a Sassenach, she might have sought him out. There was an aura of wild unpredictability about him that called to the reckless side of her own fierce Highland nature.

She had not wanted to wed him—never that. As much as she desired children of her own, she had never wished to surrender her independence to another man. Husbands brought too many controls. A wife gained respect and position, but in doing so, she surrendered her own will to that of her lord and master. Cailin had been a maid, a bride, and a widow. She greatly preferred the freedom of being a woman grown, with the right to make her own choices.

She liked men. In general, she would rather be in their company than that of females. She loved the sound of their deep, booming male laughter and the way their broad shoulders filled a doorway. She found their bluntness of speech and directness of manner a relief from the deviousness and petty jealousies of most women. She enjoyed playful flirtation and the easy camaraderie that came with knowing a good-natured man well.

And she was not immune to the intense pleasures of lovemaking. Sex was the one thing that had never been wrong with her first marriage. And since her widowhood, she had twice indulged herself with the comfort of strong arms and the whispered delights of a night of abandon.

Both of those men were dead now, she realized with a start. And for the first time, she wondered if she were a jinx. Make love to me and die young, she thought wryly. Her mouth curved into a smile. What would Sterling Gray think of that? Had anyone realized what she had done and whom she had done it with, they might have started calling her the "black widow" as they had Mary MacDonald, who had wed and lost four husbands in as many years.

Perhaps the blessing in the Eye of Mist had ebbed away, leaving only the curse, she mused. 'Twould serve her captor right if she turned some of her foul luck on him.

Her stomach growled, and she shifted in the saddle, suddenly becoming aware of a hollow feeling inside. She was hungry. The bread and cheese they'd shared at midday seemed to have been devoured weeks ago. She'd always had a keen appetite. Going without decent food had been one of the worst things about being in prison.

That and worrying if she was with child by her rapists ... She sighed with relief. That terror at least was behind her. Her body had healed, and she'd not been left with the guilt of carrying a child of shame. Had she been in the family way ... She shook her head. There was no use reliving the terrifying incident or her weeks of mental agony afterward. She only hoped that what the English soldiers had done to her had not ruined the act of love for her forever.

She'd felt rage against her attackers and a desire for revenge, but she'd known she was blameless. She had fought them tooth and nail with every ounce of her strength. They had overpowered her only because there were three of them. And what they had done to her had no relation to the natural beauty of the act between a willing man and woman. They had been worse than beasts, and she had contented herself by imagining their souls consigned to eternal hell.

She had done so logically. One by one, she had mentally brought each man before a clan tribunal. She had been the only judge and jury, but she had replayed each moment of the offense in detail. She had given them a chance to speak in their own behalf, and she had questioned them with the detachment of an Edinburgh barrister. Once their guilt had been declared, she had taken days to come to a decision about the sentence. Death, she'd decided, would be too easy. In the end, she'd stripped them of their immortal souls.

Later, she wondered if the imaginary trial had been an act of madness. Her delusions had been so real that she had been able to forget the damp stone walls and the stench of the dungeons. But dementia or sanity, her staged drama had allowed her to put her brutal violation behind her. The painful memories of her assault no longer haunted her dreams or caused her gut to twist with pain. Right or wrong, she had found her own version of justice.

"Cailin."

She started as Sterling Gray called her name. She'd been so lost in her own thoughts that she'd forgotten him.

He pointed to a cluster of structures at a crossroads ahead. "There is an inn, the White Fleece. They bake a tasty pigeon pie, and the beds are free of vermin. I mean for us to spend the night under their roof."

"So?"

"Would you rather ride in with your hands bound like a criminal or peacefully as my wife?"

She considered his offer. "Untie me."

"Do you give me your word that you won't slit my throat in the night or try to escape?"

"Aye," she agreed readily enough. This was war. Any soldier could lie to an enemy without losing honor.

"Can I trust you, Cailin?"

She flashed a wide-eyed look of innocence. "Of course. As ye say, I am your prisoner and your wife. It would make no sense for me to risk your displeasure."

"That's the part that troubles me," he said as he dismounted and walked back toward her mare.

Cailin smiled and held out her wrists.

Chapter 7

~~~~~OO~~~~~

Cailin was so weary that she could hardly keep
her eyes open long enough to eat the lamb stew
and hot baked bread the serving girl had brought
her. She sat alone at a small round table in a shadowy corner of the White Fleece Inn. Sterling had escorted her to a table, ordered a meal, and then had
gone out to oversee the care of their horses. For the
first time in months, she was not manacled or under
close guard, and every instinct bade her use this opportunity to escape.

Her family, her homeland beckoned. Each day and
each mile she and Sterling put between them and
Scotland made it more difficult for her to return to
her beloved Highlands. But her strength was gone,
her will weakened by the ill treatment of the prison
guards and the fatigue of her body. She'd not slept in
a proper bed since the dragoons had raided Johnnie's
farm; she'd gone so long without decent food that
her gums felt tender and one back tooth was sensitive.

Even her mind seemed dull and unable to respond.
She desperately wanted to go home; she wanted to
keep her promise to find Corey. But even more, she
needed to bathe and climb between clean linen sheets
and sleep for twenty-four hours straight.

Sterling had told her that Jeanne and her grandfather had gotten safely away from the farm. She had to believe that. She could not stand the death of one more person whom she loved.

How many times can a heart be broken and still beat? she wondered as she stirred the steaming food on her plate and nibbled at the bread. *Ye must be strong*, her grandfather had said. She'd heard him say those words on her sixth birthday, the morning her mother had hung the Eye of Mist around her neck and related the magical legend that accompanied it.

It was her grandfather who had taken her on his knee and confided the family secret that her father was not really Muireach Campbell—her mother's first husband—but a rogue named Cameron Stewart who now lived somewhere in the wilds of the American Colonies. This Cameron Stewart, Grandda explained, had sent her the necklace and a sum of money to be used for her wedding dowry when she was a woman grown. Since Cailin's birth date was ten months after Muireach Campbell's murder by a jealous husband, there had always been servants' whispers about her legitimacy. It was a shock to know that the gossip was true and that she was a bastard instead of the firstborn of a wealthy laird; but since she'd never known her mother's first husband, she could not mourn his loss as her father. Neither could she feel anything for Cameron Stewart, another man who had been drawn into the complicated web of her mother's life.

Ye must be strong. Her grandfather had said the same thing on the night that her mother died in childbirth, and again when Cailin's husband had died.

No wonder Jeanne is such a milksop of a woman, Cailin mused as she forced herself to take another bite of the delicious food in front of her. Meek little Jeanne. Sweet Jeanne. Jeanne's weapons were her fair face and the big blue eyes that shed tears when a voice was raised in her presence or whenever she was frightened or angry. There was no need for little Jeanne to be strong; there were always others willing to be strong for her.

And I was always first in line . . .

From the day she was born, I watched over her. I fought her battles and spoke up for her while she wept pretty tears. Jeanne has always looked so much like Mother, but her lovely shape and features are the only similarity. She has none of Mother's shrewdness or her iron will. Yet Jeanne's path has always been a smooth one.

Why couldn't I have been the sweet one? Why hadn't people said *gentle Cailin?* Why is it always taken for granted that I will do what needs to be done and save my tears for the privacy of my own pillow?

I'm tired of being strong, a voice inside her cried. *I want someone to take care of me for a change.*

"How'd ya like some company, darlin'?"

The strong smell of rum shattered Cailin's reverie as a pock-faced stranger draped his arm around her shoulder and squeezed her breast.

Without thinking, she seized her plate and hurled the contents into his face. He bellowed with rage as she leaped out of the chair, grabbed her eating knife, and faced him across the table. "Dinna touch me!" she cried. She stood trembling with the knife clutched in her hand, but her knees were slightly flexed, and she balanced on the balls of her feet as Johnnie had taught her.

The man was big and dirty with a wide nose that

had been broken so many times that it had lost all shape. He was a giant—so tall that his bald, pock-scarred head barely cleared the low ceiling beams. He wore the coarse clothes of a drover, and he smelled like a rotting sheep.

In seconds, the public room erupted around her. A dog began to bark furiously, the barmaid shrieked, and the tavern owner came running with a thick oak staff in his hands. The intoxicated lout who'd accosted her stammered obscenities as he wiped the hot stew from his face. He circled Cailin ominously, keeping just out of range of her knife.

Behind him, several comrades surged forward, hooting with laughter. "Get her, Harley!"

Harley balled a meaty fist and took a stride forward. "Drop 'at knife, bitch."

Johnnie MacLeod's words echoed in Cailin's head. *Watch a man's eyes, lass. Watch his eyes, and you'll ken what he means to do before he does.* Harley's eyes were pale blue, small and piglike in his broad face.

She sucked in a ragged breath. "Touch me again, and I'll make ye rue the day ye were born," she threatened softly.

Harley took a swing at her. She dodged aside and drove the knife up to catch him in the underside of the arm. But before the blade touched his flesh, someone coming up behind her shoved her halfway across the room. She struck the side of a table, regained her balance, and looked back in time to see Sterling land a fist to the drunkard's jaw.

The innkeeper stepped in front of her, barring her way with his staff. He reached for her knife. She handed it over without protest, then ducked past him to see what was happening.

Harley rocked back, shook his massive head, and blinked.

"You've made a mistake," Sterling said in a low, reasonable tone. "The lady you have difficulty with is my wife. Admit your error, apologize to her, and walk out of here while you can still walk."

A purple tide washed over Harley's pocked face. He let out a roar and lunged for Sterling with arms that could have lifted an ox. Sterling waited until the last second, then moved aside so quickly that Cailin was astonished. And as he did, he put out a booted foot to trip Harley.

The big man crashed into the floor with enough force to rattle the tin plates on the tables, gave a single groan, and lay still.

Sterling glanced up at Harley's companions and smiled. "Poor fellow. He's had too much to drink. Best you take him somewhere to sleep it off." His voice was amicable, but his right hand dropped to rest on the hilt of his sword.

Wordlessly, two of the men took hold of Harley's arms while the third grabbed his ankles. Sterling tossed a silver coin to the innkeeper. "That should cover any damages and pay for a round of ale for the house."

The tavern owner grinned. "Aye, sir. It will. And you have my apologies. I run a decent inn."

Cailin opened her mouth to comment on the quality of an inn where common folk felt free to lay hands on a lady, but before she could say a word, Sterling crossed the distance between them with two strides and took her arm.

"We'll say no more about the matter," he said to the innkeeper, "so long as my lady hasn't been harmed." He looked into her face. "Mistress?"

"No," she replied. "I wasna hurt but—"

Sterling nodded to the innkeeper. "Good enough. We'll have our meal in our room. Kindly send up a bottle of your best wine and plenty of hot water for the bath." He pushed Cailin firmly toward the open staircase.

"It wasn't my fault—" she began.

"Hush, *dear*," he said. "We'll discuss that later. Keep going. Top of the stairs, last room on the right."

His fingers gripped her arm, not tightly enough to hurt, but too firmly to pull free. "Ye must listen to my side of—"

"Remind me not to let you near a blade," he murmured in her ear as he hustled her up the staircase. "You wield it like an Italian assassin."

She detected a hint of sarcasm. "He assaulted me," she insisted. "I was eating my—"

"Can't I leave you alone for five minutes without you getting into trouble? Were you planning on murdering this one too?"

"Mother of God!" she swore. "Only an Englishman would be stupid enough to fight a giant with his fists instead of drawing his sword. What right do ye have to judge my—"

"Quiet. You've caused enough of a commotion for one day in the public room."

"Ye dinna believe me. That filthy swine took liberties with me. What would ye have me do? Fling myself into his arms?"

"You were minding your own business and he—"

"Aye," she answered hotly. "I was."

"If you're telling the truth, I owe you an apology."

"Aye, ye do that."

"Men make a habit of attacking you without reason."

"Aye, so it seems."

"A coincidence that this should happen while I'm outside."

"Would he dare to touch me with my ... " She started to say *husband*, but the hateful word refused to roll off her tongue. ". . . with you in the room," she finished lamely. "He deserved killing. Ye should have run him through with your sword."

He shrugged. "Many men deserve killing. If I made it my business to dispose of them all—"

"A Highlander would be ashamed to let a woman under his protection be insulted. Obviously, you English—"

"Peace, mistress. If you were wronged, I'm sorry. But when I came in and saw you about to carve that poor drover's—"

"You assumed that it was my fault—that I'm a woman who welcomes mauling by—"

"No. That's far from the truth. But I don't like killing. I've been a soldier most of my life but—"

"If he'd put hands on an Englishwoman, what then? Suppose it had been your mother?"

"I told you that my mother wasn't English, she was Indian. And no, if he'd insulted my mother, I wouldn't have killed him for it—not unless I was forced to it." He looked at her sharply. "You're certain you're not hurt?"

"Nay."

"If he did hurt you, I'll find him and—"

"Nay. He was drunk and crude. Had ye not come when ye did, I would have taught him some manners. But ye came to my aid, and for that I suppose I must thank you."

"Don't put yourself to any trouble." Sterling pushed open the door to a cramped room containing an ancient bed, a fireplace, a single oak table, and a straight-backed chair. Wedged between the poster bed and the tiny fireplace was half a wooden barrel. Interior shutters covered the only window. To open it, someone would need to climb over the bed and stand on the chair.

Cailin stepped inside the shabby chamber, and Sterling followed. Worn floorboards creaked under her feet as she moved as far from him as she could without getting on the furniture or climbing into the barrel. She peered into the container. It was empty except for a puddle of water in the bottom. "This must be my laird's bath," she said, wrinkling her nose.

"It's plain, but it will do," he replied. "The room's clean enough, and as I told you before, there aren't any bugs. You should be grateful I didn't put you in the common chamber. Up to twelve strangers share the three beds. The women's side is curtained off for propriety's sake."

"It might be better if I stayed there."

"I think not. You'll remain here where I can keep my eyes on you."

She glanced at the bed. "You expect me to sleep there with you?"

"Unless you'd prefer the tub."

"I prefer my freedom."

"Damn you, woman. Can you not give me an hour's peace? It's no wonder we've been at war with the Scots since the wheel was invented. You're all a surly, troublemaking lot." He removed his coat and hat and threw them on the bed.

"This marriage was not of my making," she said. "I've slept with three men, all by my own choice. Do ye expect a husband's rights, they will come dearer than ye reckon."

His expression softened. "Is that what frightens you, mistress, that you think I'll force you into—"

"You forced me into wedding vows."

"To save your stubborn neck."

She stared straight into his black devil eyes. "No man takes his enemy to wife for charity's sake. Give me an honest explanation, and we may come to terms."

His skin took on a darker hue, and Cailin knew she'd touched a nerve. "As I said before, my reasons are my own." He laid a hand on her arm, and she jerked away. "I won't hurt you, Cailin. I've beggared myself to keep you from harm. The last thing I'd want to do is hurt you."

She wanted to believe him, but life had taught her better. *No man acts except in his own interest.* She'd not stayed alive when others around her died by playing the fool. "Ye hurt me most by holding me against my will. I've a child waiting for me. I must return to Scotland."

"I can't let you do that, Cailin."

Frissons of excitement ran down her spine whenever he said her name. It should have sounded strange on his lips. His accent was all wrong. Instead, *Cailin* came out softer ... sweeter than she'd ever heard it spoken. Her face felt warm, her knees weak.

I'm tired unto death, she thought. My mind and body are playing tricks on me. Mayhap I've taken a chill. I had a fever earlier; maybe it's coming back.

But she knew this was no ordinary sickness. Whatever spell Captain Sterling Gray had cast over her, it had naught to do with weak bowels or a queasy stomach. She'd not shrunk from him because she was afraid of him—it was fear of herself that drove her. She liked his touch. A little wine and a warm fire and she might find herself liking more than the feel of his fingers.

"If you go to Scotland, it will mean your execution," he said.

"I'll take the chance o' that."

His brow creased in a frown. "Over my dead body."

"I hope not."

"I'm weary, woman. I want a bath, hot food, and sleep. You can lie on the floor or sit in the barrel, or you can share the bed with me. I've not the strength for anything more vigorous than a good night's rest, even if you were willing—which I take it you're not."

She shook her head. "I'd rather go to the common room. I'm nay in the habit of sharing a room with—"

He laughed. "With your lawful husband?"

"There's still some doubt as to how lawful that ceremony was."

"It better be good. It cost me every guinea I had and every one I could borrow to bribe the justice to exile you instead of—"

"You *paid* for my release?"

"What have I been saying?"

She sank into the chair. "Be ye mad?"

"There are those who think so." Her eyes widened, and he raised a palm. "No, I assure you, my irrationality isn't dangerous. I was sickened by what happened after Culloden. All my life, I've been a soldier, but I've never been a butcher. I couldn't make war on civilians, not even Scots. I've resigned my commission in the dragoons. I'm afraid I've acquired a wife at an awkward time. I haven't the faintest idea how I'm going to support you."

"Where are you taking me?" Her fatigue was over-powering. She wanted to crawl into the bed and shut her eyes, but she couldn't—not yet.

"My father's country estate. I doubt we'll find much of a welcome there, but I borrowed money from my friends, and I must repay it. I have some savings and—"

"He is a wealthy man . . . your father?"

"Yes. He's a baron, but I'm a bastard son. He gave me his name and an education. I can expect no more from him."

She couldn't keep from smiling. "That's the first thing we have in common, Sassenach. I was born on the wrong side of the blanket myself. Of course, my mother was wise enough to conceal the fact." She fingered the necklace at her throat. "All I had from my father was this and—" She broke off as someone rapped loudly at the door.

"Hot water, sir," a woman's voice called.

"Come in," Sterling answered.

A maid pushed open the door and entered with two buckets of hot water. Behind her came a half-grown boy, also carrying buckets. "Will you have your bath or your meal first, sir?" the girl asked.

"I'll have the bath," Sterling replied. "Bring the food and drink in half an hour." When the servants were gone, he glanced at Cailin. "Would you like first chance at the water?"

"You canna expect me to bathe with you in the room."

He chuckled. "If you think I'm leaving you alone here, you're crazy. You'd be out of that window and on my horse before I finished a mug of ale."

"I refuse to take off my clothes in front of you," she said indignantly. The clean water was enticing, but she was no fool. First he'd watch her bathe, then he'd expect her to climb between the sheets and provide entertainment.

"Pity. The water will be filthy after I'm done with it." He began to undo the buttons on his shirt cuff. "I hope you're not dirty by nature. I can't abide an unclean woman."

"Unclean?" She felt her throat and face grow hot with shame. "How dare ye accuse me of such a thing?"

He laughed. "I'll admit I'm a fanatic about bathing. It's my savage ancestry. The Shawnee bathe every day, regardless of the weather. In winter, even children break ice to swim in the rivers and streams."

That sounded like a tall tale. She stared at him, wondering if he believed her a fool or if he really was telling the truth about the Indians bathing in ice water.

He shoved the bed in front of the door. "Just to make certain you don't try to escape while I'm in a state of undress," he said. "Are you certain you don't want a bath?"

"No," she replied stubbornly.

With a shrug, he pulled his linen shirt over his head, and before she turned away, she caught a glimpse of deep, ivory scars crisscrossing a brawny copper chest. Sterling's shoulders were broad and corded with muscle, his belly flat, his waist neatly tapered. His chest and powerful arms were nearly free of body hair, but above the low-slung waistline of his doeskin breeches, she saw the definite shading of black curls.

"The least you could do is scrub my back," he said.

Cailin stared at the crumbling plaster wall and

tried to ignore the sounds of sloshing water coming from the tub. "I dinna find this funny," she replied.

"The water's still warm, mistress," he teased. "It feels good to wash off the dust of the road. I've real French soap, scented with lilac. A pity you're missing—"

"Stop it!" She whirled around. Sterling was crouched in the barrel so that no more of him was visible than when he'd removed his shirt. "I dinna ken what game you're playing with me," she cried. "I'm tired, and I'm sore, and I'm not in the least interested in your naked body."

He grinned lazily. "You're sure? I've not had many complaints." He lifted a dripping arm and soaped his shoulder. "I can't say about your body—since I've yet to see it—but I doubt I'll find much to complain about."

"I'm getting in the bed," she said angrily. "I'm going to sleep. And if you so much as touch me, I swear, I'll have your black heathen eyes from their sockets."

"For one so small, you're as fierce as a Seneca."

"I mean what I say, Englishman," she threatened as she kicked off her shoes.

"Sleep. I'll not trouble you. As I said before, I like my bed partners willing. You are my wedded wife, and you'll not be able to resist my charm for long."

"Don't count on it!" His laughter burned her ears as she pulled back the covers and flung herself into the feather tick fully dressed.

"Sweet dreams, wife."

She shut her eyes and drew up her knees, pulling the covers over her head. If he laid one hand on her, she'd kill him. Marriage lines or not, she'd nay be raped again.

"This water will be cold by morning," he added.

"Damn you," she muttered. But images of her husband's naked body rose behind her clenched eyelids to trouble her fitful attempts at sleep.

Chapter 8

Oxley Hall
Surrey, England

Ten days later, Sterling faced the full force of his father's rage in the quiet opulence of the great library in Oxley Hall. Sterling and Cailin had arrived at the baron's country home late the night before, after having ridden through rain for a week. Sterling had insisted that she breakfast alone in his chamber that morning while he went to confront the old lion in his den.

Years had added weight to his father's powerful frame. Henry Gray's snow-white hair was shoulder-length, in flagrant disregard for current fashion, which dictated that gentlemen shave their heads and wear wigs at all times. His eyes had once been piercing blue; now the intensity of their hue had faded, but they'd lost none of their fire when he was in high temper.

Henry, the Baron Oxley, had just launched into his second tirade. The first had begun when Sterling entered the room and had ended with the shattering of a delicate Chinese teapot that Sterling estimated would have cost the equivalent of a month's salary as a captain in His Majesty's dragoons.

"... ungrateful bastard pup!" his father roared.

"Better you'd never been born than to shame the Gray name with . . ."

Damn it, Sterling thought. Why do I let him rant on like this? He makes me feel sixteen years old again.

But Sterling knew why. His Indian heritage made him straighten his shoulders and stand there while venom spewed from his father's lips. Reverence toward his elders had been bred into Sterling for a thousand generations. It was bone and sinew of his soul. As much as he wanted to release the full force of his own pent-up anger, he bit back his words and let the filth spill over him.

Shifting his booted feet, Sterling allowed his gaze to stray through the wavery panes of the old casement window to the formal boxwood gardens that stretched out over the site of a ruined priory. King Henry, his father's namesake, had seized Oxley from the white monks centuries ago and given it and a title to a wealthy merchant in exchange for a large donation to the Crown treasury. Thus, Martin Gray, a commoner had become the first noble Lord Oxley.

"Worthless red-skinned whelp. The worse mistake I made in my entire life was to bestow a Christian name and birthright on you."

Sterling didn't need to listen. He knew his father's speech by heart.

How many times had he stood here and listened to this? he wondered. In the past, he'd usually suffered the indignity with a smarting back from the caning his tutor—and in later years his father's footman Edgar—had administered before Sterling entered the library. It had been Edgar's pleasure to lay vigorous strokes across his bare back until blood ran. His brothers cut their beatings short by crying out; he never had. Keeping silent was his single triumph.

Sterling glanced back at his father, waiting for the old man to sweep the inkstand and papers off the inlaid walnut writing cabinet that served the baron as a desk. And, as usual, Sterling wasn't disappointed. His father sent ink, quills, holders, and parchment flying with a fresh round of curses.

Now it was time for Father's tears.

"I treated you like a son. I raised you as though your skin was white," the baron proclaimed.

And the old wound ached anew, as Sterling had known it would. His father's words never failed to find a weak spot in his armor and dig deep.

He swallowed against the constriction in his throat. I am as white as you, he wanted to protest. But he never had.

In truth, he'd always been somewhat ashamed of his dark skin and exotic eyes. He'd wanted desperately to have a long, narrow nose like his brothers, but the mark of his Shawnee blood was indelible and became more evident with each passing year.

Sterling drew in a slow, deep breath. Only a few more minutes and his father would begin to lose his wind. He'd rally with a few choice insults against Sterling's Indian mother before turning to the current sin at hand.

". . . not only proved your cowardice by resigning your commission in time of war," Henry continued, "but have the audacity to bring that . . . that . . ." He sputtered, gasping for air. "That Scottish whore back . . . and tell me that she is your lawful wife."

Sterling blinked. His torpor vanished. "What did you say?"

"A traitorous Scot! A common savage. No better than the bitch who bore you."

"Father, shut up."

The port-wine flush of anger in the old man's face drained away, replaced with stark milk-white. "What? What?" The words came out in a strangled whisper.

"I said *shut up*. I owe you some measure of respect because you are my father and an old man. That's the only thing that's keeping me from smashing your ugly mouth in."

"You dare ... " Spittle sprayed from his lips. "You dare to speak to your sire in that fashion?"

"I should have done it long ago. You've no right to condemn my mother when your sin of lechery was as great as hers. And you've certainly no right to impugn my wife."

"Traitorous pup!" Henry yanked a bellpull. "Edgar! Edgar!" he shouted, summoning his footman.

Edgar sprang from his post outside the library door with more agility than Sterling would have supposed he possessed. "Yes, Your Lordship. What is it?"

Henry pointed a trembling forefinger at Sterling. "Thrash this ungrateful whelp!"

Sterling glanced at the tall, thin footman and laughed. "I wouldn't if I were you, Edgar," he warned. For all his determination, Edgar was older than the baron, and it had been many years since he'd set his hand to anything more demanding than climbing the grand staircase in the hall.

"Thrash him," Henry ordered.

Edgar stood rooted to the floor, mouth open.

"Touch me," Sterling said quietly to the startled

footman, "and I'll toss you through the window into the box garden."

"Get out of my house," his father roared. "Out, I say! You and your Scottish strumpet."

Sterling heard a sharp intake of breath behind him and turned to see Cailin standing just inside the room. "Go back to my chamber," he commanded her. "There's no need for you to hear this. This is between me and my esteemed parent."

"No longer your parent," his father proclaimed. "I disown you! I'll have your name removed from the family Bible. By God, if you—if the *two of you* think to come here and extort money from me, I'll—"

"That's a lie!" Cailin said hotly. "I didna ask to come here. I dinna know why your son brought me to this place. But I want nothing from ye. And from what I ken of him, I doubt he does either."

"Don't dare speak to me, woman," the baron cried. "Edgar, get her out of—"

"Don't touch her, Edgar," Sterling warned. "*She'll* throw you through the window." He turned on his father. "I have no intention of staying. I only came to retrieve some personal belongings, to arrange to repay some loans with my own savings, and to say goodbye. I'm going to America, and I'm taking my wife with me."

"Taking me *where?*" Cailin cried.

He glared at her. "I told you to leave the room." He directed his attention to his father again. "I can see it was a mistake to try and deal with you rationally, so I will be blunt. I want the deed to the land my mother gave me."

"You do, do you?" His father was shaking from head to toe, and Sterling was afraid the old man might have a stroke.

"Calm yourself. I ask for nothing that is not mine by law. If you remember, I asked you for the deed when I reached twenty and one. You put me off. This time, you're not getting away with it. The land is rightfully mine."

His father whirled and yanked open the upper doors of the writing cabinet, then began throwing papers right and left. "You want what *she* gave you, do you?" he sputtered. "Well, you shall have it! And not another penny! I'll cut you from my will. I swear I will. You'll be disinherited from this day forth." His fingers closed on a cylinder of rolled oilcloth, and he held it high. "Your precious mother's legacy. Naught but useless wilderness. Little good you'll have of it, boy. Nothing but trees and savages." He grimaced and threw the deed on the floor between them.

Sterling's eyes burned. "What have I ever done to make you hate me so?" he finally managed.

The baron swayed on his feet and caught himself on the corner of the desk, supporting his weight. Suddenly, he looked old and tired. "You make me ashamed every time I look at you," he said with disgust. "You remind me of *her* and of a period in my life that I've never ceased to regret."

Sterling's chest felt tight, and his head throbbed. The room had become stuffy, and it was hard for him to breathe. "I'm sorry, Father," he said. "It seems the biggest mistake was yours. A mistake for you to ever bring me to England. Why did you do it? Why didn't you leave me with my mother's people?"

"Because of your Gray blood," the baron answered hoarsely. "Because I thought good English stock would triumph over barbarian—"

"Enough," Sterling said. "There's no need to continue." He noticed that Cailin had come to stand at his side, and he grasped her arm firmly. "We'll take our leave of you, sir."

"Damned right you will. And if you ever set foot on Oxley again, I'll have you shot!"

Sterling took a step toward the door. Cailin broke free of his grasp, darted back, and picked up the oil-cloth cylinder from the floor.

"You'll need this if you're going to America," she said.

"*We* will need it," he replied.

"Go straight to hell, both of you," Oxley flung after them as they left the library.

"We'll save ye a good place near the fire," Cailin quipped. Then she scowled up at Sterling. "Be this English hospitality?" she asked. "When ye call us savages?"

"My father's idea of hospitality," he answered softly as he strode down the hall, pulling her along with him. "He was ever a man sentimental toward his children."

"Stop pretending to be asleep," Sterling said. "I know you're awake. I asked if I can trust you alone here long enough to secure passage to Maryland for us on the *Galway Maid*."

Cailin rolled over in bed and opened her eyes. It was true; she had heard his question. But she had been summoning her wits to try to deal with him.

They had been in the seaport of Dover for the best part of a week. Sterling had rented two rooms in a private home on the outskirts of the town for them. The accommodations were plain but clean, and Cailin could find no fault with their landlady's cooking.

Since she'd witnessed the angry scene between Sterling and his father in the library at Oxley Hall,

Cailin couldn't help feeling some sympathy for the man she still considered her captor. It was obvious that whatever his reasons for becoming entangled in her life, Sterling Gray was a complex and basically decent man.

"Ye canna force me to go with you to America," she said quietly. She was close enough to feel his breath on her cheek. As unnerving as it was to live in such intimacy with her unwanted husband, he'd made no improper advances toward her, and she had begun to trust him enough to catch hours of fitful sleep at night.

"You are a vision in the morning with your hair loose around your shoulders and your face all dewy soft."

Shivers ran down her spine, and she sat up, clutching the light coverlet to her chest. She looked away toward the window, where mastheads showed against the robin's-egg-blue of a cloudless morning sky.

For an instant, memories of the rape swept over her, and she saw the hungry eyes of soldiers and heard their foul words.

"Dinna fash me with such lies," she said. Sterling was not like the men who had hurt her. In her heart of hearts, she knew it. "I am not a beautiful woman, and I am past the age to believe such nonsense."

"Cailin."

He touched her bare arm between elbow and shoulder, and her shiver became a flood of sensations that she'd vowed she would not let herself feel for this man.

"Cailin," he repeated.

Her name rolled off his tongue like warm honey. There was no anger in his speech, no naked lust.

Sterling was an Englishman, but he was nothing like the soldiers who had raped her. She could not prevent her gaze from straying back to his naked chest ... his muscular, tanned arms ... his intense face.

"We are enemies," she murmured.

"Our *countries* are enemies." His lean fingers caressed her shoulder.

"I hate you." The words came out all wrong. She did hate him, she did, but her tone wouldn't have convinced a lackwit. And Sterling Gray was far from slow-minded.

"You think you do." He stroked her hair with feather-light movements, and pinwheels danced in the pit of her stomach. "Wife," he whispered. "I'm not made of steel."

"Ye knew from the first I didna want you."

"No?" He buried his fingers in her hair. She wanted to tell him to stop touching her. She wanted to leap out of bed and run from the room, but she didn't. She was so surprised that his touch didn't repel her that she waited until he lifted a heavy lock of her hair and kissed her neck.

"Don't be afraid of me."

She wasn't. The fear she'd expected didn't come. Instead, she felt what could only be desire. "Sterling."

"Aye," he teased, then kissed her again beneath the ear. His lips were warm and moist. His hand slid down to caress her shoulder and collarbone. And when he pulled her closer to him, she had not the strength to resist.

"Dinna ..." she began, but the rest of her words were lost as his mouth pressed against hers.

His kiss was tender. His lips were as beguiling as the devil's lies.

"Wife," he said. "Let me love you."

"I dinna ..." Her protests died away as she found herself inexplicably kissing him back. She sighed, a long, soft sigh. This felt good. It felt right.

She had been so afraid that the rape would keep her from wanting this ever again. But it hadn't.

He kissed the corners of her mouth, her throat, and her eyelids. She laughed, and he found her mouth again. She knew she was lost when the tip of his tongue parted her lips.

Suddenly, Sterling was no longer the man who had murdered her father or stolen her away from her homeland. He was only a desirable man, and they were together in a warm bed on a late summer morning.

It had been so long since anyone had held her this way, so long since she'd tasted the sweet nectar of a lover's kisses or felt his hands on her naked body. She closed her eyes and gave herself over to the pleasure, letting herself savor the velvet heat of his tongue and the response of her own love-starved body.

Cailin was vaguely conscious of putting her arms around his neck, of meeting kiss for kiss ... of letting him push her back against the feather tick ... of feeling the length of his hard body pressing against hers.

His black hair fell forward to brush the bare skin above her shift. "It tickles," she whispered.

He laughed and pushed the hair away, kissing the spot with his lips while his hand gently cupped her breast.

She arched her back and sighed, remembering the joy of a man's mouth on her nipples ... Remembering ... One of the dragoons had bitten her. Her right breast still bore a scar from his teeth. But Sterling wouldn't hurt her. She knew he wouldn't, and she needed his lips, his mouth to wipe away the memories of horror. "Kiss me there, please," she whispered.

"You're a bold piece," he teased. But he did as she asked, and it was all right. She felt her nipple tighten and swell. She felt a heat coil in the pit of her belly.

Tears sprang to her eyes . . . tears of joy. What those men had done to her was over and done with. She didn't have to carry the shame for the rest of her life.

Outside the open window, a bird trilled. A warm breeze carried the scent of the ocean to the bright bedchamber. Cailin closed her eyes and blocked out the ugliness and the pain. Sterling's head lay against her breast, and she felt safe.

"Such a sweet bud," he said.

Somehow, his free hand had found her bare thigh and was sliding her linen shift higher. She moved restlessly as a cold sliver of unease darted from the darkness of her mind.

It's Sterling, she told herself. It's all right if he touches me. I want him to. She tried to concentrate on the rubbing of thin cloth against her throbbing nipples.

"Am I so repulsive a husband?"

She caught his chin and raised it so that she could kiss him full on the mouth. When they were kissing, she didn't think about the soldiers.

"Ye talk too much," she said when they broke to take a breath. "If I did want a husband, 'twould never be one who cawed like a raven from dawn till dark."

He was an excellent kisser.

Cailin was no inexperienced lass. She'd been

kissed by boys and men, some sober and others drunk as lairds. Sterling was a master of the art. His breath was clean, his teeth sound, and his manners proper.

Kissing Sterling was like leaping off a bluff into the sunlit waters of Loch Shin. At first contact there was a shock, but as the kiss deepened, the mystery and the sense of abandon grew. His kiss took in more than her lips; it swept over her body like a wind-whipped tide. And like staying under water too long, Sterling's kiss made her lose track of reason.

He nuzzled her breast. "You're soft in all the right places, wife. I want you." His voice deepened to a low husky rumble. "I want you, Cailin, more than I wanted my first woman . . . more than I've ever wanted any woman."

"I'm nay your wife," she protested, but only a little, because he'd pushed her shift down to expose her round, rosy breast.

She moaned as he flicked his tongue over her nipple. "Sweet," he whispered, and gently drew her into his mouth.

Good. It felt so good. She didn't care if she hated him. It had been too long since any man had suckled at her breast. Closing her eyes again, she strained against him, stroking his shoulders and sinewy arms with her fingertips. She felt his manhood, hard and swollen, press against her leg.

I want him, she thought. I do. I want him to make love to me.

Then, Sterling's hand brushed the curls between her thighs, and her eyes flew open. Instantly, she stiffened in his arms.

"I need you, Cailin," he said huskily. "I've been too long a monk."

She shook her head, and the tears spilled down her cheeks as the taunts of the soldiers echoed in her ears. She remembered one dragoon—the leader. His cock had been huge and purple-red. He'd hammered into her when she was dry, and the pain ... "I can't do this," she cried, pushing Sterling away. "Please, don't."

"What do you mean, you can't? You wanted it as much as I did." He rolled away from her and rose from the bed. Angrily, he stalked to the chair and began to pull on his breeches. "We took vows together. Did you think I meant to sleep alone forever?"

"You don't understand." She was sobbing now, out of control.

"You're damn right I don't. There's a name for women who do what you just did to me."

"That's not fair. You don't—"

"Save it."

He was angrier than she'd ever seen him.

"Just listen to me for one minute," she pleaded.

"For what? More lies?" His face darkened. "Did you ask me to kiss you or not? What was I supposed to think?"

"It's not you," she blurted out. "I was raped. The dragoons who took me from Johnnie's farm to Edinburgh Castle raped me and—"

"*What?*" He returned to the bed and pulled her into his arms. "Are you telling me the truth?" He looked into her face, and his scowl dissolved. "Why didn't you tell me?"

She leaned against his shoulder and wept. He held her until the storm of emotion passed, then he wiped the tears from her face with the hem of his shirt.

"Damn them to hell," he muttered.

"I already did," she said.

He pulled her against him again and hugged her. "You should have told me."

"I thought it was over and done with."

"I'd have killed them if I'd known. I'd have hunted them down and killed them like the rutting boars they are."

"Really?" She sniffed.

"I killed a man before for rape."

"I did want you, just now, but . . ." She averted her eyes, and her cheeks grew warm. "I guess it's too soon. I thought I was ready, but . . ."

"You should have told me, Cailin. I would have gone slower. I thought—"

"Do ye blame me?"

"Blame you? Why should I—"

"I knew a woman who drowned herself in the loch when her husband turned her out after the English—"

"I knew a soldier who futtered a sheep, but that doesn't mean I favor four-legged partners." He stood up and walked to the window, throwing back the interior shutters and looking down on the street below. "I didn't know, Cailin," he said. "I swear I didn't know you were in that danger or I would have taken you to Edinburgh Castle myself."

She slid out of the far side of the bed, stepped behind a screen, and began to dress. "I can't go to America with you," she said.

"You can and you will." He turned back toward her. "There's little for you in England, and Scotland would be a death sentence." He dropped into the chair and reached for his stockings. "You might learn to like America, Cailin. It's a new land, without the old hatreds."

"You still want me, even though men have—"

"What happened had nothing to do with you. It wasn't your fault."

"I never thought it was. I wanted to know what you—"

"You are my wife. I've not led a saint's life myself."

"You've never told me why you married me," she reminded him as she peeked out from behind the screen.

"No, I haven't. Why isn't important. What is important is that we get on with our lives. I want to make a bargain with you, Cailin. If you'll agree to live as my wife for two years, I'll let you go after that."

"In America." She struggled with a row of tiny buttons.

"Yes. You'll be safe there."

"And during this two years, ye expect me to share your bed and fortunes?"

"My fortunes, yes. We'll have to work on the bed part."

"Aye," she replied. "I can see that."

"No more threats, and no more attempts at running away."

"When have I tried to get away?"

"When have I given you the opportunity?"

"Two years is a long time," she hedged. "I'd have to think on it."

"I'm tired of the fighting. I'm tired of the arguments. I think the offer is fair. Two years isn't much to ask, after what your release has cost me."

"I didn't ask for your help," she reminded him as she stepped out from behind the screen.

"But you pride yourself on being a woman who pays her debts."

"Who told ye that?"

The corners of his mouth turned up in a grin as wicked and sweet as stolen honey ... a smile that made her go all shivery inside. "Yes or no, Cailin? Do we have a deal?"

"How do I know you'll keep your part of the bargain—that you'll give me my freedom when my time is up?"

"You'll have to trust me," he answered.

"Aye, trust in an Englishman." She stepped out from behind the screen.

"Well?"

"Can I think on it?"

"No. My patience has run out."

"Yes," she replied.

"Yes, what? Yes, my patience is gone, or yes, we have a bargain?"

"Yes, I shall be your wife." His eyes widened in disbelief as she stood on tiptoe and kissed him lightly on the lips. "A kiss of peace, Sassenach," she said. "To prove the goodwill between us."

"And to what do I owe this sudden change of heart?" he asked her suspiciously.

"Reason, plain and simple. Why should I continue to fight a battle that was obviously long lost?"

"Were you not a Scot and a redhead, I'd find this sudden attack of logic easier to accept."

She laughed. "You should be happy. You've won."

"I know," he said. "That's what worries me the most."

Chapter 9

When Cailin and Sterling had come aboard the *Galway Maid*—a merchant vessel bound for Charles Town, Annapolis, and Boston, with a cargo of china and farm implements—she'd intended to keep the bargain they'd made in bed at the widow's lodgings.

But she'd agreed to Sterling's two years of marriage after she'd unwisely allowed him sexual liberties, and her own fierce desire for his embrace had gotten the better of her common sense.

Now, as sailors unfurled the sails and the first burst of wind filled the canvases, the finality of what she was doing hit home hard. Already, the men had pulled anchor. The bow of the *Galway Maid* swung around to the west. Ahead of them lay thousands of miles of open water; behind lay Scotland and a grieving child who watched the road for her arrival.

She had made Sterling Gray a promise, but she'd also promised Corey that she'd come for him. She could not keep both pledges. Her little brother needed her; her grandsire and her sister needed her. Whatever irrational urge Sterling had followed when he'd snatched her from the gallows, it would pass. He'd soon realize that he was better off without her. In America, no one would know that he'd exchanged marriage vows with a Scots rebel. He could choose another wife, one who would willingly share his bed and mother his children.

Willingly ... It was the willingness that frightened her. What Highland lass could take pleasure in the touch of a man who had slain her father? How could she have forgotten that Sterling Gray was her greatest enemy? Obviously, her arrest, rape, and imprisonment had impaired her senses. She belonged among her own kind. She was a Stewart by birth, a MacLeod by heart ties, and the widow of a MacGreggor. Her duty was to her Scottish kin, not to an Englishman with blood on his hands. Whatever the cost, she must return to her people.

Keeping that thought foremost in her mind, Cailin edged away from Sterling's side. In the confusion of the ship's sailing, it was easy to slip between an aging cleric and his stout wife. By the time Sterling noticed she was gone, she'd already put the great oak mainmast between them.

Dropping her cloak on the deck, she kicked off her shoes and scrambled up onto the rail. Behind her, a sailor swore and shouted a warning. Cailin balanced on the polished wood and tried to judge the distance to the choppy waves below. From the corner of her eye, she saw Sterling dash down the deck toward her.

"Cailin, no!" he yelled.

She dived over the side.

The water closed over her head, warm and embracing. Her clothing buoyed her up at first, then the material soaked through and became heavy. She opened her eyes and let herself sink, down and down. The hull of the *Galway Maid* was close, very close. The underwater wake of the vessel was strong, and it was difficult to keep herself from being swept under the boat.

When she had used most of her oxygen, she swam to the surface with strong strokes. Almost to the surface ... As she reached the top, she sucked in another deep breath of air, splashed wildly, and shrieked an outrageous lie. "I canna swim! Help me! I canna swim!"

Someone dived into the sea beside her, and she realized that it was Sterling. Quickly, she stopped kicking and let herself sink again. He came after her, and she twisted away. The water was dark and dirty. If she could put a few yards between them, he'd never find her.

Her head struck something hard; for a moment, she was disoriented, then she realized that she had hit the hull of the ship. Immediately, she swam deeper. She kept going until she reached the mucky bottom.

Her lungs were aching, her limbs were tired, but she couldn't go up for air yet. It was too soon. She forced herself to count out the seconds.

She was a strong swimmer. Johnnie had taught her to swim in the swift current of a mountain river. But the weight of her clothing drained her will. At last, she began the struggle toward the sunlight, hoping that she'd put the ship between her and Sterling—hoping he would believe she had drowned and give up the chase.

She gasped for air, blinking to clear the muddy water from her eyes, and saw to her dismay that the *Galway Maid* was coming about. Two sailors were already in the water, and a third pushed a barrel over the side. She glanced around for Sterling, didn't see him, and prepared to dive under again.

Before she could take three strokes, he came up an arm's length away from her. She tried to evade him again, but this time he grabbed a handful of her hair.

"Damn you, Cailin." The anguish on his features turned to anger, and she knew that it was useless to struggle against his iron grip. She shut her eyes and let him drag her back toward the ship. A seaman swam up beside them and took hold of her arm. When they reached the side of the *Galway Maid*, the first mate was dropping a Jacob's ladder over the rail.

Meekly, Cailin caught hold of the swaying rope and climbed slowly up the ship's side. She had failed. Now she must suffer the rage of captain and crew as well as her husband. Tears of shame clouded her vision. She blinked them away as her bare feet touched the sun-heated deck. Head up, defiant, she faced the hostile crowd.

The reverend was praying loudly. His plump wife pointed at her and sputtered platitudes. Two seamen were laughing outright, another leering at her water-soaked form, while a swarthy passenger shook his head and muttered his disgust.

From the quarter deck, the ship's master and the first officer glared at her. The captain was so furious that his nose was fiery red, and he quivered from head to boot. "What madness is this, woman?" he demanded. "I'll have no bedlamites aboard the *Galway*—"

"My apologies for my wife's shameful behavior, sir." Sterling jumped down from the railing, wet and dripping. "The responsibility is mine. I will see that she is properly chastised."

"I want no crazy woman on this ship," the captain snapped.

Cailin opened her mouth to deliver a choice response, but before she could utter a word, Sterling grabbed her and heaved her over his shoulder. "Put me down!" she said. "Sterling! Put me down!"

Ignoring her angry cries and struggles, he carried her past the mainmast to the nearest hatchway and down the steep steps to a dark passageway. "I've been patient with you because of what you've been through—but my patience is at an end."

She pounded his back with her fists. "I said *put me down!*" Fear that he might strike her made her light-headed. She wouldn't be beaten by a man—husband or not. Sterling had hit her at the gallows, and he'd not do it again. She'd not let him abuse her—not if he valued his life. "Sterling! What are you doing?"

He stopped at a cabin door and slammed it open. A lantern swayed from the rafter. By the pale yellow light, Cailin saw a harelipped serving wench staring at them.

"What do ye—" she gasped.

"Out!" Sterling bellowed.

With a terrified squeak, the maid fled the room. Her wooden-soled clogs hammered down the corridor.

"Why?" he demanded as he dumped Cailin onto the wide box of an upper bunk. "Why did you try and drown yourself? Is being married to me that bad?"

Cailin twisted around and backed into the far corner of the bed. "Keep your hands to yourself," she warned him.

"Sweet Jesus!" He turned away, tripped over an open trunk, and steadied himself against the wall with one arm. "Why? Why, Cailin? Why in the name of all that's holy do you plague me this way?"

"I wasn't trying to drown myself."

"No? You gave a good imitation." He kicked the trunk. "Why? Why did you jump over the side?"

She swallowed. "I wished ye to think I'd drowned." Her excuse sounded foolish, even to her own ears.

"You're crazy," he replied. "I've ruined my life and saddled myself with a woman who has wool for brains."

"I told ye that—" she began. "Not that I have wool for—"

"Shut up. Don't say a word." He kicked the trunk again, scattering ladies' shoes and stays across the heaped boxes. "Anything you say to me is bound to be a lie."

"Nay." She looked into his eyes, then lowered her gaze. " 'Twas my last chance. Before America. Ye canna blame me. Ye'd do the same."

"Take off your clothes," he ordered grimly.

The fear that had dimmed inside her flared again. "I'll nay be beaten, and I'll nay be raped."

"Beaten? Raped?" He made a sound of contempt. "Have I hit you? Lord knows you deserve it, but I told you before—it's not my way to use my fists on women. And believe me, rape is the last thing on my mind. I want you out of those wet clothes before you catch your death and pass it to every soul on this ship."

"I'll not be strippin' for you, Sterling Gray. And if I'm so weak that a swim in the harbor finishes me off, I'd nay live until we reach the Colonies anyway."

He swore again, and she saw the throbbing vein in his throat swell with barely controlled ire. "Do you see this room? Do you see it?"

"Aye," she answered with more nerve than she

felt. "What of it?" It was a poor, mean cabin with two sets of bunks, a bare board set into a corner for a table, and a single whale-oil lantern. The bunk she sat on backed against the hull, and the boards were damp and mossy.

"You will share this room with six other women. I don't want to see your face on deck for the next week. You can eat here, sleep here, and tend to your—"

"This place smells like a fish bucket. You expect me to live for weeks with six seasick—"

"You're lucky to have a bunk to yourself. It cost me extra."

"And you?" she flung back. "Have ye a private cabin? I vow you're not locked in some foul-smelling closet with unwashed strangers."

He flushed. "I cannot afford a private cabin for us, Cailin. The bribe I paid to save you from hanging was a year's salary."

The thoughtlessness of her tongue sobered her. "I'm sorry," she said. "I didna mean to taunt ye for the thickness of your pocketbook. Being an officer of the king's dragoons, you—"

"No more. That is behind me. I am simply Sterling Gray, a fool who tried to—"

She sneezed. "Haven't we insulted each other enough for one morning? I tried to escape, and I failed. Now, I'll stick to our bargain. Two years and then—"

"Will you?" He scowled at her. "I can't trust you. You've proved that much to me."

She shrugged. "Must ye hold a grudge? As I said, 'twas my last chance. Now, I'm stuck with ye. I can swim, but I canna walk on water."

He took a few steps toward the door and glanced

back at her. "You've no concept of honor, have you? Breaking your word means nothing."

"Honor is a man's word," she scoffed. "Women do not play such silly games. We have not the luxury of made-up rules. When we play, it is for keeps."

"You're talking riddles, Cailin. All I know is that you gave me your promise that you would live with me as my wife for two years, and then you tried—"

"Nearly got away too. Ye swim better than any Englishman I've kent."

"Your things are here somewhere in this mess. Change into them. And if you cause any problems at all, I swear I'll have you bound and gagged and stuffed into a barrel in the hold."

"Such venom," she chided.

"You made me look a fool, woman," he answered stiffly. "If Captain Daniels had refused to allow us to remain aboard, I wouldn't have had enough money to buy passage on another ship."

"I said I was sorry."

"You say a lot, Cailin, but you mean little of it. We've scarce money left to travel to the frontier and make our start in America."

"Surely, ye dinna expect me to stay below for the whole voyage. I'll die down here in this devil's hole of a closet."

"I don't want to see you, and I don't want to hear you. Stay away from me. I warn you."

"As ye wish," she answered.

He stalked from the cabin, swearing under his breath. When she'd leaped over the side of the ship, he'd been stunned. He'd not dreamed that she'd risk death to keep from fulfilling her part of the agreement. The thought that he could have lost her forever shook him to the bone. A shudder passed through him.

She was meant to be his. They were linked together spiritually. Why couldn't she see that? Since the time he'd seen her on his vision quest, he'd known, deep down, that she held his future in her hands. But now that he'd found her and altered his whole life for her, she refused to play her part. His career ... his father ... his country ... None of it meant a damn against this slip of a redheaded girl.

He came up hard against the ship's gunnel, unconsciously gripping the rail. His clothes were still soaked through, and the brisk wind chilled him, but he paid them no heed. He stared back toward the harbor, watching as anchored ships and buildings grew smaller and smaller in the distance.

"I love you, Cailin," he murmured. "Why can't you see that? And why can't you love me a little in return?"

As Cailin had feared, most of the other women who shared her cabin quickly became seasick. On the second day out, the *Galway Maid* hit bad weather, and the ship tossed and bobbed like a cork in a millrace.

Cailin turned her back to the room and tried to shut out the smell of vomit and the sounds of weeping. She'd never been at sea before, but the rocking of the ship reminded her of a galloping horse. Had she been on deck with the salt breeze in her face, instead of in this cramped cabin, she was certain she'd enjoy the voyage—even when the waves turned to whitecaps and the wind howled through the sails.

The Reverend Stark's wife was the worst of Cailin's cabin mates. Mistress Trumby and her fourteen-year-old twins were repeatedly ill, and old Agnes Williams snored constantly and suffered from flatulence. But Margaret Stark lay flat on her back in the bunk beneath Cailin's and moaned and prayed aloud for hours on end. Fortunately, her maid had a stronger stomach than her mistress, for the girl was kept busy running up and down emptying slop buckets and cleaning her mistress's foul linen.

Water dripped down the hull wall, making Cailin's blankets damp and giving the Trumby twins a cold. When the serving girl began to sneeze, Cailin could stand it no longer. She left the cabin and went topside.

Disregarding the stares of crewmen, she found a secluded spot near the stern of the vessel and let the sun and sea wash away the sights and odors of sickness. She'd not been there an hour when Sterling approached her.

She turned her head away, trying to ignore the thrill of excitement that rippled through her at the sight of his sun-bronzed features and piercing dark eyes.

He draped an arm carelessly around her shoulders. "Not planning on going for a swim, are you?" he asked sarcastically.

"Not this morning," she replied, shaking off his arm. She refused to be drawn into another argument with him. If they fought, she knew he'd send her below again. One more day of Mistress Stark's wailing and Cailin knew she'd lose her mind.

"You're not ill, are you?"

She shook her head. "Nay."

Why did looking at Sterling always make her heart race? Memories of their time together in the widow's lodgings flashed across her mind, and she felt her cheeks grow warm as she pictured him standing before the fireplace stripped to the waist. The broad expanse of his smooth chest, the swelling muscles of his upper arms, and the way his unbound hair fell over his shoulders were enough to make a holy nun forsake her vows.

And she had never been a nun.

He brushed a wayward curl away from her eyes, and she flinched at the heat of his touch.

His black gaze twinkled with mischief. "Easy," he soothed, as though she were a flighty mare. A slow grin revealed his even white teeth. "Peace, little wife. I've brought you a gift."

"I need nothing from you," she replied sharply. But she did. Heaven help her, she did.

"Trust me. You'll like this." He dug into a pocket and produced a fat green summer apple. "Eat this," he said, offering it to her.

"Is it poisoned?" The words were out before she could guard her acid tongue, but she snatched the fruit before he could take back his offer.

He moved closer, watching her with those devil eyes that seemed to burn into her skin. "You needn't worry about that. If you drive me to murder, you'll know it. You are an exasperating woman, Cailin Gray."

Cailin Gray. Was that her name now? Not MacGreggor, but Gray. How strange it sounded. She shook her head. It wouldn't do to think too much about that. Next, she'd be wondering why, if she was a wife, she wasn't fulfilling a wife's duties to her husband. "Some men have called me difficult before, but I dinna believe them," she replied.

He pushed her hooded cloak back, and his fingers brushed her temple. She shivered, but not from the cold wind off the water. Then, a sudden gust caught her linen cap, sending it flying across the waves.

"Sorry," he said huskily. "I didn't mean for you to lose your cap."

He was staring at her hair. She'd braided it into two plaits and curled them around her head like a crown. The cap had held them firmly in place, but now the wind played havoc with the wayward strands.

"'Tis just a cap," she said. "I have another." It wasn't the hat he was talking about and they both knew it. "Ye provided me with a generous wardrobe, and I am grateful."

"The other women—are they kind to you?"

She laughed. "Kind? To a Scot?" Little chance of that. Granny Williams made rude remarks when she was awake, and Mistress Trumby had forbidden her daughters to speak to Cailin. Instead, they simply stared at her with stupid, sullen faces. "We have not exchanged blows yet." She smiled up at him. "As ye bid me, I am on my very best behavior."

"See that you remain that way."

She polished the apple on her sleeve and bit into it. The fruit was sour but juicy, and she relished the sharp bite on her tongue. He stood beside her in silence as she finished the apple, and she found his company strangely comforting.

"Save the seeds, and we'll plant them on our land," he said.

"Do apples grow in America?" *Our land*, he had said. *Our land*. The notion thrilled her. "What is it like—the Maryland Colony? I've heard of the redmen and the great trees, but I ken little else. Will ye have sheep and cows? I'm a good milker, and I churn the sweetest butter you've ever tasted."

"There are mighty stretches of virgin forest," he said, "with trees as high and wide as London towers. And there are clear, fast rivers, and a bay the likes of which you've never seen. Wheat grows from the rich earth, and corn, and tobacco. It's been a long time since I've been there myself, but I remember heavens dark with flocks of geese and . . ."

Cailin found herself listening eagerly to his stories of the wilderness. For minutes that stretched into hours, she stood next to the man who was her greatest enemy and shared his dream of an untamed land to the west . . . a place where the waters teemed with fish and the hungry soil waited for apple seeds. And for a little while, both of them forgot their grievances, and they laughed together and talked like any newlywed couple bound for a new life and a bright future.

Far to the north of Dover, in Scotland, on the outskirts of the settlement of Fort William, a small boy watched the road and wiped tears from his grimy face with the back of his hand. "Cailin said she'd come for us. She promised."

Big Fergus stopped and mopped the sweat from his broad face. The rock balanced precariously on his shoulder weighed more than a six-month calf, but that worried him not nearly as much as the child's anguish. Thinking came hard to him. He was slow; he knew it. He'd always known it. And he'd long ago given up trying to figure things out for himself and just concentrated on following orders.

The Lady Cailin had entrusted the little chief to his care. "Go with him and protect him," she'd said. "More than God, I count on you." Those were her very words. Fergus had repeated them over and over in his mind. He didn't like to remember the rest of what she'd said ... the part about the ghost hounds eating him skin and bones. Fergus didn't like scary stuff like silkies and haunts.

Just plain dead people didn't bother him. He'd seen a lot of dead men and women in his life—more this past year than ever. But he'd found good work in digging graves since they came to Fort William. No, dead folk didn't bother anyone. But ghosts ... A shiver came over him just thinking about them.

"Fergus! Get to work! Do ye think this wall will build itself?" Artair Cameron shouted.

He shouted more too, bad stuff about Fergus being as stupid as a rock, but Fergus didn't listen to that. He just dropped the stone into place and went to pick up another. He liked building stone fences. All he had to do was lift and carry. Somebody smarter would tell him where to put the rocks.

Fergus glanced back at Corey. He was a wee mite to be the MacLeod of Glen Garth, but Fergus guessed he'd grow in time. Corey was smart. Thinking never bothered him, and he never called Fergus names either. He'd make a laird a man could be proud to serve.

"You boy!" Artair yelled. "Stop sniveling and tote that water bag over here."

Fergus frowned. Artair was mean to Corey too. He didn't care that Corey was heir to Glen Garth or that his father had died at Culloden Moor. He'd paid Lady Cailin's kin, the Stewarts, for the boy's indenture, and now he was working the lad hard. Corey had cried a lot when Artair had sold his pony. And Artair kept threatening to get rid of Corey's sheepdog. Corey thought a lot of that dog. Fergus didn't think the boy could stand it if Artair killed his dog.

"Big Fergus. Big Fergus!"

Fergus looked down. Corey was tugging at his arm. Fergus smiled at him and bent down to look the lad square in the eye. "Aye, little laird, what is it?"

"Something's happened to Cailin," the bairn replied.

"What?" Fergus's mouth dropped open. He straightened up and stared around him. "What's happened to Lady Cailin?" he asked in astonishment. He didn't see anything amiss. The only thing moving along the road was a flock of sheep.

"She said she'd come," Corey insisted. "She promised. If she didn't come, it's because something's wrong. She needs our help, Fergus."

Fergus blinked. Artair was yelling again, but he didn't pay any mind to him. Corey had said that the lady needed his help.

"We're going home," Corey declared. "Home to Glen Garth."

Fergus chewed at his lower lip, trying to remember if the lady had said anything about *not* going home. While he was studying on it, Artair ran over and backhanded Corey. A black wave of anger swept over Fergus. "No!" he cried. "Dinna hit the bairn!"

Corey got to his feet. Blood was running down his chin, and his lip was swelling up like a pig's bladder. "I'm going home!" he cried defiantly.

"You'll do as I say, you little bastard," Artair said. He swung his clenched fist at Corey's head.

Fergus's arm blocked the blow.

Artair turned on him. His hand went to the dirk at his waist. The knife slipped out of the leather sheath with a hiss, and the steel blade winked in the hot sun.

"Big Fergus!" Corey screamed.

Fergus meant to knock the weapon out of Artair's hand. But the knife sliced a gash in his forearm, and the pain made him react without thinking. When the black fog receded from his head, Corey was pulling on his leg and Artair lay against the stone wall.

Artair wasn't moving.

Something told Fergus that Artair wouldn't get up—not then or later.

He looked down at the boy. "I hurt him, Corey. I hurt him bad. What do I do now?"

Corey's small fingers entwined with his. "We're going to Glen Garth to find Cailin and Grandda James."

Fergus glanced at Artair's sprawled form again. "I hurt him bad."

"He was a bad man."

Fergus's throat felt funny. "You're not mad?"

Corey shook his head. "You did right."

"The lady won't set the ghost hounds on me?"

"No, she won't. I promise you." He whistled to the black and white sheepdog. "Come on, Big Fergus. We're going home."

Chapter 10

Annapolis, Maryland Colony
December 24, 1746

Huge white snowflakes drifted lazily down to dust the ship's yards, frost the rails and bowsprit, and lay in frothy heaps amid the stacked bales and barrels that crowded the deck. Cailin stood amidships, wrapped in her woolen cloak, oblivious to the salt-raw air and the raucous cries of seagulls that swooped overhead.

Passengers and crew crowded the railing, staring and pointing at the cluster of buildings just beyond the market square, and waving at people on shore. In the midst of all the excitement, Cailin felt as alone and confused as she had ever been in prison.

We're finally here, she thought. So this is the Maryland Colony we've come so far to reach. Months had passed since the *Galway Maid* had sailed from Dover. Since then, the crew and passengers had weathered storms and becalmings, cholera, measles, and smallpox. A French pirate schooner had fired on them off the coast of the Canaries, and two Spanish sloops had chased them for days in the warm Caribbean waters.

Illness and bad luck had taken a toll on Cailin's cabin mates. Old Mistress Williams had given up the ghost halfway across the Atlantic; one of the Trumby twins had died of fever, and Reverend Stark's maid had fallen overboard and been eaten by sharks one day out of Jamaica.

Cailin had remained remarkably strong. When she'd discovered that Agnes Williams had brought two cows aboard the *Galway Maid,* she'd volunteered to care for the animals and milk them morning and night. The milk was supposed to supply the captain's table, but Cailin made certain that she drank her share. The sea air had stimulated her appetite, and she was constantly hungry. Most of the women would leave the ship pale and wan-looking; she had regained muscle and curves that she'd lost in the dungeons of Edinburgh castle.

Scotland and the tragedy at Culloden seemed almost a lifetime ago. In so much time, her grandfather might have passed on. Her sister, or even Corey, might be dead. She turned her hand palm up and watched as snowflakes lit and melted there. Were the graves of her loved ones white with snow as well? she wondered. Or had they found a way to survive under Butcher Cumberland's fist?

She glanced around the deck but didn't see Sterling. He was probably still with that deckhand, she decided. In the Canaries, the *Galway Maid* had taken on a new crewman, Beck Erikson, a native of Lewes on the Delaware Bay. The sailor had been a farmer before going to sea and was able to answer many of Sterling's questions about planting seasons and crops in the mid-Atlantic Colonies.

Sterling had written down all that Beck had told him in detail in a journal. "I lived in America as a child," Sterling had explained to her on one of the occasions when they had shared a few hours together, "but I don't know much about agriculture other than what I've read in books. My mother's people raise corn and beans, but the fields are considered women's work. Shawnee men are hunters and fishermen. I've a lot to learn if I want to become a successful planter."

Other than short periods on deck, and once when they'd gone ashore in Jamaica, Cailin had seen little of Sterling. They were not important enough to be asked to the captain's table for dinner, and Sterling could hardly come to the crowded women passengers' cabin to talk with her. Since he slept in the fo'-c'sle with the crew, she could not venture there if she'd wanted to—which she hadn't. At least, that's what she'd convinced herself.

Although she and Sterling had had little opportunity to be together on the voyage, she felt that she knew him much better than she had when they'd set sail from England. He had a quick mind, a good sense of humor, and an obvious passion to learn whatever would aid him in his new life. Despite their differences, she'd found much to admire in his self-control and strength.

He desired her. She saw it in his face; she heard it in his husky voice. She read it in his dark, piercing gaze that seemed to sear her skin more than the relentless sun overhead.

He wanted her, but he had not forced himself on her sexually. He was her lawful husband, but he'd not used his right to her body as a weapon against her. If he had, she could have summoned all her will to fight him. As it was, she thought about him day and night.

He haunted her dreams.

She found herself unconsciously spinning fantasies

that made her blush crimson in the light of day. They were lewd, blatantly sexual flights of fancy that no decent woman could ever admit to conceiving, even with her husband.

And they had become worse since the day the ship had anchored in Kingston, Jamaica, to take on fresh food and water. Most of the passangers and crew had gone ashore, and she'd accepted Sterling's invitation to spend the afternoon on dry land. It had begun innocently enough.

But she'd allowed herself to be caught up in the excitement of seeing the island town, and she'd behaved foolishly. Even now, bird wings fluttered in the pit of her stomach when she thought of the delicious meal and the bottle of wine she and Sterling had shared at a tiny inn overlooking the harbor.

Vivid colors and exotic smells swirled in her head as she remembered the hot sun, the swaying palms, and the throb of African drums and Spanish guitars. She'd devoured the fresh fruit, crusty bread, and hot roasted pork that a dusky-skinned serving wench had brought them, then watched scandalized as the same girl had shed her blouse and skirt and danced barefoot in a scarlet-flowered petticoat and bodice that barely covered her from nipple to mid-thigh.

The woman—hardly more than a child—had tossed her long dark hair and moved her body in ways that Cailin would not have believed were physically possible. Huge gold rings dangled from the dancer's ears; her brown feet were long and narrow, her toenails painted a garish red. Her eyes were languid slits, as black as sin, and when her gaze met Sterling's, the trollop's lips shaped an unspoken promise of wicked delights.

Cailin's appetite had suddenly vanished. The

heated rhythm of strings and drums sounded harsh in her ears. Green peppers and onion that had seemed so spicy and delicious turned to clay in her mouth. Sterling didn't shout or tuck coins between the dancer's high, upthrust breasts as some of the other customers did, but Cailin noted the quickening of his breath and the predatory gleam that had filled his eyes as he watched.

"Take me back to the ship," Cailin demanded.

"So soon? We don't sail until the evening tide," he replied.

"No doubt ye will find something or someone to fill the time," she spat back at him. "I'm sure ye can have her for the price of a new dress—or perhaps ye'd nay have to pay her at all. The two of ye seemed to—"

He laughed at her. "You're jealous."

"Of what, may I ask?" Her voice was louder than she'd intended. The couple at the next table were staring. Embarrassed, she rose and fled the inn by way of open French doors that led to a garden.

Sterling followed her, moving more swiftly than she'd anticipated. He caught her when she'd gone only a few steps down the twisting red-tiled walk. Caught her and spun her around, then yanked her against him and covered her mouth with his own and kissed her with all the unleashed passion aroused by the Jamaican woman's dance.

Cailin was too stunned to struggle. With one hand, Sterling fumbled with her cap and set free her heavy hair. With the other, he pressed the center of her spine, holding her tightly as his kiss scorched her with the burning intensity of the island sun.

He tasted of wine and hot peppers, and he smelled of tobacco and leather and clean, virile man. And there was a scent of something more ... something that she could only vaguely define as the scent of carnal heat. "Cailin," he whispered hoarsely. "It's you I want."

Desire lanced through her.

She knew she should rebuff his rude assault. Cry out for help ... strike him ... But the heady scent of the orchids was overpowering ... the cadence of the drums too compelling ... and his embrace too sweet.

The wine, she thought, the unwatered wine was Spanish and stronger than she was used to. But the palpitation of her heart was not caused by the wine. And neither was the trembling in her limbs.

He broke off the kiss and stared full into her eyes. And when he leaned toward her again, she parted her lips to receive the heated thrust of his seeking tongue.

He ran his fingers through her hair, and each touch sent a new river of emotion racing though her veins. And when he cupped her breast in his strong fingers, she felt herself grow hot with wanting.

"Cailin ... Cailin," he murmured.

She reached up and stroked his tanned jaw. Strange, she thought, how smooth it was for a man long past his third decade. But Sterling's lack of beard did not detract from his appeal; instead, she found his difference oddly compelling.

Somehow, they had covered the few steps to a brick-walled fountain. Sterling sank down on the wide ledge, pulling her with him. Ivy grew over the mossy bricks, and the drops of water spraying from a marble dolphin's mouth splashed over Cailin's gown. He was kissing her again. She leaned against him with her head thrown back wantonly and her arms around his neck.

He's so beautiful, she thought. Black English devil that he is, he has the face and form of a fallen angel.

"You are my wife," he was saying. "My wife."

He'd slipped a hand under her skirts. His hot, lean fingers caressed her bare leg. "How long must I wait?" he asked her. "How long, Cailin?"

She felt his fingers brush her inner thigh. She groaned and tried to pull away, but her body betrayed her. Instead, she shifted her weight so that his seeking fingers could touch her most intimately.

He kissed her again, and she closed her eyes, caught in a languid web of erotic pleasure as he thrust two fingers into her and gently stroked her. She sighed, and tears gathered in the corners of her eyes.

"You want me as much as I want you," he whispered. "Cailin, I can't—"

And then she heard a woman's throaty laughter. Stiffening, she looked back at the inn and saw the dancer coming down the walk arm in arm with a sailor.

"Oh," Cailin cried. Mortified, she twisted away from Sterling and turned her back on the couple while she tried to bind up her hair and make herself presentable. Sterling put an arm around her, but she threw it off.

"Don't," she pleaded with him. "Don't make it worse than it is."

The black girl's laughter turned to shrill giggles, then faded as the sailor's footsteps grew fainter.

"Cailin, you are my wife. There's no sin in kissing your husband," Sterling argued.

She whirled around and blamed him for her own confusion and wanton behavior. "Think ye that I'm a common lightskirt—to dally with a man in broad daylight in the courtyard of a public house?"

He chuckled. "Not common. Never common. But you cannot claim you were forced."

"The wine went to my head," she lied, snatching up her linen cap and tying it over her hair. "It won't happen again, I assure ye."

"Oh, but it will, my little Scottish hellcat. You've too much loving inside you to keep it—"

"Never!" she'd insisted. " 'Twas a mistake. I'll nay lie with ye. Not now and not ever! Not with you, Sassenach. And the sooner ye realize that, the better for us both."

She'd run from the garden back to the safety of the ship, and for weeks afterward she'd kept her distance from him. But she'd not forgotten. Nay ... The memory of that heated encounter with Sterling remained as hot as butter in a flame-licked skillet.

She had dreamed of that courtyard a dozen times. Dreamed of the sun-warmed tiles and the scent of tropical blossoms ... Dreamed of Sterling's embrace and the feel of his hard body locked with hers ...

And she'd imagined herself dancing half-naked as that native girl had danced, not for a room full of people but for Sterling alone ... dancing in the steamy tropical sun to the beat of a primitive drum, and then allowing him to bend her back against the stone fountain and fill her with his hard, thrusting love. As long as they were aboard the *Galway Maid*, she had been able to hide from him, but now that they had reached Maryland the rules would all change. She would be alone with him for months to come. And she didn't know how she would avoid his demand that she come to his bed, or even if she still wanted to ...

Taking a deep breath of the cold air, she pushed back her hood and looked around her. Annapolis

Harbor was a busy spot, despite the fact that it was the day before Christmas. Men, women, and children bustled along, shouting, swearing, and laughing. Dogs and boys scampered along the wooden dock, defying gravity and straining the patience of their elders. A team of oxen strained under the weight of a high-wheeled cart while two black men struggled to load a barrel into a dinghy that was already riding low in the water. A pot-bellied donkey wandered loose, nibbling at whatever took its fancy and adding its loud braying to the din of creaking wheels and groaning timbers.

Cailin counted eleven other vessels of all sizes and types in the harbor, some riding at anchor, others sailing to and from the small port. As she watched, a crude boat cut from a single hollowed log and boasting one patched sail drifted into the path of the *Galway Maid*. Cailin was certain that wind and tide would sweep the merchant ship over the log boat, crushing the farmer's cargo of children, squealing hogs, and chickens. The *Galway Maid*'s first officer bellowed an order; sailors heaved at the ropes, and the officer spun the great wheel to starboard.

To Cailin's great relief, the *Galway Maid* missed the smaller craft by an oar's length. The farmer shook his fist and cursed, the sailors cursed back, and the small boat slid into open water.

"That was close," Sterling said.

Startled, Cailin saw that he'd come up on her left side without her noticing. "Ye sneak up on a body like a cattle reiver," she said, trying to hide her inner trembling.

He pulled her hood up over her hair. "You're getting wet," he replied.

His deep voice sent ripples of excitement down her

spine, and she found it hard to breathe. "I'm fine," she protested.

He smiled. "I'd not want you sick for your first Christmas in Maryland."

"I don't take ill from a few flakes of snow." She pushed her hood down again. "What I am sick of is this boat and those infernal women in my cabin. Even your wilderness will look good to me."

He nodded. "And to me. Smell this air. It's so clean."

She sniffed. "I smell salt and wet canvas."

"Close your eyes. What else do you smell?"

She did as he bade her. "Tar. No, there's something else. Pine. I smell pine trees."

"Yes! Pine and oak, beech and—"

She laughed. "You can't tell the scent of beech trees from oak, not this far away."

"Maybe not," he agreed, "but they're there. Chestnut and cedar, willows and poplar. More trees than there are fish in the sea. I'm home, Cailin. God help me, I never thought I'd feel like this. I can't wait to set foot on land." He swallowed and she saw the raw emotion flickering in his eyes. "Because of you, I'm home."

And I'm not, she thought. A wave of sadness swept over her, bringing bittersweet memories of the familiar scents and sounds of Glen Garth.

"We've reached Maryland, but we can't set out for my land in midwinter," he continued. "There's nothing there. No shelter for us or our animals. We'll start in the spring. For now, I'll seek lodging for us with Lord and Lady Kentington. The old earl is a distant cousin to my father. I'm sure we'll be welcome in their home. They were kind to me after my mother died. The captain tells me that they were both alive and in good health when last he anchored in Annapolis."

"Would this great English lord be so generous if he knew that your father had disowned ye?" Cailin asked. Her brief stay at Sterling's father's estate still rankled, and she had no wish to go somewhere else where she was clearly not wanted. "He may not be pleased to learn that your *wife* is a Scots rebel."

Sterling grinned. "I doubt that will bother Lord Kentington or his lady. I have been away for many years, but one thing I can tell you. Maryland is not England. Things are done differently here. Ties of blood, even distant ones, are taken seriously."

"As they should be anywhere," she agreed.

"Lord Kentington is nearly my father's age," he continued, "but he's nothing like him in disposition or behavior. And his wife, Leah, the Lady Kentington, is half-Scottish. I'm certain you will like her. Everyone does."

A red-haired sailor caught Cailin's attention, and for a few seconds, she stared at him, completely losing track of what Sterling was saying. The seaman looked so much like Alasdair from the back that her heartbeat quickened. Then reality caught her up short. It could not be her big, brawny cousin, the man who had single-handedly thrown the three MacDonald brothers into the loch; he was long since dead.

". . . Kentington ships some of the finest tobacco in the Colony. I know I can benefit from his advice." Sterling touched her arm. "Are you listening to me?"

"Do as ye please then," she murmured. "You will anyway." Tears gathered in her eyes as the image of Alasdair's freckled face formed in her mind's eye. What would I give for an hour with him again? she thought. Alasdair had never failed to make her laugh or to raise her spirits.

Sterling took hold of her shoulders and gave her a long, searching look. "Have I treated you so badly, Cailin?"

"Nay," she admitted.

"You've a shell as tough as a hickory," he said. "But crack that shell, and the meat underneath is sweet and tender. I mean to be the one to find that tender center."

"Unless ye smash your fingers in the trying," she warned. "For I've not a mind to be swallowed up by a Sassenach, whole or piecemeal."

But later, as she followed Sterling down the gangplank and onto solid ground, a strange thing happened. The sailor she had taken for Alasdair passed close to them, and he was laughing, a full-blown roar of mirth so like her cousin's that she stopped and looked at the man in astonishment.

And then, inside her head, she heard Alasdair's booming voice repeating the words he'd said to her at her mother's funeral. *Dead's dead, Cally. Love her, remember her, but dinna crawl into that grave wi' her. For if ye dinna savor every bite of life that's left to ye, ye mock your Maker. Heaven or hell waits fer each o' us. Today, our duty lies in livin'.*

Sterling took her arm and hustled her out of the way of a team of horses. "Cailin? Are you all right?"

She nodded, hurrying to keep up with him. Alasdair was right. When she'd stepped off that ship, she'd cut the cord to her past. There would come a time to cross the sea again and return to all who waited for her. But for now, she must live as best she could. If she didn't, she'd face Alasdair's scorn and tempt God's wrath.

Hell might wait for her, she mused, but for today, she must savor every bite of life.

As Sterling had predicted, they were offered hospitality at Lord Kentington's grand plantation on the Chesapeake. Neither the earl nor his lady wife was in residence, but their youngest son, the Honorable Forrest Wescott, and his bride, Lady Kathryn Wescott, received them like long-lost kin.

"You just missed Father," Forrest said, clasping Sterling's hand with genuine warmth. "He sailed for England not a fortnight ago. It is my brother's last term at Oxford, and Father wanted to tend to some legal matters before he saw Brandon get his sheepskin."

Forrest was tall and well-favored, with curling brown hair and brilliant blue eyes, a gentleman that Cailin supposed would be as comfortable in the saddle of a blooded horse as here in the hall of this richly furnished mansion.

Somehow, in less time than it would have taken to tell, Cailin found herself sitting before a fire in the great hall of the manor, her feet on a stool and a cup of Christmas punch in her hand. Her hostess, the young Kathryn Wescott, was a red-cheeked colonial lass whose obvious pleasure at having unexpected guests for the holiday could hardly be contained.

Cailin didn't have to talk; Kathryn chattered on as brightly as a sprite, asking questions about the ocean voyage, ordering servants to prepare a chamber for Sterling and Cailin, patting her two spaniels, and laughing at her husband's jokes.

"Did your mother go to England as well?" Sterling asked when he could get a word in.

Both Forrest and Kathryn—Kate, as she asked to

be called—seemed intelligent, friendly, and greatly suited to each other. Often, one would begin a sentence and the other finish it, whereupon the first would seize the storyline and run with it. Cailin liked them at once, but decided she had never before met anyone who could talk as much as this pair of newlyweds.

"Mother? To England?" Forrest laughed and winked at his wife. "Not—"

"Likely." Kate giggled. "She's off to visit her family. We were married—"

"—In October," Forrest said. "Then they both said we should be alone here. But—"

"—Christmas isn't Christmas without guests," Kate put in. "We have my sisters and their families, and Papa and Mama, and the neighbors coming tomorrow for—"

"—For dinner," Forrest added. "But it isn't the same as having houseguests. You must consider this your home until the weather breaks and you can leave for the frontier."

"Cailin is welcome to stay until you get your house up, or whenever it suits," Kate said breathlessly. "She must stay. The frontier is no place for—"

Cailin held up a hand. "We couldn't impose on ye," she said. "Not for so long. We just—"

"But it's not an imposition," Kate insisted. "At home, I had four sisters and two brothers, and the cousins. Forrest is such a dear, but this house is too big for the two of us. Servants don't really count. I know how homesick my cousin Mary was when she came from Dublin last year. Annapolis seemed the end of the world. Now, she loves it, and you'll soon feel the same, Mistress Gray."

Sterling waved away a maid offering him another drink. "If your father was here—"

"Nonsense," Forrest said. "You came to learn about tobacco, didn't you? I don't know as much as Father, but our foreman taught him most of what he knows. Whatever you need to learn, Jock can show you."

"Lord Kentington left Forrest in charge of the plantation and all his affairs," Kate said. "You are family, and there are four—no, five bedchambers standing empty. And we have all this staff to look after the two of us. My father-in-law would be greatly offended if we showed you less courtesy than he would himself."

"Your parents were good to me when I was a boy," Sterling explained. "I only thought—"

"I will consider it an insult of the gravest kind if you do not accept Kate's invitation," Forrest said. "Do stay, at least through Christmas and Twelfth Night. You can hardly take Mistress Cailin to a public inn. They are all mobbed. In a few weeks, if you're bored with us, we can help you make other plans."

Since it was snowing harder than it had been before, Sterling was in no position to argue. An hour later, after they had eaten and shared another glass of wine with Forrest and Kate, a footman showed Sterling and Cailin upstairs to a spacious bedchamber and adjoining parlor.

"Shall I send one of the girls up to help the lady, sir?" the boy asked.

Sterling glanced at Cailin.

"No." She shook her head. All evening he'd been devouring her with his eyes. His message was very clear. His patience had come to an end. "I . . . can manage for myself tonight."

"Very good, m'lady." He left the room, pulling the door closed after him.

Sterling sat down on the bed. "It feels somewhat softer than my bunk aboard the *Galway Maid*." He patted the satin coverlet. "Join me," he said. "Unless you plan to sleep in a chair."

Goose bumps rose on her arms. She could not resist a smile as she went to the hearth and held out her hands to the crackling fire. It was time and past time for this marriage to be consummated. She wondered when she'd made the decision, and decided it didn't matter. She wanted him as much as he wanted her.

She turned to look around the elegant chamber. The room was large, with windows overlooking the bay; at least the view would be of the water in daylight. Tonight, snow piled on the sills and sleet tapped against the glass panes.

She sighed and smiled at him. "Your cousins live well for colonials," she said, stalling for time. She didn't know what sleeping with Sterling would do to her plans for returning home. She was tired of fighting him and her own desires. Despite the chasm between them, Sterling was a very, very attractive man.

And she had slept alone for a long time.

"Do you intend to demand your rights as a husband?" she asked him teasingly.

"Cailin."

He was looking at her with that gaze that seemed to penetrate her deepest thoughts. She could not stay still. She left the fire and went to a window. She could see nothing but swirling snow and darkness.

"This game is played out between us," he said.

"Aye," she agreed. "It is." Her skin seemed too

tight for her body. Her breasts tingled; her palms felt as though they were burning up.

"And now ..."

"Now what?" Excitement made her giddy. She was stone sober, but the floor seemed to sway beneath her feet.

"Now it's time to clear the board and set up the pieces for a new game." He crossed the room and stood very close to her.

"What are the rules?" She swallowed. Her heart was racing; each breath was an effort.

"We make them up as we go along," he said. He touched her cheek, and she shivered.

"There must be rules," she whispered breathlessly.

He brushed his forefinger along her lower lip. "A new game," he repeated.

The husky tremor in his voice made her weak.

His face softened in the firelight. "We are the first to play." Lowering his head, he brought his lips to within inches of her own and slid his fingers into her hair. "Cailin," he murmured.

With a low cry, she flung her arms around his neck and kissed him full on the mouth.

Chapter 11

Her crumbling resistance melted away in the incandescent flame of that fevered kiss. Warmth suffused Sterling's body as he lifted the weight of her red-gold hair off her nape, and his lips trailed hot kisses down her neck and throat.

"Cailin," he whispered hoarsely. "I want to see you ... all of you. Let me undress you." For months, he'd dreamed of this moment, imagined her rosy and bare in the firelight. Now that his dream was about to be fulfilled, he wanted this consummation to be perfect. "Cailin?"

She made a muffled sound that might have been a protest, but she didn't stop him as he began to undo the tiny buttons at the back of her neck.

"Take down your hair," he said. He wanted her so badly that he was already in agony. The scent of her ... the feel of her warm, soft curves was enough to bring him to a fever pitch. Raw instinct bade him throw her down on the floor and drive his cock into her sweet, wet cleft, but he forced himself to maintain control.

If he rushed her, he'd lose her willingness. And he wanted to please her nearly as much as he wanted to satisfy his own powerful urge.

She looked up into his face.

"Please. You have such beautiful hair." He kissed

her bare back and undid another button. "Take out the pins. Let your hair fall, Cailin."

She shivered.

He brushed her neck with the tip of his tongue, and she inhaled sharply. "Oh."

She smelled of violets. He sucked in a deep, shuddering breath. "I want to see you in nothing but that glorious hair."

Trembling, she reached up to pull an ivory hairpin loose. And when her necklace tangled in her curls, she jerked it impatiently. The worn silver chain snapped in two, and the pendant she always wore slid down to rest against the hollow between her breasts.

He touched the amulet. To his surprise, the metal felt hot enough to scorch his fingers. "Your necklace broke," he murmured.

She yanked the pendant away and threw it across the room. "I don't want it anymore," she said. "Little luck it's brought me. It's nought but superstitious nonsense."

He turned her in his arms, and she lifted her face to meet his kiss. He knew he should be tender with her, but when his mouth touched hers, flames leaped between them. He ground his lips against hers fiercely, thrusting his tongue deep inside her willing mouth and closing his mind to everything but the physical pleasure of taste and texture, and the woman scent of her.

He crushed her so tightly that he could feel the heat of her body through the layers of her clothing. He ran a hand down her back and clasped her closer, molding her to him as his burgeoning shaft throbbed with aching.

She clutched his shoulders and whispered his

name. He kissed her again and again. Her breath
came in ragged gasps.

He fumbled with the last button. There was a little
pop as the thread parted. The button hit the wide
plank floor and rolled away. Cailin didn't seem to
notice. She was thrusting into his mouth with her
tongue and tangling her fingers in his hair.

He slipped her gown off one shoulder and then the
other. She gave a small cry, deep in her throat. He
tore at her petticoats and clasped one round buttock
as the heavy material pooled around her ankles.

"Sterling . . ." she whispered. The sound of his
name on her lips nearly undid him.

In an effort to slow the pace, he caught her hand in
his, turning it over so that he could kiss the pulse at
her wrist. "I love you, Cailin. God knows why.
You've given me little cause . . . but I do."

Half-laughing, half-crying, she held out her arms
to him, and he drew her into another embrace. He
kissed her mouth again, and then turned his attention to the soft hollow between her breasts. He
flicked his tongue against her bare skin, and she
moaned with pleasure.

She reached up and took his face between her
hands, running her fingers over his chin, his nose,
and the high, sharp lines of his brows. And all the
while, he stared into her eyes and savored the sweet
frissons of sensation that settled in the pit of his
stomach.

God knew that gentling Cailin had taken time, and
more endurance than he'd ever believed he'd possessed. But this was worth every lonely night that
he'd lain awake wanting her. She was his. His. And
no other man would ever touch her again.

He tugged at the silken cords that held her stays

and pulled the stiff garment free. Now all that lay between them was her linen shift.

Sterling dropped to his knees and buried his face in her full breasts. His hands cupped and squeezed them: his fingertips teased her nipples to hard nubs. "Ah, woman," he murmured. There was an innocence about her that drove him wild. And yet, at the same time, he sensed a depth of passion he'd never found in another woman's arms.

She closed her eyes and whimpered with longing.

"You have beautiful breasts," he whispered. "Beautiful nipples." He kissed first one, then the other, drawing each taut bud between his lips and sucking until she writhed with desire.

The throbbing of his swollen phallus grew ever stronger. He gritted his teeth and willed his body to obey. Never had he experienced such exquisite torture. Never had he been so determined to give his partner a gift of complete fulfillment.

Firelight flickered, casting a golden glow over her lightly sheened skin. Her breasts were high and thrusting, the perfect nipples pink and swollen. He cupped one soft globe in the palm of his hand and lifted it to his mouth. She shuddered and arched against him. Her hands fluttered like birds, touching his face and hair and brushing against his shoulders.

Dropping to his knees, he caressed her back and stroked her small, round buttocks. He'd dreamed of this, but his dream hadn't matched the woman in his arms. He groaned as waves of white-hot desire flooded his veins. He wanted to fill her with his seed ... to mark her as his own forever.

Cailin gave a little cry, and her fingers tangled in his hair. Whispering love words, he continued to tease her breasts with his tongue until she covered his hands with her own, urging him on.

"Harder, harder," she moaned.

He lowered his head, nipping her gently with playful love bites across her belly and the curve of her hip. She gasped as his lips grazed the soft red curls above her cleft.

"Please," she murmured. "I . . . can't."

"Can't what?" He touched her love-swollen folds and nestled his face against her moist heat.

"Can't stand up . . . if ye . . ."

He slipped a finger inside her. She was wet and ready for him. "Sweet Cailin," he said, delving deeper.

Shamelessly, she opened to his exploring fingers. "Oh," she gasped. "How can I . . . If ye . . . Oh!" Bright sensations rippled through her, and she felt suddenly faint.

"Does that feel good?" he asked her. "I've something for you that will feel better than that."

She felt her cheeks grow hot with shame, but she did not stop him. Could not. She dug her nails into his shoulders as shudders of hunger shook her body. She was out of control. Never . . . never before had she felt like this.

"I want to taste your sweetness," he said.

In desperation, she glanced toward the bed. His lips brushed her cleft, and she gasped. "No," she cried suddenly. It felt good—it felt wonderful, but . . .

His hot tongue caressed her most secret spot. "Devil take you," she cried. "I'll reach a climax before ye ever get me to the bed." Her fingers clutched at his bulging biceps.

He threw back his head and let out a roar of laughter. Then, standing, he gathered her in his powerful arms. "I was afraid you meant to tell me no again," he said. "I am not a man to force a woman, but if you'd refused me this night, I swear I could not—"

"Nay," she answered, laughing with him. "I'll not tell ye no. But if ye don't pleasure me soon, I may kill ye."

"Then we must remedy that," he answered, carrying her to the bed.

She held tightly to his neck as he dropped her against the heaped pillows and covered her face with teasing kisses.

When he pulled away, she felt a sense of loss and held out her hands to stop him. "Don't leave me," she begged. "Not now!" God in heaven! She was a strumpet. No whore had ever demanded a man's lust so brazenly.

"Shhh, shhh," he whispered. "I'll not go far." His back was to the fireplace, his craggy face in shadows as he deliberately began to undress.

Boldly, she watched his every movement. And when he stepped out of his breeches, she drew in a deep, ragged breath, but still did not take her eyes off him.

"Do I pass muster?" he asked.

"Aye," she replied after long seconds. He was more than well-endowed, a great broth of a man, long and thick, in perfect proportion. And he was definitely aroused. "Come to bed, husband," she whispered hoarsely. "I want to see if it works as good as it looks."

She wanted to touch and taste him . . . to run her fingertips over his naked thighs . . . to feel the iron sinew beneath his bronzed skin. She wanted to trace the swell of his shoulders and caress the ridge of his collarbone. And she wanted to stroke his taut belly and savor the nest of dark hair below. She wanted him to fill her with his erect member.

He must have read the desire in her eyes. "You are a caution, woman," he said.

But she knew that he was pleased. She laughed softly as a new understanding passed between them, but her passion had not dwindled. His next touch proved that.

I'm lost, she thought as he pressed his hard palm against her most sensitive place. Desire flared and set her blood aflame.

"Where was I?" he asked. He slid his hand provocatively up her leg beneath her shift, and she could not hold back a whimper of delight.

"Sterling . . ."

"I like the way you say my name." He lowered his head and kissed the inner curve of her thigh. "Nice," he whispered as he moved his fingers between her damp folds.

"Oh . . ." She buried her face in his thick, clean hair and stroked his bare shoulders. His black hair was so soft and silky . . . not coarse . . . His skin was as smooth as raw silk. And the scent was his alone.

Sterling thrust two fingers deep inside her.

Cailin tossed her head from side to side and tried to control the surge of emotion that coursed through her. "Ye do this like you've had experience," she said breathlessly.

"Do I?" Without warning, he threw himself over her, seizing her wrists and pinning her to the mattress. For the space of a heartbeat, she felt unreasonable fear, but then he rolled over onto his back, pulling her atop him, and the terror receded.

This is Sterling, she told herself urgently. He won't

hurt me. No matter what I do or say, I'm safe with him.

"It's your game, Cailin," he said lazily. "Your move."

If she said no now, if she pulled away, he'd not force her. She knew it in her heart, and the knowledge gave her courage.

"Must I make all the moves?" she dared. Leaning over him, she kissed him with slow, exquisite pleasure.

He groaned with arousal and clasped her around the hips, urging her to move against him. "Don't stop," he said. "Touch me."

Cailin laughed. Sitting astride a man was a new sensation, and she liked it. The sweet aching between her thighs was driving her wild, and knowing that he wanted her so badly made her excitement all the stronger. She wanted him to kiss her breasts again . . . but this time without the shift between them. Slowly, she wiggled out of the garment and tossed it aside.

He touched her bare breast.

"That feels good," she said, leaning down so that he could reach her with his mouth. His swollen shaft throbbed hot against her leg. She arched her back. "Kiss me," she begged him. "Kiss my breasts."

He tongued her nipples until she writhed and cried out with desire, then drew a hard, erect bud between his lips. Bright colors danced behind her eyelids, and she felt herself being swept up into a swirling vortex.

"Now! Now!" he cried, lifting her hips with his powerful hands.

She took him deep inside, and he filled her with a love and satisfaction that she had never known existed. Slowly, he withdrew and plunged into her with wild, sweet abandon. She met his tumescent power thrust for thrust as her hands clasped and caressed his sweat-sheened body. Together, they rose and fell in a primeval hymn of life, giving and seeking fulfillment, locked flesh to flesh and soul to soul in an eternity of rapture.

And when the earth fell away beneath them, she clung to him, so that the wind carried them through the abyss and dropped them, as lightly as thistledown, back into reality.

"Cailin, sweet Cailin," he groaned. "God in heaven, woman ... you are ... you are ..." His words trailed away, lost in the damp kisses he bestowed on her face and throat.

She laughed and curled beside him, laying her head on his chest and listening to the slow, steady beat of his heart. "You'll do, Sassenach, you'll do," she teased.

"I love you," he said hoarsely. "More than my own soul ... I love you."

She sighed and closed her eyes. She did not want to think about tomorrow. She only wanted to savor the moment ... the utter peace and joy of being held like this.

"I've never met a woman like you." Carefully, he wound a strand of her hair around his finger. "Our married life begins here," he said quietly. "Here, this night."

"Shhh," she answered. *Dinna ask me to promise what I cannot give. Tonight is ours ... Tomorrow ... Who knows what tomorrow will bring?*

"I've spent a lifetime running from you," he admitted. "But now that I have you, I—"

"Shhh," she said, putting her fingers over his lips.

"Don't talk, Sterling. Just hold me. Just hold me like this forever."

And he did hold her through the long, cold night, until the first rays of purple dawn spilled across the gray waters of the Chesapeake and the first call of a wild goose echoed across the winter fields.

On Christmas morning they awoke to the faint knock of a servant. But when the maid entered for a few seconds to bring a tray loaded with hot food and a pot of steaming tea, they ignored the breakfast bounty. Sterling pulled the coverlet over their heads, and they rolled and kissed and touched until play became passion.

"Are ye never satisfied?" she asked him. "This makes the third—"

"We've a lot to make up for."

"Within reason," she teased.

"Am I hurting you?"

"Nay," she cried. "It's just that I've never known a man to—"

"Are you willing?"

Her answer was a kiss that led to other things and kept them abed until the sun was nearly straight overhead. Finally, eyes heavy-lidded and lips bruised and puffy from lovemaking, they dressed and went downstairs to celebrate the remainder of the day with Forrest and his bride.

In spite of her earlier reluctance, Cailin found herself drawn to Kate Wescott. The younger woman seemed not to care that Cailin's clothes were plain and out of fashion or that Cailin was Scottish.

"Lady Leah's clothes will fit you as though they were made for you," Kate declared. "I know we'll find a gown suitable for our Christmas ball."

Cailin was shocked. "I couldna wear—"

"Nonsense," Forrest said. "My mother would insist if she was here. She has far more in her wardrobe than she will ever wear. There's a green velvet that will make you the toast of Annapolis. With that hair, Mistress Gray, you will break hearts, I promise."

"As long as they remember that she's my wife," Sterling muttered.

"I have not agreed—" Cailin began.

"Quiet, woman," Sterling ordered with a grin.

Thus, despite her arguments, Cailin danced the night away—not only in her husband's arms, but in her host's arms and also in the embrace of many of his friends and neighbors.

No one seemed to care for politics here in the colony. No one asked her about Prince Charlie or the rebellion, and no one looked down their long English noses when they heard her Scottish accent. Men and women alike were cordial, and she could not help but respond in kind.

That night, she and Sterling retreated to their chamber and spent the evening in each other's arms. She did not think of what would come of their marriage or what would happen when winter receded and they had to go west into the wilderness. She didn't think about the future at all. She lived only for the moment, for Sterling's kisses and whispered words of love.

In the days and weeks that followed, Forrest and Kate taught Cailin much about life in the Maryland Colony. In the magic of her happiness, it was easy to forget that Sterling was her sworn enemy and that life on Lord Kentington's estate was a far cry from how she would live as the wife of a poor tobacco planter.

Kate's life was a whirlwind of duties and pleasures. Together, the two young women rode horseback across the frozen fields, visited with Kate's many relatives, explored the shops in Annapolis, and shared late-night suppers, card games, and laughter with their husbands.

Cailin saw little of Sterling during the day. He spent long hours studying tobacco culture, discussing the merits of various crops and the problems of shipping product to England. He inspected tobacco prize houses, drying barns, and land set aside to raise the young tobacco plants from seed.

"I need to learn all I can," he explained to Cailin when they were alone in bed. He pulled her against him and stroked her hair. "Forrest learned all this from the time he could sit a horse. I'm long past thirty."

"Hardly a toddling graybeard," she teased.

"Old to be starting on virgin land. From what I remember, we've some meadowland, but most is tall timber. Forrest says there's a good market for masts if I can float the logs down river. A white oak mast suitable for His Majesty's man-of-war will bring twenty pounds."

"Kate and I rode to the river crossing today," Cailin said. "You'll never believe what she told me. She said that her mother-in-law Lady Leah bathes there every day—even in winter. Have you ever—"

Sterling chuckled. "Yes. I do believe it. If you ever get the chance to meet the earl's wife, you'll see why. She's an unusual lady, to say the least."

"But to swim in winter? She must be mad."

"Not mad. She is half-Indian."

"What? That's nay possible."

He laughed. "Anything is possible. Look at you,

here in my bed—as cozy as a woodchuck. Three months ago, would you have believed that?"

"Nay." She shook her head. He was stroking her leg in a way that made it hard for her to follow the conversation. Sterling's desire for her seemed insatiable, and she wanted him so badly that sometimes she counted the hours until they could discreetly close their bedchamber door and shut out the world. Some days, they could not wait. She giggled aloud as she remembered the close call they had had on Sunday last.

The minister had come to conduct services at the plantation in the morning and share the bountiful dinner afterward. But between the closing prayers in the great hall and grace in the dining room, Sterling had lured her into the buttery, tossed up her skirts, and performed what could only be described as a remarkable feat before the butler discovered them still in each other's arms. Only the servant's discretion prevented a scandal. Still more shocking, she was as guilty of the sin of lust as Sterling, and as unrepentant. Neither cared a fig that the good cleric had waited so long for their arrival that his soup was cold before he got to taste it.

She was mad for her husband's body. The thought was troubling, and she pushed it away and tried to remember what Sterling had been saying to her. "You said Lord Kentington's wife is half-Indian, but surely, he canna have wed a savage."

"You did."

"I see little Indian when I look at you," she observed, "other than the color of your hair and eyes—and your dark skin."

"You've named me devil often enough. There's a

saying here, half-breed—not just half-Indian and half-white, but half-devil as well."

"That much seems reasonable, although your arithmetic doesn't add up."

He kissed her then, long and lingering, so that butterflies tumbled inside her and she no longer wished to fence words with him. Instead, she kissed him back and pressed her naked body close to his.

Much later, before they fell asleep, she remembered their discussion of Lady Leah. "Great English lords do not wed little red-skinned girls," she said. "They may lie with them but—"

"Lady Leah was herself born of noble blood. Her father was a Scottish earl. Remember, I told you that she was half-Scot."

"Half-Scot, ye said, but nothing about the Indian blood."

"It wasn't important."

"Nay, I suppose not. But all the same, I'm eager to meet her, this noble savage who swims in the river in winter and runs this grand household."

"From what Forrest tells me, his mother is more interested in her people than she is in the plantation. Lord Kentington has good servants. And now that Forrest has wed Kate, she is the real mistress here."

"Mmm," Cailin said, snuggling down beside him. "But I still have to see her with my own eyes to believe it."

"You will," he promised. "You will."

January passed and then February without Lady Leah's return. And as spring approached, Sterling became more and more anxious to leave the settlement and travel to his own land.

"Cailin should stay here with us," Kate insisted.

"At least until you have a house up. You can't expect her to sleep on the ground while you cut logs to build a cabin."

"That's exactly what I expect," Sterling said. He glanced across the table at Cailin. "I want you with me," he told her.

Her throat constricted. She'd not imagined that he'd leave her behind. They were still as hot for each other as they had been since they'd first consummated their marriage.

"It's not really safe," Forrest said. "There are rumors of unrest with the tribes. Mother—"

"I want her with me," Sterling repeated. "Cailin?" He looked into her eyes, and any fears she might have had vanished.

"Aye," she agreed, lifting her glass of wine in salute. "In for a penny, in for a pound."

"Then it's settled," Sterling said. "We'll leave the second week of March."

"You don't know what you're letting yourself in for," Kate argued. "The wilderness is not Annapolis."

Cailin laughed. "And neither are the Highlands. I'm used to hardships. And if Sterling insists on being massacred by savages, where else should I be but by his side?"

Chapter 12

The Maryland Frontier
May 15, 1747

Sleeping on the ground has merits that I never thought about before, Cailin mused as she snuggled closer to Sterling's solid warmth. It was very early in the morning, still an hour before dawn according to her sleepy reckoning. And it was either May 15 or 16. Keeping a calendar was not so easy in this vast wilderness. Yesterday, Sterling had led her to a patch of ripe wild strawberries. Yes, it was definitely mid-May. Past time for planting, yet they were still cutting and burning trees to clear a field.

She rolled onto her back away from him and stared at the blue velvet sky above. Crystalline stars shone in the canopy of heaven. So bright they were ... In all her nights, she had never seen stars so close or so big and brilliant.

God, but it would be easy to forget Culloden, to let Scotland and her family fade away as though they had never been. It would be natural to accept this good man as her husband, to nurture and love him, to bear his children and grow old beside him.

No man had ever set her afire as Sterling did. His touch ... Hell! One glance of those piercing black devil eyes, and she melted inside.

Theirs had been a honeymoon to equal any. Nay—to best any time of love and laughter spent by a bride and groom. He had carried her off to an enchanted land of giant trees, pure ice-water brooks, and deep, swift rivers. Never had she lain in grass so thick and green or breathed air so sweet and invigorating.

Sometimes she thought that this land was the Eden the Bible spoke of. Everything was larger than life here in this Maryland forest, even the man who claimed her as his wife. Each day, it seemed, he found a new wonder to share with her: a doe coming down to the river to drink in the morning mist, a raccoon sitting on its hind legs and washing its breakfast before it ate, a sunset of flaming orange and purple so colorful it looked as though it had been painted on a blue-gray canvas.

Sterling could read the forest floor like a book. Crouching, he would point to the slightest indentation in the leaf-covered earth and tell her of an animal's passing. "Here, see this," he would call out. "A bear and two cubs crossed here just before dawn. She's old and she's missing a toe on her left hind paw, but she's still spry. Her cubs are strong and fat. See here, where they walked along this log."

He knew each bird by the sound of its song, and he could imitate their calls. He could catch fish without a hook and line, and snare rabbits with a few twists of handmade bark cord.

One afternoon, he'd led her to a wind-fallen hollow tree large enough to stand upright in. But they'd not stood in its cavity for long. He'd stretched full length in the warm sunlit cave and pulled her onto his lap. They'd wrestled playfully until she was on her hands and knees and Sterling—

Sweet Mary! Had any maid been so happily and thoroughly swived in so many different places? Sterling's education had been far more extensive than her own. She had not dreamed that feathers or even commonplace items such as apple tarts could be put to such wanton uses.

Sterling made a soft sound in his sleep and reached out a hand. As soon as he touched her, he relaxed. His breathing deepened and became more regular. She knew that he would spring up fully awake at the slightest hint of danger, but now there was nothing more alarming than the hiss of the fire and an occasional hoot of a far-off owl.

How different this marriage would have been if the past several years could be erased, Cailin thought. If Prince Charlie had never made his last attempt at regaining his throne and the Battle of Culloden had never been fought . . . If so many of her dear ones had not died under the English guns . . . Had she come to Maryland and met Sterling not as an enemy dragoon but as the colonial he truly was, she could have loved him unconditionally.

Still, she had to admit that Sterling was not the same man she'd been forced to wed at Edinburgh Castle. With every mile they'd traveled away from the bay country, civilization had slipped from his shoulders. His senses seemed keener, he laughed more easily, and his step was lighter. He moved through the wilderness as silently as one of the wolves that shadowed their camp.

Sterling had always carried himself erect, with the proud bearing of a military man. Years in the saddle as a dragoon had given him grace and a commanding manner with horses and men. Those attributes had only increased since they had reached the trackless forests; now, he moved with the assurance of a crown prince.

Except that she'd never heard of a crown prince who could appear and disappear at will. Sterling had developed the most exasperating habit, partly as a jest and partly ... Truth was, she didn't completely understand how or why he would be standing talking to her one minute and vanishing into the trees the next. It amused him to find a spot and sit as still as a stone, watching her from his hiding place as she worked, without her awareness of his presence, until he tired of the game and spoke her name.

Even his speech, still deep and resonant, had softened with a colonial accent since they'd arrived in Annapolis. He no longer spoke like an Englishman. And, at times, she'd even caught him singing.

He spared himself no physical effort. Day after day, she'd watched him, stripped to the waist, wielding a broadax and chopping down trees. His hands had blistered from the oak handle; sweat had run off his back in rivulets. He'd never complained and never slowed his pace. Four hired men had come with them from Lord Kentington's plantation, and Sterling had outworked every one of them. At first, the laborers had been surprised and unsure of how to react to a master who swung an ax and rolled stones into place to make the foundation for a house. But they'd soon learned that Sterling expected his orders to be carried out. He was fair but unyielding. And if he drove himself to the limit, he expected a full day's work from his men as well.

His skin had quickly darkened in the sun to a deep bronze, and every spare ounce of flesh had dropped away, leaving him a lithe, sinewy Adonis who laughed and loved with a greater zest than Cailin would have believed possible.

When Sterling had forced her to marry him and taken her to his father's house in England, she had thought him to be a willful, even stubborn man. But he had also seemed troubled, at times uncertain of purpose. Now, she saw only determination and focus. Lines caused by years of care and cynicism had vanished from Sterling's face. In their stead, she saw hope and the fulfillment of a dream.

"You should have come back to America years ago," she'd told him one afternoon. "You look younger here, more alive than I've ever seen you."

He regarded her intently with those riveting hell-black eyes and slowly grinned. "If I'd come back years ago, I'd not have you," he reminded her.

"You don't have me now," she answered.

"Don't I?" He leaned his ax handle against a tree and ran a hand possessively down her back to fondle her bottom.

"For two years only," she reminded him, trying to wiggle free. She'd been carrying a basket of clothes to the river to wash them.

"We'll see," he'd said, tilting her chin with his other hand and covering her mouth with his. "We'll see about that."

Cailin sighed, remembering what had happened to the wash, and how late supper had been that night. Sterling was impossible . . . and wonderful. And she was hopelessly addicted to his kisses and the loving that always followed them.

If she had half the sense God gave a goat, she'd forget revenge, duty to family, Prince Charlie's accursed rebellion, and every vow she'd made to return to Scotland. Sterling had offered her a share in his dream, and it didn't take a vast amount of imagination to know that she could find happiness as Sterling's wife and partner in this new world.

"Ye be the most obstinate lass it has ever been my misfortune to ken," her husband MacGreggor had told her the last time she'd seen him alive. That was her failing and her weakness. Once she made a promise, she must keep it or die trying.

"Oh, MacGreggor," she murmured into the darkness. "Why did I ever let lust and a handsome set of legs lead me to the altar?"

She'd not thought of MacGreggor in weeks. He'd been a good catch for a woman without wealth, or so everyone had said. He was young and full of vinegar, and his kisses made her head spin. "Marry or burn," the priest proclaimed. And her cousin Jane had just given birth to a beautiful baby boy.

"Long past the age to wed," a neighbor had told her.

"She'll end up old and sour, caring for her sister's children," Aunty Meg had predicted. "She's too choosy by half, that one."

Reasons . . . some foolish, some wise. MacGreggor had been willing to have her, sharp tongue and all. He'd offered her a ring and a household of her own, and she'd accepted him. Later, she'd found that he was the father of three little bastards by three different women. And that the mischievous smile that had captured her still charmed other fair lassies.

First, she'd caught him with the shepherd's wife. Next, they'd had a public shouting match at the spring horse fair when he'd let his hands roam too freely over the flanks of a gypsy fortune-teller. And finally, MacGreggor had tried to turn her over his knee when she'd questioned him about the woman's red satin garter she'd found in their own marriage bed.

He'd tried to explain and had failed most miserably. She'd not believed the lie that the single garter was a gift he'd bought for her. In the argument that had followed, they'd broken the pitcher and washbowl and torn the hangings from the poster bed, but it was MacGreggor who'd gone down to breakfast in the hall with an eye as black as the devil's cod and scratches on his face that did not fade for a fortnight.

If she'd quickened with MacGreggor's babe, perhaps they would have come to terms before parting. But she hadn't. And the pleasure of his company was not enough to overcome her shame and anger at his roving eye. So she'd packed her trunk and returned to her stepfather's house.

She'd remained there, a little wiser but no less stubborn. So complete and scandalous was their separation that MacGreggor's death brought sadness and regret, but no real heartbreak.

A wolf howled nearby, and Cailin flinched.

"Shhh," Sterling soothed. "They'll do us no harm. The pack is hunting deer, most likely." He pulled her close, and she relaxed and let her eyelids drift shut.

When I married MacGreggor, I was a woman in body but still a child in my mind, Cailin thought. Why couldn't it have been Sterling whom I met at that wedding? If he had kissed me instead of MacGreggor ... if he had asked for my hand in wedlock ...

I would have slapped his face and set the dogs on him.

She caught her lower lip between her teeth.

If I was too young to recognize MacGreggor for

what he was, I wouldn't have been mature enough to see beyond Sterling's enemy uniform.

Sadness swept over her. Two years she had promised Sterling Gray, and two years they would have. She would give her body willingly and take sensual joy in his. But theirs was an arrangement. When the time had passed, she would keep her vow and return to Scotland.

And regret leaving him for the rest of her life.

She was still tired from yesterday's long day's work. She had carried branches all afternoon and helped to dig the foundation trench for the cabin. She'd rolled rocks and carried water from the stream for the thirsty men to drink. She'd cleaned and cooked for seven men, and in an hour or two, she'd rise and begin all over again. But this morning—in the darkness before dawn—sleep eluded her.

Restlessly, she turned and wiggled. Something didn't feel right. An odd, prickly sensation spread up the back of her neck. Uneasy, she opened her eyes and stifled a cry of alarm. Beyond the fire, in the stygian blackness of the forest, red eyes glowed.

"Sterling." His name came out a bare whisper, but she felt him tense.

"It's all right," he said. "It's just a wolf."

Cailin's mouth was suddenly dry. "A wolf? Just a wolf?" She shrank back against him. "Aren't you going to shoot it?"

"He's just curious."

As she watched, the animal's eyes grew larger. "*Sterling.*" Gooseflesh rose on her arms.

"He won't hurt us." Sterling sat up. "Greetings, Brother M'wai-wah."

The creature took a few steps closer to the fire, and a huge gray form emerged from the darkness. Cailin's teeth began to chatter. The wolf's legs were long and surprisingly slender, its coat gray-black. White hairs sprinkled the ruff of its neck and encircled its muzzle.

A cold wind rustled through the trees. A log on the fire cracked, shooting sparks into the air. White teeth gleamed in the beast's mouth.

"Sterling!"

"Shhh." He moved to kneel between her and the wolf. *"M'wai-wah, ili klecheleche?"*

For a long minute, he and the wolf stared into each other's eyes. Slowly, Sterling smiled.

The wolf lifted one paw as if to salute them, and then dropped to its haunches and gave a low, doglike whine.

Sterling extended both hands, open to show that he held no weapons. *"Auween khackey?"* Who are you? he asked.

The wolf opened its mouth, letting a red tongue loll. Its eyes were yellow now, as bright as molten gold, and it was close enough for Sterling to hear its breathing.

Sterling was puzzled. He'd told Cailin that there was no reason to be afraid of the wolf, and normally that would be true, but this animal was not behaving as it should. It didn't look sick or mad, but wolves were generally shy of humans, and it was late spring, a time when there were many young birds and animals, making food easier to come by for predators.

Sterling slowly reached for his rifle. He'd not shoot unless he or Cailin was in danger. Instinct told him that the wolf wouldn't attack, but he couldn't be sure. He'd never seen or heard of a wolf coming so close to fire.

"Are you someone's pet?" he asked.

The animal maintained eye contact.

"What are you saying?" Cailin asked.

With a start, he realized that he'd been speaking in Algonquian . . . thinking in it as well. How long had it been, he wondered, since he'd ceased to reason in his native tongue?

He kept his gaze fixed on the yellow eyes. Finally, the wolf lowered its head. Then Sterling glanced toward the second fire on the far side of the clearing where the workmen were sleeping. Not a soul was stirring. When he looked back, the wolf had gotten to its feet and was strolling off into the trees.

"It's going away," Cailin whispered.

The animal stopped, stared back at them, then trotted off. In seconds, it vanished into the underbrush.

Sterling noticed that the wind, which had come up quickly, had calmed. The fire was burning steadily; the flames flickered low. He would need to add more wood to keep it going until dawn.

"Sterling."

He looked down at Cailin. She was visibly shaken, and he wondered if he'd been selfish to bring her with him to the frontier. "I told you that it was all right," he said. "Probably a pet."

"A pet wolf?" She sounded unconvinced.

He laughed. "Well, it's no stranger an explanation than having a wild one come sit by our fire."

"Ye spoke Indian, didn't ye?"

She still clung to his arm, and he liked the feeling. When he was near Cailin, it was hard to think of anything but her. He was nearly overwhelmed with a desire to protect her—to make up for all she had suffered.

"Ye did speak Indian."

Her insistence pulled him from his reverie. "I suppose I did," he agreed, hugging her.

Strange how he'd seen her image so many years ago when he'd gone out to seek his spirit guide. Having a white woman appear in his vision—when he'd hoped for a bear, a hawk, or a mountain lion— had been a great trial to him. But now that he'd found her again, she seemed as much a part of him as his right arm. It didn't matter what nonsense she prattled about going back to Scotland. She was his. Call it coincidence, Indian magic, or fate, Cailin was his woman. He'd never let her go.

He kissed the crown of her head. Her hair was soft and sweet-smelling. "It's not wolves or bears you need to watch out for here in the woods," he said, "it's two-legged beasts. Unless you frighten a sow with her cub or come across a sick animal, they will give you a wide berth."

"It sounds a wee bit like Gaelic—your heathen talk—but I dinna ken a word of it."

He kissed her on the forehead, then got up and put several logs on the coals. "I don't know why I started speaking Shawnee. I've gotten out of practice. My father threatened to whip me for forgetting to use English. I wasn't even sure I remembered much Algonquian."

She moved closer to the fire and laid a hand on his arm. "What did ye call it?"

"Algonquian. It's a language used by most of the tribes along the Atlantic and west to the Great English Lakes. The Iroquois speak their own tongue, and so do the Cherokee in the south. But most of us between the ocean and the Mississippi River speak Algonquian. Each nation has a slightly different accent, but we can usually understand each other well enough. I've a few words of Iroquoian—at least I used to—but their speech is nothing like ours."

"So you are Shawnee, but you speak Algonquian."

"My mother was Shawnee," he corrected. "I told you, I'm a half-breed. I like to consider myself English now."

She sniffed. "I'd prefer ye to be Shawnee, I think. I've known none of them, so I have no trouble with them." She looked over her shoulder anxiously. "Will the wolf come back, do ye think?"

"I doubt it."

"So ye say."

He fancied the Highland lilt of her husky voice. Her *come* always sounded like *comb* and her *back* like *bock*. "Think of that wolf's visit as an adventure. Something to tell our children on winter nights, when we're safe inside thick walls." He smiled as he thought of her holding his son to her breast.

"I doubt there will be any bairns."

"Why not?" he demanded. He'd never thought of being a father before—never thought of himself as a man who could settle down. That had changed at Culloden Field. Now, he couldn't imagine *not* having children. Why else was he carving a plantation from virgin forest, if not to leave it to his sons and daughters?

"I had none with my first husband. And . . ." She blushed faintly. "I told ye that there were . . ."

"Other men." He pushed back a primitive wave of jealousy and waited for her to go on.

"Nay so many," she said. "At least not willingly."

He shook his head. "I'm sorry. I didn't mean it like that. The fault wasn't yours." His chest tightened as black rage surged up within him. Had he guessed what was in store for her, he'd have accompanied the soldiers to Edinburgh. And had he known later, he'd have tracked them down and given each one a slow, painful death. "What happened before we wed is your own concern. God knows I've been no saint."

"I only wanted to say that I dinna think I'm a fecund mare to quicken with babe easily."

"I'll get you with child, Cailin. I swear I will." He took her in his arms again and looked into her face. "I've no babes that I know of either, but that doesn't mean we can't make a baker's dozen between us." He kissed her lightly on the lips. "Come to bed," he coaxed. "Dawn will come soon enough."

She followed him willingly to their bedroll and lay down in the circle of his arm. He pulled the wool blanket around them and rubbed the small of her back.

"I like sleeping next to you," she admitted. "You're big and warm, and you're a good back scratcher."

"Flatterer," he said. "There's something I have for you." He'd picked up the necklace she'd thrown away in the bedroom weeks ago and taken it to a silversmith to have a new chain made. "I was planning to save it until the house was finished, but—"

"A present? What it is?" she demanded.

A wolf's howl echoed through the clearing, and she began to tremble again. "Shhh," he said. "I won't let anything harm you, Cailin. I promise." He reached for his leather shot bag and dug inside. "Here." He pulled out a small bundle of velvet cloth and gave it to her.

She unrolled the velvet, and the necklace gleamed in the firelight. "My amulet," she said with surprise. " 'Tis called the Eye of Mist."

"It has a name?"

"Aye, it does."

"When the pendant struck the bricks on the hearth,

some of the paint chipped away. I took it into Annapolis and had it cleaned and strung for you."

"I thought it was gone for good," she said.

"The pendant is solid gold, but I suppose you knew that. The merchant said it's older than anything he's ever worked with. He thought the markings on it might be Saracen." He'd wanted to buy her gold earrings to go with the necklace, but they'd been too dear. What money he had left had to be stretched to cover draft animals, seed, and glass for the windows of the house. "Are you sorry I—"

"Nay." Her voice choked with emotion. " 'Tis not Saracen. 'Tis Pictish, my mother said. Handed down from mother to daughter for thousands of years."

"It's a family heirloom, then?"

"Aye, ye might say that. It's all I ever had from the man who sired me." She unfastened the clasp and put it around her throat. "I said I didn't want it anymore, but . . ."

"Why was it covered in that awful blue paint—a fine piece of gold jewelry?"

"To keep the English from stealing it."

"Ouch. I asked for that."

"So ye did, Sassenach."

She snuggled against him, and he went all soft inside. "Someday I'll buy you pearls," he promised.

"I'm glad to have it back. I forgot it the next morning, and when I did remember to look, I couldn't find it," she admitted. "I thought one of the maids might have taken it, and I was too ashamed to say anything."

"I took it while you slept. I didn't know it was valuable, but I knew you always wore it."

"Thank ye. It's the nicest gift you've ever given me."

"The only gift," he corrected. "But there will be more, Cailin. Trust me. I'll look after you. You have my word on it."

She slipped her hand under his hunting shirt. The warmth of her palm against his skin made his groin tighten. " 'Tis not your word I want now," she teased.

"No? And what do you want?" He lowered his head and kissed her mouth. She tasted sweeter than wild honey.

She laughed and brushed his nipple with her fingertips. He groaned as his cock hardened and began to throb.

"I'm cold," she whispered.

"Not for long." He cupped a rounded breast. Her skin was like satin. Already, he could imagine himself driving into her soft, wet sheath, burying himself deep inside her, and pumping until she cried out with joy.

He loved her screams of satisfaction when he futtered her. Each sound she made increased his own pleasure twofold. He freed her breast and took her nipple into his mouth.

"Yes . . . yes," she murmured as he sucked harder.

He kissed her lips, and she opened her mouth to take in his deep caress. Their tongues met and parted, then entwined again as she wound her bare legs around his. "God, but I can't get enough of you," he groaned. "I love you."

"Sterling . . ."

He caught her hand and brought it to his tumescent cock. "Like this," he whispered. "Stroke it." Her soft hand slid along the length of him, lingering on the throbbing head and slipping down to explore his heavy sacks. "Cailin," he murmured.

"Shall I stop?"

"No . . ." He writhed under her touch, thinking how lucky he was. Cailin was a sensuous woman and an adventurous bedmate. She never failed to set his blood to boil when she teased him like this.

"What is this I've found?"

"I'm not sure," he answered, playing her game. She was stroking him faster now. His prick felt as if it were going to explode. He ran his palm down over her flat belly and spanned a bare hip.

She turned to face him, putting her arms around his neck and lifting her head for his caress.

"Cailin." His heartbeat quickened, and the urgency in his groin grew more intense as a light film of perspiration broke out on his skin. He was panting now; the hot woman scent of her was driving him wild.

Her fingers played up and down his rod.

He exhaled softly. "You know what you're doing to me?" He pushed her back and knelt between her legs. "Are you ready?" He knelt over her, rubbing the swollen tip of his erect phallus against her wet, silken cleft.

"Yes! Yes! I want it," she replied.

His first thrust was hard and deep. He caught her arching hips and lifted her. She was tight and hot, and her eager pleas gave him strength to plunge still deeper. Far off, a wolf howled, but the sounds of the forest were lost in the heated frenzy of their mutual rapture.

Chapter 13

Isle of Skye, Scotland
May 1747

Duncan MacKinnon stepped into the shelter of the overhanging porch and shook the rain off his ragged cloak. He was dressed in worn woolen breeks and a homespun shirt of indiscriminate color. He wore no kilt, no plaid of any sort. The tartan had been banned on pain of death.

Naught but death and destruction reigned in the Highlands today, Duncan mused. By the devil's bowels, he'd smelled his share of slaughtered cattle and burning men. He'd get not a wink of honest sleep until he'd put the shores of Scotland behind him.

"Jeanne," he called softly. " 'Tis me."

"Duncan?"

"Aye, I said it, didn't I?"

His young wife rose to meet him, and he was shamed at how threadbare her gown was. The skirt was burned in two places and torn along the hem; her bodice had seen better days.

"Did ye get it?" she asked anxiously. "The bread?"

"Aye, and a bit of cheese to go with it. As luck would have it, MacCrimmon needed help to geld two colts. There's enough here to last us today and tomorrow. We'll be on the ship the following day. Donald promised that we'll get daily rations."

She reached for the bread and eagerly crammed a little in her mouth. "We'll save the cheese for Jamie," she said. Pushing aside the blanket, she showed him his son's sleeping face. "I think his cheeks look fuller today, don't ye?"

Duncan gritted his teeth and turned away, as hot blood flushed his fair skin. The world was upside down when a MacKinnon had to beg day work to feed his wife and child. "I brought you milk for the bairn last night. I'll do it again tonight."

"Stolen," she accused softly. "Taken from MacCrimmon's cow in the dark of the moon."

"Silence," he warned her. "I do what I must, Jeanne." He'd done worse than steal a noggin of milk to get them safely here from Johnnie MacLeod's farmstead. He'd murdered two men to escape after he'd been captured by the Hanoverian troops, and he'd killed again before he reached the place where his wife and infant son were hiding. He'd kept himself from starving by eating raw horseflesh, and he'd stripped dead Scots of their shoes and clothing. And now—as a last resort—he'd sold both himself and his wife into servitude for three years to buy passage to Canada.

"I don't mean to blame ye. It's just that I keep thinkin' about my grandfather and Cailin. Cailin would fault us for leaving Grandfather behind."

"Your sister didn't have to listen to a hungry baby cry, did she? She didn't sleep in caves without a fire or go days without a crust of bread." He took hold of Jeanne's shoulders and pulled her against him. "I do what I must, woman, to save the three of us."

"But Cailin—"

"I want to hear nothin' more about your sister. She's gone, God rest her soul. Hanged at Edinburgh Castle."

Jeanne began to weep quietly.

"Dinna ..." Duncan begged her. "Do ye think I want to hurt ye more than you've been hurt already? But ye must face the truth. What we're doin' is for wee Jamie. He'll have a new start in Canada. No one there will know or care what side I fought on at Culloden Moor."

"Cailin may be dead but Grandfather ... 'Twas nay right to just leave him standing by the road last summer. And there's still Corey, waitin' somewhere for us to come and fetch him. He's just a wee boy."

"Your grandfather was old and blind. His time was past. He knew it. He urged us to go on without him—didn't he? If we'd brought him with us to Skye, do ye think any man would take his indenture? We've no money to pay our own passage, let alone his."

"Cailin promised Corey she'd come for him. We should have tried to find him."

"I'm as sorry as sorry can be for Johnnie MacLeod's boy, but your sister made the promise—not you. Corey MacLeod's not our responsibility. He should go to the MacLeods for charity. He's their blood. Johnnie was naught to you but a stepfather."

Tears slid down her cheeks. "I ... I don't want to ... go ... over the ocean ... to a strange land full of savages," she sobbed.

Duncan swore under his breath. "We've gone over and over this. Would ye rather see me hanged for treason and our son with his brains dashed out on some rock?"

"No! No!" she cried. "I just—"

"You'll just pray for the old man's soul, and for the lad, and you'll take ship with me for the Colonies. 'Tis Jamie's future we must think of now. And the only chance for us is Canada."

A week later and thousands of miles west across the Atlantic in the Maryland Colony, Jeanne's sister, Cailin, stood thigh-deep in the river watching the laborers shingle the roof of a new log house. Nathan cut each cedar shake by hand, and Joe bundled them up and carried them to the ladder, so that Sterling and the free Negro, Isaac Walker, could nail them in place. They would have been finished by now, Sterling had told her, if the other two workers hadn't gotten scared and sneaked away in the night.

"Injuns is bad out this way," Isaac had said when it was discovered that the hired hands had fled. Isaac had rubbed his bald head and looked pointedly at Joe. " 'Course I don't got to worry like some about being scalped." Joe's hair was long and corn-silk white in color. "I hear tell yellow scalps bring top money in Canada."

Sterling had quickly put an end to the teasing. "Enough of that talk," he said sternly. "We've not seen a single Indian, peaceful or hostile. I hired the lot of you to finish the job. By running off, those two have forfeited their wages."

Cailin bent over and let the clean river water wash the suds from her hair. The temperature was cool, but not uncomfortably so, and Sterling had brought her a plant he called soapwort and showed her how to pound the roots to make shampoo.

She had been familiar with herbs and flowers that grew in the Highlands, and had often used them for medicinal purposes. Sterling knew of dozens here in the Colonies that she'd never heard of. "My mother knew of hundreds of useful wild plants," he'd said. "Many are women's medicine, and others I never bothered to learn. There are no apothecaries in the woods. I'd match a Shawnee shaman against a European trained physician any day. The Shawnee, and especially their cousins, the Delaware, can cure more wounds with roots and herbs than most English surgeons can with scapels and bone saws."

Cailin looked back at the cabin with pride. It was small, only one room and a hall downstairs, and one long room on the second floor, but there were real steps and bull's-eye glass in the windows. A stone chimney covered most of the north end. There was a huge fireplace downstairs and a smaller one upstairs. The peak was steep, the walls log, and the roof neat cedar shakes.

The floors were made of wide pine boards, sawed in Annapolis and hauled there at great expense along with a walnut table, four straight-back chairs, a six-board chest, and a bedstead. A few basic cooking pots, an iron spit for the kitchen hearth, and pewter dishes had been brought in by oxcart. As Sterling had told her more than once, they were starting out close to the bone. But he'd assured her that when he had time to trade with the tribes for furs and bring in a crop, they'd start to accumulate financial security.

"It's not as though the land isn't mine," he'd explained. "I hold directly through the Crown, not by leave of any royal governor. My father took pains to ensure that my mother's gift would be safe from greedy hands. The king owed my father a favor. By giving us the land outright, His Majesty satisfied an old debt without spending a shilling of his own money."

Land ... Cailin turned her head and stared east along the river. Their property ran that way farther than she could see; it ran in every direction farther than she could imagine. Thousands of acres of forest, stream, hills, and meadows belonged to Sterling ... and to her too, she supposed. Enough land to put many a Highland laird or English lord to shame. Enough land to feel free of rules and quarrelsome neighbors.

She sighed with regret. It wasn't really hers because she didn't intend to stay with Sterling. He belonged here; she didn't. Where were the open fields of heather? The stone crofter's huts and herds of shaggy Highland cattle? The castles and enchanted hollows? Maryland was too big, too green—and yes, even too wild for a Scotswoman.

What I'd give to hear Jeanne's babe cry now, she thought ... or even to hear her sister complain about something. She missed her family terribly.

Absently, she fingered the amulet at her throat. "You've brought me far and far," she murmured. " 'Tis true that I've been cursed ... but where is your blessing?"

A loud hurrah sounded from the house site. When she turned back, Sterling was waving at her. "We're finished!" he shouted. "Come light the first fire!"

The first fire ... Another ritual to ensure luck for the house. They'd already buried a shiny new shilling under the front doorsill and hung horseshoes over each entrance. Sterling had thought that the horseshoes were silly superstition, but Isaac had agreed with Cailin. "A new house needs protection from witches and other evil spirits," she'd said. "My grandfather was an educated man, but he believed it.

If it's good enough for him, it's good enough for me."

She'd made a joke of it, but horseshoes over the doorway were customary among the people she knew. She would have felt strange if they didn't hang them. It went along with the old saying that guests should always leave the house by the same entrance they'd come in, and the one that insisted the first visitor on New Year's Day should be a man rather than a woman. If a woman came in the door first, people at home thought that meant the wife and not the husband would rule the household until the following year.

Isaac had climbed the ladder to nail the horseshoes, open side up, to keep the luck from falling out, before the doors were even hung. "It don't pay to fool around with witches," he said. "Out here in the big woods—who knows what haunts there might be?"

Cailin wasn't sure about ghosts, but she had seen a witch with her own eyes. Old Granny MacGreggor could take off warts and heal burns overnight. And she had the sight as well. People for miles around used to bring their newborn bairns for her to bless. Granny was a Christian, she was sure of that. Granny never failed to pray before each laying on of hands. But her religion was the old kind, and Granny had powers that few people were born with. Ghosts— maybe so or maybe not, but Cailin knew about witches. Besides, she told herself, the horseshoes would do no harm, and they might do good.

"Cailin!" Sterling shouted. "Are you coming?"

She closed her eyes and turned her face up to the sun. Truth was, she hated to leave the river. The sound of the rushing water was soothing to her ears.

The sunshine was warm, and the music of birdsong came from every direction. Here, for the first time in weeks, she'd been able to step back from all the hard work and lose herself in her thoughts.

"I'm torn," she said with a sigh. "I'm torn by wanting him and knowing it canna last." But part of her wished it could last ... wished her life could start over here in this clean, cool river.

Straightening her shoulders, she opened her eyes, took hold of a thick section of her hair, and squeezed the water from it. "I'm coming," she called.

The sandy bottom felt good under her bare feet as she turned toward shore. She'd have to change into another skirt and bodice; this one was soaked through, but—

"Holy Mother of God!"

Coming directly at her—not twenty yards away— was a boat full of feathered savages.

"Sterling!" she screamed.

The birch-bark canoe shot forward, cutting between Cailin and the riverbank. Kneeling in the bow was a copper-skinned man wearing little more than a scrap of deerskin around his loins. His head was shaved except for a rooster crest, from which several eagle feathers dangled in the back. He held a paddle in his hands, but a long rifle lay propped against the side of the boat.

Behind him, in the center, Cailin saw an Indian woman of indeterminate age, with a face as beautiful as a rose-marble madonna, dressed all in red with a white beaded headband decorated with black and white feathery plumage. She was armed with a rifle as well.

The paddler in the stern of the boat was the fiercest-looking one of all. His face was painted with yellow slashes, and he wore his black hair long and streaming around his tattooed shoulders. Around his neck hung a string of bear claws, and his fringed leather vest bore bits of hair that Cailin feared might be human scalps. In his ears gleamed ornaments of bone, and a silver pin was thrust through the soft underpart of his nose.

He drove his paddle deep into the water, and the canoe glided to a halt. He said something in Indian to his companions, and the man in the bow traded his paddle for the rifle.

Cailin froze. "Sterling!" she cried again.

The Indian woman smiled at her and lifted a hand, palm out. "Do not be afraid," she said in perfect English. "We mean you no harm."

Cailin was so startled that she couldn't speak. Her heart was pounding so hard that she was certain the Indians could hear it. "Who . . ." she began. Her voice cracked, and she tried again. "Who are ye?"

The Indian woman's smile widened, and her dark eyes twinkled. "I had heard that Ko-nah had taken a Highland wife."

Cailin's eyes widened in astonishment. Had she heard a trace of Scottish burr? "I am Cailin MacGreggor," she said. Then she corrected herself. "Cailin Gray. I dinna ken this Connor."

The lady in the canoe laughed. "Ko-nah Ain-jeleh. In Shawnee, it means Snow Ghost. It is what we call your husband, Sterling Gray. Moonfeather greets you, Cailin Gray."

Cailin swallowed. "Moonfeather? Be that your name?" It fit her. A beautiful name for a beautiful woman. She was not as young as Cailin had first thought. When she looked close, she could see a sprinkling of gray frost in her ink-black hair, and there were tiny laugh lines around her eyes. But her face ... Cailin had never seen such oval perfection. True, her nose was strong and her eyes faintly slanted like those of some Oriental queen, but her skin was russet silk and her features in exquisite balance.

She nodded her head graciously, and Cailin lost her fear. Moonfeather radiated trust. Despite her wild companions, it was natural to believe that this woman came in peace.

"Come ashore," Cailin said. She wasn't certain how one made Indians welcome, but Sterling would know. "Can I offer you something to eat?" Feeding guests must be universal ... at least if they ate the same kinds of food as the English and Scots.

Moonfeather said something to the paddler in the stern of the canoe. He frowned but steered the boat toward the bank.

Cailin splashed after them, suddenly conscious of how she must look, hair wet and stringing, clothes soaked through. A fine hostess I am to greet our first visitors, she thought.

"Moonfeather!" Sterling hurried toward the canoe with open arms. "Moonfeather! Kitate. Chee-tun-ai, it's good to see you."

The men brought the light craft as close to the bank as possible, then one stepped out and lifted Moonfeather in his arms. He set her lightly on the grass and returned to help the brave wearing the bear claws beach the canoe.

"Cailin." Sterling took her hand and helped her up the bank. "We are honored by a visit from Lady Leah." He draped an arm around Cailin's shoulder. "Cailin ... Moonfeather, Lady Leah."

"I dinna ken—" Cailin said.

Moonfeather laughed. "Call me whatever you like. Leah will do if Moonfeather sits uneasy on your tongue. But here in my mother's land, this person does not need the title of *lady*."

"Moonfeather is Lord Kentington's wife," Sterling explained. "I told you that her father was a Scottish earl."

"My mother was Shawnee," Moonfeather said. "Only with the English do I bow to my husband's wishes and follow his customs. Here this one is only—"

"A peace woman," the shaven warrior growled. "The peace woman of the Shawnee."

Sterling smiled. "A great lady in any tongue. We are pleased to welcome you here to our home."

Any doubts that Cailin might have had about Moonfeather's identity were quickly extinguished as the workmen snatched off their hats and bent their heads in salute to their mistress.

"Lady Leah," Isaac said. "Good t' see you, ma'am."

"And you, Isaac," she replied.

"Your Ladyship." Joe's Adam's apple bobbed up and down as he clutched his cap.

"Ladyship," Nathan echoed.

Moonfeather responded to them graciously, calling each by name, and asking after Isaac's family.

"Your son and his wife were very kind to us," Cailin said when the laborers stepped back. "I'm afraid we took advantage of your hospitality for several months this winter."

Moonfeather smiled. "Forrest wrote to me. I'm glad that he remembered his manners. If he had done any less, I would have scolded him severely. Isn't his wife a treasure?"

"I liked her very much," Cailin replied. She wondered why Sterling hadn't told her that Lady Leah dressed like a savage and lived in the woods. It was all very puzzling. But there was no time to worry about that now. She brought out the food that she'd been planning to serve for the noon meal and put water over the fire to boil.

Within minutes, she, Sterling, and their guests were seated under a large beech tree, sipping mugs of steaming tea. Cailin had offered chairs, but the Indians declined. Instead, the five of them sat on the ground. Indians, Cailin decided, liked a great deal of precious sugar in their tea.

"Tea is one custom that this woman grew fond of in England," Moonfeather exclaimed after an exchange of gifts and appropriate thank-yous. She had presented Sterling with a magnificent knife with a carved bone handle and a beaded sheath and belt. Cailin had received a beautiful basket woven of pine needles. Sterling in turn had produced powder horns full of gunpowder for the men and a small silverplated French pistol for the peace woman.

"I'm afraid I canna offer ye cream or lemon," Cailin said. "We've no cow yet, and lemon is too dear for us to afford."

Moonfeather laughed. "Milk is one of the other European customs I've not adjusted to. I find it . . ." She spread her hands expressively. "Rather repulsive."

"I meant to come to the village as soon as the house was finished," Sterling said, changing the subject. "I've heard a lot of rumors of unrest among the tribes, and I wanted to hear what you thought about it."

The Shawnee with the bear claw necklace, the man called Kitate, glowered. He had not spoken since they'd left the canoe. Now, he said, "It is not wise that you build a house in this place." Cailin noticed that his English was good but heavily accented.

Moonfeather waited until he had finished. "My son speaks truth," she agreed. "This is not the time to cut this earth for planting tobacco."

"The land is mine," Sterling insisted. "Mine from my mother and by the king's own hand."

Kitate's scowl became darker. "Land cannot be owned. From your mother came hunting rights, not the right to carve up the forest."

"King George—" Sterling argued.

"King George is far away," Moonfeather said. "His moccasins have never walked these trails. He has not the blood of the people—he is not Shawnee. The English king does not matter."

"You, Snow Ghost, have returned to us," Kitate said. "But you do not come as our brother. You come as one of them."

"War is coming between red man and white," the second warrior said. "Which side will you choose, Snow Ghost? Will you fight against your mother's—"

Sterling's features became as hard as Kitate's. "Half of me is Shawnee," he said, "and half is English. The peace woman knows my heart. I am torn between mother and father."

"My father was a Scot," Moonfeather corrected softly. "Not English. My children are more European than Shawnee. Those closest to me have pale skin and light eyes, but I always knew my loyalty lay with my mother's people."

"My mother was Shawnee as well," Sterling said. "I honor her memory and would never lift a hand against the Shawnee or the Delaware."

Moonfeather gave him a long, pensive look.

"If they leave me and mine in peace, I'll be a friend to them," Sterling added. "But I will build a plantation here. I mean to keep what is mine."

Moonfeather handed Cailin her cup, and when she leaned forward to take it, her amulet slid from her damp bodice. Instantly, Moonfeather's gaze became fixed on the pendant. Her eyes widened, and she drew in her breath with an audible gasp. "So," she murmured.

Self-consciously, Cailin clasped the necklace. Hadn't she heard something about Indian giving? If Moonfeather liked the Eye of Mist and wanted it, what should she do? Lady Kentington had been good to them, but she didn't want to hurt Sterling by giving away the necklace either. Quickly, she tucked the amulet back under her clothing. "Would you care for more tea, Lady Kentington?" she asked to cover her distress.

"Where did you get that?" Moonfeather asked.

"She's had it since she was a child," Sterling said. "It's a family keepsake. Now, about this land . . . I have no intention of forbidding the Shawnee to cross it, to fish and hunt here. I—"

Moonfeather would not be distracted. "Who gave you the necklace, wife of Snow Ghost?"

Cailin answered stiffly. "It was a gift from the man who fathered me, Cameron Stewart."

"So." Moonfeather rose to her feet and smiled. "The circle is closed," she said mysteriously.

Confused, Cailin glanced at Sterling. He seemed as bewildered by his guest's remark as she was.

"Come to the village and talk with the elders, Sterling Gray," Moonfeather said. "There will be a high council meeting on the night of the next full moon.

You should hear what has happened between Shawnee and the whites in the years since you left." She looked directly into Cailin's face. "If you are ever in need, come to me, Cailin Gray. Two days' walk along the river. This woman would be your sister."

The two braves leaped up.

"There's no need for you to go," Sterling said. "We can talk—"

Moonfeather suddenly grasped his hands and stepped close to him. "Heed my words. War between the English and the French is coming to this land. This woman fears that the rivers will run red with blood."

"If war does come, will the Shawnee stand with the English or the French?" Sterling asked.

Moonfeather shrugged. "When hawk and eagle clash, small birds scatter."

"You must choose between them. The French only want furs and to convert the tribes to Christianity. The English colonists have come to stay. They've sunk roots here. They won't be driven out," Sterling replied. "The French can't win. If the Shawnee choose the wrong side—"

"Some of my people fear the English settlers more than the soldiers," Moonfeather replied. "The soldier comes with cannon and shot, but the farmer sinks deep roots in the earth."

"We can learn to live together—English and Indian," Sterling argued. "You've spent your life making peace. You must believe in the possibility."

Moonfeather sighed. "To make a lasting peace, both sides must agree. So long as the Indian claims land that the *Englishmanake* wants, there can be no end to the fighting."

"You can't put all the blame on the whites, Moonfeather. Your greatest enemies, the Iroquois nation, were here long before the first European set foot in America."

"My enemies?" She shook her head. "You believe in your heart that you are English, Sterling Gray, but your mother carried you under her breast. She gave you life. It is her heritage that runs strongest in you. You cannot turn your face from your Shawnee brothers and sisters."

"I'm not ashamed of my Indian heritage."

"Then I have wronged you," she said. "You are a good man, and I would offer you no insult."

Sterling's face flushed beneath his tan. "The English and the Shawnee don't have to be at each other's throats," he said. "There's land enough here for us all."

"Aye," she answered. "So my husband and father believe. But when this one looks into the sacred fire, she sees the flames of war and hears the footsteps of a passing people." She released his hands. "I sense a change in you, Sterling Gray," she said quietly. "Something has happened."

He didn't answer. Cailin glanced from one to the other. Moonfeather's warning had been ominous, but now ... A chill passed over Cailin.

The peace woman's eyes darkened to pools of liquid obsidian, and when she spoke again, it was in the Indian tongue. "Na-nata Ki-tehi," she whispered.

There was more, but uttered so softly that Cailin could hardly hear her, let alone comprehend.

"Are you sure?" Sterling asked.

"Aye," Moonfeather said, switching back to English. The fey look left her face, and she smiled.

"Come to the village," she said. Then she turned and walked toward the river, followed by her men. After a few steps, she stopped and glanced back. "Thank you for the tea, and do not forget to bring your wife with you when you come to the council fire. There is much that I would know of her."

"What did she say to you?" Cailin asked as the braves guided the canoe into deep water and began to paddle upriver against the current. Moonfeather turned to wave, and Cailin waved back. "What a strange woman," she murmured.

"Trust her," Sterling said. "No matter what comes, remember that you can trust her. She is a great lady and the wisest woman I've ever known."

"What did she say to you?" Cailin repeated. "Just before she left—when she spoke in Indian."

He gave a small sound of disbelief. "It makes no sense at all."

"What doesn't?"

"She told me that my Shawnee name is no longer Ko-nah Ain-jeleh—Snow Ghost. My new name is Na-nata Ki-hehi—Warrior Heart."

Cailin chuckled. "She can change people's names, can she?"

"She is a peace woman. There's no English equivalent, but she's a spiritual and political leader, not just of one tribe, but of the whole Shawnee nation. A peace woman is born, not appointed, and there's never more than one in a generation. She can damned well give me a name if she decides to."

"She's that powerful?"

He nodded. "She could have a royal governor killed with a flick of her hand. She could declare war or end it. It's an Indian thing. I don't expect you to understand."

"You take this seriously, don't ye?"

His mouth tightened to a thin slash.

" 'Tis odd, certain," she said, "but I'd like to try and understand. She called ye Ko-nah at first. Who gave you the name Sterling? Your mother?"

"No. My father called me Sterling, after his grand-father. Snow Ghost was my child name. I should have been given a new one when I received a vision and completed my initiation into manhood."

"And for some reason, ye didna."

"No. My initiation was ... somewhat irregular. Usually, a boy has a vision of the animal that will be-come his spirit guide—his protector. My naming was postponed. Then my mother died, and my father took me to England."

"And today, Lady Kentington—Moonfeather—has decided to give ye a new name."

"Crazy, isn't it? A man's name is never given to a warrior who doesn't have a proper spirit guide." He grimaced. "I told you that you wouldn't under-stand." Sterling draped an arm around her shoul-ders. "What say we light that fire and start moving our furniture inside? We'll sleep under our own roof tonight."

"Will you go to the Shawnee village?"

His mood became somber again. "We'll have to. There's an old war trail that crosses our land. If trou-ble comes, I'm afraid we'll be in the thick of it. I can't really spare the time now, but as soon as our first crop is in and the stable is finished ... yes, I'll ride west to the village and hear what the council has to say."

"She said on the next full moon."

"There's been talk of all-out war between the Indians and the English since before I was born. If the news is good, it won't hurt to wait to hear it."

"And if it's bad?" Cailin asked.

"We'll learn the truth of that soon enough."

Chapter 14

Moonfeather's visit troubled Cailin so that she took only a little pleasure in the lighting of the first fire in the cabin and in moving the furniture into place. Supper was roast venison and trout, supplemented with fresh greens, oatcakes, and applesauce made from dried apples packed in from Annapolis.

Sterling and Cailin sat together at the table enjoying a late cup of tea after Isaac and the others had climbed the ladder to the loft to sleep. Sterling filled a long-stemmed pipe with Maryland-grown tobacco and puffed at it thoughtfully.

"Why don't the Shawnee want you to build a plantation here?" she asked him, voicing the question that had bothered her all afternoon.

"We're on the edge of prime hunting ground. If I build here, they're afraid other settlers will come and push them off their lands."

"Will they?"

He watched the smoke curl upward from the bowl of his pipe. "Yes."

"Then we're hurting the Indians by what we're doing."

"There's no stopping settlement, Cailin. This summer or next, cabins will start springing up along the river. If we're not here to establish our claim, squatters will try to move in on my land. Cheap acreage is

185

hard to find along the bay. They keep coming from England, Ireland, and Scotland. Most are poor men determined to cultivate a plot of their own—they've made great sacrifices to come to the Colonies, and they won't be denied land."

"But the Shawnee will blame you along with the others—even though you have a legal deed?"

"Yes, they will. They don't look at land ownership the way we do. They think the earth belongs to God. Men and women just have the use of it."

"Will they go on the warpath?"

"I hope not." He laid down his pipe. "I doubt it. Moonfeather will talk hard for peace. But still . . . there's a thing I need for you to see." He motioned her to come to the fireplace. "Just listen to me. Don't argue. What I have to show you may save your life someday."

Puzzled, she followed him to the hearth.

"The stone is warm. Don't burn yourself," he cautioned. "Look up the chimney and to the left."

She did as he instructed and saw what looked like narrow steps of rock jutting out of the back corner of the fireplace. "I still don't—"

"Higher."

Shoulder high, too high for anyone standing in the great room to see, was a ledge set into the side of the chimney. "It's a priest's hole," she said. "What in God's name—"

"It's for you," he said. "You and our children. There's room for you to hide. We purposely made the chimney wide enough to hold a hidden compartment. If the fire's burning when you need to climb up, it will get warm enough, but you shouldn't be hurt. Don't tell a soul about it. No one knows about this but Isaac and me."

She ignored the part about the children. Having a baby was the last thing she wanted now. A babe would tie her to Sterling forever. And she couldn't give him forever ... no matter how she might want it. "Why would I want to hide in a fireplace?"

"Keep your voice down. Remember, there's only a single layer of floorboards above us. Someone could be awake in the loft. The hiding hole's useless if anyone else learns the secret."

"Who am I supposed to hide from?"

"It's insurance, in case the plantation is ever attacked."

"You think the Shawnee are going to attack us?"

He shook his head. "No, I don't think that. I wouldn't have brought you out here if I didn't believe my mother's Indian blood would protect us from the Delaware and the Shawnee. But there are always men outside the law. White or red, they're no different from raiders in Scotland. Forrest warned me that deserters from the military burned a farm on the Eastern Shore. They murdered a man and his wife and stole the livestock and the slaves. We're isolated here. We don't have to worry about pirates like the plantations on the bay. But there aren't any neighbors to call on for help. I want you to have a way to survive if anything bad happens."

"And you? Will ye be hiding there too?"

His jawline tightened. "If I'm here, I'll be fighting or dead. But if there is trouble, I could be off hunting or cutting trees. I won't always be within earshot." He pulled her back away from the flames. "I'm not trying to frighten you," he said gruffly. "But I've seen too much violence to—"

"As if I have not seen my share?" She thought a moment. "I'll want a big dog for protection."

He nodded in agreement. "I've already put in a bid for two of Forrest's mastiff pups once they're weaned. You never said, but I had hoped you liked dogs."

"Aye, I favor them. We had a sheepdog at home that was as smart as most men. I sent him with Corey." For an instant, the child's tearstained face formed in her mind. She pushed it away and looked back at Sterling. His expression was grim.

"I should have warned you what you were coming to. If you're afraid to stay here—"

"Mary and Joseph!" she exclaimed. "Wolves walk into our camp. Indians pop up out of nowhere and tell us that the river is going to turn to blood. Then ye show me this hole in the chimney and tell me to hide when the beasties come. How could a sensible woman not be afraid—will ye tell me that?"

Clouds swirled in the depths of his dark eyes. "Do you want to go back to the bay country—to Annapolis? I'll not put your life in danger unless you—"

"Nay." She gripped the warm, solid flesh of his hand, marveling at the thrill that passed through her. What was there about this Sassenach that made her forget common sense and loyalty to her family and country? A body would think he was the only man alive, she scoffed to herself.

"I want you here, Cailin," he admitted, "but—"

"No more of that," she said, fighting the desire to stroke his clean-shaved cheek. Sterling needed to shave only twice a week, but he never let stubble show on his face. She liked that.

She stepped closer and put her arms around his neck. "After all the rocks I've carried for ye . . . after all the work we've put into this house, do ye think I'll cut and run?" she asked him huskily. "Two years

I've promised ye, and two years you'll have. I'm no coward, I vow."

"I never thought you were." He sat down in the chair and pulled her into his lap. "I love you." He leaned down to kiss her tenderly on the mouth. "I want to keep you safe," he added after the next kiss. He rubbed the back of her neck with strong fingers . . . slow, provocative motions that made her go all giddy inside.

"Sterling. We shouldn't," she whispered, struggling only a little. The heat of his callused palm felt marvelous on her sore muscles, and she didn't want him to stop. "One of the laborers might come down to . . ."

He brushed her lower lip with the tip of his tongue, and even her token protests ceased. She put her arms around his neck and parted her lips eagerly when he kissed her again. His tongue touched hers, and she gasped at the sensation.

It was suddenly hard to breathe.

She clung to him, letting him fill her mouth with his tongue, taking sensual pleasure in the taste and scent of him. And with each kiss, she forgot more and more of where they were and that they might be interrupted by one of the workmen coming downstairs to answer a call of nature.

He slipped a seeking hand under her petticoats and caressed her thigh above her stocking. She sighed and then pulled loose the leather thong that tied his queue in place as he nestled his face in her bosom. She loved to touch his hair. "Ye should have been born a lass, with such lovely hair," she teased. The strands slipped through her fingers, as soft as black velvet.

"I think not," he said. "We'd make an odd pair."

She laughed. "I didna mean that ye were womanly, although ye do have nice legs. I'd like to see ye in a kilt."

"I wore a loincloth until I was fourteen," he said. "That's as close as I intend to get to wearing a skirt."

"A plaid is hardly a skirt," she admonished him.

"You're not drawing me into a battle tonight," he said, raising his head and kissing the tip of her nose.

"You're insatiable," she replied, but she couldn't keep the laughter from her voice. And she couldn't keep her pulse from racing. Cuddled against him, she felt as giddy as a new bride.

"I admit it," he said with a devilish wink. "I can't get enough of you. When I saw you washing your hair in the river today, I wanted to strip off my clothes and join you." He nibbled on her earlobe. "Mmm," he murmured. "It's not too late to go for that swim."

"Swimming? In the dark—with wolves and wild Indians?" She pursed her lips. "You're mad—even for an Englishman."

He laughed again, a deep rumbling sound of contentment that made her heart leap. He kissed her throat, then began to undo the lacing on her bodice. "Why must you women wrap yourselves in such a tangle of clothing? It's enough to drive a man out of his mind."

Above, in the laborers' bedchamber, a board creaked, and someone coughed.

Cailin stiffened and glanced up. "Sterling, someone's awake."

"They're sound asleep."

"If they should come down, what would they think?"

"They won't come down."

"But . . ."

"Shhh." He sighed as he covered her hand with his. "See what you've done to me?" He pressed her fingers against his straining garment. His shaft throbbed hot against her flesh.

"Lecher," she accused. But the tremor in her voice betrayed her own desire. "Be that all ye think of?"

"No . . . not all." He whispered a scandalous suggestion into her ear, and her eyes widened with astonishment.

"For shame," she whispered. "At least let us get into bed." The thought that someone might come down and catch them in intimate circumstances was exciting, but also disturbing. She didn't really want Joe to see her with her skirts up to her thighs and her bodice all undone. At least she hoped she didn't.

Sterling kissed the top of her exposed breast. "I want you near the firelight, so I can see your face when I enter you . . . when I'm deep inside you."

Her heart skipped a beat. Each time he kissed her, she flushed with inner heat. Already, moistness pooled between her thighs. She wanted him . . . wanted his hands on her . . . wanted him to fill her with his hard, thrusting shaft.

He loosened the top of her stays and freed one breast from the linen and whalebone garment. She drew her breath in sharply as his wet tongue flicked over her tingling nipple.

She moaned softly, imagining what was to come.

He encircled the swollen nub with slow, sweet kisses, then slowly drew her nipple between his lips and sucked gently.

Her nails dug into his shoulders as waves of sweet sensation flooded her veins, washing through every inch of her body ... intensifying the molten heat at her core.

"Sterling," she gasped. "Take me to bed. I—"

Another bout of coughing echoed from the chamber overhead. Sterling swore softly as she stiffened in his arms and covered her breast with her hand.

"I can't," she said.

He groaned. "Cailin, please."

"I'm afraid they will—"

"Shhh, love." He kissed her neck and her ear, but the spell was broken.

"Not here," she said.

"Where, then?"

She pulled her gown up over her breast and stood up. "I want ye too," she admitted.

He rose to his feet. "See what you've done to me," he said. He glanced down at his breeches. "I can hardly walk in this state."

"I'll come outside with ye if ye want," she suggested boldly.

"Will you swim with me in the river?"

"Aye, I will."

He laughed and grabbed her around the waist, lifting her high and turning around. "I'm mad for you, woman. I have no intention of letting you go—not in two years ... not in two lifetimes."

"Put me down," she protested weakly. In truth, her knees were like jelly and she wasn't sure they would hold her long enough to walk the length of the room. She wanted to tear off his shirt and touch his bare chest. She wanted to savor the hard ridges of his body, to taste the salt of his skin.

Still laughing, he threw her over his shoulder and carried her out the door into the cool May night.

"I said put me down," she whispered.

Sounds of frogs and insects came from the forest and river. There wasn't a breath of wind, and if the temperature was lower than that inside the cabin, it wasn't enough to make her uncomfortable in her state of undress.

Sterling sat her feet lightly on the ground a hundred paces from the house. "Look at that sky," he said, pointing up with one hand while the other arm held her against him. "See that moon."

Cailin looked up in wonder. The pale shimmering disk was larger than she'd ever seen it, so close that she almost felt she could reach up and touch it.

"They call that a Shawnee moon," he said. "It makes the forest trails as bright as day. When the moon glows like that in the heavens, the Shawnee travel by night. They swoop down on their enemies and capture fair maidens." His rich voice had taken on a teasing note, and she joined his game.

"And will one of these Shawnee warriors carry me off tonight, do ye think?" she asked innocently. She wasn't looking at the moon; she was looking at him.

He laughed. "That might be arranged." He let his hand slide down her shoulder and close around her fingers. "Come with me," he ordered.

Eagerly, she followed him across the open clearing to the river, and then downstream, along the deer trail that followed the bank. The surface of the river winked with the reflection of the brilliant moon; the stars glowed with the heat of a thousand candles. Beneath her feet, the moss was as soft as any carpet, and the air smelled of pine, and cedar, and wildflowers.

"This must be a taste of heaven," she murmured. They had spent many nights here by the river, but always, she'd remained near the fire. Now that the wilderness night had enveloped her, she was enchanted by it—nay, not enchanted, intoxicated.

"I missed the forest sky in England," he confided to her. "The moon shines there, but it's not the same moon. It can't be." He pointed at a group of stars. "There are the Brothers, and over there is the Great Bear . . . and there . . ." Sterling's voice grew husky with emotion. "There is the Star Bridge of Souls."

He stopped and pulled her into the circle of his arms. "I want you with me for the rest of my life," he said hoarsely. "And when we die, I want our lights to shine side by side in the Star Bridge for our grandchildren and their grandchildren to see. I want you beside me, Cailin . . . for all eternity."

Before she could answer—before she could tell him no—he kissed her. And the heat of that kiss drove everything from her mind but the wanting. Trembling, she allowed him to undress her. Item by item, he removed her clothes until she stood proudly in front of him, hair unbound, garbed only in a dusting of moonlight.

"Now you," she said. The aching between her legs grew more intense. When he took off his shirt and boots, she dropped to her knees and gently stroked his hard belly and the mat of curling black hair along the waistline of his breeches.

His quick intake of breath made her daring, and she found the ties at the small of his back. "Don't move," she said. "Stand where ye are and let me do it."

She pressed her lips into his belly, feeling the texture of his hair against her lips. He smelled clean with no hint of sweat . . . only a subtle scent of honest masculinity that awoke something wild and primitive within her.

"Cailin . . ." He groaned.

She drew her fingers down, tracing the lines of his loins, gently teasing the growing tumescence. Then she slid the breeches over his slim hips so that his hard shaft was no longer encased in his garment.

"Cailin."

"Shall I touch ye?" she asked. "Does it please you if I do this? And this?" Lightly, she brushed the length of him with slow, sensuous strokes. He uttered a sound of desperation, and she pushed his breeches down over his knees. "Ye must help me," she reminded him. Obediently, he stepped out of first one leg and then the other. "Your stockings," she said.

He reached a hand to her, but she shook her head. How beautiful he was in the moonlight, she thought, a great bronzed devil of a man. His broad, muscular chest; the sinewy shoulders and massive arms; the neatness of his hips; his well-formed legs. And his rod . . . She smiled and moistened the tips of two fingers with her tongue.

"Which feels better?" she asked, caressing his straining phallus. "When I do this? Or this?" She leaned closer and parted her lips.

"Woman," he grated. "Another second and I—"

She could not answer with words . . . being currently occupied with other pursuits, but his groan of pleasure made her certain that he approved. Other parts worked as well as deft fingers, she decided.

His hands tangled in her hair, and he gasped as she drew him into her mouth.

Sterling shuddered and tried to grab hold of her arms to pull her up against him, but she was too quick. Twisting away, she laughed and jumped into the river. In the space of a heartbeat, she heard a second splash. She dived under and swam into deeper water.

When she surfaced, he was in front of her. He seized her shoulders and kissed her. She wrapped her legs around his waist and lay back in his arms so that he could find her breasts with his mouth.

They went under together and came up laughing. The river water was warmer than the air, but not as hot as her skin . . . nor as hot as his erection.

He pressed against her, fiercely seeking entrance to her cleft. But she would not be caught so easily. She twisted away and went under, letting the current carry her along. She came up for air, laughing so hard that she got a mouthful of water.

He seized her and dragged her splashing into the shallows. Waist-deep in water, they stood up, blending limbs and souls as their playful kisses became deeper and more fevered. And when neither of them could wait another instant, she closed her eyes and gave up all resistance.

He entered her with all the glory of a spring sunrise, and her laughter became cries of delight. Each thrust brought her closer to the brink of fulfillment. She wanted desperately to prolong the act—to make certain that she pleased him as well as herself, but her need would not be denied. Rapture exploded within her.

To her surprise, Sterling continued to move, and Cailin found herself responding to his impassioned strokes. Swiftly, her excitement grew until once again searing, all-consuming tremors of luminous ecstasy rocked her body.

On the far bank, a doe, coming to the river to drink, froze in its tracks and stared at them.

Cailin saw nothing but Sterling. She heard nothing but his whispered words of love, and cared for nothing but this night of exquisite happiness illuminated by the haunting magic of the forest moon.

Chapter 15

A week passed, and then two. With each day, she and Sterling seemed to grow closer. Cailin had never felt like this before. Sterling was a wonderful lover, but her affection for him went far beyond sexual desire. He made her laugh, and he shared plans and dreams with her as he would with a close male friend. When she looked into his eyes, she saw respect, even admiration. And she knew that in another time and another place, she would have pledged her immortal soul to him.

Work on the plantation continued from early dawn to twilight's dusk. Only Sunday was set aside as a day of worship and rest. Her husband, she was surprised to discover, was a man of deep spiritual faith. He began each Sabbath morning with a prayer and a short reading from a well-worn Bible. Those who labored for them were welcome to join in the ritual or not, according to their own consciences. Cailin had been christened and raised in the Holy Roman Church, but she saw nothing in Sterling's prayers to offend even the strictest Catholic. And she found that setting aside a time for worship filled a long-neglected need within her.

Sterling had delayed plans to construct a stable and put all his efforts into building several smaller cabins for the workers on the far side of the clearing.

"So that you may have your privacy behind our bed curtains," he'd teased her.

Several days ago, another boat had come upriver from the bay, bringing more household goods and the loan of a half-dozen more bond servants from Lord Kentington's plantation. Forrest Wescott had also sent two riding horses and a team of oxen by the land route.

"A man with any pride would return the horses and oxen," Sterling had said on the afternoon they'd arrived. "God knows when I'll be able to return the favor."

"Ye canna do it," Cailin whispered. "To throw the gift in his face would be to make an enemy of a good friend."

"You're right," he agreed. "But I'll not rest until I've settled my debts."

"You're a proud man and a generous one," she'd added. "Perhaps you need this lesson to learn how to receive as well as to give."

He'd scowled and grunted something at her, then hurried off to see the precious animals properly confined.

Among the new servants were two married couples. The women, Franny Simms, wife to Hob Simms; and Phoebe Smyth, Simon the carpenter's wife, were both experienced in cooking and caring for the needs of large groups of men.

Franny was nearly six feet tall, plain of face and sparse of hair. She towered over her sour, whip-thin husband. Phoebe was of middling height with dark brown curling hair and laughing green eyes. Phoebe's infant son, Jasper, was the image of his mother. Jasper was too young to walk, but he managed to get whatever he set his eyes on by creeping to the object and patiently pulling himself up with chubby, dirt-smeared hands. He was cutting his second tooth and spent much of his time gnawing on anything or any-one that he could capture.

Cailin was delighted to have the companionship of women again and to be relieved of the heavy chores. It was good to talk of small household matters and to hear a babe's crowing laughter again. Even the hard-faced lumbermen grew foolish around Jasper and vied to see who could make the silliest faces for the child's amusement.

Yesterday, she and Phoebe had planted a garden in a small cleared area. They'd marked off the rows with string and cultivated the hand-dug area with hoes and then their fingers, shaking out clumps of grass and tree roots left from the new plowing. Care-fully, Cailin had sown turnip seed, radishes, kidney beans, corn, and squash. The corn, as Sterling had suggested, was planted Indian fashion in six-inch-high hills. First, Phoebe raked up individual mounds of rich soil and buried a fish deep in each one. Then, Cailin thrust kernels of corn into the center and sur-rounded the hills with squash seeds.

She and Phoebe had had a conflict of opinion about how many kernels should go in each hill, but Phoebe was firm. "One for the worm, one for the crow. One for God, and one to grow," she insisted. "Four kernels in all." Cailin found it impossible to ar-gue with such colonial logic and agreed to risk an ad-ditional seed in each mound.

At the edge of the garden, Cailin had directed Joe to dig a hole to plant her first fruit tree, a golden pip-pin sapling that Kate had sent wrapped carefully in damp cloth. "Can you bake an apple pie?" Sterling had asked when Cailin had taken great pains to tamp the tiny tree in and water it properly.

"Aye," she'd replied. "I can." But she'd not added that by the time the first apple swelled on the branch, she'd be far away across the sea in Scotland.

That morning, she'd taken a quick look at her garden, admired the sturdy little apple tree, and left preparations for the midday meal in Franny and Phoebe's capable hands. Taking her new pine-needle Indian basket, Cailin had followed the game trail through the woods to the meadow to hunt for any late-ripening strawberries. Phoebe claimed to have a rare talent with bread and pastry, and Cailin wanted her to make berry cobbler for supper.

When Cailin reached the place near the river where Sterling had shown her the patches of wild strawberries, she found only a few, and those she ate. The solitude was wonderful after being with a group for so long; the sun was warm and the field knee-deep in wildflowers.

The soothing sounds of running water added to her laziness, and she couldn't resist taking off her shoes and stockings. After she was barefooted, it was impossible to resist the temptation to sit on the sun-baked rocks and dip her legs in the cool river. As she gazed at the shimmering blue-green surface, a great blue heron unfolded its wings and rose into the air on the far bank.

"Cailin!"

Sterling's call broke into her peaceful reverie. She turned and waved. He stepped out of the shadow of the tall oaks and entered the meadow. "Here I am!" she answered, waving again.

I should have saved him some strawberries, she thought as memories of a late afternoon tryst they'd spent in this very spot brought a rush of blood to her cheeks.

He strode toward her, his raven-black hair gleaming in the bright sunshine, and she went all soft and fluttery inside. Sterling had been cutting timber all morning, and he was stripped to the waist, wearing nothing but his breeches and heavy boots. In one hand, he carried a steel broadax, and in the other, his cocked hat.

"Now, there's a sight to turn a maid's thoughts to lust," she murmured too low for him to hear. "Damn me, but he's as bonny a rogue as any Highlander."

"I've been swinging this ax for five hours, and you're whiling away the day like a countess." Mischief lit his devil eyes, telling her that he was teasing.

"Had ye a mind to go for a dip?" she asked as he drew closer.

He grinned. "I don't know if I'd have the strength to go back to the lumbering after I swam with you."

"Coward."

"Call me a coward, will you?"

"Aye."

"We'll see who's the coward." He propped the ax against a rock and laid his hat on a flat outcropping of shale.

Cailin scrambled up and started to him, then stopped when she heard an unusual sound—the faint tattoo of seeds shaken in a dry gourd. Instantly, the hair rose on the back of her neck. "What's that—" She broke off as terror turned her limbs to wood.

A huge red-brown snake with a flat rust-colored head and triangular-banded markings undulated across the loose rock and lashed out at Sterling's arm.

Cailin screamed.

The serpent coiled and struck again.

Cailin caught a glimpse of gleaming fangs in the gaping mouth. Sterling leaped back, grabbed the ax, and dispatched the snake with three quick blows.

"Jesus and Mary," she exclaimed.

The snake was as thick around as her arm and longer than a man is tall. Decapitated and chopped into three separate pieces, the horrible creature continued to writhe and twist, making ugly patterns in its own blood against the rock. The odd vibrating continued from the severed tail section, not quite the same but near enough so that she realized it was the snake that had made the noise she'd heard.

Still tasting the metallic bitterness of fear in her mouth, Cailin flung herself against Sterling's chest. "Holy Martyrs," she cried. "That was close." She clung to him so tightly that she could hear the pounding of his heart.

The thought of what could have happened sickened her. Sterling's hand had been within inches of the creature's yawning mouth—of those gleaming curved fangs. "What kind was it?" she asked. "Be it venomous?"

He looked down at her with a strange expression on his face. Beneath his tanned features, his face took on an unnatural gray hue.

"Be it venomous?" she repeated. Icy dread knotted her belly, and she began to tremble. "I was so scared. I thought that it—"

Sterling pushed her gently away, tossed the ax down, and took several steps backward. "It's a copperhead," he said quietly.

She shuddered. The tone of his voice answered her question. She tried to say something, but her mouth was too dry. She licked her lips and managed to say, "Thank the Lord neither of us was bitten. I canna—"

He thrust out his right arm. Midway between wrist and elbow on the outside were four tiny spots of blood.

"It got ye."

"Twice."

"Mother of God." This was a nightmare. Any second, she'd wake up and find that they were safe in their bed. "What shall I do?" She sounded breathless, as though she'd been climbing a steep hill. "Shall I run to the house for help?"

Sterling shook his head. "No, stay." He dropped to his knees and then lay full-length in the grass.

She could not contain a small whimper of fright.

"I'm not dying yet," he snapped. "I need to lie still to keep the poison from reaching my heart." With his left hand, he drew his knife from his beaded scabbard. "Undo my belt and bind it tight just below my elbow," he ordered. "Then use the knife point to cut slits directly over the bites."

She untied his belt and removed the razor-sharp weapon with shaking hands. "How do ye feel?" Putting the knife between her teeth, she wrapped the leather around his arm and knotted it once.

"It burns like hell, but my mind's still clear. If I pass out, remember to loosen the belt every quarter-hour. Too much pressure and I could lose the arm." She made the knot tighter. "There, that's good," he said as she twisted the binding. "Now make the cuts."

Gritting her teeth, Cailin poised the steel blade over his arm. Reason told her that what she was doing was dangerous and foolhardy. A knife used for surgery should be passed through fire to drive away demons and cut the pain. She should have soap and bandages—men to hold him still while she did what must be done. But an older instinct bade her act before it was too late.

"Do it!" Sterling ordered.

Cailin swallowed hard. The area around the bites was already turning dark and swelling. Blood welled up as she pressed the keen steel into his flesh. The first slice went deeper than she wanted it to go, but Sterling didn't flinch.

Tears clouded her vision, and she blinked them away. The second incision was easier. Yellow venom welled up on either side of the puncture as she dug into the wound. "Two more," she said.

Sterling cursed, but kept up his courage. By the time she reached the last bite, his arm ran red, and she was afraid that she was going to be sick. "Done," she said. He gave a sigh of relief. When she looked into his face, she saw that he was sweating profusely.

"Now run and get Isaac," Sterling rasped. He put his mouth against the bleeding wounds and began to try to suck the poison out.

"Let me do that for you."

He spat. "No. Go for help."

"Are ye going to die?" It still seemed impossible. One moment, he was laughing and teasing her, and the next . . .

He spat out another mouthful of blood. "Not if I can help it."

"I can do that," she said.

"Damn it, woman! For once, do as I say. Run!"

"Don't ye die on me, you bastard. Don't ye dare!" No longer able to hold back the tears, she turned and dashed across the meadow toward the path that led through the thick forest to the house.

She was ten yards from the tree line when she heard the first shots and then a woman's scream, followed closely by a long, drawn-out, unearthly screech. She skidded to a halt, ran a few more steps, and stopped again.

Two more rifle shots rang out.

She glanced back over her shoulder, then plunged into the woods. Halfway down the trail, she heard the footfalls of someone running full out. Ducking off the path, she crouched in the shelter of a wind-damaged cedar tree.

Another whoop shattered the air. Then Franny's ungainly form came pounding through the forest. Her dress was bloody and ripped to the waist. Half of her face was gone, and one big hand was a scarlet ruin. Right on her heels came two howling savages.

Cailin watched in horror as the lead warrior—a huge man with his face painted black and white to resemble a skull—hurled a tomahawk at Franny's back. The bondwoman groaned, staggered to her knees, and then fell full-length on the forest floor. The ax handle quivered as Franny writhed in agony.

With a wild cry of triumph, the painted brave leaped forward and planted a moccasined foot on the dying woman's spine. Franny uttered a bubbling groan, and her eyes rolled up in her head until Cailin could see nothing but white. Seizing a handful of Franny's meager, graying hair, the Indian wrenched her head cruelly back until her neck snapped, and slashed down across her forehead with a fourteen-inch butcher knife.

Cailin shut her eyes. When she opened them again, Franny was motionless, and the skull-faced monster danced around her body brandishing a crimson mat of hair.

Cailin held her breath and remained motionless. The scent of crushed leaves and fear filled her nostrils. She perceived a salty taste on her tongue, then vaguely realized that it was her own blood. Exploring her inner mouth, she found she'd bitten the inside of her cheek, but strangely, she felt no pain. She felt nothing at all; she was numb all over.

Then the second warrior—a brave wearing a blue loincloth and tall red plumage at the back of his shaved head—pointed directly at her and let out a yelp of triumph. Instantly, both Indians lunged toward her hiding place.

She sprang up, whirled, and ran through the trees. Howling like wolves, they sprinted after her. She paid no heed to the sticks and briers, or the fallen logs and underbrush. Cailin yanked up her skirts and fled as if the hounds of hell pursued her.

Branches scraped her face and tore at her hair. She dodged under low-hanging tree limbs and dashed around obstacles. She sucked in gulps of air as her lungs screamed for oxygen. And when she saw the thick boughs of a cedar grove ahead, she plunged headlong into it. Ducking this way and that, she crawled and scratched her way deep inside the morass of evergreens.

It was only when she stopped for breath that she remembered she was still clutching Sterling's knife. When she realized what she held, she almost laughed out loud.

She wasn't defenseless.

The knife gave her strength. Hope flooded through her, and she began to think rather than just react for the first time since she'd seen Franny fleeing down the wood's trail. She forced herself to take deep, quiet breaths, and she listened.

The shouts had ceased. Instead, she heard the buzz of men's voices and the snap of branches. She looked down at her cumbersome skirts and sliced through the lacing of her gown without a moment's hesitation. Pushing the garment off her shoulders and over her hips, she let it pool to the ground. Next, she cut through her petticoat strings, leaving her garbed in nothing but her shift and stays.

She wasn't afraid of rape. She'd been raped once, and she knew that she'd die before she let men put their hands on her like that again. She had the means and the will to take her own life if she was backed against the wall. But she was far from suicide. The fierce legacy of millenniums of Highland warriors drummed in her blood. She was a Scot, by God. And if she forfeited her life to these painted barbarians, it would be at dear cost.

Her naked feet were bruised and wounded. A splinter as thick around as a quill protruded from her instep. She jerked it out and pinched the flesh shut to quell the bleeding. She ignored the throbbing. What was a little discomfort when Sterling's life and her own hung in the balance?

He wasn't at the farmstead. She'd left him in the meadow, by the river. He was sore hurt, true, but he was strong. He might well survive the snakebite, even without assistance. The war party couldn't kill him if they didn't find him. All she had to do was lead them away from the meadow. She simply needed to escape in the opposite direction. And when they were gone, she'd find her way back to Sterling, nurse him to health, and—

The boughs parted an arm's length away, and the Indian in the blue loincloth backed into the shelter of the big cedar. One of his arms was raised as he tried to extricate his crested red topknot from a tangling branch. He was cursing the tree—at least it seemed so to her. She could comprehend none of the strange dialect he muttered.

Wide-eyed, she stared at his exposed back.

For no longer than the blink of an eye, she gazed at him. Then she drove Sterling's knife up with all her might, plunging it into the savage's flesh, just to the right of his backbone. By rights, his ribs should have deflected the blow, but in her haste, she'd turned the blade so that the steel slid between his bones.

He stiffened, gasped, and crashed forward. His weight nearly pulled Cailin's arm from its socket, but her fingers were locked on the bone handle, and the weapon came free.

She gazed at her fallen enemy in shock.

"God forgive me," she whispered in her native Gaelic.

And like Lazarus rising from the dead, the Indian lurched up and snapped his head in her direction. His eyes bulged, and blood ran from the corner of his mouth. He twisted around and clawed at his belly. Before she could move a muscle, his arm shot out, and bloody fingers clamped around her wrist.

She slashed at him with the knife. He screamed, and she twisted away. An answering shout came from the left. Cailin didn't wait to see if her victim was dead or alive. She dived back into the hole she'd crawled through to reach this spot. Branches crashed behind her.

Then, a shriek of unbridled rage told her that Skull Face had discovered his companion. She kept going, found a break in the thicket, and burst out into the open forest again.

She began to run in earnest. Uncertain of direction, forgetting caution, she ceased to reason. She concentrated on putting one foot in front of the other and not dropping her knife. And when she heard the war whoop directly behind her rise into a bone-chilling bay, it was joined by a chorus of additional yowls from either side.

Cailin ran harder.

Chapter 16

Cailin ran until she thought that her heart would burst from the strain. She didn't know how long she'd been running, but she knew that her pace was slowing and her hunters were growing closer with every step. Skull Face was twenty yards behind her, shrieking like some fiend from hell and swinging his tomahawk around his painted head. Two more savages closed in on her right. She didn't know how many were on her left, but they were farther back.

A stitch in her side had become a red-hot poker that jabbed deeper into her vitals each time her foot hit the ground. Sweat and blood from scratches on her face ran into her eyes and threatened to blind her. Her fingers had clutched Sterling's knife so long and with such fervor that she could no longer feel the bone hilt in her hand.

Her prayers had dwindled to a desperate litany consisting of a single word, uttered over and over with each strangled exhale. "God ... God ... God ..." She fixed her eyes on a single object, a tree, a fallen branch, or a pile of leaves. All she had to do was to run a few more feet, another wagon's length ... an easy task, even for a clumsy child. And when she reached that goal, her gaze sought another, and that became her prize.

Still, she knew that she could not keep running. She must turn and fight. But where? How?

A swirl of bagpipes sounded in her head. For an instant, she smelled the smoke and heard the cannons of Culloden Moor. Madness ... Madness beckoned to her like a mirage of sparkling water to a woman dying of thirst. She had only to yield to the siren call of the piper's tune, and she could rest beside the fallen Highlanders. She could laugh again with all those dear ones and feel the touch of her mother's hand on her cheek.

Instead, she forced her weary legs to a burst of speed, leaped over a rotting windfall, and darted under a low branch to find herself in the wild strawberry meadow.

She stared around her in shock, then stumbled and nearly went down. She'd believed that she was leading her tormentors away from Sterling. Instead, she'd guaranteed his discovery and death.

"Yi-yi-ya-yee!" Skull Face cried.

She glanced back over her shoulder. He was so close that she could see the engraving on his silver nose ring. His nostrils were flared; his hooded ebony eyes gleamed with bloodlust.

Defeat sliced through her sinews and washed over her in a choking black tide. There could be no escape from Satan's hellhound. Cailin opened her mouth to utter her death scream and watched as Skull Face tripped and sprawled full-length in the grass.

Her own bittersweet laughter lent wings to her feet. She sprang away and began to run again. Just ahead, not a hundred yards from the forest edge, a giant oak reared from the sea of wildflowers. There! There she could stop and make her stand with a solid wall at her back and Sterling's steel blade in her hand.

She barely heard the war cries to her right. If she could just make the safety of the tree—

A musket blasted the serenity of the sunny meadow. Not a heartbeat later, Cailin heard the distinctive whine of a lead ball. Suddenly, a stripe-faced warrior appeared in front of her. She saw the gleam of an ivory spike as a jagged club hurled toward her head.

Running too fast to stop, Cailin threw herself to the ground and rolled, expecting at any instant to feel the crushing blow of the savage weapon. Instead, the brave screamed and vanished from her line of vision. She brushed a hand across her face. And when she looked again, a half-naked form stood over her with an ax in his hand.

She slashed out at his legs instinctively, then realized that somehow, in the midst of her fall, she'd lost her grip on the knife.

"Get behind me!" Sterling ordered.

She closed her eyes and opened them again. Had there been red paint spattered across his bare chest before?

"Get behind me!" he repeated.

On hands and knees, she tried to obey. Her knee struck something hard in the crushed grass. Scooping up the knife, she scrambled behind him. Another musket went off. More Indians rushed at them. Sterling's broadax cut a terrible swath of vengeance.

"Back!" he commanded her.

A brave threw a tomahawk. It missed Sterling by a hairbreadth. Indians were all around them.

Somehow, the oak was behind her. Sterling was still on his feet, but his strength was clearly failing. A man with a stuffed raven on his head lunged at Sterling's side. She jabbed the Indian with her knife. He let out a groan, then seized her arm and tried to twist the weapon from her fingers. Sterling went to his knees. Oiled copper-skinned bodies swarmed over them, and the blackness took her.

Something wet dripped down Cailin's face. The rumble of cannon made her open her eyes. The flash of a lightning bolt nearby made her close them. Rain. The spatter of drops became needles. She groaned and tried to move, but she couldn't. Her eyelids felt as though they were weighted down by lead coins.

Someone was crying.

She forced her eyes open and found that she was sitting on the ground. Her wrists were tightly fastened to the tall wheel of an oxcart, and her ankles were tied together. The rising wind carried the strong smell of charred wood. It was raining so hard that it was difficult to see more than a few yards away. But she knew that the figures moving around in the twilight were Indians.

She was cold. Soaked through. Her head hurt so much that it was impossible to think. Something . . . something. She had to remember.

The wailing persisted. A baby. It sounded like a baby's cry. But how . . . Jasper. Was that Jasper crying? Cailin tried to focus, but the day was dying fast, and the increasing force of the wind gusts bent small saplings double and tumbled leaves and debris across the clearing.

Why didn't Phoebe go to the child and comfort him? she wondered. She was a good mother. It wasn't like her to— Jasper stopped crying. Cailin

heard nothing but the wind and the rain . . . and the
sound of her own teeth chattering.

Sterling. Where was Sterling? She wanted to
scream his name, but even as she parted her lips, she
knew it was useless. She'd seen him fall. She'd seen
him go down. He was as dead as all the rest. She was
simply too much of a coward to admit it.

A paint-smeared image loomed out of the rain,
inches in front of her. Skull Face. The white lines had
run, and the circles around each eye had become
only smudges, but she recognized him by the silver
nose ring and the pronounced bump on the ridge of
his nose that told of an old break, long healed.

"So. You not die so easy, Fire Hair," he said in
badly accented English.

She made no response, merely stared at him.

"You run good for woman."

"Aye," she answered defiantly. "Better than you."

He backhanded her so hard that her head banged
against the thick wagon spokes. "Hold tongue," he
growled. "Or Ohneya cut it out." He tapped his
chest. "Ohneya master. You slave. Obey master or
die."

She shut her eyes. Had that been blood dripping
down his chin? she wondered. Had—

He pinched her arm cruelly. "Ohneya!" he shouted
at her. She glared at him. "Ohneya," he repeated.
"Say it."

"Ohneya," she muttered. Her lip was swelling, and
her jaw felt as though he'd cracked it when he hit
her.

"Hmmph." Then his expression became sly. He
raised his left hand. In it, he held what looked to her
like a piece of beef liver. Grinning, he took a bite and

chewed loudly. "Not for woman," he said. "For warrior."

Had they slaughtered the oxen?

"*O-wa-rough,*" he said. "*Rong-we ka-hon-ji.*" Then he laughed again. "Brave enemy; eat spirit of enemy, make Ohneya strong."

"Rot in hell," she replied.

Ohneya struck her again. Then another warrior called to him in the guttural Indian language. Ohneya answered briefly, then walked purposefully away.

Cailin drew in a long breath and offered a silent prayer for the souls of those murdered by the war party. Tears trickled down her cheeks and mingled with the rain. She refused to think of Sterling. Not of his death, or of what they might have done to him after he'd ceased to breathe. For herself, she was beyond caring. Nothing Ohneya could do or say to her could hurt her more than she was already hurting inside.

The worst of the storm passed, but it continued to drizzle rain. The Indians built a small campfire in front of the unfinished cabins Sterling had been building for the bondsmen. Cailin thought she counted more than twenty warriors, but there was no sign of any other captives. The raiders laughed and talked to one another, and roasted what looked like the haunch of a horse over the coals before rolling up in blankets.

She couldn't understand why the Indians chose to make a wet camp instead of sleeping inside the house. That section of the clearing was dark. She saw no light from the window, heard no sounds of activity. It was puzzling. It wouldn't be so hard to reason if her head didn't hurt so much. She couldn't remember being hit. So what was wrong with her, and how had she been injured?

Jasper. She fought off the urge to drift into unconsciousness. Who was caring for the baby? He was alive. She'd heard him crying. She almost wished that she'd asked Ohneya to let her tend the infant. She hoped they hadn't left him lying in the rain. A darker suspicion nagged at the corner of her mind, but she wouldn't let herself imagine that possibility. Surely the Indians would show mercy toward a helpless child. If they hadn't killed him during the attack, they must mean to do right by him.

Minutes passed and then hours. No one came to her, and no one stirred. She thought she slept for short bits of time. On the far side of the clearing, she heard two Indians call to each other, but they were too far away for her to see in the dark. Sometime later, she heard an owl hoot, but she wasn't certain if it was a real bird or some signal.

Suddenly, she was fully alert as a sense of being watched came over her. Fearful, she looked around, straining at her bonds. And to her surprise and relief, the wet leather ties on her left wrist loosened.

She knew she should try to escape, but the overwhelming impression of eyes staring at her was unnerving. She held her breath and peered intently into the tangled shadows of the forest ... and heard a slight rustle of twigs.

Cailin's skin prickled as the outline of a wolf materialized from the darkness just beyond the cart. Her sanity wavered as familiar glowing eyes flickered red, catching the reflection of the firelight.

"You," she whispered. "Go away."

The creature crouched down and crept closer until

she could hear its heavy breathing. She wanted to scream, but she didn't dare.

Could this be the same wolf that had come to the campfire before Sterling had finished the house? Was it a pet as he'd suggested, or had it come to feast on the dead or the living? "Go away," she pleaded.

"Cailin." Sterling's voice was slurred and weak, but she knew him instantly.

"Sterling?"

"Here. On . . . on the cart wheel."

For a moment, that confused her. "But I'm . . ." she began. Then she realized that he was tied to the wheel on the opposite side. Had he been there all along? "You're alive?"

"Have you lost your wits, woman? Do I sound like an angel?"

She almost laughed. Then she sobered, remembering his snakebite . . . remembering how she'd seen him last, overwhelmed by the enemy. "How bad are ye hurt?" She yanked frantically at her wrist bindings, slipped her left hand free, and began to work on the other one.

"It doesn't matter."

Men. They were all as crazy as bedlamites, she decided. "What do ye mean, it doesn't matter? Of course, it matters." She squirmed and dug at the cruel rawhide knot, but the lashing held, cutting deeper into her wrist.

"My arm . . . is swollen as thick around as my leg."

She gave up on the wrist ties and concentrated on getting her ankles loose. "Wait," she said. "I'll come to ye." She kicked hard, and the final thong snapped. Still attached to the wheel by her right hand, she squirmed under the cart and strained to touch him. "I'm here," she whispered. "Can ye—"

Warm fingers brushed her, and she grabbed hold of them. Sterling groaned.

"Oh. Is that your . . ." She didn't finish. It was his bad arm. His fingers were swollen beyond belief. "Be the pain bad?" She felt a shudder ripple through his hand.

"Not so bad," he said.

She knew he was lying. "Ye should have hidden," she said quickly. "Ye shouldn't have tried to fight them."

He gave a scornful chuckle. "You didn't do so bad yourself," he said. "For a Highlander."

"Sterling, dinna . . ." A lump rose in her throat. When she'd thought he was dead, when she'd expected to die at any second, she could maintain some control. But now that she'd found out he was alive and possibly dying . . . She lifted his poor hand to her cheek and tried to hold back the sobs. "I was wrong," she admitted. "I didn't love ye when I could . . . and now . . . Oh, Sterling, don't leave me." She kissed his palm and found the flesh torn and ragged. "Please," she begged him. "Don't die on me."

"Cailin. Listen to me." His tone was suddenly frigid.

"I'm almost free," she interrupted. "I'll get ye loose, and we'll escape. We'll cross the river and—"

"Cailin."

Softly, he spoke. But each word was a knife thrust into her heart. "Don't say it. We'll get away together," she insisted.

"I can't walk."

"Of course, ye can walk. I'll help—"

"No. Do as I say. For once, Cailin. There isn't much time."

"The wolf is back," she said. She wouldn't pay

heed to what he was saying. He wanted her to escape without him. But that was crazy. "Did you see the wolf, Sterling?"

"I see him. He's been here since the storm."

"Just let me get my other hand—"

"Cailin. I can't walk, and you can't carry me."

"I'll think of something," she sobbed. "I'll drag—"

"I want you to untie yourself and go to the house," he continued, as though she'd not spoken. "They tried to burn it, but the storm put out the fire. Hide in the chimney. Don't come out, no matter what you hear. Wait until the war party is gone, then go to the Shawnee village and find Moonfeather."

"Go to the village? When the Shawnee came here and—"

"These aren't Shawnee, Cailin," he said harshly. "These are Iroquois, Mohawk to be exact, come down from New York for scalps and booty. The Iroquois are blood enemies to my mother's people."

"But Kate told me the Iroquois have a treaty with King George. They're friendly—"

"Kate is a fool if she believes that. The Iroquois have spent the last three hundred years trying to make slaves of the Delaware and the Shawnee. They are friendly all right—to their own interests. And they'll slaughter English settlers or soldiers with as much enthusiasm as they will the French. Go to the Shawnee. You'll be safe with them."

"You expect me to leave you—"

"I do."

"Nay." It was unthinkable.

"You can do nothing for me but live."

"I don't want to live without you," she whispered brokenly.

"Everyone is dead. Men, women, they're all dead."

"But they kept us alive," she argued. "Why—"

"They kept us for sport. You don't have much time. If you run, they'll track you down, but they'd never find you inside the chimney. Now, get into that damned hole in the bricks and stay there."

"I can't leave ye," she pleaded. "Why should I—"

"I understand a little Mohawk, Cailin. At dawn, they mean to head north to their own hunting grounds. But before they leave, they intend to burn us both at the stake."

Chapter 17

It was mid-afternoon on the following day before Cailin ventured from the priest's hole in the chimney. She was torn between not knowing Sterling's fate and the overwhelming dread that she would find his mutilated body waiting for her. Her feet were swollen and so painful that she could hardly walk on them, and she was plagued by thirst and hunger.

She'd not heard any sounds of humans for many hours. Overhead, a mockingbird perched on the chimney and chirped a saucy refrain. Cailin could wait no longer. With bated breath, she climbed down into the blackened hearth and crept across the great room floor.

The door stood open. Trembling, Cailin forced herself to step outside. No amount of self-control could stop the single scream that ripped from her throat when she saw buzzards flocking around the sprawled bodies in the yard.

"No!" she cried. "Leave them alone!" She ran at the scavengers, waving her arms like a madwoman. She didn't stop running until she reached the river and waded into it. She dropped to her knees and drank, trying to ignore the stinging in her feet.

And then she realized she'd seen nothing that looked like a torture stake. Laughing hysterically, she retraced her steps, going from body to body, identifying each man. She found Joe and Isaac's mutilated remains and those of Phoebe's husband. But there was no sign of Jasper or his mother ... or of Sterling.

She ran to the cart. On the side where she'd been tied were the remains of the leather thongs that had held her to the spokes of the wheel. On Sterling's side, she saw nothing but muddy earth and fresh hoofprints mingled with the marks of moccasins and the deeper indentations of Sterling's boot heels. And a short distance away, she saw what looked like a single pawprint.

Cailin's mind reeled. Sterling couldn't walk. Was it possible that the Mohawks had carried him away on horseback? Did that mean that they'd changed their plan to burn him ... or did it mean simply a delay in the execution?

She couldn't accept that possibility. For whatever reason, her husband was alive, and he would remain alive until she saw his dead body with her own eyes.

She went to the well and leaned over to lower the bucket ... and found baby Jasper.

Rage brought her back to full sanity. She hadn't the strength to bury all the dead, but she'd be damned if she'd leave Jasper in the bottom of the well. Getting him up took nearly an hour. Finally, when all else failed, she used a branch to make an open loop in the end of the bucket rope and snagged one tiny leg.

She wrapped him in the remains of her cloak and made a deep nest for him in the garden. The pippin apple would do for a headstone, and rocks would keep the scavengers from his remains. She tried to pray, but her words sounded hollow. An innocent child would have no need of her prayers to find God's mercy. In the end, she commended his soul to the Lord and sang an old Scots lullaby that Corey had always liked to hear at bedtime.

Then she set about dragging Sterling's people into the house. It was nearly dusk when she rolled the last one over the sill. The stuffing of feather ticks provided the tinder, her remaining furniture the fuel. Using flint and steel, she struck a spark. When the cabin was blazing, she turned away and began to follow the river west.

Moonfeather had told her that the camp was two days' march; it took Cailin three and a half. She'd been unable to get her shoes on, so she'd walked the distance barefoot. And by the time a Shawnee hunter found her, she was out of her head with fever and exhaustion.

Cailin was only partially aware that a man had plucked her from the shallows of the river and was carrying her into the village. And when Moonfeather's face hovered over hers, Cailin wasn't sure if she was real or a dream.

"We were attacked," she whispered hoarsely. "Mohawks. Sterling ... said ... Sterling said they ... were Mohawks."

"Is he alive?" Moonfeather demanded.

Cailin nodded. "I think so. He said they were going to burn him, but they didn't."

"They took him captive?" the peace woman asked.

"Aye. I saw hoofprints in the mud. He couldn't walk. He was bitten by a snake."

"Do you know what Mohawks they were? Of what band? Did Sterling tell you a name?"

"Ohneya. One man's name was Ohneya. I think he was the leader."

"Ohneya." Moonfeather's brow furrowed. "This

one has heard of Ohneya. He is a war chief ... a man who has taken many scalps."

"Aye. I saw him take another."

"How many dead?" Moonfeather asked.

"All of them ... all of them." Cailin seized her hand and peered into her face. "Even Jasper. He was a baby ... a baby. He was crying, and then ... " She shook her head. "It's nay right. Not a wee bairn."

The Indian woman touched her cheek. "Nay," she agreed softly. "It's wrong to hurt a child, white or red. Children belong to the Creator." Her great liquid brown eyes glistened with moisture. "You're certain Na-nata Ki-tehi—Sterling—wasn't killed? Ye couldn't have missed his body?"

"Nay. We have to find him before—"

"We will call a council," Moonfeather assured her. "Now, you must eat and sleep. Your feet are badly injured. Rest now, you are with friends. We will care for you."

"But Sterling," Cailin insisted. "Sterling is—"

"He is Shawnee," Moonfeather said. "He belongs to us, and we look after our own."

Cailin lost track of time. Night came and then morning ... or was it afternoon? She could see the dappling of sunlight play across the hard-packed dirt floor of the hut. She slept on a wide, soft bed. And when she lay on her back and looked up, a roof of bark curved pleasingly overhead.

Any fears she might have had of being helpless among the Indians soon faded. Gentle hands spooned soup into her mouth and covered her with a light blanket in the night. Anxious copper-skinned faces stared back at her whenever she opened her eyes—some old and wrinkled, some young. But every face showed only compassion. And if she couldn't understand the soft, lisping words, she needed no translator to tell her that her visitors were offering comfort.

At first, Cailin was conscious of a throbbing agony in her feet that lessened when someone bathed them and rubbed ointments into the blisters and sores. She heard Moonfeather's assurances that she would be all right, and came to accept the steady beat of drums above the rushing sound of the river.

Sleeping and waking, Cailin smelled the unfamiliar scents of dried herbs and the contents of mysterious baskets hanging from the hut framework. Delicious odors of corn cakes baking on flat rocks drifted through the open doorway. It seemed as though all she did was eat and sleep, lulled by the rhythm of the peaceful village.

Until she opened her eyes to find a white man standing over her, holding her amulet. Cailin sat bolt upright.

"Easy, easy, child," he cautioned. He let go of the necklace and moved back. "I'll nay harm you," he said.

Nearly buried beneath the fine speech of an English gentleman, Cailin heard the Scot's Highland lilt. "Who are ye?" she demanded.

The smiling man was no longer young; his hair had turned an iron-gray, and his face was lined with experience. But his shoulders were still broad, and he was still handsome enough to turn a woman's eye.

"Do I know ye?" she asked.

Moonfeather entered the wigwam and pulled the doorflap closed. "Someone special has come to meet ye," she said.

"I can see that," Cailin said, sliding her legs over

the side of the platform. She was decently dressed, she was glad to discover. In place of her ragged shift was a robin's-egg-blue dress of cotton with a darker blue underskirt. "What I'd like to—"

"What is your name?" the stranger asked her. "I know you're the wife of Sterling Gray, but what was your maiden name, and where exactly were you born?"

"What business is it of yours, sir?" she replied.

"Your mother. Who was she?"

"I've no wish to play your game," she replied sharply. Something was not right. Nervously, she glanced at Moonfeather. Sterling had said that she could trust Lady Kentington, and Cailin's own instincts agreed.

The peace woman smiled reassuringly. "Na-nata Ki-tehi, who you call Sterling, told me that your necklace was a family heirloom. Do you know where it came from?"

Cailin clasped the amulet. It felt curiously warm to the touch, almost alive. Oddly, the sensation was not disturbing; instead, it made her feel safe. "I don't understand why you're so interested in my pendant."

"The Eye of Mist," the gentleman said. "It has great power—I wonder if you realize how much."

She looked into his face. His cheeks were stained with tears.

"The Eye of Mist is Pictish gold," he continued. "According to legend, it must be handed down from mother to daughter. I only wish you to tell me if it came from your mother's family of—"

"It was a birth gift from the man who sired me," she snapped. "A man I have never seen, but one who wished me ill."

"Nay," he answered huskily. "Never that."

"If ye ken so much about the necklace, then ye must know that it is cursed," Cailin said.

"And blessed," Moonfeather put in.

Cailin stiffened with resentment. "I've seen little of the blessing."

The man covered her hand with his. "The blessing is that ye will be granted one wish. Whatever you ask you shall have—even unto the power of life and death."

"Who are ye?" Cailin demanded, snatching her hand away. "And how can ye ken so much of my affairs?"

"I am Cameron Stewart," he said. "And you are the child I got on the fairest lass in all the Highlands, my cousin, Elspeth Stewart."

"Ye lie!" Cailin felt the blood drain from her face. "It canna be."

"It is, child," he said. "On my mother's soul, I vow it's true. You are the babe Elspeth and I conceived, and she brought forth and raised alone."

"You lie. My mother's name was not Stewart when I was conceived," Cailin protested hotly. "My mother was the wife of another."

"Not the wife, but the widow," Cameron corrected. "And she was in danger of losing all she had to her husband's family because there was no lawful heir."

"Do ye tell me that yours was a love match? You and your *cousin?*" It was easy enough for Cailin to believe her mother could do such a thing—she was ever an easy piece with an eye to her own best advantage. Elspeth had been widowed young, birthed Cailin ten months after her husband's funeral, wed another, and buried him before she became Johnnie

MacLeod's wife. Jeanne had been born somewhere in between. She wasn't Cameron Stewart's or Johnnie's child. Where her sister had come from, Cailin had never had the courage to ask her mother.

"Second cousin, twice removed, lass. You're not the result of incest, just of two old friends who wanted to right a wrong and keep a lady from losing her home."

"By making a bastard."

Cameron chuckled. "Hard words, lass. Hard words. The Shawnee have a kinder way of speaking."

"That's true," Moonfeather said. "Among my people, there are no illegitimate children. Descent comes through the mother. Clan and kinship are reckoned by maternal blood. Fathers come and go, but mothers are as true as rain."

It was Cailin's turn to scoff. "It's plain ye never knew Elspeth. She was true—to herself."

"Be not so harsh on her," Cameron said. "She was always a lighthearted lass, and she loved where she pleased. But she cared for her children. When I learned of your birth, I sent the necklace and silver for your raising. I offered to take you, but she refused. She said you were hers, and she'd keep you."

Cailin shook her head in disbelief. "For all this love between you, ye never thought to marry her yourself?" she asked sarcastically.

"I had a wife at the time," he replied.

"So you cheated on her as my mother cheated her dead husband?"

Cameron laughed. "Her husband had little need of what we shared. And as for my wife, Margaret and I were wed when I was sixteen and she ... Well, let me say that she was older and that it was a marriage of convenience."

"Convenient for you, sir," Cailin shot back, "if you could forget your vows so easily and make a child with the likes of Elspeth Stewart."

"My lady wife was a good woman who had the misfortune to be born different. Our arrangement was an honest one and—"

"She and your father had not shared a bed in many years when you were conceived." Moonfeather put in delicately.

"How do you know so much of his affairs?" Cailin asked the peace woman.

"Suffice it to say that she does," he said. "I have no secrets from Moonfeather."

"So I am to accept you as my long lost father," Cailin said. "Miraculously restored to my side in my hour of need, here in the wilderness. 'Tis the stuff of children's fairy tales, sir."

"True, nevertheless."

She scoffed. "And you happened to be driving by in your coach ... from London?"

He sighed. "You have the right to be upset. It's a lot to hear, and from what Moonfeather says, you've been through a terrible ordeal. I left London before you were born. I have several plantations on the bay. I came to the Colonies to be near ... near family."

"I know of the amulet," Moonfeather said. "I knew he would want to see you. I wrote to him soon after I met you."

"I would have come sooner," Cameron said, "but I was in Williamsburg on official business. I just received the message."

"Now you've seen me, now what?" Cailin asked.

It was impossible to think of this man as her father. She'd known the name Cameron Stewart for years. She'd known that he'd sired her. But Johnnie MacLeod was her real father, and nothing could change that fact.

"I'm nay such a fool as to expect you to fall into my arms, lass," he said. "There are too many years between us. I should have come to you—or at least written. I did not, because I didn't know if your mother had told you the truth or not. If you had a full life, I didn't want to interfere. Now, it seems, I can be of some real use to you."

"The council has decided not to declare war on the Mohawk," Moonfeather said. "At least, not yet. I'm going north with trade goods to the Mohawk village. If Sterling is alive, it's possible that we can ransom him. Your father insists on going with me."

"You mean to try and buy Sterling back?" Cailin asked.

"Aye." Moonfeather nodded.

"But you're putting yourself in great danger."

"She is," Cameron agreed, "but not as much as you'd think. Moonfeather is a peace woman of the Shawnee."

"Sterling told me that," Cailin said. "But how—"

"Even the Mohawk respect her power. And . . ." He pursed his lips thoughtfully. "I expect they're a little afraid of her too."

Cailin looked from one to the other. A sinking thought had just occurred to her. "I don't know if Sterling had any silver left to use as ransom," she said. "He put every penny into tools and supplies for the plantation. Unless he could raise money on the worth of the land . . ."

"Ye must not think of the cost," Moonfeather assured her. "Na-nata Ki-tehi is Shawnee. We do not abandon our own. We will bring him back peacefully, or we will paint our faces and take up the tomahawk. If he lives, we will find him."

"And if he's already dead?" Cailin asked.

"Then we will seek vengeance."

Cailin nodded. This was the code of the Highlands, a way of life she understood all too well. "When do we leave?" she asked.

"You will stay here," Cameron said. "You aren't fully recovered from your injuries."

"Sterling is my husband. I must go."

"No," Cameron said sharply. "That's not possible. If you don't want to stay here, I can arrange for you to be escorted back to my home."

"I'm going," Cailin insisted.

"If her heart tells her that she must come," Moonfeather argued, "then she must."

"Damn it," he said. "You can't take her into Iroquois territory. She has no concept of—"

"Aye, but I do," Cailin said, remembering Jasper's pale, cold face. "I ken men like Ohneya well enough. But I will come, with ye or on my own."

Cameron folded his arms over his chest. "I say no and no again. This is bad business. I'll not take the responsibility for endangering Cailin's life."

"I appreciate any help you can give to restore my husband's freedom, sir," Cailin retorted. "But what risks I choose to take are my own affair. May I remind ye that you have no authority over my actions, and if you wish our acquaintance to be more than passing, ye will cease from—"

"She survived the raid," Moonfeather said. "If she travels with us, she will be under my protection and that of the Shawnee nation."

"You're two of a kind," Cameron said. "Stubborn and willful women."

Moonfeather laughed. "And when have you ever loved any other kind?"

Chapter 18

～◯◯～

Glen Garth, Scotland
June 1747

Big Fergus hunkered down and splashed water
on his face, then lifted the bucket and drank
long and deep. Corey stood, arms akimbo, watching
him and trying not to cry. Corey's belly hurt; he
couldn't remember being so hungry. They'd dined on
a chicken two days ago, but he'd had to share his
portion of the skinny bird with his dog, Lance. All
day, as they'd gotten closer to home and the country-
side became more familiar, Corey had thought about
home and all the good things cook would make to
eat. *Glen Garth. Glen Garth.* The words had sounded
over and over in his head. But now that he and Big
Fergus were here, nothing was the same as he remembered.

The rambling stone house stood as black and
empty as the rotten husk of last autumn's walnut. No
voices called from the courtyard, no horses whin-
nied, and no dogs barked to welcome Lance.

When they'd reached the home place, Corey had
run and peered into the burned interior of the hall
and shouted for Cailin. Her name had echoed spook-
ily through the ruins, becoming fainter and fainter
until it was only a whisper. He'd called again and

again until Big Fergus got scared and began to mutter about ghosts.

Next, Corey had hurried to the stables. They stood vacant, without horse or cow or saddle. The pigsties were open and still. Not a single goose hissed or a pigeon fluttered in the yard.

"Where's Cailin?" Corey had demanded of Big Fergus. "Where's Jeanne and Grandda? Where's your brother, Finley? Where are all the servants?"

Fergus hadn't answered. Instead, he'd gone to the bell at the corner of the house. The rope had burned away, but the bronze bell hung where it had been since the days of the great Rob Roy. Still not saying anything, Fergus picked up a broken paving stone from the walk and handed it to Corey. Then he caught Corey around the waist and lifted him to his shoulders.

The bell had only been rung in time of trouble. This was trouble. Even Big Fergus could figure that out. Corey took the rock in both hands and struck the bell as hard as he could.

Twelve times he hit the metal, and twelve times the bell pealed out. Twelve for the twelve apostles of Christ, Big Fergus said. Then he set Corey back on the ground, and they sat down by the well and waited until the afternoon shadows cast patterns on the deserted compound.

Corey wanted to ask Big Fergus what they should do if no one came. He wanted to know where they'd sleep and what they'd find to eat, but he knew that thinking wasn't Fergus's duty. Corey himself was laird of Glen Garth, and head of the MacLeod clan. Fergus was more than a servant; he was a man-at-arms, sworn to follow the commands of the MacLeod laird as long as he lived. But no man-at-arms, especially Big Fergus or his twin brother, Finley, could be expected to make decisions.

Corey rubbed his eyes with the backs of grimy fists. Since they'd left Artair Cameron by the unfinished stone wall, he, Fergus, and Lance had had a purpose. They were coming home. But now that they'd reached Glen Garth, it wasn't home. Corey knew he was too big to cry, but the thought of sleeping another night on the road without supper was enough—

Suddenly, Lance's ears went up and his tail began to wag. He let out one sharp bark, then tore off around the house.

"Lance! Lance!" Corey leaped up and ran after the dog. Big Fergus thundered after him, claymore drawn and ready. As Corey rounded the corner, he saw a familiar figure walking toward him with a gnarled hickory staff in his hand.

The old man came slowly but steadily on, tapping the ground in front of him as he walked. Lance whined with excitement and ran circles around him.

"Grandda!" Corey said. "Grandda!" He hurled himself against his grandfather's knees, nearly knocking him off his feet.

"Corey? Be that my Corey?"

Corey cried and laughed and tried to talk, all at the same time. Big Fergus was so relieved to see his old master that he folded his arms over his broad chest and did a Highland jig without benefit of a piper.

"Ah, laddie, who brought ye home to me?" Grandda asked, when the excitement had died down enough for them to talk again.

" 'Twas me," Big Fergus declared, beaming with pride. "Big Fergus. Watch over the wee laird, the lady bid me. And I did."

"He did," Corey agreed. "We slept in hedges and hid from the English soldiers in the daytime and walked by night. When I was hungry, Fergus caught a chicken and cooked it over a fire."

"Artair Cameron was a bad man. He was mean to the young laird, so I hit him," Big Fergus explained. "We come home to Glen Garth. We shouted. We didna find a soul. We thought maybe they were all dead."

"Nay, not all dead," Grandda said.

Corey thought his grandfather's voice sounded tired. "Cailin promised she'd come for me," he said. "She lied."

" 'Twas nay her fault, lad," Grandda said gruffly.

"I watched the road. Every day, I watched, but she never came." Corey squeezed his grandfather's seamed hand.

"There's much to tell ye of what happened. The soldiers came and burned us out. But that can wait," Grandda said. "I imagine you two could use a bowl of good oat porridge."

"Aye, sir," Big Fergus said. Then he tugged at his ear. "Did I do right? Bringin' the wee laird home, Master James?"

Grandda ruffled Corey's hair. "You did good, Fergus. And you, Corey. 'Tis proud I be of ye both."

Fergus's chest swelled. "I want to tell Finley. Have ye seen Finley?"

"There's no easy way to tell ye, man. Your brother's dead. He died defending Glen Garth, struck down by the dragoons."

The big servant looked stricken. "Dead? My Finley dead?"

"Aye, dead and buried. But Father John said the words over his grave."

Fergus shook his head. "Finley be my twin. Borned together, die together, Mam always said."

"Nay," Grandda said. "Finley did his duty, and so shall you. Cailin told ye to watch over the young master, and so ye must. Ye must be the eyes and strength for me, Fergus. I'm old and I'm blind, but I'm all Corey has left."

Corey's belly got a hollow feeling, worse than the hunger. "Is Cailin dead like my father?" he asked. "Did the soldiers kill her and Jeanne too?"

"Nay, nay," Grandda said. He cleared his throat, and Corey looked up to see he was crying too. He'd never known his grandfather to cry; he didn't know the blind could cry.

"The same English dragoons who burned Glen Garth and murdered Finley took Cailin away. I thought she might be dead, but just last week, Robert Gunn came by the cottage—I'm living in the shepherd's hut back of the hollow—Robert Gunn came by to bring me a bag of oat flour. I pay him—it's not charity, Corey. Your sister had the sense to bury a bit of silver before the thieving British came. Anyway, Robert told me that his cousin, Tormod Gunn—the short one who never grew right—was in Edinburgh. The English meant to hang Cailin, "but they didn't. Instead, they made her marry an Englishman, Sterling Gray. Remember that name, boy. Sterling Gray."

"Is she coming home?" He wanted to ask about Jeanne and the baby, and about Glynis and the others, but he was awfully hungry and tired.

"I know Robert Gunn," Fergus said, "but I don't know Tormod. How little is he?"

"Not much taller than Corey here. He's a dwarf," Grandda explained patiently. He always took time to answer questions. It was the thing Corey liked best about his grandsire.

"I saw a little man one time. He was a Gypsy," Fergus said. "Is Tormod Gunn a Gypsy?"

"No," Corey said. He didn't want Fergus to start asking about Gypsies. Once Fergus started on Gypsies, he would keep on till dark. "I'm hungry, Grandda."

"Me too," Fergus chimed in. "I could eat a horse trough of porridge."

"A washtub is all ye'll get from me," Grandda replied. "We'd best get back to the cottage. We've a long day ahead of us tomorrow."

"Doing what?" Corey asked.

"We're going to England to find your sister," he said.

"To England?" Corey looked up at the old man in surprise. "Cailin or Jeanne?"

"Cailin, of course. Jeanne's gone away with her man. She'll not be back. She's left us to our own devices. Not that I'll have ye blame her, lad. Times are wicked, and each must do as his or her heart bids."

"We're going to England?" Fergus asked. "To see King George?"

"To find Cailin," Corey corrected. "Can we, sir? Can we find her?"

"I'll not die until I put ye into her arms. Rest assured on that," Grandda said. "She's wed the son of an English lord, Baron Oxley by name. The parson who performed the marriage will have the name and place of Sterling's home parish. We go first to Edinburgh and then to England."

"All the way to England?" Corey murmured. " 'Tis far and far, be it not?"

"Be it so far as hell, it matters little." Grandda's

fingers stroked Corey's hair. "Till ye rang the bell, I thought to sit in that hut until I died. But I see now that God has work for me yet. Glen Garth is finished, but you're just beginning, Corey MacLeod. Wherever your sister is and whatever her future brings, she'll make a place for ye. She'll see ye get the proper learning and make ye into a fine man that your father, rest his soul, would be proud of."

Corey sighed with relief and smiled. If Cailin was alive, everything would be all right. She liked to make decisions. All they had to do was find her, and the three of them could do that. Grandda had said so, and he was old enough to know everything. "Come on, Lance," he called to his dog. And he held on as tight as he could to his grandfather's hand as they turned and walked slowly back to a hot supper.

In Penn's Colony, an ocean and a world away, Sterling put his head back and opened his mouth in an attempt to quench his thirst with rainwater. It was long past midnight, and he was tied upright to a tree trunk on the edge of the Mohawks' night camp.

The rain had started a short while ago, and so far, he'd not gotten enough water to moisten the inside of his mouth. His fever had passed; the snakebite had left him weak and disoriented, but the swelling in his arm had gone down.

When the Mohawks had found that Cailin had escaped, they'd been as angry as a nest of ground wasps. Sterling had feared that the Indians would track her to the cabin, but another rainstorm just before dawn had covered any trace of her passing. The loss had spoiled the war party's morning so much that they'd decided not to burn him right away, but to hold off until they reached the safety of their own land. Since he couldn't walk, they'd thrown him on a horse. Last night they'd cut the horse's throat and grilled choice portions over the fire.

No one had thought to feed the prisoner. And no one had brought him water. He'd not had a drink since the horse had swum a river and had lost its footing on the rocks, nearly drowning both of them. The horse had been a fine-blooded animal, but he'd have eaten its flesh gladly, had he been given the opportunity.

By his count, he'd been traveling with the Mohawks for three days. During that time, he'd been beaten, stripped naked, and burned with the muzzle of a red-hot gun barrel, all for his captors' amusement. And somewhere along the trail, the English dragoon, Captain Sterling Gray had gotten lost, leaving a Shawnee brave named Na-nata Ki-tehi in his place.

He wasn't certain how or where the transformation had taken place; he only knew that he was thinking in Algonquian and he was reasoning like an Indian. Na-nata Ki-tehi—Warrior Heart—blood enemy to the Iroquois. How Snow Ghost had gained a new name was a mystery, but Moonfeather, the greatest peace woman in his tribe's history, had the right and the authority to give it to him. He wondered briefly if she'd known that capture and death by torture lay ahead of him. A Shawnee brave with such a future needed a powerful spirit protector and a strong name if he was not to shame his ancestors under the Mohawk knife.

The Iroquois were highly skilled in the art of bringing a man pain. Death after such exquisitely delivered agony would be welcome. Sterling did not expect to live—his hope was to die well with a death song on his lips and triumph in his heart.

Cailin had escaped. Bound to the cart wheel, snakebitten, and wounded, he'd managed to save the woman he loved ... the woman who'd become his whole world. His wife ... his lover ... his spirit guide ...

Strange that a Scottish woman with red-gold hair could come to him in his youth vision, but the years had proved the truth of his seeing. He had found Cailin again on the field of battle in a far-off land, and she'd led him back to the country of his birth, where he'd found a peace and happiness he'd forgotten existed.

He'd spent a lifetime trying to become an Englishman. He'd rejected his mother's blood and tried to forget the tongue that had taught him the wisdom of an ancient people. His mother had sung him to sleep at night, had encouraged his first steps, and had praised his first hunting success. He could still remember her shouts of pride when he'd snared his first rabbit. She had cooked the animal into a stew. Adding spices, vegetables, and other meat, she'd created the center dish for a feast in his honor. Even the chief of the tribe had eaten a little of his rabbit, and a boy's heart had swelled with joy.

His mother had not been as small a woman as Cailin, and she had been pleasantly rounded. Her eyes had been as bright as ripe blackberries, and her hands had never ceased their constant motion. And her singing ... How she could sing. He remembered the words to one such lullaby now ...

High flies the red hawk over the river,
Over the forest and over the meadow,

Sweet sounds the river and sweet sounds the hawk,
But sweetest of all is the sound of your laughter
Over the forest and over the meadow ...

His early memories of his father were not as clear. Once, he'd come to the village with a man in black—a cleric of the Church of England, Sterling had realized years later. The strange white man had sprinkled water on his head and declared that the child was now a Christian. It was the first time that Sterling had heard his English name spoken.

He'd seen his father once more, when he and his mother had gone to Annapolis to trade for needles and gunpowder. His parents had spoken to each other, argued, and then Sterling had been hurried away. His mother had wept bitterly—he remembered that clearly. It was the only time he'd ever seen her cry. Sterling had not set eyes on the baron again until after his mother's sudden death of a high fever.

"Why did you take me away from these forests—from this earth?" he whispered into the night.

Eyes glowed in the darkness, and Sterling knew instantly that it was the wolf who'd been shadowing the Mohawk raiders since they'd left the plantation clearing.

"You again," Sterling murmured. *You'd best get far from here, or you'll end up part of a Mohawk breakfast.* The old wolf had obviously attached himself to the group for a reason. Perhaps it was too old to hunt and hoped to find scraps around the camp.

Then, the answer to his question rang through his brain as clearly as if his father were standing beside him. *Why did I take you from the Indians? Because you were my son. Because you carried my blood, and it was my duty to bring you to Christianity and to return a Gray—even a Gray of mixed heritage—to civilization.*

It was all Sterling could do to keep from laughing aloud. All his life, he'd tried to be what his father wanted, and in all that time, his father had not seen him as a person, only as a possession.

Why hadn't he guessed the truth before? Among his mother's people, children belonged to the Creator, while the Europeans considered them possessions without rights or free will.

The wolf stepped closer.

Sterling blinked and tried to fathom the logic of a wild creature willingly coming close to its only mortal enemy. Then one of the Mohawks groaned in his sleep, and Sterling snapped his head toward the sound. When he looked back, the wolf was gone.

Sterling waited, fully alert. The rain came down harder, lapping over his body like a warm bath. He tilted his head and let the delicious liquid sluice down his throat. The warm downpour soothed his wounds and washed away his confusion.

Cailin is safe. If she lives, I live as well.

With his mind at ease, he drifted into a peaceful sleep and dreamed of the strawberry meadow and Cailin ... dreamed of the scent of her hair and the taste of her berry-stained lips ... and of the feel of her bare, silken skin pressed tightly against his.

Chapter 19

Moonfeather stalled for another two days before she led Cailin, Cameron Stewart, and six warriors out of the Shawnee village. Cailin's feet were still tender, and Moonfeather had serious doubts that the Scottish girl could make the journey to the Mohawk village near the big lake the English called Ontario.

Learning the war party's destination was a piece of luck that Moonfeather thought could only have come as a direct blessing from Inu-msi-ila-fe-wanu, the great spirit who is a grandmother. Moonfeather had heard of Ohneya, the Mohawk Cailin said had captured and terrorized her, but the Iroquois were as numerous as the leaves of the trees. There were many Mohawk villages. Since the Shawnee were presently at peace with the Iroquois, she could have gone to the first Iroquois village she saw and asked Ohneya's whereabouts. But she had little faith that she would have received a truthful answer.

Instead, she found out the name and location of Ohneya's camp from a Lenape warrior named Lachpi who had been born beside the great salt ocean at the mouth of the Delaware River. Lachpi had once hunted whale with his grandfather from a twenty-man dugout, and he had lived to see his family's homeland claimed by Swedish and later English settlers. Now, he no longer speared fish by torchlight on the Delaware, and the only whales on which he used his knife were those he carved of cedar. Lachpi had drifted farther and farther west as his people died of the white men's sicknesses and he watched their culture fragment. Last summer, he had become the husband of a Shawnee widow and a member of Moonfeather's clan by marriage.

Two years ago, before Lachpi had met his wife-to-be, he and his grown son had been trading beaver skins north of Lancaster. This same Mohawk Ohneya had attacked Lachpi, stolen the furs, and taken Lachpi's son back to his village. Lachpi had trailed them to the camp, but it was too late to save his only son. Now, Lachpi was eager to lead Moonfeather north to the Mohawk town.

"If you seek revenge in blood, this may not be the time," Moonfeather had warned him. "This woman goes in peace to try and negotiate a prisoner's return."

"A father's memory is long," the man replied. "A debt must be repaid. You have the word of Lachpi that he will not fail you. In exchange, this man would have your word. If Ohneya the Mohawk must be killed, let me do it for you."

"A peace woman does not seek violence," she answered softly.

"Storms come before the rainbow."

She had nodded at that, thanked him for his information, and agreed that Lachpi should go with them into the domain of the Mohawk.

The animosity between the Shawnee and the Iroquois nation stretched back hundreds of years, since the Iroquois had first claimed the huge chunk of land in the center of the Algonquian-speaking tribes' hunting grounds. The Shawnee were blood cousins to the Lenape, or Delaware as the English called them, and the Mohegan, thus they were honor-bound to support and defend one another. This common kinship of language and intermarriage extended to the Nanticoke, the Powhatan, and other nations such as the Ojibwa, the Menominee, the Fox, and the Miami.

The powerful Iroquois Confederacy, consisting of the Seneca, Cayuga, Onondaga, Oneida, and Mohawk, had realized the military importance of forming strong ties with the Dutch, the English, and the French in the early seventeenth century. The Iroquois had used their political might and their new white friends to conquer or destroy the neighboring Indian tribes around them. The Mohegans had been completely destroyed; the traditional homeland of the Delaware was now in English hands—sold to the British by the Iroquois, who never had rightful claim to the hunting grounds along the Delaware River. And now the Iroquois were trying to extend their rule into the heart of the Shawnee territory, the Ohio River country.

The Iroquois were enemy to the Shawnee, and the Mohawk tribe was the greatest enemy of all. The Mohawk called themselves Ganiengehaka, People Who Live in the Land of the Flint. The Delaware called them Mohawk, Eaters of Men, after the custom of ritual cannibalism practiced by the Iroquois, and the Mohawk in particular.

Moonfeather knew that if they did not arrive in time, Sterling would meet a hideous death. Still, she had waited for Cailin to gain strength and for her own inner feeling that it was the right day and the right hour for their departure. Moonfeather had spent the time in prayer and meditation. She had offered tobacco to the sacred council fire, and she had cleansed her own body by fasting and ritual bathing.

Her vote against war had kept the Shawnee council members from passing the black string of wampum and seeking revenge with tomahawk and long rifle. The strike at Sterling's plantation had been more than an attack on an English settler; it had been a blatant insult against the Shawnee. Sterling's land was Shawnee hunting ground. Ignoring the raid would mean accepting Iroquois domination; contesting the affront could mean a long and bloody war against not just the Mohawk, but the entire Iroquois Confederacy.

But if a Shawnee peace woman could go to the Mohawk village, recover the prisoner, and demand apology and token payment from the Iroquois without being slaughtered or taken captive herself, then the shaky peace would hold a while longer. No Shawnee children would be orphaned, and no women made widows before their time. Shawnee cornfields would ripen, and the old men could sit in the sun, smoke their pipes, and speak of times when the world was a better place.

Moonfeather glanced back at Cailin. The girl was breathing easily and having no obvious problems keeping her place in line. Tomorrow, the pace would be faster, but Moonfeather had quietly told her men that they would start out slowly and make up time as Cailin proved her ability. A final glance over her shoulder assured Moonfeather that Cameron was holding his position at the rear.

Relieved that all was well, she let her mind slip back to the conversation she'd had with Cameron last night. She remembered every word and motion with crystal clarity.

"What chance of success do we have?" Cameron had demanded.

She'd spread her hands and shrugged. "A chance."

He'd looked skeptical. "You put a lot of stock in Iroquois honor."

"Some. They do ken honor, not English honor or Scot, not even Shawnee honor, but we are more alike than even you realize."

"I don't like this," he said. "I'm sorry about Sterling and for Cailin, but there's no need for you two to die trying to get him back."

She laughed softly. "Who was the first to say he would go?"

Cameron shook his head. "That's different. I'm an old man. My joints hurt in the morning, and if I ride too long, my back kills me. I've had a long life—a good one. There's little enough I've done for this daughter. I owe her."

"You're a rogue, certain," Moonfeather answered. "A little gray around the ears, mayhap, but not yet too old to seek out adventure. You're bored. The Chesapeake's too tame for ye."

He smiled, and she saw again why Cameron Stewart had broken so many women's hearts. "This journey will give the two of you time to see into each other's souls."

"You should have told her the rest of it," he said.

Moonfeather paused in packing her medicine kit and looked up at him. "Have I lied to Cailin?"

"No." He uttered an exasperated sound. "You just didn't tell her all the truth."

"The Shawnee have a saying, 'Truth is a knife with a sharp edge. Take care where you stab it.'"

"That's not Shawnee, it's Chinese."

She shrugged again and laughed. "Wisdom has many faces. It's better that she doesn't know everything at once."

"She has the right."

"Nay." She shook her head. "The right must be earned. She has the Eye of Mist. She must prove worthy."

"I've said it over and over. You're a stubborn, willful woman. Your sister Anne was never this difficult."

"I'm more hardheaded than even my sister Fiona?"

"Aye. You are. You know you are."

"And you are a man of reason."

"Aye, I am," Cameron agreed. "But it still irks me to have you call me by my Christian name."

"I've called ye—"

"We won't dig up old misunderstandings. You are a grandmother, and I'm a great-grandfather. We both need to have our heads examined for willingly going into Iroquois land."

She tucked a packet of dried trillium into the otter-skin pouch and tied the closures tightly. It was true that she was no longer a young woman, but the lure of an unknown trail that led to danger still brought a youthful excitement to her heart. She had a good husband and loving children who understood that they could be part of her world, but not all of it. If she didn't return from this mission, they would mourn, but they wouldn't blame her for going.

"I am the peace woman," she said simply. "Who else could do this?"

"We could contact Mountain Standing of the Onondaga. He could attempt negotiations."

"In time. Meanwhile, Sterling could be bound to a

stake, have his eyes burned out with hot coals, and have his insides wrapped around—"

Cameron swore.

"I only speak aloud what we both think," she answered softly. "Although, if they mean to prolong torture, they would leave his eyes until last—so that he could—"

"Enough." His mouth tightened and his eyes took on a steely hue. "I'm no coward, but you know how I hate torture."

"We are reaping the harvest of your sowing," she said. "Is this the last? Or have you sprinkled daughters in the Far East as well?"

"I cut the Eye of Mist into four pieces when you were a child. Four parts of the whole. I can only think that there are four daughters." He ran lean fingers over his eyes. "I've loved many women, Moonfeather. That's been my curse and my blessing."

A cold chill passed through her, and she stared into his eyes. "Ye dinna believe that you will return this time, do ye?" she asked. Unconsciously, the heavy burr of her childhood speech had crept into her voice.

He tried to laugh off her sudden fear. "I like to be ready for any possibility. I've written a new will. Cailin will be provided for, whether or not her husband survives."

"English gold cannot make her happy."

"Do you deny that Brandon's wealth has made your life easier—and that of your tribe?"

"My husband's inheritance has provided many things, but my mother's legacy has given me more."

"Most women would trade their immortal souls to be the beloved wife of Lord Kentington."

"Aye, that may be so," she agreed, "and my heart

is his, but my soul has never been for sale. You taught me that."

"Another moment and we'll all be weeping like sailors at a bosun's funeral. I don't agree with your decision, but I'll keep your secret for a while longer."

"When the time comes for her to know—if it comes—I'll tell Cailin myself."

He reached out and laid his hand on her cheek. "I love ye, lassie. Have I ever told ye how much?"

"You have," she replied. "But ye may say it again as often as ye like." She smiled up at him and hoped her earlier chill was not a premonition of heartbreak to come.

Moonfeather felt none of that dread this morning. All her doubts had been pushed from her mind. It was too late to consider what they might have done; she had made a decision. She would follow her instincts until they successfully rescued Sterling or until the mission was lost. And if she or Cameron or even Cailin was meant to die trying, then it was already written in the star path, and nothing could prevent it.

Cailin lay awake staring up at the stars long after Moonfeather and Cameron Stewart were asleep. Her body was exhausted, but her mind refused to stop working long enough for her to relax. So much had happened since she and Sterling had laughed together by the river. First his snakebite, then the massacre, and now this man who claimed to be her father.

She supposed she should summon affection or even resentment toward him from the depths of her being, but she couldn't. Her emotions were drained. She had no reserve of strength left to deal with him. If he said he was her sire, she accepted his word. She'd not question how or why he'd found her—she'd simply use him and his wealth to try to save Sterling's life.

A shadow moved in the trees. Behind her, a night hawk called. The sound was answered.

Mentally, Cailin counted the sleeping figures around her. Six. Seven, if she included herself. Two braves were keeping watch. One of them was the fierce Kitate who had come with Moonfeather to visit the homestead in May. Sterling had told her that Kitate was Moonfeather's Shawnee son, born before she married Brandon, Lord Kentington. Cailin could see little resemblance between the hardened warrior and his mother. He seldom spoke or smiled.

Cailin felt at ease with Moonfeather, but not with Kitate, who watched her every move with heavy-lidded black eyes. She didn't like him, and he made no attempt to hide his distrust of her.

The other Shawnee were Ake, a tall, light-skinned brave with a wide mouth; a short, husky man who went by the Christian name of Joseph; a seasoned warrior with graying hair called Pukasee; and Koke-wah, a boy of about sixteen years of age. Koke-wah walked directly behind Cailin on the day's march, and once, when she'd nearly tripped, he'd caught her arm, smiled reassuringly, and steadied her balance. The sixth member of their guard was a Delaware brave named Lachpi. He had never said anything to Cailin, but he laughed so easily that he reminded her of her cousin Alasdair, and she couldn't help but be drawn to him. Lachpi was the other man standing guard duty with Kitate.

They'd not built a fire. Moonfeather had explained that they would rest for a few hours and then travel on through the early morning before dawn. Supper had been water from a fast-running stream and a mixture of dried meat and berries that had a strange consistency that Cailin found surprisingly filling.

No one had undressed. They had simply spread blankets on the ground and gone to sleep. Cailin had wanted to remove her high-laced moccasins, but she was afraid that if she did, she'd be unable to get them back on her swollen feet. She was the only one garbed in European clothing, a plain wool skirt and a bodice of Lincoln green that Moonfeather had given her.

The braves wore little more than loincloths; Cameron Stewart had traded his fine broadcloth shirt and silk waistcoat for a homespun shirt, fringed leather vest, and doeskin breeches. He wore high elkskin moccasins, much the same as her own.

No one would recognize Moonfeather as an English lady of high degree. She looked every inch a barbarian princess in a cream-colored fringed skirt and laced short-sleeved vest and quill-worked moccasins. Her long dark hair was braided into two thick plaits and held in place by a beaded headband. Strings of tiny shells hung from her ears, and her throat was covered with a scarf of brown silk embroidered in exquisite Indian designs. Slung over one shoulder was a bag made of the skin of an animal, complete with the head, and over the other, a light French rifle set with silver inlay. Around her waist, she wore a belt with a sheathed knife and a holstered pistol.

"For a peace woman, ye go well-armed," Cailin had remarked early that morning.

"Those who love peace most are wise to be prepared for violence," Moonfeather had answered smoothly.

Cailin wondered about that now. No one had offered her a weapon, and she'd not thought to ask. Was that because they thought she was too stupid to shoot a rifle?

She'd been given only a small pack to carry. Each of the warriors was weighed down with a heavy bundle of trade goods, but that hadn't slowed down the march. She had begun the morning confident of her ability to walk as far and long as anyone, but by the time they'd stopped to sleep, she was struggling to keep up.

So now, why can't I stop thinking and fall asleep? she agonized. In late afternoon, Joseph had pointed out the trail of the Mohawk war party. Sterling was alive and still with them, Cameron had assured her.

"They mean to take him to their home camp," her father had said.

"For certain?" Cailin had asked him. She'd not missed the warning glance Moonfeather had thrown to the older Scot.

"Nothing's for certain with Indians," he'd admitted. "But he's alive now. I'd stake my hair on it."

"You might do that," Pukasee had said in plain English, and several of the men had laughed.

A mosquito buzzed around Cailin's head, and she rolled over onto her side. Doubtless, she would have been eaten alive by insects if it hadn't been for the oil Moonfeather had given her to rub on her skin. So far, the potion had worked. She hadn't been bitten, but it was still hard to ignore the high-pitched whine.

She tried to clear her mind, but all she could think of was Sterling. She wished she'd attempted to get him loose from the cart wheel . . . insisted they try to escape by the river, or at least hide together in the chimney. Why had she gone along with his plan?

Oh, Sterling, she thought. I was so unfair to ye. He'd offered her nothing but kindness, and she'd thrown his love back in his face.

Now she'd lost him, along with all the others she'd cared for . . .

No. She couldn't think that way . . . she wouldn't. She'd fix her mind on the fact that he was alive and that they would attempt to rescue him. Surely, Moonfeather wouldn't come all this way if she didn't think they had a good chance of success. If she was as important as the Shawnee considered her, wouldn't the Iroquois respect her position as well?

Cailin shifted again, wiggling until she dislodged the stone that dug into her hip. She knew she was drifting . . . suspended in the twilight between consciousness and sleep. Her breathing became deeper, and for an instant, she could smell the sweet perfume of wild strawberries and feel the warm sun on her face.

"Cailin! Cailin, here's some."

Sterling's voice . . . echoing across time.

She extended her hand, and his strong fingers closed around hers . . . real and alive.

"Are you blind, woman, that you can't see those ripe ones there?"

She stared into his face. "Sterling?"

Laughing, he caught her around the waist and tumbled her into the high, soft grass. And the memory possessed her . . . pulling her back to a precious afternoon when all the world stretched out before them . . .

Chapter 20

"*S*terling," she protested between giggles. "How can I pick strawberries with you lying on top of me?"

"Excuses, excuses," he teased, straddling her and leaning his weight on his elbows so that his face was inches from hers . . . so close that she could read the flickering light of desire in his eyes.

He smiled, a lazy, heart-catching smile that made bird wings flutter in the pit of her belly. She tried to wiggle out from under him, but all she succeeded in doing was crushing the grass beneath her, filling her head with the sweet, familiar scent of new-cut hay.

"Scoundrel," she accused. "You promised to help me fill my basket, and you've done nothing but eat the ones I pick." Her skirts were flung indecently up around her knees, and she could feel the hard length of him pressed against her. "Ye set a poor example for the help, dashing about half-dressed." He wore only boots and breeches; his shirt and waistcoat had been discarded somewhere in the meadow. "My kitchen maids spend half their time trying to catch sight of you stripped to the waist, all brawny and full of ginger."

He laughed. "What maids? I hadn't noticed that I'd provided you with any, wife."

"Well, they would do nothing if I had them. A master is supposed to be old and wizened with legs like broom-

sticks and arms as stringy as old mutton." She sighed, se-
cretly admitting to herself that she was the one who
watched him—couldn't keep her eyes off him. Face it, she
told herself, you're smitten with your own husband.

He plucked a clover blossom and brushed it slowly
across her lower lip. "I do have nice legs," he agreed. "I
believe I'll order some clocked stockings to show them off
to advantage next time we're invited to the governor's
house. Maybe in a bright orange."

She giggled, picturing him in orange stockings and
dainty gentleman's shoes instead of the military boots he
favored. "Nay," she said. "Your calves are attraction
enough without decking them like a mating peacock."

He concentrated on tickling her lip with the stalk of clover. "You have strong opinions for a wife," he said.

She made one last futile attempt to squirm away, then
surrendered and relaxed. "Bully," she accused.

He didn't take her seriously for a moment. "For once, I
have you where I want you," he gloated.

The warmth of the earth under her was comforting, and
the bright sun on her face made her so happy inside that
she felt like bursting into song or doing handstands in the
wide expanse of golden buttercups. "Is the sky bigger here
in Maryland?" she asked. "I canna remember ever seeing
it so high or wide in the Highlands. Or so blue . . ."

He traced her upper lip with the clover, and it tickled.
She licked at her lip. "Stop that," she told him.

He obediently removed the offending clover and replaced
it with his lips, kissing her with so much fervor that she
was certain the ground swayed and the carpet of wildflowers swirled around her, all pink and blue and purple.

"Mmm," he murmured when he broke for breath. "You
have a mouth made for kissing, Cailin MacGreggor Gray."

She savored the taste of him, letting her eyes drift shut.
He was, she decided, a very demanding lover. Not that she

minded ... She found it exciting and wonderful that he wanted her so much. "Are all Shawnee men so ... so attentive to their wives?" she asked him as she rubbed his cheek with her open palm, marveling at the smooth texture of his weathered face.

He laughed. "I can't tell you about all Shawnee men, but making a wife happy is considered vital in an honored warrior of my mother's people."

He was toying with the laces of her bodice, and his slow, deliberate touch sent shivers of anticipation rippling up and down her spine. "I think I like that custom," she said softly.

"It's you," he answered. "I've never felt this way about another woman. You make me like this, Cailin."

"It's the same for me," she confided. "You make me feel more alive than I've ever been."

He leaned so close that the tips of their noses touched, and devilment twinkled in his eyes. "Shawnee men cherish their wives," he pronounced solemnly. "And this is one of their secret love practices that drive women mad." He rubbed her nose with his, and she giggled like a twelve-year-old.

"But we came to pick strawberries," she reminded him. She had picked some, along with violets, shooting stars, and wild sweet William. Her basket had overflowed with flowers, even before she'd dropped it.

"So we did, woman." He reached over and dug a plump crimson strawberry from the pile strewn in the clover beside her overturned basket. "As red as your lips," he mused, then used the berry to follow the natural curves of her mouth. "I fear I've made a stain," he said, then touched her lower lip with his tongue. "I'll fix it."

His seeking fingers found the swell of her breast as he licked away the traces of berry juice from her lips.

"Ummm, nice," he whispered, reaching for another strawberry.

Her hands would not be still. She tried not to run her fingers through his hair . . . fought and lost the struggle to keep from twining her fingers through his thick dark locks and pulling him closer as his mouth found her nipple and teased her willing flesh until she moaned with passion.

She strained against him, shamelessly arching her back to mold her hips and thighs to his . . . helping him raise her skirts still higher. His heavy breathing stirred the wanton in her, and she met his probing kisses with open mouth, sucking at his hard tongue and digging her nails over the surface of his nipples until they were as love-swollen as her own.

He took another berry and dripped the juice in the hollow of her throat, then licked away each drop. She gasped. And when he put his mouth to her other breast and began to suckle harder, she writhed wildly, nipping his neck and chest with her teeth, feeling for his throbbing member and freeing it from the confines of his breeches.

He moaned, and a flush of heat washed over her. His hands were doing wonderful things . . . His mouth . . . his mouth . . .

"Don't stop," she whispered hoarsely.

He laughed and crouched lower. "Lie still, woman," he ordered. "There is more berry juice that must be washed from your body."

She wanted to spread her legs to welcome his hard thrusts, but daring tempted her, and she lay back among the wild violets and stared at the clouds overhead. His lips brushed her belly, and she shuddered with longing.

"You have been very naughty," he murmured. "It will take time to wash away—"

Her breathing was coming in broken gasps. Waves of rapture threatened to wash over her, but she held them *back by watching a circling hawk climb higher and higher into the pristine blue sky. Her loins were aflame. She could feel the moistness pooling there. His warm, teasing tongue . . . his hands . . . were driving her mad.*

"Please . . ." she begged him.

"What is it? What do you want?"

"Ye know," she moaned.

"Say it."

She looked full into his proud face with his black devil eyes, his broad jutting nose, high chiseled cheekbones, and square chin, then lower, at his wide shoulders and sinewy chest, bronzed by the sun and sheened with a faint layer of perspiration. His scarred arms bulged with muscle; his hands were strong enough to wield a steel broadax for hours on end, yet gentle enough to make her body tremble with desire. He is a beautiful man, this husband of mine, she thought . . . as beautiful as God's first creation, Adam.

"Say it," he commanded.

Shivers ran under her skin as she allowed her gaze to caress the hollow of his taut belly, the dark shadow of hair below his navel, and the glory of his erect male organ. "I want ye to love me," she whispered.

She opened to receive him as naturally as the flowers around them opened their petals to the sun, taking him joyfully, sharing the beauty and passion of simple, wild lust. She clung to him, crying out with eager abandon and letting loose the primitive fierceness of her own searing passion.

Again and again, they came together, until rapture coursed through her veins in a flood tide of ecstasy. He slowed his thrusts until her intense pleasure became a warm contentment, then slowly stroked and teased her to the brink again. This time, when she let the pulsing storm spiral to culmination, he gave a shout of triumph and rode the wind with her, holding her safely against his heart until they found sweet, velvet serenity together.

Then, he lay back in the tall grass and pulled her down with him, and she listened to the lazy buzz of bees and the melody of birdsong. In the distance, Cailin could hear the sighing of the river and the rustle of leaves in the solitary oak tree that stood near the center of the meadow.

"Did I make you happy, Cailin?" he asked.

"Ye rolled on my berries and mashed them all," she said.

"So I did." A slow grin spread across his face. "And I suppose I have juice stains all over me."

"Ye do."

"There's only one way to fix that," he said. "And it's up to my loving wife to—"

"You're not suggesting that I—" she began.

"Ordering you."

She laughed. "Give me a while to rest and then . . . mayhap . . ."

"I'll take that as a solemn oath," he said, placing her hand on the part of him that had only recently relaxed and was now taking on a new firmness.

"I love you," she said.

He gave a mock growl and pretended to bite her neck. "You're sweet enough to eat, woman."

She put her hand on his chest and nestled close to him. "Hold me," she begged him. "Hold me like this and never let me go."

"Cailin, I—"

"Cailin. Cailin, wake up."

It was a man's voice, but no longer Sterling's. Confused, she blinked her eyes. She could still feel her husband's arms around her, but the sensation was fast fading. She didn't want it to stop.

"Cailin, it's time to go."

Cameron leaned over her and shook her gently.

"I'm awake," she said. But she wasn't, not really. She'd been dreaming, and the dream was better than reality. She wanted to stay there in the meadow with Sterling. Instead, she rose, shouldered her pack, and took her place in line.

They walked in almost total darkness, following a narrow game trail that seemed nonexistent to Cailin. They kept going as the stars twinkled out, one by one, and a purple mauve spread across the eastern sky.

By mid-morning, heavy clouds had gathered overhead. Cailin concentrated on putting one foot in front of another. She couldn't forget her dream ... or the overwhelming sensation of Sterling's arms around her.

Have I lost him forever? she wondered. She began to feel the same slight nausea she'd experienced the morning before. She swallowed, determined not to give in to her weakness.

Could it be possible? Her breasts were unusually tender, but then she was sore all over. The lack of appetite and the occasional dizziness might be signs of pregnancy, or they could be just the lingering results of her ordeal.

She had suspected that she might be carrying Sterling's child before she left the Shawnee camp, but she hadn't said anything to Cameron or Moonfeather. If they guessed, they might send her back, even now.

She did want a baby desperately. If Sterling was dead, it would give her something of his to hold on to—some part of him that she could keep.

How could she have changed so much in so short a time? She'd convinced herself that a child would bind her to Sterling ... would prevent her from returning to Scotland and fulfilling her duty to her family. That wasn't true. A babe would give her something to live for ... someone to cherish. She would remember Sterling whenever she looked into the laughing face of their child.

"Cailin." Cameron touched her arm.

"Oh." She jumped.

He smiled. "You were about to walk on without us. We're stopping to eat," he said.

She thought she was too tired to be hungry, but she'd not admit it to him or let Moonfeather, a woman old enough to be her mother, outwalk her.

To her surprise, the Delaware Indian Lachpi led the way up a steep brush-covered hill to a cave. Joseph and Pukasee were already there. They'd built a fire, and were roasting some type of wild fowl over it.

Gratefully, Cailin sank down against a far wall. The floor was bare rock, but she didn't care. Cameron went to the back of the cave and returned with a brimming cup of cold water.

"There's a spring back there," he said. "Drink this."

She took the offering and drank. The water was clear and sweet, the best she'd ever tasted. "Thank you," she said.

The rest of the group crouched around the fire and began to share the meat. Kitate seemed as taciturn as ever, but the others laughed and talked. She felt strangely at ease with these half-naked Indian warriors. Not a single one had looked at her with lust in his eyes or had offered her any affront. Instead, she'd been shown nothing but good humor and kindness, even when she was certain she was slowing the march down.

Ake and Joseph began to talk quietly in the Indian language. Koke-wah, the boy, came to sit near Cailin. He smiled shyly but didn't speak.

"Koke-wah is a new man," Moonfeather said. "This is his first journey since he became an adult."

Color tinted the youth's tanned cheeks.

"He completed his trial of manhood only weeks ago," Moonfeather explained.

Koke-wah spoke softly in Algonquian, and the peace woman translated. "Koke-wah wants you to know that the bear is his totem. He has asked his spirit guide to protect you as well."

"Thank you," Cailin said.

Koke-wah ducked his head and blushed, then whispered something else to Moonfeather.

"You have an admirer," Moonfeather said. "Koke-wah wants to know if you have any unmarried sisters. It seems he is thinking of taking a wife."

"Tell him I said he is too young for marriage," Cailin replied.

The boy obviously understood, because he wiggled uncomfortably, then made a show of standing up, stretching, and walking to the mouth of the cave.

Cameron took his place and sat cross-legged, beside Cailin.

"I hope I didn't hurt his feelings," she said.

"He'll get over it." He pursed his lips. "I'd like to talk with you awhile," he said. "Regardless of what you think of me, there are things you need to know."

Instantly, she stiffened. "I appreciate your concern, but I've no wish to—"

"Patience," Moonfeather said, coming to sit with them. "We've time to pass. We'll rest here until dark. The rain is coming, and no one will see our fire." She handed Cailin a browned drumstick. "Eat. Ye canna keep up if ye do not eat."

Cailin bit into the meat. Even without salt, it was delicious. She was hungrier than she thought, but still, she didn't miss noticing the meaningful look that passed between Cameron and Moonfeather. "You two seem to be old friends," she said.

"We are," he agreed.

Cailin wished that Cameron was not so charming. It was hard to dislike him, and she wanted to. He'd abandoned her when she was a babe. She didn't need a father now. It was years too late for him to ease his conscience.

"Cameron has been my friend as long as I can remember," the Indian woman said. "I was a small child when he first told me the story of the Eye of Mist. Have ye never wondered why it was given to you?"

She had, but she wouldn't admit it. She'd not make it easy for this man who'd forced himself into her life—who wanted more than she could give him.

"It was my mother's," Cameron said, "and her mother's before her. Always passed down through the daughters, for two thousand years and more."

"A magic necklace," Moonfeather added softly in her lilting English. "A thing of great power, come down to you from long ago when the world was young and innocent."

"Pictish gold," Cameron continued. "Did you—"

"I dinna believe in fairy tales," Cailin said flatly.

"Then why did you keep the necklace?" he asked. "It's solid gold—worth a fortune. There must have been times when you were tempted to sell it."

"She could no more sell the Eye of Mist than her

right arm," Moonfeather said. "You felt the power in it, didn't you?" she asked.

Cailin glanced at Moonfeather. She felt drawn to this mysterious woman, but she was still an enigma. It was unnerving to hear Moonfeather's distinct Highland burr, and she could not shake the feeling that they had met before. But that was impossible. Cailin had always believed the American Colonies were full of wild beasts and savages. To find such a great lady in an Indian village was beyond her comprehension.

"You must believe what we tell you," Moonfeather said.

"I realize that ye mean well, but the legend concerning the Eye of Mist is nothing but a story. It isn't true. It's an old and beautiful necklace, nothing more," Cailin said.

"Blessed," Moonfeather insisted. "Did ye ken? Those who possess the necklace are granted one wish, any wish—even unto the giving of life or—"

Cailin stood up. "No more." She snatched the chain off over her head and tossed it into Cameron's lap. "Here, take it back," she said. "I don't want it. It's given me nothing but pain."

He shook his head. "I can't take it back, Cailin. It belongs to you. To my true daughter, my mother said. It was hers, and whatever you think of me, she was your grandmother. You carry her blood and her fire. You would have liked each other, you and my mother." He pressed it back into her hand.

"Where we are going," Moonfeather said, "is a place of danger. You may need the Eye of Mist. It may make the difference between your survival and—"

The amulet pulsed in her hand. She wanted to

throw it to the floor, but she couldn't. Slowly, she dropped it over her head again. "I'll keep it for your . . . for my grandmother's sake. But you have to know that whatever power it might have possessed, it's gone now. I tried to use it when my mother died. I sat with her and watched as she died in childbirth . . . as her life's blood gushed from her body. I called on the power of your precious necklace then, and it didn't work. My mother died just the same." Hot tears stung her eyes, and she blinked them away. "So ye see, I dinna believe in magic anymore. And sometimes . . . sometimes, I'm not even sure I believe in God."

"He's real enough," Moonfeather assured her. "And no matter what you believe, He will never stop loving you."

Chapter 21

It was the first week of July by Sterling's reckoning when the deer trail widened to a well-worn path. His Mohawk captors had paused in midmorning to repaint their faces and bodies with red and black stripes, and Ohneya had fashioned his eerie skull face with the aid of a lady's mirror stolen from a Dutch farmhouse.

Fresh scalps dangled from Ohneya's belt; three brown, one russet, another white ash-blond. The stench turned Sterling's stomach. Two days running in the hot summer sun with only brief smoking over a campfire made for poor curing.

He had not witnessed the deaths of the Dutch farmer, his wife, and his servants, but he had heard the screams of the women and the ceaseless wail of a baby. The babe was still crying when the war party had jogged away. Sterling wondered if a quick death would not have been more merciful for the infant.

One Mohawk carried a prisoner on his shoulders, a sweet-faced boy of six or seven. The child had not wept or uttered a single word, but his stare was vacant. Sterling had whispered to him at the morning stop, but received no reaction. Either the small captive didn't understand English or the shock of what he'd seen had caused the temporary loss of his wits.

Sterling was heavily laden with booty taken from

the farmhouse and the isolated cabin the war party had destroyed a week earlier, but he had no trouble keeping pace with the Mohawk. His strength had returned in the long days of walking, and despite his captors' efforts to starve him, he'd managed to snatch enough meat to keep himself from suffering.

Yes, he mused, it was either the last of June or the beginning of July. The first part of the forced march had been hazy; he couldn't be certain how long he'd been out of his head. But he'd counted the days since his mind had cleared. July 3, he decided. Right or wrong, it would give him a date to reason from.

Ohneya stopped short and emptied his rifle into the air. His companions were quick to imitate their leader, and Sterling found the barrage of firing near deafening. Off to the right, out of sight, an answering volley of muskets and then cheering echoed through the trees.

The war party began to chant at the top of their lungs. Someone produced a small hand drum; another brave struck the flat of a tomahawk against the stock of his rifle. A woman carrying an armload of wood appeared from the forest. She dropped her firewood and fell in behind the last brave, dancing from side to side and clapping her hands in time with the drum. Ohneya strode proudly in front, chest out, chin up, grotesque painted features immobile.

The path dipped into a gully, then climbed a rough grade to open into a clearing. Sterling felt his heart plummet as he sighted the high stockade surrounding the Mohawk town. Double walls of upright logs honed to deadly points followed the circular course of a swift-moving river. Another river, or a second channel of the first, came in from the right so that the palisade was surrounded by water except for a narrow strip of grass that jutted out at the front. That tongue of land was guarded by a triangular wall of logs with no visible entrance. Hundreds of wooden spikes of various lengths were set into the earth at an angle, to form a wicked barrier around the perimeter of the fortified town and to guard the land approach.

Women and children came running from the cornfields. Men waded the river, waving and shouting cries of welcome. Ohneya and his warriors pretended not to hear them and continued their fierce song as the war party moved on toward the village. More people spilled out of the palisade and clustered around the returning braves.

Sterling watched in silence as a dark-skinned woman in a blue dress ran to Ohneya and hugged him. A boy shouted "ra-ken-iha," the Mohawk word for "father."

The war party reached the crossing and began to wade across the stretch of river in front of the stockade. Icy water lapped up to Sterling's chest, but the bottom was gravel and offered firm footing. He was still naked, but the swift current felt good as it washed away the dust and sores of travel. Taking advantage of the river, and not knowing when he'd be given water again, he lowered his head and drank. A brave behind him hit him in the center of the back with the butt of his rifle. Sterling pretended to stumble and went under, reveling in the cold, clear water.

Another brave grabbed Sterling's carrying strap and yanked him up. Sterling resumed his place in line and tried not to show emotion as a half-grown girl in braids splattered an egg on his bare chest. Instantly, a group of jeering children surrounded him. One boy dashed in and whipped him across the buttocks with a switch; another flung a stone that glanced off his elbow.

Cur dogs ran barking at him, then slunk close to growl and snap at his ankles. He kicked at the nearest animal. An old woman beat the dogs off with a beanpole, and when the animals fled yipping, she used the pole to try to trip him. Sterling jumped the stick and laughed, setting off a flood of verbal abuse from the hag and other gapers.

As the procession neared the vee of logs, Sterling saw that a curtain wall concealed the entrance. He had to crouch over and squeeze through a low doorway, then zigzag through a narrow passageway to the outer stockade. Two reinforced gates led into the town, which covered more than an acre of ground. Rows of bark-covered longhouses stretched in precise patterns inside a third fence of six-foot-high stakes woven tightly together with vines.

Ohneya led the way past a group of eight multiple-dwelling houses on one side and seven on the other, all marked over the doorways with clan symbols. A blind ancient, so old that Sterling couldn't guess if he was male or female, sat in the shade of one hut smoking a pipe while babies played in the dust by his feet. Turkeys scratched for insects, and a tame owl swiveled its head around to stare as the war party strode by.

The deep boom of a log drum echoed through the town. Everywhere, the people left their chores to come and gaze at the returning warriors and prisoners. Sterling kept his eyes fixed on the center of Ohneya's back, but he could not ignore the smells of drying fish, Indian tobacco, and baking bread.

The village of his Mohawk enemies smelled surprisingly like the Shawnee towns of his boyhood.

Sterling swallowed the lump in his throat. So many years wiped away in an instant. A small child ran out of a house and was quickly snatched up into the arms of a pretty Iroquois woman who could have been Sterling's mother. Until she spoke ... Not the soft lilt of Algonquian but the guttural tones of the Mohawk tongue.

Most of the rough Iroquois phrases he could not understand—but some meanings lingered in the shadows of his memory, left over from a grandfather's stories of captivity among the Cayuga. *Prisoner. Englishman. Kill.*

The war chief, Ohneya, had ceased to sing. Now, he was boasting loudly of his deeds as he strode across a wide, hard-packed dirt street, and then led them past another cluster of longhouses bearing wolf effigies. In the middle of the town was a large open square with a charred post set in the center. Sterling saw three drummers near the torture stake. One man beat a repetitive rhythm on the hollow log drum, while two others were just taking their places beside a large round water drum with a taut-stretched, painted skin cover.

At the far end of the clearing stood an imposing longhouse of logs. Seated on mats in front of the structure was a solemn group of elaborately dressed Iroquois elders. Ohneya made one complete circle of the square in what Sterling could only assume was a final display of his triumphant procession before coming to a halt in front of the dignitaries.

A gray-haired man in a red military coat and tall beaver hat rose to his feet and began to speak to the war party, obviously praising Ohneya and his followers. The villagers crowded close, cheering whenever the sachem paused in his oratory.

Suddenly, a crow screeched, and a hunched figure in a carved wooden mask scurried from the longhouse. He was dressed all in black with a red waist-length horsehair wig. The mask, painted red and black, was a grotesque oversized caricature of a human face with round exaggerated eyes, a broad nose, and hideous teeth.

The onlookers shrank back and grew silent. Only the war party and the men and women on the mats seemed unaffected by the strange apparition.

The medicine man stared directly at Sterling and shook a turtle-shell rattle. *"O-neg-we-a-sa!"* he hissed.

The word echoed in Sterling's brain. *Blood.* The masked man shook his rattle again and drove his staff of office—a black-painted stick with the carving of a raven on the top—into the soft earth. He left the staff quivering there and began a curious side to side shuffling around Sterling. He circled twice, then produced a handful of ashes, seemingly from thin air, and tossed them into Sterling's face.

Sterling had closed his eyes when the medicine man had thrown the ashes. Now he opened them and glared back at the face behind the mask.

A child began to cry and was hustled away. As the two moved through the crowd, people muttered. A woman cried out the name Jit-sho, and another Mohawk word that Sterling recognized as meaning "shaman."

The medicine man, whom Sterling now assumed must be this Jit-sho, brought the carved face close to his and whispered ominously.

Sterling summoned up his entire Mohawk vocabulary. *"Jit-sho, wah-et-ke-a,"* he replied. *"Wah-et-ke-a o-ne-soh-rono."* Jit-sho, you're an ugly devil!

The medicine man jumped back as though he'd

been hit, and a murmur rippled through the war party. Ohneya spun around and struck Sterling across the face with the flat of his tomahawk. He fell to his knees. Ohneya swung the weapon over his head to deliver a death blow.

The old high chief in the tall beaver hat spoke.

Ohneya halted in mid-swing, muttered something in Mohawk, and turned away. Sterling got to his feet and spat blood from his split lip.

"How is it that an Englishman speaks in the language of our brothers the Cayuga with a Shawnee voice? And how is it that he knows the name of our honored shaman, Jit-sho?"

Sterling had known his accent was atrocious. He was surprised that anyone understood him at all. "My father is English," he explained. "My mother was daughter to the Shawnee. At her fireside, I learned some of your language from one who had been a captive of the Cayuga."

"So." The gray-haired leader turned to the woman beside him and said something in Mohawk. She whispered back. He glanced at a second woman sitting two positions down on his right. "*Egh-ni-ta?*"

She nodded. "Shawnee mother," she said in bad English. "Shawnee son."

The medicine man spat out an objection, but the old chief shook his head. "You are Shawnee," he said to Sterling. "Now let us see if you are a man." He looked at Ohneya. "Make for him a gauntlet," he said. "We will see if mother's blood or father's flows stronger."

Shrill cries rang from the throats of men and women alike as the Mohawk hurried to form a double line down the left side of the open square. Armed with lengths of firewood, whips, and war clubs, they laughed and taunted him, waving their weapons and daring him to pass between them.

Someone cut the straps holding the pack to Sterling's back, and the heavy bundle tumbled to the ground. He strained against the leather thongs that bound his wrists behind his back, but they held tight. Ohneya shoved him toward the howling column. Only men had taken their places in the game, but the women would miss none of the sport. They rushed at him, shouting insults and pointing rudely.

"I want his gourds," Ohneya's woman called to him in English.

"And the rest of it?" the war chief retorted. "Shall I pluck it for you, wife?"

"Yes!" Her companions shrieked with laughter. "I'll make you a tobacco pouch of it," she promised.

"Run swift and straight," the sachem advised.

Ohneya's wife darted in and jabbed Sterling sharply in the ribs with the butt of her wooden corn pestle. "Run well," she echoed. "If you do, we will burn you at the stake."

"And if you do not," Ohneya said, "we will skin you alive and then burn you until your eyes roast like chestnuts on a winter fire."

Sterling glanced back at the chief. The fear had left him, and he felt strangely calm, almost as if he were watching another man face the Mohawk gauntlet. "What is your name, sir?" he demanded.

"Bear Dancer."

Sterling nodded in respect.

"How is it that you do not know our leader?" the masked man hissed. "And who are you, a death-marked slave, to question him? What use has a dead man for names?"

Sterling gave the medicine man a cold stare.

"Among the Shawnee, knowing a man's name gives you power over him. Is it not so, Jit-sho, mighty shaman of the Mohawk?"

"Who told you my name?" The ugly mask bobbed up and down as if the man behind it quivered with rage.

"I have a powerful spirit guide," Sterling answered. "Perhaps I learned your name—"

"Enough!" Jit-sho said. "You are nothing, and you will die as nothing."

"You are wrong," Sterling answered softly. "I am Na-nata Ki-tehi, Warrior Heart of the Shawnee, and I will teach the Iroquois how to die like a man."

Cailin shifted her shoulder pack and looked nervously around her. That morning, not long after they'd started the day's journey, she'd seen a huge wolf standing in the trail in front of her. Lachpi, the Delaware, was walking at the head of the column. When the beast appeared without warning, directly ahead of him, she'd tried to cry out a warning. To her dismay, no sound came from her throat, and then the animal leaped into the trees and was gone as silently as it had come.

She'd been so shaken that she'd stopped short in her tracks and pointed. To her dismay, Lachpi claimed he hadn't seen a wolf, and neither had anyone else.

"You're tired," Koke-wah said.

Ake had made a joke. "The white woman sees wolves behind every bush." No one had laughed.

"Whatever it was, it's gone," Moonfeather said.

They had resumed the march. For several hours, Cailin scanned the trail and the forest. She'd nearly convinced herself that they were right, that she was tired, when she saw the same wolf crouched on a rock overlooking the gully they were traversing.

"There," she'd called to Moonfeather, pointing.

"What? What did you see?" the older woman asked.

"A wolf. It was right there. Didn't you see it? Didn't any of you see it?" she'd demanded of Cameron and the others.

Pukasee shook his head. Joseph glanced at Kitate, and the dark man frowned and muttered something to his companions in Shawnee.

"We saw nothing," Lachpi said.

"I'm not mistaken," Cailin insisted. "I saw a wolf watching us."

"Wolves are naturally curious," Cameron said.

But as they continued on, Cailin couldn't help wondering if her mind was playing tricks on her.

At noon, Moonfeather called for a rest beside a stream. They ate dried meat and berries, and a little fish caught the evening before. Cailin washed and dried her feet in the stream. They were fully healed now, hard and callused from the days of marching. She felt strong, as though she could walk as long as anyone. But then, sitting in the shade, she drifted off to sleep and dreamed of the big wolf.

Mist surrounded her, making the forest unreal. She could hear the wail of bagpipes and the roar of cannon. Yet somehow, when the boughs parted, the face that appeared was not human, but that of a gray wolf. She tried to scream, tried to run, but she was frozen. Helplessly, she watched as the animal padded closer and looked into her eyes.

For a moment, she had the strangest feeling that the ghostly specter would speak to her, and she found herself waiting to hear what it would say. "What? What is it, brother?" *she asked, not with her voice but with her mind.*

And the answer came back in the same way, not in words, but in curiously pulsing thought. "Na-nata Ki-tehi. Warrior Heart. He is in great danger. Lend him your strength."

"What strength?" *she begged silently.* "How can I help him? How—"

She blinked. An acute awareness spread through her body. She was conscious of the weight of her limbs, of the texture of the gravel under her bare leg, of the breeze kissing her cheek. She looked around quickly, trying to guess how much time she had lost, but it must have been only seconds. Pukasee was still scraping the tobacco from his pipe, and Moonfeather was licking crumbs off her lip as she had been doing before.

Cailin was afraid to mention the dream. Terrified, she studied every turn of the trail, every shadow for the image of the wolf, but it didn't return.

Minutes passed, then an hour. She thought that her madness had passed as her heartbeat slowed to normal, and her anxiety began to fade. She was walking behind Joseph with her father following her. Then, abruptly, she stumbled on the trail and fell to her knees, bringing the whole party to a halt.

Her father was the first to reach her. He put an arm around her shoulders to help her up, but she pushed him away. "No," she stammered. "No." She covered her face with her hands and tried to shut out the waking dream that consumed her.

This time she wasn't asleep. She was wide awake, but she could no longer see Joseph, Moonfeather, and the others who had been walking ahead of her.

Instead, she saw a hard-packed field of dirt beneath a

blazing sun. Drums pounded in her head, drowning every-thing but the fierce cries of Indians.

She caught sight of Sterling. Running. Running. She felt blows on her arms ... her back. Something tangled around her ankles, and she fell to the ground. "Sterling!" she screamed. A red film clouded her eyes. She felt the weight of a heavy object strike her head.

"Cailin!" The voice came from far away. It was not Sterling's voice, so she shut it out.

"Sterling?" She could no longer see him for the blood. Blindly, she reached out with both hands.

And found him.

His hands gripped hers and held on.

"Cailin." As had happened with the wolf, she heard him in her mind, not with her ears. "Cailin, help me."

"I'm here," she answered, clinging to his fingers. "I'm here."

And then a weird red and black face surrounded by a mat of crimson red hair peered at her. Closer and closer it came, until it filled her vision, and she felt Sterling's hold begin to weaken. "Sterling!" she screamed. Then he slipped away, and Stygian blackness took her.

Chapter 22

❧

Sterling stumbled and fell to his knees under a torrent of blows. Nearly blinded by his own blood, he fought excruciating pain and the ingrained Indian acceptance of his own fate.

This is how it ends, he thought. I'm dying.

Black clouds of smoke and ash swirled across his field of reason. Another object slammed into his head. He continued to struggle, but the heart had gone out of him.

There is no shame in dying an honorable death, the stoic voice in his brain intoned. *A warrior's death, a death that the Iroquois will sing of on long winter nights.*

Then another entity spoke, not as loud as the first, but utterly compelling. It was a voice that he had heard only once before, long ago, during his youth vision. "Open your eyes, Na-nata Ki-tehi!"

Sterling did not have the strength to oppose that command. He opened his eyes and looked directly into the face of a gray wolf.

With the raw power of a lighting strike, a firestorm leaped between them. And in the jagged bolt of energy, Sterling felt Cailin's touch and heard her cry his name.

And took from her the will to live.

With a last mighty surge of strength, he heaved himself to his feet amid the howling blood-thirst of the mob. His wrist bonds snapped, and he seized a club from the hands of the nearest Mohawk warrior and laid the man senseless with his own weapon. It wasn't until the brave was falling that Sterling realized that he'd defeated Ohneya.

Sterling had little time to gloat. There were still more Iroquois screaming for his blood. With a shout of triumph, he waded into them.

The element of surprise gave him the precious seconds it took to regain his reason. He sprang forward, blocking the descent of a spear shaft, elbowing the youth wielding it, and twisting left to jab another warrior in the pit of his stomach with the end of the knobbed club.

Strike. Twist. Duck. Swing. Sterling moved down the shifting channel of the gauntlet with the vengeance of a Greek hero, oblivious to the beating he was taking . . . until he reached the far end of the line and there were no more opponents to face.

He gazed around him in bewilderment, then caught sight of the torture stake. He reached it in three strides, set his back to the solid oak post, threw his hands high over his head, and defied them all with a chilling Shawnee war whoop.

Instantly, the scattered throng converged on him in knots of outraged fury. "Kill him!" a woman screamed.

"He cheated! He took Ohneya's war club!"

"Death to the Shawnee dog!"

A graying elder shook his fist skyward. "Burn him!"

The masked shaman snaked out of the seething crowd. "I smell a witch!" he cried, waving his staff of office. "We saw the prisoner fall to his knees. No mortal could rise against such odds. Only one in league with demons could leap up and complete the gauntlet. I tell you, this is foul Shawnee witchcraft!"

"Burn the demon!" A brave staggered forward with swollen face and forearm bent unnaturally. "I, Rax-aa, saw ghosts around him. I will light the fire!"

"My husband! My husband is dead!" screamed Ohneya's wife. "He is a witch! He knew our shaman's name, didn't he? Who but a witch would know?"

Ohneya lay moaning in the dust, obviously still very much alive, but the fact did not dampen his wife's ardor for Sterling's scalp.

"Look at your war chief!" she wailed. "See your fallen leader. Will the Mohawk let such a witch live?"

Jit-sho shook his turtle-shell rattle at Sterling. "Niyoh the Creator cries for this demon's blood!" he shouted. "His nostrils long for the scent of burning flesh! Will the Mohawk suffer a witch to live?"

Two men helped Ohneya to his feet. Through bloodied lips, he mumbled something and then pushed through the angry mob. "This white-skinned Shawnee ran the gauntlet with dishonor," Ohneya croaked. "Give me a knife, and I will cut his manparts—"

Sterling silenced him with a scornful laugh. "Is this the war chief of the Mohawk? This pissing dog's vomit who hides behind his woman's skirts?"

The shaman hissed in disapproval and shook his rattle again, but many villagers cast sidelong glances at Ohneya.

"His insults are but the foolish bleating of a dead man. He broke the rules," Ohneya said. "He tricked me with black magic and stole my weapon. He is not worthy—"

"Bear Dancer will say who is worthy," the old sachem said in English. A pathway opened for him, and he came to stand near Sterling. "Ohneya thinks to speak for the Mohawk. When I am dead, he may speak for you. But here I stand, and you will listen to my words."

"Listen to Bear Dancer," Sterling said. "Not to the unworthy one who seeks power. A coward who murders infants and does battle against helpless women. A coward who thinks to take Bear Dancer's staff. A dung-eating weakling who dares not fight a man."

"What man?" Ohneya's wife shouted. "I see no man. Only a Shawnee witch." She put out her hands to Bear Dancer. "Father, I am your only child. Will you see my husband wronged and not take vengeance? Burn the witch, I say!"

"Yes, burn him," cried one of Ohneya's supporters.

"Bear Dancer is old," Ohneya said. "My wife's father's heart has become as soft as his head. Listen to our shaman, not this Shawnee offal."

Bear Dancer turned to glare at Jit-sho. "What say you, mighty shaman? Do you fear this Shawnee?"

The little man stiffened; the wooden mask tilted on an angle. His moccasined feet began to step back and forth as an eerie flood of garble issued from the snarling mouth. Then the spew of syllables became a high-pitched chant. "Jit-sho fears no witch. Jit-sho fears no demon. Jit-sho is mightier than the storm."

The circle around Sterling tightened. Warriors and a few women drew closer, while other mothers tugged their children away.

Overhead, thunder grumbled. Someone looked up and pointed. What had been a cloudless sky had darkened.

"Witchcraft," a stout woman moaned.

"See! The storm comes to do battle."

Another whispered. "Jit-sho challenges the elements."

The wind began to pick up, forming spouts of whirling dust that rose to the height of a longhouse. A black feather came loose from Jit-sho's carved mask and tumbled away. A half-grown girl screamed and fled toward the huts.

Thunderheads rolled in from the north. The wind gusted and began to blow in earnest, sending drying racks, mats, and household articles spinning.

"Jit-sho boasts that he is mightier than the storm!" Sterling shouted.

Lightning cracked. To the north, a fiery finger reached down to shatter a pine tree.

More villagers ran from the square to shelter. Old Bear Dancer ignored the wind and stood staring at Ohneya. "Is my daughter's husband afraid to fight the Shawnee witch?" he demanded. "He says that I am old. I say that a Mohawk war chief should fear no one—man or ghost."

A wolf howled nearby, so close that men looked around nervously and women clutched their children.

"Fight me!" Sterling dared. "Fight me, Ohneya, or prove that your courage is water and you are not worthy to call yourself Mohawk."

"You will die!" Ohneya screamed. "You will not trick your way out of the torture stake! Your flesh will—"

"Do you fear him?" Bear Dancer said.

"No, but—"

Bear Dancer's head snapped around, and he looked into Sterling's eyes. "If you are a witch, Shawnee, you must die. I do not know if what you did in the gauntlet was bravery or treachery. This I know. You will fight Ohneya to the death."

"And if the witch bests Ohneya?" Jit-sho shrieked. "What then, noble Bear Dancer?"

The old chief's lined face grew stern. "Then we will consign him to the fire and eat his roasted heart to share among us the courage of a worthy Shawnee warrior."

Her father's face was the first one that Cailin saw when she opened her eyes. She threw her arms around him, desperately wanting the comfort of human touch, forgetting for the moment that she had vowed to show him no affection. Forgetting that he could never be more than a father in name to her.

"Shhh, shhh," he crooned soothingly. " 'Tis all right, lass. 'Tis all right."

His arms were strong despite his years, and it was easy to lean against him. The images in her mind were not so easy to dispel. "I dreamed . . ." she stammered. "But it wasn't a dream." She pushed back and met his worried gaze. "Am I losing my mind?"

"Did you see the wolf again?" he asked.

"No . . . yes." She shook her head and covered her face with her hands. "It's all mixed up. A nightmare—but I was wide awake. I swear it."

"Ye had a waking vision," Moonfeather said, laying a cool hand on Cailin's shoulder. She smiled. "Do not fear the power. It is the gift of your amulet." She glanced at Cameron. "I think this is best spoken of between Cailin and this woman, don't you?"

He nodded. "Talk to Moonfeather," he said. "If anyone can ease your soul, she can."

Cailin let go of him and slowly let out her breath.

Cameron touched her cheek. "It will be all right,

lass. I promise. Listen to what she has to say with an open mind." He got up and motioned the men out of earshot.

Cailin rubbed her eyes. "You must think I'm crazy," she said to Moonfeather.

"Nay, I dinna think that. Tell me what happened today. Tell it all," the Indian woman urged. "From the beginning." She unslung a water skin and offered it to Cailin. "Come, we will sit over here on this rock in the shade, and you will say what ye saw."

Cailin's legs were shaky, and she was grateful for the solid granite. Murmuring thanks, she took a sip. The liquid was warm, but it wet her dry mouth. "I can go on," she said. "We are wasting daylight when we should be walking."

"This is more important," Moonfeather replied, clasping Cailin's hand in hers. "Tell it, leaving nothing out."

"If you're sure," Cailin said. She glanced toward the men, but they had taken off their packs and settled down to wait a distance away. "It began with the wolf," she said. "I saw him on the trail . . ."

The peace woman listened without comment as she related the strange events of the day. "I think I'm with child," Cailin said in apology. "I've heard that it addles the brain for some women."

Moonfeather smiled. "No, you are not mad. This is something very different. Tell me more about the face ye saw in your vision. Was it human, or could it have been a wooden mask? Something like this?" She picked up a stick and drew a crude image in the sand.

"Yes," Cailin agreed excitedly. "Only there was . . . hair. Not real hair, but a red stringy mass around the face." She took a deep breath and let it out slowly. "Could it be the heat, or do ye think I'm fevered?"

"No," Moonfeather assured her. "You are not ill. You have the sight. Surely, a Scotswoman has heard of—"

"Yes, of course. But I never had it before. Why—"

" 'Tis your love for Sterling."

"Ye mean I saw something in the future. Or was it the past?" A sudden chill passed through Cailin. "He's dead, isn't he? I saw him fall." She shook her head. "Nay, more than that. I *felt* him fall."

"Past, future, they are the same," Moonfeather murmured. "Your ties to him are very strong. That's why you felt as though you were there with him. But I dinna think he is dead. We must hurry. The face you saw was an Iroquois mask, probably a shaman's magic."

Gooseflesh rose up on Cailin's arms. "Magic. Shamans. What's a shaman?"

"A physician. Medicine man. They also deal in magic, sometimes what you would call black magic. Good ones have power."

Cailin's eyes widened. "They're in league with the devil?"

Moonfeather laughed. "Indians don't believe in the white man's devil. That's not to say we don't have a few demons of our own. But if the Creator is all-powerful, which He is, how can a devil steal away His souls? The Shawnee believe that evil or good comes from a man's heart. The Great Spirit can only be good and offer good. If we choose to turn our backs on what we know is right, we can go astray. But we cannot blame our fall on a devil. Each man or woman is responsible for his or her own actions."

Cailin pulled her hand free and ran her fingers

through her hair. She was feeling much better physically, but all this talk of sight and magic was as hard to fathom as her waking dream. "But you said these ... shamans ... can do black magic."

Moonfeather chuckled. "There is no black magic or white. There is only magic. And a few tricks. Most shamans I have known use more knowledge of men's weaknesses than real magic."

"What about the wolf? There was a real wolf that came to our plantation before we built the house. At least, I thought it was real. This looks like the same animal, but that's impossible. And now, I'm dreaming that the beast talks to me."

The Indian woman's eyes narrowed. "The wolf is real, but I believe it is Sterling's spirit guide, not a flesh and blood wolf. It is a powerful totem."

"A ghost wolf." Cailin shook her head. "I don't believe it."

Moonfeather shrugged. "You don't have to." She hesitated and then went on. "But ye should know that Sterling dreamed of you ... long ago, on his vision quest."

"How do you—"

"It is my business to know such things. I am peace woman to the Shawnee. Every boy must seek a spirit guide to become a man. He goes off alone to a high place for days to fast and pray. To each new man comes a vision and a spirit protector. Sterling saw you."

"Impossible. That must have been years ago. I was in Scotland ... still a child."

"Yet, he saw the woman you would become. His journey was longer than most, but you led him home to his spirit wolf protector. Now the circle is complete, the vision whole."

Cailin got up and shook her head. "This is non-sense. Indian superstition."

"Perhaps," Moonfeather agreed. She spread her hands gracefully. "Perhaps not. You did see the wolf and hear his words of wisdom."

"It was a nightmare," Cailin insisted stubbornly.

"In any case, the time grows short," Moonfeather said. "You are strong enough to walk?"

"Aye. Of course. I'm sorry if my weakness made me—"

"Visions come to the chosen. You are unused to seeing them. Next time, it won't be so frightening."

"There won't be a next time."

"Perhaps," Moonfeather said.

The men were making ready to continue the march. Cailin looked from one bronze face to the other, wondering how she'd come so far from the glens and lochs of Scotland. A few more years, and she'd begin to believe all this nonsense about ghost wolves and amulets that could raise the dead.

The first rumblings of thunder rolled across the hills, and Cameron shaded his eyes and looked up at the clouds. "It looks like a bad one coming. Maybe we'd best look for shelter."

Cailin moved close to him. "Thank you . . . for what you did . . . before. I don't know what to say. Nothing like that has ever happened to me before."

"What did your . . . What did Moonfeather say about what you saw?"

"Nonsense, really. She's as superstitious as the rest of them."

Cameron's brow wrinkled. "She's a wise woman. I'd take most of what she says as gospel."

Cailin forced a smile. "If you'd heard it, you wouldn't say that. Spirit wolves and—"

He sighed. "I pride myself on being an educated man, but I've lived long enough to know that life isn't as simple as it seems. There are things and things under heaven, lass. Moonfeather is a rare person. At home, we'd call her fey. My grandmother was like that. Oh, none dared call her witch, but we all knew she had something. She foretold her own death."

"An old woman with the sight is a far cry from ghost wolves," Cailin argued.

He shrugged. "Come, lass, it will be raining buckets any minute. Let's get under cover while we can."

The entire group took refuge under an overhanging ledge while the storm raged. One hour passed, and then two. Cailin ate, and slept in short catnaps. Rain fell into the night, but finally, the wind ceased to blow and the deluge tapered off.

Before they set out again, Moonfeather changed into a dress of white doeskin, adorned with tiny shells and porcupine quills. She slipped a cascade of minute silver bells into each earlobe and settled a white embroidered headband over her forehead. Kitate shouldered her pack so that she was unburdened as they headed north through the dripping forest.

Cailin watched the trees on either side of the trail for wolf eyes in the night, but she saw nothing. They walked steadily until the first light, when Cailin saw that they were following the shoreline of a wide lake.

"Are we getting close?" she asked Moonfeather.

The Indian woman nodded. "A few more days if Inu-msi-ila-fe-wanu smiles on us. We are in the heart of Iroquois country now."

"But we haven't seen a living soul."

Moonfeather nodded. "And I hope we won't. The

Shawnee are at peace with the Iroquois League, but that doesn't mean we couldn't meet with a hunting party who would rather not have us here. If we simply vanished, who would know?"

"We would," Cailin answered.

"Nay, my friend. If they catch us unawares, we will be beyond knowing or caring. My mother had a saying, 'Better dead than captured by the Iroquois.' "

"That's a comforting thought."

"Aye," Moonfeather agreed. "It is, isn't it."

Chapter 23

Frenzied barking by the village dogs woke Sterling soon after dawn. He strained against the cords pinning him to the earth and turned his head to try to see what the commotion was all about.

Mohawks began to spill from the longhouses as the guards on the walls beat an alarm on small hand drums. Armed warriors dashed across the square, and old men and women demanded in shrill, peevish tones why they had been awakened at such an hour. Babies squalled and children shouted, adding to the confusion.

Jit-sho, the shaman, appeared without his mask, his sparse hair partially covered with an owl-skin cap, his eyes sleep-swollen. Right behind him came a tall, untidy woman hastily braiding her hair and glancing around nervously "Is the town under attack?" Jit-sho cried. "Who comes?"

A flea bit Sterling's neck, and he cursed the creature to a fiery hell. Fleas from the moth-eaten deerskin he was lying on made his existence miserable, and a man bound hand and foot couldn't scratch.

Four days he'd lain here naked, burned by the sun and wind, ridiculed by the camp women and children. Four days, lying in his own waste, so that Ohneya's injuries might heal enough so that they could do battle.

No one had tended Sterling's wounds. His hip and shoulder were the worst. Hot aching told him that the cuts had festered, and he knew that only the heavy rain the day he'd run the gauntlet had prevented his cuts and scrapes from becoming running sores.

Yesterday, he'd insulted an old woman carrying a bark bucket of water from the river until she'd tossed the contents over him. If he shut his eyes, he could still taste the water on his parched lips and swollen tongue.

A few more days and he'd be unable to stand, let alone fight Ohneya. If he was too weak to stand, they'd not give him a chance to wipe the smirk off the Mohawk war chief's face. They'd simply tie him to the stake, skin him alive, do as many other nasty things as his living body would permit, and then light the faggots heaped around his feet.

He'd seen what was left of a burned woman in the Scottish border country when he served in the dragoons. Someone had accused the poor lack-wit of being a witch. It wasn't a sight or a smell he cared to remember. Especially since Jit-sho had taken it into his warped mind that Sterling was a sorcerer because he'd managed to survive the gauntlet and deliver a few good knocks to the Mohawk.

He wished the shaman was right. If he were a witch, he'd have been glad to use whatever supernatural powers he could summon to get him the hell out of here.

Instead, he waited, rehearsing his coming battle with Ohneya in his mind, imagining himself facing the war chief with a knife or tomahawk. Swinging. Dodging. Using feet and fists and head to knock Ohneya off balance and delivering the coup de grâce before twisting around to finish off that little shit, Jit-sho, before the Mohawk swarmed over him and killed him.

Sterling wasn't particularly curious about the cause of the excitement among the Mohawk this morning. He greatly doubted that it was his friend, George Whithall, leading a mounted company of His Majesty's finest to the rescue. Like as not, the visitors were more Iroquois, come on a holiday outing to witness the burning of a white Shawnee witch.

One thing he could be certain of—the distraction would prevent his keepers from feeding him any time soon, or from providing food and water at all. It didn't take much to deter them; meals were few and far between for captive slaves. He decided he ranked somewhere below the dogs in the social order of the village. Yesterday, they'd given him some burned corn mush; it was hard to swallow without salt or sugar. This morning, he'd gladly eat the sticky porridge and the rotten deer hide under him, given half a chance. He was hungry enough to devour Jit-sho, wooden mask and all, even though he suspected the little man would taste like crow dung.

When Sterling understood enough of the shouted Mohawk to realize that the village turmoil was due to the arrival of a delegation of Shawnee, he was stunned. He'd never imagined that any of his mother's people would come to try to rescue him.

"Peace," one of the Iroquois women cried. No, he reasoned, it wasn't *peace* she'd said, it was *peace woman*. Surely, he'd misunderstood. It couldn't be— but it was. There was another shout, and he saw Moonfeather's small proud form leading an honor guard of Shawnee warriors.

Behind her . . . Sterling swore under his breath and

shut his eyes. The sun was getting to him. He'd almost thought that he recognized another slim figure amid the Shawnee. He forced himself to take another look and groaned as realization hit him. It was Cailin. There was no mistaking that wild mane of red hair shining in the sunlight.

He shut his eyes.

Minutes passed before he heard her call his name. "Sterling."

He opened his eyes to see her standing over him. "What in hell are you doing here?" Heat flooded his neck and face. He was naked, filthy, and helpless. Of all the people in the world, the woman he loved was the one he least wanted to see at this moment. "You stupid wench," he said. "I left you—"

Cailin dropped to her knees and took his face between her hands. "Dinna say what ye may regret, Sassenach," she whispered. Tears were streaming down her cheeks.

"Don't touch me," he flung back at her. Sweet Jesus. He strained at the ropes that held him fast. Not even the thought of Mohawk torture could cut him as deep as having her here. If they hurt her, he'd crack . . . he knew he would. He'd beg . . . He'd kiss Jit-sho's skinny brown arse to save her. And it would be as useless as pleading for the sun to rise in the west tomorrow.

Not Cailin here. He couldn't stand it. Not when he'd imagined her safe on the Tidewater . . . Not when he'd summoned up the courage to sing the Shawnee death chant and meet his end like a Shawnee warrior . . .

It was more than a man could bear. He closed his eyes and shut her out, retreating behind a wall of stone where her voice or her touch couldn't find him.

Bear Dancer shouted an order, and two tattooed Mohawk warriors bore down on Cailin. She stood and faced them, bracing herself for the hard hands on her body. But before they could touch her, Moonfeather spoke.

"The flame-haired woman is my sister. She travels under my protection. Harm her, and you tempt the anger of the spirits."

"Shawnee spirits!" snarled a man wearing a red and black wooden mask. "What cause do the Mohawk have to fear Shawnee ghosts?"

But the Mohawk braves stopped in their tracks. Trying not to show fear, Cailin left Sterling and ducked past the enemy warriors to Moonfeather's side. Despite the threat from the fierce braves, she couldn't take her eyes off the masked man. The face was the same one that had loomed up in her waking dream. The peace woman had been right when she'd said that Cailin had the sight. Days and miles away, she'd seen that mask—as horrible and bright as it was today.

Her insides felt as though they had turned upside down. Her mouth was dry, and her hands and feet were numb. It took her another minute to realize that the man wearing the mask was the one Cameron had pointed out to her near the stockade wall as being the infamous Mohawk shaman, Jit-sho.

Cailin tried to focus on what Moonfeather was saying, but she was speaking to the Mohawk leaders in their own language, and Cailin couldn't understand a word.

Cameron stepped close and shot her a reassuring glance. She wanted to seize her father's hand and hold on tight, but she didn't dare. She stood motionless in the center of the clearing with the morning sun on her face and tried not to look at Sterling as the throb of Iroquois drums turned her blood to ice.

Damn them! she thought. Damn them all to a bottomless hell. Look at what they'd done to him. Sterling was thin; his body was covered in welts and gashes. He was lying in his own filth like a cur dog. Worse than the English, they were. Even her terrible cell in Edinburgh Castle had not been so foul.

She didn't care that he'd cursed her. She didn't care that he stank like last week's uncured cowhide. Let him rant and rave like a bedlamite if he wanted to; all she wanted was a chance to wash his poor wounded body and feed him a hot meal. He was alive! Alive! Finding him strong enough to snap at her was a taste of heaven.

The Mohawk sachem's voice had taken on a steely thread, but Moonfeather never flinched before his tirade. She seemed so small beside the Mohawk leader, but her tiny, erect stature did nothing to diminish the effect she had on these savage Iroquois. It was impossible to look at her and not feel the power radiating from her. Despite the hopelessness of their situation, Cailin was certain that the peace woman had never looked as beautiful or as dangerous as she did at this moment.

Behind her, Moonfeather's Shawnee stood like lead soldiers, faces stern and emotionless, shoulders back, heads high. Each man had decked himself in his finest attire. Eagle feathers dangling down their scalp locks, faces painted, they stood as proudly as if they were honored guests of the Mohawk. But no lead soldier had ever had eyes so black or shining with defiance as those of this honor guard. Old Pukasee's weather-worn features were as hard and fierce as the gray wolf that had shadowed Cailin's trail. And even sweet Koke-wah, the boy, had taken on the demeanor of a seasoned warrior.

Cameron leaned closer to Cailin. "She says that the Shawnee and Iroquois are brothers of the peace pipe, and that she will not allow the foolish actions of one young war chief to jeopardize that treaty. She says that Bear Dancer is known from the Ohio to the mountains of the Cherokee as a man of honor. And she offers gifts of friendship to smooth the tempers of his people. She says that she does not come to buy back the captive but to retrieve a Shawnee warrior unjustly taken."

"And what does he say?" Cailin whispered. It was plain to her that the Mohawk chief wasn't happy with his guest's speech, and that the masked man was even more enraged.

Cameron swallowed. When he looked into Cailin's eyes, his gaze was sorrowful. "Bear Dancer says that the white Shawnee—Sterling—killed many Mohawk warriors. He says that their souls cry out for revenge. He insists that Sterling must fight Ohneya in a battle to the death. And if he survives, the sachem has promised that Jit-sho can burn him at the stake. Jit-sho has convinced the Mohawk that Sterling's some kind of a witch."

"That's nonsense," she replied. "He's as good a Christian as I've ever met."

"Indians take witchcraft seriously. My Iroquois is rusty, but Bear Dancer said something about a wolf and a storm that Sterling called down on their heads."

A cold hand squeezed Cailin's heart. She had to struggle to breathe. The awful threat of Sterling's burning had shadowed her since the raid, but she'd pushed the fear back once they'd reached the village and found him still alive. She'd been certain that the Mohawk had changed their minds. Now the terror returned with renewed fury. "What about the wolf?" she asked. "What's that about?"

"Later. Shhh," he cautioned. "Bear Dancer seems to be coming to a decision."

The sachem raised a hand and said something to the gathered Mohawks. There were outcries and grumblings. One Mohawk brave threw his bow onto the ground and kicked it in frustration. The masked shaman shook a turtle-shell rattle and howled in frustration.

Bear Dancer cut the air with his hand in a final gesture that plainly said there would be no more discussion. Then he clapped his hands, and two squaws came running. The younger one approached Moonfeather, touched her own forehead in salute, and motioned for the Shawnee peace woman to follow her.

Moonfeather glanced back at her people. "Come," she said. "We are to be honored with a feast of dog meat." Cailin's face must have registered her disgust, because the peace woman's answering look brooked no argument. "You'll eat it and smile," she said.

The hell I will, Cailin thought. "What about Sterling?" she said. "He's hurt. He needs—"

"We will be permitted to administer to his injuries," Moonfeather answered. "Come with me now."

Cailin looked back at Sterling. He was lying just as she'd left him, eyes clamped shut, unmoving. Her heart went out to him. She wanted nothing more than to cut his bonds and bathe him with her own hands. "But—"

Moonfeather's stern gaze silenced her. With a final glance back at her husband, Cailin followed the peace woman into the big log longhouse at the end of the open square.

The Mohawk woman led them through the high-roofed structure to a partially secluded room at the eastern end of the building. Raised platforms ran along the walls, obviously meant for sleeping, much the same as those inside the smaller Shawnee dwellings. Baskets, rolled blankets, and a few copper kettles were stacked on the floor and beds. Strings of dried tobacco, corn, pumpkin, squash, and beans dangled from the roof rafters. A fire pit in the middle of the room was lined with blackened rocks, and there was a stack of dry kindling, but there was no fire lit. The floor was hard-packed clay, swept as clean as any Highland cottage, but tanned skin rugs lay scattered around the hearth and heaped in one corner.

The Shawnee piled their packs on one side of the room and took up guard stations around Moonfeather, Cameron, and Cailin. Moonfeather signaled that they should remain silent until the Mohawk squaw left them alone. As soon as she did, the peace woman settled onto a deer hide and motioned Cailin to join her.

"They will take Sterling to the river and let him bathe, then they will take him to a place where we can care for him," Moonfeather said.

"Not here?" Cameron asked.

Moonfeather shook her head. "This longhouse is reserved for honored guests. They consider Sterling . . ." She shrugged. "They don't trust us enough to let us have him."

Cailin licked her dry lips. "I thought they'd be willing to sell him to us."

Moonfeather sighed. "Ordinarily, they would. But this talk of witchcraft has frightened them."

Cailin swallowed at the constriction in her throat. "Cameron . . ." She tried again. "My father said that they're threatening to make Sterling fight Ohneya. And that . . ." She couldn't say the rest.

"Aye. I believe he'll have to fight. Bear Dancer seemed unmoving on that."

"Ye willna let them burn him?" Cailin begged.

Moonfeather's liquid eyes filled with compassion. "That is where we differ—this woman and the Mohawk sachem. This woman has no intention of letting that happen. You must remember that Jit-sho is our greatest enemy."

"And Ohneya," Cailin said. "Don't forget him."

"Aye. Ohneya. He is a formidable warrior, but Jit-sho is different. He pressures Bear Dancer to renounce me. He says that because of my white blood, I do not deserve the respect of my office."

"If the Mohawk won't accept you as peace woman—" Cameron began.

Moonfeather spread her hands, palm up. "Then it could become very uncomfortable for us all. But to do that, he must discredit me—prove that this woman is without power."

"If he does?" Cailin said.

Lachpi the Delaware tapped his tobacco pipe against a bed frame. "Then we all die at the stake. Those who cannot fight their way out of this walled town."

Kitate grunted.

"But ye do have power?" Cailin asked. Anxiously, she glanced from the peace woman to her father. "Ye are who ye claim to be."

"Perhaps," Moonfeather said calmly. "That rests in

the hands of Inu-msi-ila-fe-wanu, the great spirit who is a grandmother."

"And Sterling?" Cailin pleaded.

Moonfeather nodded. "Call him Sterling or Nanata Ki-tehi, he is the same man. And his fate rests with Inu-msi-ila-fe-wanu most of all."

Later, the same Mohawk woman escorted Cailin to a longhouse bearing the totem of the bear over the door. A surly brave, armed with a rifle and a hatchet, barred the entrance. After several verbal exchanges between the Mohawk woman and the guard that Cailin couldn't understand, he reluctantly moved aside to let them pass.

Cailin noticed that, unlike most of the other longhouses, the bark on the outer walls of this hut was loose and badly in need of repair. Once inside the dusty interior, she realized that this building was used for storage rather than as a dwelling.

Sterling was in the last room, chained to a newly set post by iron wrist manacles. His hair hung down his back, tangled and dripping, and he was still naked.

"Be quick," the Mohawk squaw said, then turned and strode swiftly away.

Cailin threw herself at Sterling's chest and whispered his name hoarsely. She would not cry, she promised herself. She'd not.

It was like hitting a wall of ice. He didn't embrace her ... didn't speak ... didn't acknowledge her presence at all.

Hurt, she shrank away from him and looked into his face. "Are ye daft?" she demanded. "I ken that you're angry with me, but—"

"Angry? Angry?" The ice wall shattered in a flood

of profanity so original that Cailin couldn't help but laugh at him.

"That's better," she said. "I thought they'd beaten the wits out of ye. How bad are ye hurt?"

"I've felt better," he snarled. "That doesn't excuse your stupidity! How could you disobey me in this, you stupid jade? You're an idiot. A total feather-brained lunatic!"

She sniffed. "A fine thanks I get for coming to rescue you."

"Rescue me?" His face darkened until she thought he'd have a stroke. "Is this what you call a rescue? You'll never get out of here alive. None of us will."

"I might have known you'd say that," she retorted. "Typically English. Give up as soon as a noose begins to tighten. Where's your ballocks?"

"Still where they belong, thank you," he flung back. "Although how long they'll stay attached is any man's guess."

For a long moment, they glared at each other, then he looked away and swore again.

"Say you're glad to see me," she murmured.

"I'd sooner see Beelzebub."

"You're lying through your teeth, Sassenach."

A shudder ran through him. "I thought you were safe, woman. Can't you see that? I thought you were safe. No matter what they did to me, I—"

She touched his shoulder, running her fingers gently over the swollen, torn flesh, caressing his skin until he turned back, and she saw tears welling in his dark eyes. "Don't ye ken that I'd rather die here with ye than live not knowing if ye were dead or alive?" she said. "I love ye, Sterling Gray. Heart and soul, body and mind, I love ye. And if it was stupid to come here, then I'm stupid, but I had to chance it."

"Cailin." The agony in his voice cut her to the quick. "Cailin ... darling," he continued raggedly.

She threw her arms around his neck and pulled his head down. His mouth crushed hers, and she clung to him until she grew faint from lack of oxygen.

"I love you," he said when they drew far enough apart to breathe. "You're still an idiot, but I do love you."

"And ye are glad to see me?"

"No. I'm not. And if I die a sniveling coward, it will be your fault."

"You're not going to die," she promised. She was afraid to kiss him again. Once he started kissing her, she'd lose the reason to think. And she needed her wits if they were to survive. "Moonfeather's going to trade for your freedom. I'm under her protection—we all are."

"Diplomatic immunity?" Sterling grimaced. "Don't look for the niceties of honor among the Mohawk."

"Well, we're alive so far. They're preparing us a feast of dog, and they've agreed to let me clean up your injuries." She inspected the angry gash down his thigh. "By all that's holy. 'Tis a wonder you've not taken the rotting sickness. Look at this." She took a step back. "I've brought medicine, and some dried meat and water. I brought a loincloth too, if you think they'll let you keep it."

"Put the damned thing on me. It's not much protection, but it worries a man to have his most precious possessions dangling in the breeze."

She chuckled. "And I thought I was your most precious possession." She handed him the water skin.

"A wife who doesn't obey her husband. Not likely." He took a long swallow of water. "The biggest mistake I ever made was stealing you from the hangman in Edinburgh."

"If that's the worst ye ever make, we'll both live to rock our grandbabies," she said. The inflammation on the leg was leaking pus; it would need lancing and washing. "This is going to hurt," she warned.

He shrugged. "Have at it, woman. You're not the first to enjoy torturing me. And the Mohawk have had more practice at it."

She had administered to his leg and was just putting the final stitches in his shoulder wound when the Mohawk squaw returned.

"You come now," the woman said in stilted English.

"Just a little longer," Cailin stalled. "I need time to—"

"Come now!"

Cailin whirled and gave the Indian woman her fiercest look. "I'll go with ye when I bandage this, ye blackhearted daughter of Satan."

"No! Not wait. Now."

Sterling nodded. "Go along, lass. No need to set off fireworks over a few more minutes."

She wanted to kiss him again, to wrap her arms around him and not let go, but his face had taken on that Indian look again. Instead, she smiled and mouthed the words *I love you* as she hastily bound a dressing over his injury.

"You come feast," the squaw said. "Tomorrow, Shawnee witch fight Ohneya."

"Tomorrow?" Cailin's gaze met Sterling's.

The Mohawk woman smiled slyly. "Ohneya great warrior. Kill witch and take his wife for slave."

"What?" Cailin asked. "What did you say?"

The Indian woman laughed. "Is Mohawk custom.

Witch win, take Ohneya's wife. Ohneya kill Shawnee witch, take enemy's wife to his bed. Is fair, yes?" She motioned toward the entrance. "Go now. Eat white dog. Tomorrow, when your man's head hang on Ohneya's lodgepole, you eat scraps dogs leave behind." She rolled her eyes and smirked. "If Ohneya not keep white woman too busy to eat at all."

Chapter 24

"**T**omorrow he may die," Cailin whispered urgently to Moonfeather. "Ye must help me find a way to go to him."

The two women moved away from the smoky hearth to talk, so they wouldn't disturb their sleeping companions. Cailin had lain awake for hours; she guessed it must be sometime after midnight, but all she could think of was Sterling and the danger he was facing.

Except for the occasional cough, or the cry of an infant, the Iroquois camp was quiet. A Mohawk stood guard outside the entrance to the ceremonial longhouse, and Lachpi the Delaware squatted inside the door with a rifle cradled in his arms. Both warriors were too far away to hear what she and Moonfeather were saying. The men kept watch so silently, without moving, that they might have been another pair of upright oak columns that stood in pairs down the center of the massive log structure.

"Your heart is troubled," Moonfeather replied, placing a warm hand on Cailin's shoulder. "Mine too. I do not trust the Mohawk. They are as truthful as the English. A promise made today may not be kept tomorrow."

Hope surged in Cailin's breast. "Then they may not force Sterling to fight Ohneya?"

Moonfeather made a doubtful sound with a click of her tongue. "That is a promise I expect they will keep. They are bloodthirsty people. The other tribes of the Iroquois Confederacy are not so cruel. I would feel better if Bear Dancer were an Oneida or an Onondaga. He would have more control over his warriors. I see the young men look to Ohneya. If Bear Dancer's authority as sachem is uneasy, he may sacrifice us all to keep his position." She made a sound of derision. "Weak politicians are worse than evil ones. Even a wicked man will sometimes listen to reason. Thus I would rather deal with a strong, bad leader such as Ohneya than a good, weak one."

"How is it that they listen to you at all?" Cailin asked. "Ye be Shawnee, not Iroquois, and ... and ye are a woman."

Moonfeather spread her hands gracefully.

In the light of the glowing fire, Cailin was struck again by just how regal the peace woman appeared. She could be a Spanish princess, Cailin thought.

"The Iroquois are a race of conquerors and our blood enemies," Moonfeather whispered softly, "but they are not barbarians. Far from it. They recognize the honored place of women as the Europeans do not. Their women have traditionally wielded great power among them. Normally, they would discount a Shawnee female, but—"

"Aye," Cailin replied impatiently. "Ye be a peace woman, but I still don't understand what that means. Are ye a shaman, like Jit-sho?"

Moonfeather chuckled. "Better, this woman hopes."

"Are you a chief?"

"Nay. A chief can be replaced, while a peace woman cannot be. She is born to the title, not chosen by the Shawnee. She is a councilor, not just to a single village, but to all who call themselves Shawnee. There can be but one, and she must die before another is recognized."

"Will the office pass to your daughter?" Forrest had mentioned an older sister, but Cailin had not met her. She still had trouble believing that Moonfeather was the wife of an English earl. There were so many questions she wanted to ask her, but this was not the time or the place.

"That is not given for me to know."

"That Mohawk woman who took me to Sterling said that I belong to Ohneya if he kills my husband. Is that true?"

"So." Moonfeather's voice was thoughtful but noncommittal.

Cailin was beginning to realize that the Shawnee told what they wanted and left out the rest. Getting an aye or nay was sometimes harder than hiking uphill through a thunderstorm. "If Sterling wins the encounter," she continued, "this Bear Dancer says they will burn him. There's no way out for us. I must be with him tonight."

Moonfeather nodded. "That much this one can give you."

"How?" Cailin asked. "We are guarded, and so is he."

"It is not important for you to know how it is done," Moonfeather said. "Do you remember the way to the place where he is held prisoner?"

"Of course, but—"

Moonfeather gripped her shoulder with surprising strength. "Do not speak. Do not utter a sound. Do not touch the Mohawk guards. And remember that you must return to this longhouse before the first light of dawn. Do you understand? You must follow my instructions exactly."

"I ken your words, but how am I to do this? Ye canna make me invisible."

The peace woman's chuckle was low and warm. "Aye, my friend. Something like that. It is an Indian thing that ye canna fathom. Think of the wolf and place your feet as he does, silently. Go to your husband. Quickly. But be back before the sky lightens. This charm will not hold in daylight."

"Witchcraft," Cailin murmured. "I canna—"

"Ease your heart, little Christian sister. A peace woman does not bargain with the prince of darkness. Above all, she must follow the way of the light. Your soul is safe enough. Go now. And offer prayers to your Jesus that your husband fights well tomorrow."

Cailin shook her head. What Moonfeather was telling her to do was impossible. Stupid. A madwoman's ploy. No one could make her invisible. If she tried to set foot outside this building, the Mohawk would seize her—maybe even strike her dead.

But she wanted to be with Sterling—had to be with him if it was humanly possible.

Gritting her teeth, she took a deep breath and began to walk through the darkened longhouse toward the entrance on the east end. It was a chilly night, cool for summer, even damp, but sweat beaded on her face and trickled down the hollows of her throat.

Lachpi will stop me, she thought. I'll get as far as the doorway, and Lachpi will bar the way. Surely, the Delaware brave wouldn't let her step past him into danger.

She could hear the rhythmic sound of Lachpi's breathing now, see the glow from the end of his clay pipe, smell the Indian tobacco. Moonfeather had warned her not to speak. She hadn't said what to do if her heart was pounding loud enough to wake the village.

Cailin hugged her folded arms against her body. She swallowed, wanting to clear her throat, but she was afraid to make a sound. As a child, when she walked the haunted hallway at Glen Garth, she would whistle to drive away the ghosts. Tonight, she could only keep walking.

Past Lachpi . . . through the entranceway.

Moonlight shone on the Mohawk guard's craggy face. His breastplate of shiny metal glittered with cold fire; the steel head of his war club rose and fell with each deep breath he took. She could smell the fish on his breath, almost feel the slick bear grease on his skin.

Her own skin prickled as she waited for his shout, as she waited for him to lift that terrible club and bring it crashing down to crush her skull.

He passed wind.

Cailin wrinkled her nose and stopped short, ready to die, too emotionally wrung out to take another step.

He stretched and yawned, then scratched beneath his loincloth. A rude noise sounded. The brave sighed with relief as a cloud of evil-smelling gas fouled the air.

Cailin found the courage to move. She held her breath as she darted around the end of the longhouse and stopped again to listen for his footsteps in pursuit.

She heard nothing but the faint creak of a fish drying rack in the night breeze.

Think of the wolf, Moonfeather had said. *Place your feet as he does . . .*

The moonlight made the way clear. She hurried between the communal dwellings, past sleeping dogs and turkey roosts. No one stopped her; no cur yelped a warning, and no bird squawked.

Ahead, she saw the guard at the entrance of Sterling's prison. He was a tall, wide man with a shaven head and an immense, sagging belly. Cailin recognized him as one of the members of the original war party that had attacked the plantation.

Would he see her? Tension made her giddy, but she'd come too far to give up now. Chin high, certain that he would see her and raise the alarm, she walked straight toward him.

He gave not the slightest indication that she existed, and she ducked past him and into the musty-smelling storage building.

Inside, there was no moonlight and no fire. She had never been a fainting woman, but gray fog churned in her head, and her knees felt too weak to hold her up. Praying silently, she extended her arms out in front of her and put one foot in front of the other, hoping against hope that she could stay in the center passageway.

The Iroquois longhouses were much bigger than the Shawnee wigwams, one room wide and four or five long. Moonfeather had told her that among the Iroquois, families of the same clan shared a house, each individual group living in one compartment around a separate hearth. When she'd been led to Sterling before, she'd had to thread her way through piles of tanned hides, stacked baskets, metal kettles, and other stored household belongings. In the dark, it was difficult to find her way without tripping over something, but she was heartened by the knowledge that each step took her farther from the guard at the door and nearer to Sterling. Twice, she brushed against a protruding wall and tangled in a mass of cobwebs; once, she nearly walked into a center post.

Just a wee bit farther, she told herself. Then, she heard the faint rattle of a chain ahead and guessed Sterling must be awake. He didn't call out, but she sensed that he was aware he was no longer alone in the longhouse. She froze, straining to see in the blackness.

"Cailin?" He whispered her name. "I know it's you. I can smell your hair."

She didn't hesitate. She ran to him and slipped under his manacled wrists into the circle of his arms. He moaned softly and squeezed her against him.

"Cailin, Cailin, what are you doing here?"

Moonfeather had told her not to speak. She was afraid that if she did, the spell would break, and they'd be discovered. She answered him with her lips, her touch, her body molded to his.

He groaned and lowered his head.

His kiss was the sweetest thing she'd ever tasted.

"This is madness," he protested. But he kissed her again, and she clung to him.

"Woman, what will I do with you?" He uttered a sound of despair, but he kept kissing her until the feel and scent of him made her giddy and she forgot where she was and what was to come.

"Do you realize what you risk to come here?" he rasped.

She didn't care what he said. She knew that he needed her here in his arms. She parted her lips and allowed his tongue to slide deep into her mouth.

"Why aren't you saying anything?" he asked her later when they were both breathless.

She put three fingers over his lips.

"Damn it, I love you," he whispered. "I'll always love you. Remember that . . ."

She turned, still inside the circle of his arms, and leaned back against him. Taking hold of his right hand, she lifted it to kiss the place where the iron manacle bit into his flesh.

He clenched and unclenched his fingers.

"Speak to me," he begged her.

Her tears fell on his bruised flesh. She opened his hand and turned it to kiss the callused underside of his palm.

"Don't," he said. "Do you know how it rips my gut to have you see me chained to a post like an animal?" He made a sound that could have been a sob. "You can't think about me, Cailin. I'm a dead man. You've got to survive."

Sterling! Sterling! She shouted his name in her heart, but no sound issued from her throat. It didn't matter. She was here—with him. She twisted around to face him, stroked his hair, ran her fingers down his cheek, and traced the lines of his mouth and nose. She wanted to memorize every inch of him, to brand his image on her soul so that no matter what happened, she could never forget him.

His hands were bound with cruel fetters of iron, but hers were free. Free to caress his neck and shoulders . . . to brush his nipples and follow the contours of every scar and bulge on his chest . . . to blaze a trail of scorching kisses down his bare skin.

"Cailin," he gasped. "Don't . . ."

She paid him no heed.

Always before, it had been Sterling's touch that had set her desire aflame. Now it was her own.

She wanted to tell him that she was his, that nothing would ever part them. She wanted to press his hands against her womb ... to let him know of the gift she sheltered there.

Instead, she let passion fill her with languid warmth and a boldness that was almost wanton. Shamelessly, she ran her fingers over his flat stomach and narrow hips, lingering only briefly on the swell of his loincloth before following the hard muscles of his buttocks and thighs.

"Woman ..." He drew in a strangled breath. "What are you—"

She silenced him by kneeling at his feet and resting her cheek against his swelling member. She hugged his leg, massaging the knotted sinew of his calf, before retracing her path to do the same at his thigh. And as she leaned against him, she felt him tremble.

His manacled hands tangled in her hair. He rubbed the nape of her neck with his fingers, making slow, sensual circles that made her skin tingle and her nipples pucker to hard, sensitive buds.

Gently, tenderly, she placed kisses on his most vulnerable spot, adding her own fervent excitement to his.

He let out a long sigh of longing.

It was a simple matter for Cailin to undo his rawhide belt and let his loincloth fall away ... to cup his sacks in her hands and lift their weight ... to explore the fullness of his straining shaft.

How can this be a sin? she wondered. He is my God-given husband. The warmth in her loins had become waves of white-hot heat. She no longer felt the cool air, only the fevered pulse of her blood.

A smile played over her lips as she explored his length, marveling at the smooth texture of his skin and the throbbing power beneath her fingertips.

Groaning, he arched against her.

She moistened her lips and then tasted him. Salt . . . and something more. Her breasts tingled and grew heavy.

It all comes down to this, she thought. Not even fear of death could stop the overwhelming drive to mate with him—to seal their love in primitive abandon.

She stroked him tenderly, and his intense reaction made her bold. Teasingly, she flicked her tongue along his engorged flesh, then took him into her mouth. Delicately. Provocatively.

Sterling's taut body shuddered.

And her own body would no longer be denied.

He could not lie down because of the short bonds that held his manacles to the post . . . but he could kneel. And though his wrists were chained . . . his mouth . . . his lips . . . his tongue were not.

And she was free.

Her seduction became a mutual loving, an act of union that swept them from the confines of this dark prison to a world of their own making.

Yet, even in the throes of ecstasy, she did not speak, did not need to speak as he fulfilled her wildest fantasies and healed the wounds in her heart that had ached for so long.

Hours later, satiated with lovemaking, exhausted and at peace, Cailin rested her head against his bare chest. She knew that time was passing . . . that she must leave, but she could not.

This might be the last time he could hold her, the last time she could hear him whisper love words into her ear.

"Love of my life," he said. "Do you know how many times I cursed you?" His chuckle warmed her heart. "It was your image that appeared during my manhood trial. I didn't want it. I tried to deny you, but I couldn't. I wanted an animal guardian spirit—a bear, a mountain lion, even an otter. The other boys boasted of their spirits, and all I had to tell about was the image of a white woman with red hair."

She closed her eyes and snuggled closer, trying to imagine Sterling as a slim, uncertain youth waiting for a vision.

"I tried to forget you, but it was impossible," he continued. "After my father took me to England, I never stopped searching for you," he murmured. "I never passed a woman on the street that I didn't look into her face. And when I saw you on the battlefield, I knew I couldn't let you escape me again."

She sighed. Dawn would be there soon. She wondered if it would be better to stay and be caught so that they could die together.

"I wanted a guide, and the spirits gave me you."

She laid her open hand over his heart and felt the strong throb of his life's blood.

"Half a lifetime it took me to recognize a gift when I had it in the palm of my hand."

She wanted to ask him how he could believe such superstitious nonsense, but she was afraid of breaking the spell of silence. And then she nearly laughed aloud as she realized that the spell she was weaving at that moment would make any witch nod in approval.

"I have accepted Christianity," he said, "but I can't cast out the old ways of my mother's people. And I can't believe that all of them are bad. After all, they brought you to me."

He leaned down and kissed her love-bruised lips.

"The old ones say you can't escape the path the spirits have chosen for you," he said.

Perhaps not, she thought. With an aching heart, she kissed him a final time and hurried from the longhouse in the first purple flush of dawn.

She hadn't forgotten that Sterling might die today and that she might die as well, but the realization that she was truly loved by a good man erased her fear for her own safety.

If Sterling met death at the hands of the Mohawk, she would survive as best she could for the sake of the child she was certain that she carried. She would live out the days of her life, doing her duty to Sterling's son or daughter and all those who depended on her. But all the while, she would know in her heart that Sterling waited ... and no power under heaven could part them. Not even death could destroy a love as strong as theirs or keep them from spending an eternity in each other's arms.

But ... Oh, how could she stand the nights between now and then? How could she bear the emptiness of the days, once she'd buried her heart and soul with the only man she'd ever love ... a man she'd once believed was her mortal enemy.

When Cailin reached the safety of the log ceremonial house without being seen, Moonfeather pulled her, smiling, into her arms. And for a brief time, both women wept, unashamed.

Chapter 25

Cailin thought the day was the longest of her entire life. After she returned from meeting Sterling, she slept fitfully until mid-morning, when Moonfeather bade her rise and come to the river to bathe. Escorted by a bevy of giggling girls, Cameron and the Shawnee, Moonfeather and Cailin retraced their steps to the outside of the walled town.

The men turned their backs while Moonfeather and Cailin entered the river to wash. The water was cold and bracing; it cleared Cailin's head but did nothing to ease her worry for Sterling. After a short time, one of the Mohawk girls led the two women to a private spot near the wall to see to their personal needs.

Once the group returned to the ceremonial longhouse inside the palisade, there was more waiting before they were finally summoned by the council to an afternoon of talk and feasting. Cailin had little appetite despite the lavish spread of smoked fish, eels, duck, elk, corn, succotash, squash, beans, berries, and all manner of flat cakes baked from corn flour. Her stomach was queasy; she could think of nothing but Sterling and his coming fight with Ohneya, the Mohawk she still thought of as Skull Face.

What hunger she did have fled when she saw that the main course consisted of roasted dog with the head left intact. Moonfeather and Cameron ate the repulsive flesh, but it was all Cailin could do to keep from being sick. She drank water and nibbled listlessly on a corn cake while the Mohawk chief droned on in his own tongue.

The sun was hot, but that didn't seem to bother anyone else. The villagers crowded so close that she could smell the bear grease on their bodies. They smelled different than the Shawnee, she thought, and almost laughed. Had she been with Moonfeather's people so long that she was beginning to think herself one of them?

Greenhead flies buzzed around Cailin's head. A dog wandered too close to the food, and someone smacked it with a wooden ladle. The dog yipped and ran, tail between its legs. Bear Dancer stopped talking when his voice became hoarse, and he sat down. Another gray-haired Mohawk wearing a silver nose ring took his place.

Hours passed, and still the speeches continued. Cameron was seated across from her between two Mohawk elders. Moonfeather was concentrating on the speakers. Cailin wanted to scream. If she sat here any longer, she'd shame herself and the Shawnee by becoming hysterical.

Then, before she could completely lose control, the last Mohawk orator extended a hand toward Moonfeather, and she rose. She looked very small to Cailin in the midst of the hardened Mohawk warriors and grizzled old council members.

Moonfeather looked at each of the dignitaries and saluted them in their native Iroquoian. Cameron repeated her words in English so that Cailin could understand what was being said. It soon became evident that Moonfeather had no intention of rambling on as the others had done.

". . . a peace between the Shawnee and the Iroquois, a peace that we all vowed to keep," Moonfeather said softly. Her voice was not as loud as those of the previous speakers, but Cailin could see that the Mohawk were listening intently.

"Ohneya and his war party broke that peace," Moonfeather continued. "No one could have blamed the Shawnee if they dug up the black-feathered tomahawk and sought vengeance against the Iroquois League. But the Shawnee are not so quick to turn their backs on a promise. Instead, this woman has come to offer gifts for the return of the white Shawnee, Warrior Heart. He is a brave man, a man who ran the Mohawk gauntlet, a man worthy of being set free."

The medicine man leaped to his feet and shouted opposition. Immediately, there was an outcry from his supporters. Bear Dancer glared at the shaman, but the little man would not be silenced. He shook his raven staff at the chief and returned a volley of angry words.

Cameron stood and began to translate the medicine man's tirade into English. "Our sachem promised that the prisoner must fight Ohneya! Can a man remain high chief who lies to his own people? I say he cannot. I say that it is time Ohneya took his rightful place as the head of this village."

Bear Dancer's lined face darkened to puce. He rose and made an angry chopping motion with the flat of his hand. The crowd went wild.

Cailin looked back at Cameron, but he shook his head. She didn't need his words to know that the old chief was giving in to the shaman.

Men began to push and shove. Someone raised a clenched fist and trilled a Mohawk war cry. Moonfeather's Shawnee closed a wall of protection around her. She called out in Algonquian, and Lachpi motioned to Cailin.

Cailin couldn't move. On the far side of the town square, she saw two Mohawk braves enter the compound clearing with Sterling between them. Panic seized her as she watched them drag him toward the charred wooden post.

Cameron grabbed Cailin's arm. "There's nothing more we can do," he said. Quickly, he hustled her into the circle of Shawnee to Moonfeather's side.

Ululations rent the air. The booming of the big drum added to the clamor of the whooping Mohawks. Ohneya stepped forward and raised his hands over his head. Cheers pierced the drumming. Excited women began to gather up the trays and bowls of food; children ran shrieking, and the village dog pack added to the uproar with howls and frenzied yapping.

Within minutes, the center of the clearing was empty. The masked shaman drew a wide circle in the dust with the butt of his staff. Sterling's guards shoved him into the open space, and Cailin gasped as she got a good look at his swollen face.

"He's hurt. He's in no condition to—" she began, but Moonfeather cut her off.

"No," the peace woman admonished. "You can do nothing for him now. He must fight. Do not show him a wailing woman. Give him heart. Show him that you believe he will win."

Cailin pushed between Joseph and Ake. The Mohawks gave way to let her reach the edge of the circle. Sterling looked up and saw her. For an instant, they stared intently into each other's eyes. Hot tears threatened to overwhelm Cailin, but she forced them back, grinned and waved at him, and cried, "Give him hell, Sassenach!"

A Mohawk warrior laughed, and then another shouted good-naturedly. Murmurs of approval rippled through the throng. Vaguely, Cailin was aware of her father coming to stand at her right side and Moonfeather at her left.

Sterling surveyed the audience with the haughty composure of a Roman gladiator. When Ohneya stepped into the dusty circle, Sterling raised his middle finger in a crude gesture of defiance.

Ohneya screamed in fury. He thrust out a hand, and his wife put a knife into it. He opened his other fist and took a double-edged tomahawk. Chanting fiercely, he began to dance, working himself into a fervor of bloodlust.

Lachpi shouldered his way onto the field and handed Sterling his skinning knife and tomahawk. Sterling lifted both high and gave a Shawnee war whoop.

Other drummers joined the beat of the first. Women called out to Ohneya and raised their children to see him. The masked shaman climbed on top of a large, flat boulder and shook his rattle at Sterling. Then the medicine man began to sing a wordless high-pitched whine of gibberish.

Sterling and Ohneya drew closer to each other. Both wore moccasins and loincloths and were near in size. Ohneya was a few fingers' width taller and at least a stone's weight heavier, Cailin guessed. Ohneya's head was shaved except for a scalp lock wrapped in red cloth, while Sterling's hair hung uncombed around his shoulders.

The Mohawk war chief's face had been hastily painted; the outline of his skull features were slightly crooked, and one eye ring drooped at the corner. Still, Ohneya was a formidable sight as he thrust out his muscular chest and taunted Sterling in Iroquoian.

"You don't have to witness this," Cameron whispered to Cailin. "It could be very bloody."

She shook her head. She couldn't bear to stand here and watch, but hiding would be worse. Whatever happened to Sterling, she had to know. "I'll be all right," she answered.

"You're tough, like your mother."

She took her eyes off Sterling to glare at her father. "I'm nothing like her."

"Don't be so sure. You young ones are quick to judge. Whatever she did, she loved her children. She always cared for you, didn't she?"

"How would you know?" The words were out of her mouth before she could think.

Instantly, Cameron's faded eyes registered hurt. Then, he hid his feelings with a wry chuckle. "I can't argue that, lass," he admitted.

Cailin glanced back at Sterling. He crouched motionless, waiting, a weapon in each hand. Ohneya didn't disappoint him. He dashed at Sterling, whirling his hatchet in a wide arc over his head. Sterling feinted right, then ducked to the left as the Mohawk swung at his face. Cailin saw only a blur as Sterling's arm moved, but it was all too fast to comprehend.

Ohneya spun around and faced Sterling again. A thin red line opened along the war chief's right hip. Cailin was puzzled. Had Sterling cut the Mohawk with his knife?

The Indian charged again. This time, Sterling didn't dodge away. He blocked the blow from

Ohneya's tomahawk with his own and slashed at the Mohawk with his knife.

The mob roared as the two slammed together and locked, sinews straining, steel weapons flashing in the sun. Sterling's back was to Cailin. Cords of muscle stood out across his shoulders and back, and down his thighs. Sweat poured off both men, and Sterling's night-black hair clung to his damp skin.

Cailin's blood turned cold. Unconsciously, she fingered the amulet around her neck.

"Don't be afraid to use it," Cameron urged her. "The power of the Eye of Mist is real. It can save his life if you call on it."

Cailin dropped the pendant as if it had burned her. Such talk was superstitious nonsense, as foolish as Moonfeather's story about a ghost wolf. She'd not let herself believe it.

She'd tried before—when her mother lay dying. She'd tried and failed, and the bitter taste of failure and loss had never left her.

No, she'd not make that mistake again. Sterling must live or die by his own strength. All her love and prayers were as useless to save him as this heavy gold pendant.

A roar went up from the onlookers as Sterling went down with Ohneya on top of him. The Mohawk drove the ax into the earth inches from Sterling's skull. Then Sterling's knife cut a gash across Ohneya's forearm. There was a brief, violent struggle, and the two sprang apart to rise and face each other with hate-filled eyes.

Blood caked with dirt smeared Sterling's forehead. Cailin had been certain that the tomahawk had missed him, yet a thick red path continued to slide down the left side of his temple. Ohneya's wounds were bleeding as well, and the sight of blood aroused the crowd to a fevered pitch. Stamping and yelling, they pressed closer, constricting the area of combat.

Ohneya hurled his tomahawk. Sterling ducked, straightened, and threw his. Neither weapon found its mark, and the Mohawk threw his knife at Sterling and pounced on Sterling's tomahawk. In the split second he took to pry it from the dirt, Sterling buried his knife in Ohneya's right upper arm.

Ohneya stumbled to his knees and seized the blade to pull it out. Sterling darted forward and drove his weight into the war chief's back. Ohneya fell with Sterling straddling his prone body.

Cailin clapped a hand over her mouth.

Somehow, in the midst of his attack, Sterling had seized the tomahawk. He raised it over Ohneya's head with his right hand and pinned Ohneya to the ground with his left. The Mohawk onlookers fell silent, waiting for the death blow to fall.

"Kill him!" Lachpi urged.

"Finish it!" cried Kitate in Algonquian. "Finish him now!"

Sterling glanced toward Bear Dancer and the council. "I claim this life!" he shouted in the same language. "And I trade his life for that of my wife."

Ohneya's woman shrieked in lamentation and crawled toward Bear Dancer on hands and knees. "Give me my husband's life," she begged. "The father of your grandchildren. Spare him."

Bear Dancer nodded. "We will release the white woman unharmed."

Sterling got up cautiously and stepped back, tomahawk ready in case of any trickery on Ohneya's part. The Indian's wife scrambled out of the dust and ran to him. Sterling backed away and threw down the tomahawk.

"Why didn't you kill him?" Cameron whispered hoarsely.

Cailin could stand still no longer. She rushed toward Sterling, but before she could reach him, a brave tossed Ohneya a lance. Cailin screamed as the Mohawk raised his arm to cast the spear at Sterling's back.

Time seemed to stop for her. She could feel the agony of her own scream, see the confusion in Sterling's eyes, and smell the stench of death. She extended her hand, but the motion was so slow that it was unreal.

Then she heard the long, drawn-out howl of a wolf. Not far off, but here in the midst of the crowd. Sterling heard it. She could read the knowledge in his face.

And Ohneya heard the wolf as well. His white-rimmed eyes widened with fear. The lance fell from his fingers. He clutched his throat and staggered back.

The medicine man cried out. "The Shawnee witch has proved his courage! Burn him!"

Suddenly, everything was happening at once. Cailin watched stunned as the Mohawks surrounded Sterling. She could no longer see Ohneya. She tried to get to Sterling through the throng, but Cameron caught her and yanked her back. "Don't shame him, or yourself," he told her.

She struggled against him. "Let me go to Sterling," she insisted. "Let me go to him."

"No." Pulling her against his chest, he forced her back to where Moonfeather stood watching impassively.

"Stop them!" Cailin said. "You must stop them!"

Signaling to her men, Moonfeather ordered them to clear a path for her to the rock where the medicine man stood. With brawn and nerve, and the butts of their long rifles, they did as she asked. Kitate grabbed her around the waist and lifted her onto the natural platform.

"Burn him if you will," she shouted in Iroquoian, "but know that the price is war with the Shawnee."

"What is she saying?" Cailin demanded of her father.

"She tells them the Shawnee will go to war if they kill Sterling," Cameron translated.

The masked man howled, shook his rattle, and began to berate Moonfeather loudly.

"He says that she is no true peace woman," Cameron said. "He says that she is an imposter and cannot make good on her promise of war."

Bear Dancer shouted something.

"He is telling the shaman that he's still the leader," Cameron explained.

Jit-sho pointed at Moonfeather with his staff and hurled insults.

"Witch." Cameron continued to translate. "They are both witches. Kill them all."

Kitate, Lachpi, and the rest of Moonfeather's Shawnee cocked the hammers on their rifles and put solid rock at their backs.

The Mohawk ceased their clamor and stared at Moonfeather and Jit-sho. When the peace woman spoke, her words rang out with authority.

"She challenges Jit-sho to a test of fire," Cameron said. "If he dares to accept, he must risk the loss of his immortal soul. She promises to send him into the place of ice and eternal darkness, beyond the ... something about a ghost swamp."

The shaman's scornful acceptance needed no translation. He thumped his staff and shook his rattle as Kitate helped Moonfeather down.

"What does it mean?" Cailin asked her father. "What is a test of fire?"

"This woman must walk over hot coals," Moonfeather explained softly.

"So will the Mohawk shaman," Koke-wah put in.

"That's impossible," Cailin replied, wondering if they'd all gone mad. "No one can do that."

"A peace woman can," Lachpi the Delaware assured her. "A true peace woman has the power."

"And if this ... this trickery doesna work?" Cailin asked.

"Then she'll die," Cameron answered. "And so will the rest of us."

Chapter 26

The drums kept up their savage cadence until Cailin thought she would run shrieking from the longhouse. War cries mingled with yelps and bursts of chanting as the Mohawk prepared for the spectacle of two opposing shamans in public combat.

Night had fallen. Cailin had seen nothing of Sterling since the Mohawk tied him to the torture post and drove the Shawnee delegation back into their quarters. Even Moonfeather's quiet good sense seemed to have left her. She'd not spoken more than a few words to Cailin after she offered Jit-sho the fire challenge. Now, she too was gone. She'd left the ceremonial building with several older Mohawk women, leaving Cailin alone with Cameron and the Indians.

She knew that Cameron was extremely upset by Moonfeather's decision. Worry was etched on his face. For the first time, he looked like what he was, an aging man out of his own element. Wordlessly, he paced up and down, driving a fist into his other palm, saying nothing.

The Shawnee were stoic. Lachpi smoked his clay pipe and stared into the tiny fire; the others sat with folded legs and expressionless features, waiting.

Twice, Cailin had tried to go to Sterling. She'd walked boldly to the doorway and been stopped by the guards. No amount of pleading or anger swayed them. Whatever force or accident had made her invisible before was no longer working.

When the sound of the incessant drumming made her feel as though her skin was too tight, she leaped to her feet and tried to pass a third time. To her shock, the Mohawk brave grabbed her by the hair and yanked her within inches of his chest. Tears of pain filled her eyes, but he continued to twist the handful of hair until her neck was bent at an unnatural angle. Then he sneered and shoved her away. She fell heavily against a support post, got to her feet, and backed away, half-expecting him to pursue her.

By the time she reached her friends, her fear had turned to anger. She'd never thought of herself as a violent person, but she wanted to strike out and hurt the bullies holding them all prisoner.

Cameron stopped his pacing, looked into her face, and pulled her gently against his chest. For long seconds, she allowed herself the luxury of human comfort, then pulled away.

"This is hard on you," he said.

"Will any of us get out of here alive?" she demanded of him. "Will Sterling? Will Moonfeather?"

He shook his head. "God knows. I pray so. This much I do know. I've made a new will leaving my plantation, Scot's Haven, to you."

"I don't want anything from you."

"You have my grandmother's eyes ... and her dimple."

She took a deep breath. She didn't want to talk about this now. He hadn't been there to care for her when she was a child; she didn't need him now. "This is all a little late, isn't it?" she said coolly.

"Nay, lass," he said with a gentle burr. " 'Tis never too late. I found that out with your sisters."

She stared at him in astonishment. "I have half-sisters?"

"Aye." He chuckled. "Three of them, all living, here in the Colonies. The youngest but you, Fiona, looks much like you do. And she's as feisty as you are."

She turned away from him. Sisters ... three more sisters. It was hard to imagine. "I have a sister in Scotland," she said. "I don't need any more."

He laid a hand on her shoulder. "What I've done to ye is none of their doing. And when your temper cools, you'll ken that," he said, lapsing into a Highland brogue he'd not used for many years. "Sit ye down, lass, and hear what I have to say. With things as they are, there may not be another chance to tell ye what ye should know about me."

"I told ye, I dinna care," she protested.

"I am your father, and you'll listen," he said firmly, pushing her back until she sat down on the platform that ran along the wall. He took a seat beside her. "Listen and don't interrupt. Did that stepfather you dote on teach ye no manners?"

"He did."

"Good." He flashed her a smile that nearly melted the frost that surrounded her heart. "Since time out of time, 'tis been the Stewart way to marry into good fortune," he began. "I was sixteen and the sole hope of a widowed mother and younger brothers and sisters. Aye, I had a title, but we were poorer than our crofters. Many a time, I saw my mother go to bed hungry. So when a cousin arranged a marriage of convenience for me, I did as my mother bade me and accepted the lady's hand and her great wealth."

"And I suppose she was as happy as you with this arrangement?" Cailin asked wryly.

"Margaret's parents were ambitious. They had acquired gold and land through commerce, and they wanted their only child to have the title of countess. I am an earl, if it matters to you."

"It doesna," she replied. "Born on the wrong side of the blanket, what care I for your titles?"

"It wasn't a bad agreement for either of us. My family was secure, and Margaret had a boy husband who was too naive to interfere in her private life or to question her tastes."

"Your bride wasn't such a great bargain?"

"Margaret was a good woman," he answered sincerely. "We never loved each other, but we became the best of friends. She taught me how to please a woman, and strange to say, I think she made a man of me."

Cailin stared at the bark wall and didn't say anything. She didn't want to think about Cameron; she wanted to concentrate on Sterling.

"I was sixteen, Cailin. Sixteen to Margaret's thirty. She wanted a child, and I needed an heir. We tried, but all of our babes were stillborn, blue, shriveled little mites. Margaret bled terribly with each pregnancy until her physician told me that another childbirth would kill her. I was twenty then, wed to an older lady I could not bed."

"You could have had your marriage annulled," Cailin said. She couldn't help picturing in her mind a dashing young Cameron unable to have normal relations with his lawful wife. And she couldn't help the rush of compassion that followed.

"I took vows. I swore to be her husband so long as we both lived." He sighed. "I've made my share of mistakes, lass, and I've disappointed a lot of people, but I couldn't cast off my barren wife like a worn-out servant."

"You stayed together?"

"After a fashion. We maintained the appearance of a respectable couple. Margaret could entertain and be entertained in the highest circles, and I had unlimited use of her funds for my own pleasures. She never minded my lady friends, and I never begrudged her hers."

Cailin glanced back at him to see if she'd heard correctly. "Ye dinna mean . . ."

"Aye, but I do. I kept her secret as long as she lived, and I'd not shame her now. Margaret preferred the caresses of women rather than men."

"I've heard of men like that, but never women. Is it true?" she asked.

"Margaret was smart and witty, and we had much in common. God made her the way she was. Who am I, a sinner who fathered four daughters out of wedlock, to judge her? She never betrayed a friend or turned a hungry person from her door. You'd have liked her; I know you would."

"She's no longer living?"

"Margaret died of natural causes. I wasn't with her at the end, but her dear companion of many years was. Margaret left Alice well provided for, and the rest came to me. I have given all my other daughters wealth and land. For you, I would do no less." He chuckled. "I think Margaret would approve of her money passing to women, don't you?"

"Sterling has land."

"Wilderness. Virgin forest. A hundred years from now, it will be fertile farmland, but not in your life-time. Scot's Haven lies along the Chesapeake. Two thousand acres of cleared, rich earth and another thousand of woodland. You'll have your own dock and three ships to carry your tobacco and grain to England. The house is modest by London standards, but grand enough to host the royal governor himself. Ease an old man's heart and conscience, lass. Take it for your children and grandchildren, if not yourself. After all . . ." He smiled and squeezed her hand. "A husband can love a rich wife as well as a poor one."

She nodded. "I suppose, but you'll be needing your home yourself for many years to come."

He grinned. "Aye. I do intend to. I just wanted it settled between us that I've not left you penniless."

"You've given me much to think on," she admitted.

"So long as I'm clearing my conscience, I want you to be less harsh on your mother. She was very young when you were conceived, Cailin."

"You loved her, didn't you?"

"In a special way. I've loved many women—but none was the same, and I cherished my love for each of them."

" 'Tis better that you cared for each other, I suppose, than my being born to a married couple who despised each other." She grimaced. "But knowing my mother, I'd wager she'd not have been so eager to lie with you if you'd not been a comely rogue."

"As to that, I canna say. I always thought my charm had something to do with it," he answered smoothly.

Lachpi approached them and said something to Cameron in Shawnee. Cameron frowned and answered in the same language.

Cailin glanced from one to the other. They were

talking about her, she was sure of it. "What is it?" she demanded. "What are ye saying?"

Kitate joined the group and added his harsh comments. As he rarely spoke and hardly ever looked directly at her, she was puzzled.

Cameron exchanged a few more words with the two of them, then nodded and turned to Cailin. "Lachpi says that regardless of what happens to Sterling, you're still in danger."

She sniffed. "Since when is that new? I believe we've all been in danger since the attack on the farm."

Lachpi shook his head. "No," he said firmly. His English was soft and precise with a peculiar melodic ring. "This man Lenape—Delaware tribe." He motioned toward Kitate. "Shawnee. There is still peace between Mohawk and Shawnee and Delaware. You white woman. No peace with Mohawk. Danger for white woman."

"Why is that any different than Cameron?" she asked. "He's white."

Kitate make a clicking noise with his tongue.

"Not exactly," her father said, unbuttoning his shirt cuff. He pushed back the full white linen sleeve to reveal a tattoo on the inside of his forearm, just below the elbow. "Many years ago, I was formally adopted into the Shawnee nation."

"I still don't understand . . ." she began. Lachpi silenced her with a look.

"Mohawk strike Cailin. You Shawnee, he not do this thing," he said. "Lachpi take you as sister. Make you Delaware. Give white woman . . . " He shook his head and searched for the right English words. "Will make Cailin more safe."

"Lachpi has lost his entire family," Cameron explained. "When he dies, his blood line will die out. And he has a bad feeling."

The Delaware spoke at length in the Indian tongue.

Cameron translated. "He was born into the Turtle Clan of the Lenape. On the trail here, he saw a turtle and a crow together. He believes that the turtle came to tell him of his impending death. He wants to adopt you into his family, to give you his sister's name and clan. Then even if you are held prisoner, you will have some position." He exhaled softly. "In other words, the Iroquois doubt you possess a soul. If Lachpi makes you a Delaware—that's what we call the Lenape—you will gain status and become a human being."

"He wants me to become an Indian?" she asked.

"Aye. Normally, you'd be born—rather, brought into the tribe—by a woman. But this is an emergency. Lachpi assures me that such adoptions have been done before and have been recognized by the civilized tribes."

Cailin shook her head. "I appreciate what you're trying to do, Lachpi, but I'm Christian. I could never—"

"It's not just for you," Cameron said. "It's to preserve his family. His children are dead, his sister and brothers. His parents. If you will accept his sister's name, his line will continue."

"I still don't see—"

Lachpi put two fingers over her lips. "You carry a child," he said. "You white slave of Mohawk. Child of white slave must be given away to good Mohawk family to be raised as human. Child of Lenni Lenape, First People, remain with mother even if she is captive. You become Lenape, no one take your child from you."

Cailin put her hands over her belly protectively. "How did you know about the baby?" she asked. She couldn't imagine being a prisoner long enough to have her baby, but the thought that Sterling's bairn might be taken from her was chilling. "I'm still not sure I am," she hedged. "Did Moonfeather tell you?"

Lachpi smiled. "Your eyes tell this man." He touched her cheek with one finger. "Face tell him." He nodded. "You with child. Must think of child."

"Take his offer," Cameron urged her. "It will do you no harm, and it won't endanger your Catholic soul. Many Delaware are Christians."

She glanced at each face in turn. "Why does it have to be Delaware? Why not Shawnee, if I must be an Indian?" she asked.

"There is no difference," Kitate said. "Our cousins the Delaware have joined with us since the English drove them from their home by the sea. To be Delaware is a great honor. Besides . . ." He shrugged. "Lachpi is willing to take responsibility for you."

She looked at Cameron. "I don't see why you couldn't—"

"Descent is reckoned through the female line," he said. "My mother was Scot. She had no clan. It has to be Lachpi."

"All right," she agreed. "Whatever makes ye happy." She'd only thought of Sterling, not of what might happen to her if he died. Pray God, she never had to.

The ritual was short. Cameron held her arm steady while Lachpi scratched the outline of a tiny turtle on her left shoulder. Cailin gritted her teeth as the sharp knife point bit into her skin. When Lachpi was satisfied, Cameron rubbed ashes into the figure.

Next, the Delaware poured a gourd full of water

over her head. "Should be sweat bath and river cleansing," he said. "But Turtle will understand."

Cailin wiped the water out of her eyes and stood with dripping hair as the gnarled old warrior laid his hand on her forehead.

"From this day, you are no longer white, born without a soul," he said solemnly. "You are Lenape n'hackey, Indian, of the Lenni Lenape, and your name is Wing-an O-tah-ais, Sweet Spring of the Turtle Clan, and brother to Lachpi." His heavy-lidded eyes narrowed. "And you must remember to show proper respect for your totem."

"Never eat or injure a turtle," Cameron finished. "In fact, you show more respect for your totem if you refrain from mentioning his name."

"I think I can manage that," Cailin said. Her shoulder was smarting, and she felt foolish. A turtle, she was a turtle named Wing-an O-tah-ais. She tried not to smile. Her cousin Alasdair would have thought this all hilarious.

Instantly, the image of Alasdair's freckled face rose in her mind and she laughed aloud. A warm feeling enveloped her. Alasdair was dead, but he could still make her laugh ... and as long as she remembered him, he wasn't really gone.

She looked at Lachpi. He'd obviously loved his sister as she'd loved her cousin. And he was trying to live with his loss as she was. She smiled at him. "Thank you for the honor," she said sincerely. "I will try to be worthy of your sister."

He nodded. "Sweet Spring has gained wisdom," he said. "Tell your son of Lachpi, so that he will not be forgotten."

"If it's a boy, he'll be your nephew," Cailin replied.

"You'll always be welcome under our roof and at our table. You can tell him yourself."

The Delaware shook his head. "The wind calls this man's name," he said.

"Don't—" she started to say, but was interrupted by the abrupt arrival of the surly Mohawk woman.

"Come," the squaw ordered. "Watch death of your peace woman."

Kitate led the group out of the ceremonial long-house into the dark night. They walked through the chanting, shouting Mohawks, past Ohneya and his followers, to the place where Moonfeather stood near the center of the clearing.

Cailin's frantic gaze sought Sterling and caught a glimpse of him still tied upright to the stake. His eyes were open, and he looked alert. She wanted to call out to him, but she knew that he'd never hear her voice above the thunderous drumming and the wild cries of the inflamed Iroquois.

Instead, she whispered a prayer under her breath and tried to keep pace with Cameron, who held her firmly by the right arm. Lachpi strode directly in front of her, his rifle cradled in his arm.

Cailin had wondered why the Mohawk hadn't stripped the Shawnee of their weapons, but Cameron had told her that it was a mark of arrogance on the part of the Iroquois. "They don't think of us as a threat," he'd explained earlier. "We're outnumbered twenty to one. One reckless move on our part, and our scalps will decorate a Mohawk lance."

Cailin didn't think that Kitate, Lachpi, and the others looked particularly peaceful. The Shawnee had painted their faces and appeared as savage and bloodthirsty as the Mohawk. Young Koke-wah's chin jutted out defiantly, and his eyes glittered in the firelight as fiercely as any wild creature's. Joseph, a solid wedge of coiled muscle, kept one step behind the boy, planting each wide foot with deliberate purpose, and eyeing the Mohawk with black hatred.

Moonfeather looked up and smiled when she saw them coming. Her features were tranquil. She wore no paint, and her hair was covered with a fringed shawl of blue and red. Her feet were bare.

Stretching out in front of the Shawnee peace woman was a bed of glowing coals, a yard wide and four yards long. The Mohawk medicine man stood at the far end of the fire pit. He was garbed in an overpowering bear skin and a wooden mask of black and yellow with tufts of black hair and teeth of bone. The carved mask was huge, at least a third the size of his body. Jit-sho raised his staff and shook it defiantly at Moonfeather.

She ignored him and extended a hand to Cailin. "Sister," she said softly.

Cailin embraced her. "You can't do this," she whispered. "There has to be another way."

Moonfeather chuckled. "Believe me, I wish you were right." She looked into Cameron's face. "Don't worry," she said. "A peace woman can walk on fire." She glanced back at Cailin. "Bear Dancer has promised me that Sterling and the rest of us can leave if Jit-sho is proved wrong." She nodded to Kitate and said something to him in Shawnee.

He growled a reply, and Moonfeather repeated her statement. Kitate shrugged and shoved a small French pistol into Cailin's hand. "Don't shoot your foot off," he warned. "It's loaded."

Moonfeather smiled.

Bear Dancer came through the crowd and stopped midway between the peace woman and the Mohawk shaman at the edge of the white-hot coals. A group of dignitaries joined him. One motioned to the Shawnee.

"Go," Moonfeather said.

Bodies pressed in around Cailin. Hands pushed and tugged at her; strange Mohawk eyes glared at her. She and Cameron were separated by the mob, and she found herself only a few feet from the Mohawk leader, Bear Dancer, in the midst of Ohneya's warriors.

A hard hand settled on the nape of Cailin's neck. She twisted around to see the war chief Ohneya glaring down at her.

"You will learn to like my touch, Fire Hair," he said. "Please me, and I will make you my third wife."

"Go to hell," she spat. Diving between a wrinkled old woman and a Mohawk warrior in a military coat, she looked around for her father.

"Here," Cameron called. He put a hand into the middle of a seasoned warrior's chest and thrust him back. Cailin wiggled into the spot between her father and Bear Dancer. The Mohawk stiffened. Cailin flashed him a wide smile, and he blinked in astonishment.

Bear Dancer raised his arms over his head and began to speak. This time, his words were few. When he dropped his hands, the Iroquois shouted something that sounded like "Hoo!", then they fell silent.

The drums stopped.

Several of Ohneya's braves pressed through to the edge of the fire pit. Others surrounded Bear Dancer and the council members. The old woman that Cailin had jostled was lost from sight.

It was so quiet that Cailin could hear the breeze through the fish-drying racks, hear the hiss of the fire and the breathing of the Mohawk around her. Lachpi trod on the heels of a council member, and when the man stepped forward, the Delaware moved into the vacant spot directly behind Cailin.

"Courage, little sister," he murmured.

Cailin looked down at the carpet of fire.

It was impossible for Moonfeather to walk over that and not be horribly burned. Cailin wanted to scream, to do anything to stop her. Instead, she waited with bated breath and thudding heart like the rest of them.

Kitate began to chant, one Shawnee voice in a sea of hostile Iroquois. The Mohawk shaman shook his rattle.

Moonfeather stepped out onto the bed of coals as lightly as a dancer. Cailin shut her eyes. When she opened them again, the peace woman was directly opposite. Her eyes were closed; her lips were curved into a faint smile.

Cameron's whisper filled Cailin's head.

> *"She comes, the peace woman,*
> *See her come, walking lightly,*
> *Hear the wind call her name,*
> *See her, holy woman of the Shawnee,*
> *Walking lightly, on the rainbow . . . "*

Gooseflesh rose on Cailin's arms. Why wasn't the fire scorching Moonfeather's bare feet? Why? What was happening?

Then the peace woman reached the end of the fire pit, stepped onto solid ground, opened her eyes, and smiled.

The Mohawks shouted in approval.

Bear Dancer spoke.

The Mohawks cheered.

"She is worthy," Cameron called. "The chief has declared that we are to go in peace."

A Mohawk brave shoved Jit-sho. His rattle fell onto the coals. Instantly, the air was filled with the scent of burning turtle shell.

"Jit-sho!" a woman cried.

"Jit-sho," echoed a man with one arm.

The carved mask trembled.

The shaman began to sing in a thready voice, a voice that did nothing to hide the fear in the man's heart. A warrior gave him a push. Jit-sho shrieked and leaped into the fire pit.

His scream filled the night. Cailin shuddered as the bearskin caught and became a sheet of flames. She tried to imagine the high-pitched squeal as something other than human, the awful stench of charred flesh as burning pork. Sickness rose in her throat.

She shut her eyes for a moment, and when she opened them, she saw that Moonfeather was bending over something black and smoking. Her hands were touching what could have been a man's head.

The wailing had ceased, but his feet thrashed. When the peace woman stood up, he was still.

The Mohawks shrank back.

Cailin heard a sharp hiss of breath. She turned her head and saw the gleam of a metal blade in the firelight. Ohneya twisted the knife in Bear Dancer's back, and the old sachem's eyes widened. He sagged forward, and one of Ohneya's braves caught him.

Cailin seized Cameron's arm and pointed.

Ohneya leaped into Bear Dancer's place and raised a clenched fist. "The Shawnee have murdered our sachem and our shaman!" he shouted. "Burn them! Burn them all!"

Chapter 27

An Iroquois war whoop shattered the night, and the angry Mohawks surged around them. A shot rang out. A woman screamed.

Cameron swore in Gaelic.

Cailin couldn't understand Ohneya's words, but she had seen him stab Bear Dancer with his knife. And when the war chief seized her left wrist and yanked her against him, she brought her right hand up and jabbed the barrel of her pistol into the soft place under his chin. "Breathe and I'll blow your head off," she threatened as she cocked the weapon.

The ominous click of the hammer stopped Ohneya in his tracks.

Cailin caught a glimpse of a flailing war club and heard an agonized groan. Another musket boomed. Fighting broke out around the fire pit between Shawnee and Mohawk warriors.

Suddenly, Cameron was beside Cailin, aiming his pistol at the war chief's ear. "Tell them to back off," her father ordered breathlessly.

"You cannot escape me!" Ohneya snarled.

"Maybe not," Cailin said, "but we can give it a try, can't we?"

Ohneya barked a command, and the Mohawks around him halted their attack on the Shawnee.

347

Gradually, those at the back of the mob stopped shouting and grew still.

Cailin poked Ohneya's throat with the pistol. "Free Sterling," she said.

"The white Shawnee," Cameron added hoarsely. "Let him go. And let the others join us. Now!"

Ohneya called out to his people in Iroquoian. A group parted, and Cailin saw Joseph and Kitate moving toward them with Moonfeather. Joseph's face was covered in blood.

"This man will get Na-nata Ki-tehi," Lachpi shouted. Boldly, he strode through the enemy ranks to the torture stake and slashed the leather thongs that held Sterling prisoner.

Kitate stepped behind Ohneya and knotted his lean fingers in the war chief's scalp lock. Bending Ohneya's head back, Kitate laid the razor-sharp edge of his knife at the Mohawk's exposed throat. "Leave this one to me," he growled.

Cailin glanced into her father's face. He nodded. "Kitate will hold him fast for us."

Slowly, she lowered the pistol. Her hand was shaking, and she felt cold. Pukasee's voice came from the right. Mentally, she began counting the Shawnee. Kitate, Pukasee, Joseph, and Lachpi. Where was Koke-wah? And Ake?

Then Sterling's strong arm wrapped around her shoulders, and she cried out with relief. He murmured her name, and his fingers dug into her arm. "Don't fail me now, Highlander," he said.

Releasing her, he grabbed a rifle from a scowling Mohawk. "Kitate," he called. "Tell him to have them throw down their weapons." When Ohneya passed on the order and the Mohawk obeyed, Sterling picked up a tomahawk, a knife, and a powder horn and shot bag from the gathering heap.

Using the war chief as a human shield, the Shawnee party began to move toward the outer gate of the village. Lachpi went ahead with Sterling and Ake on either side of the two women. Cameron and Pukasee followed, rifles cocked and aimed at the crowd. Kitate and Joseph brought up the rear with Ohneya, Kitate never loosening his grip on their hostage. Amid the Iroquois' howls of rage, the small band hurried past the darkened longhouses.

One by one, they filed through the gate. As they passed the wall and stepped out into the open, an Iroquois guard fired from the top of the palisade. Lachpi took a musket ball in his thigh. Sterling swung around, aimed carefully, and picked off the sniper. Lachpi's wound bled heavily, but he didn't slow his pace. He crossed the river and stood waist-deep in the water, watching for other marksmen on the palisade.

When Cailin saw that Sterling was waiting for the rest to pass, she stopped.

"Go on!" he shouted. "Don't wait for me."

"I'm nay leaving ye to them again," she warned.

"I've no intention of staying. Do as I tell you, woman. Stay with Moonfeather—no matter what. Stay beside her." He waved his arms and shouted in Mohawk.

"He's telling them that if anyone crosses the river, Ohneya is a dead man," Cameron said. He squeezed her hand. "Come, lass. And I hope you're as good a runner as Moonfeather. We must move like the wind to keep ahead of these devils."

When they all reached the shelter of the forest on the far side of the river, Kitate slammed Ohneya across the back of his head with the flat of his tomahawk. Ohneya crumpled to the ground and lay as though dead. Sterling took hold of Cailin's arm, and they began to run through the pitch darkness.

For nearly half a mile, they ran. Cailin's lungs burned and her legs felt like lead. She made no effort to speak; she just ran, keeping on the trail by watching the faint glow of Moonfeather's white doeskin dress ahead of her.

When they reached an outcropping of loose rock, Lachpi stopped. "There!" Cameron said. "It's up there to the right."

Sterling pulled her off the trail and took a firm grip on her hand. Together, they climbed a steep incline to a spot where a freak windstorm the winter before had felled dozens of giant trees. She remembered Moonfeather pointing it out to her on the way to the Mohawk village.

"It's a natural fortress," Cameron explained when they reached the top. "We'll hold them off here." He was breathing heavily, and Cailin wondered how a man of his advanced years had managed to keep up the pace.

"We can't fight them all," Cailin protested. "The Mohawks must have close to a hundred warriors. We've got to keep going. We'll be trapped here."

"We're not all going on, lass," her father said. He sat down heavily behind a downed oak and began to fumble with his powder horn.

Moonfeather spoke in Algonquian. Cameron answered her in the same language, then Kitate said something.

"What are they saying?" Cailin demanded of Sterling. "I can't understand."

"Quiet," he ordered. Then he too spoke in the Indian tongue. After a few exchanges, he turned and pulled her into his arms. "Listen to me carefully," he said, speaking slowly, as though to a small child. "I want you to take off your clothes and put on Moonfeather's doeskin dress."

"Why? That doesn't make any sense," she protested.

Moonfeather materialized out of the blackness, wrapped in Lachpi's blanket. Her beautiful ceremonial garment was draped over her arm. "We are going to split up," she said. "I want you to wear my doeskin because that will make the Mohawk believe you are the peace woman."

"That's crazy," Cailin said. "I'll nay put ye in danger for my sake. I canna—"

"You can and you will," Sterling said harshly. "Moonfeather tells me that you are carrying our child."

"Yes, but that doesn't make me a cripple. I'm still—"

"Kitate, Joseph, and this woman will flee east and then south to the Dutch," Moonfeather said. "In your clothing, I can pass myself off as Lady Kentington and receive safe passage to Annapolis. In Shawnee dress, this one would only be a target for white long rifles."

"Then we should stay together," Cailin insisted. "I can—"

"Listen to those who know what they're talking about," Cameron snapped. "You and Sterling will go west to the friendly Algonquian-speaking tribes. The Mohawks will expect us to go south. If we do, we're all dead."

"What of you and the others?" she begged. Something didn't sound right. This was giving her a bad feeling. They weren't telling her everything. She knew it. "Why aren't you going with us?"

"Pukasee, Ake, Lachpi, and I will hold the Mohawk off here, long enough to give both parties a head start," Cameron said.

Sterling's arm tightened around her shoulders. "Be strong," he murmured.

"No," she cried. "That's suicide. I won't let you stay—"

"What you want isn't important," Cameron said coldly.

Frantically, she turned to Moonfeather. "Ye canna let him do this. Tell them! They'll listen to you! Tell them it's crazy."

Moonfeather held out the dress.

"How can ye be so heartless?" Cailin begged. "He's my father. He's an old man."

"And he's dying," the peace woman said in a throaty voice. "He took a knife between the ribs back in the village."

"Dying?" Tears welled up in Cailin's eyes. "He can't be," she sobbed. "He's my father."

"And mine," Moonfeather replied softly. Catching Cailin's hand, she brought it to her own throat.

"You can't be my—" Cailin gasped as her fingers touched a necklace so like the Eye of Mist in weight and shape that she released it and grabbed her own to be certain Moonfeather wasn't playing a cruel trick. "That's impossible," she said. "How—"

"Do you never listen, lass?" Cameron said. "There is little time. We can't waste what we do have in talking. I cut the Eye of Mist into four equal pieces. If it weren't as black as the devil's arsehole in this woods, you'd see for yourself. Moonfeather's necklace is a match to yours. They fit together perfectly. Each of my daughters has one; Anne, Moonfeather, Fiona, and you. You are the baby, Cailin . . . a gift I never expected to receive at the end of my life."

"But . . . but . . ." Cailin struggled to understand the reality of what her father had just said. "Moonfeather, my sister? Why didn't ye tell me sooner?"

"'This woman wanted to wait until we were friends . . . until you proved your heart," Moonfeather explained. "Quickly, now. The dress."

"I won't do it," Cailin replied stubbornly. "If Cameron—if Father's hurt, we must do something. We canna—"

"Take those clothes off," Sterling said, "or I'll rip them off."

"You must," Moonfeather said.

"But if the Mohawks think you are me, I'm putting you in danger," she argued.

"Put on the damned dress!" Sterling grabbed hold of the hem of her skirt.

"All right, all right. I'll change with ye. But I'll nay leave Cameron. If the rest of you are too cowardly to stay with him, I'll stay by myself. I can shoot a rifle."

Moonfeather didn't answer. Instead, she helped Cailin out of her English clothing and into the deerskin dress. It was so dark that Cailin didn't give a second thought to disrobing in front of the men. Only the white fringed gown was visible in the starless night.

"Don't forget the shawl," Cameron reminded them. Moonfeather made a sound of agreement and draped the cloth over Cailin's hair.

Cailin dropped to her knees and embraced Cameron. "I'm nay going to leave ye," she promised. "We can patch up your wound, carry ye, and—"

Cameron's arms encircled her. He hugged her hard, then kissed her on the forehead. "Go with God, child. And don't worry about me. I'd rather meet my maker smelling of gunpowder than being wheeled into heaven in a dogcart."

"No . . . no," she protested.

Moonfeather knelt beside them, and for a long minute, Cameron hugged them both. "Ye must go for the sake of the babe," her new sister reminded Cailin. "Our father's life is used up; the little one you carry has yet to draw breath." She tucked a shell bracelet into Cailin's hand. "Wear this, so that all who are not Iroquois know that you are kin to a Shawnee peace woman. If anything happens to Sterling, that bracelet will bring you safely home. You can go to any village. As long as you do not offer violence to the tribes, you will be welcomed as a daughter and given aid."

Sterling tugged at her arm. "It's time, Cailin."

"I canna," she sobbed. "Dinna make me."

"Remember what I said about your mother," Cameron reminded her. "She loved you as I have come to love you."

As Sterling pulled her to her feet, Cailin felt another hand on her other shoulder.

"Among the Delaware are no words for goodbye, my sister," Lachpi said in his quaintly accented English. "Follow sun's path west and do not forget another who loved you."

"Lachpi . . ." Words failed her.

"This man stays to give good fight," the Delaware said. "Mohawk will sing about this place and the Shawnee who held it."

"No! No!" Cailin cried. But Sterling's hand was welded to hers.

"We must go now," Sterling said harshly, "or they will give their lives in vain. Make it worth something, woman. Make their sacrifice count."

Blindly, Cailin stumbled after him. "Take care," she murmured. "Take care."

"And you, little sister," Moonfeather called after them. "Do not forget the power of your amulet. Use it to bring your new son safely to the Chesapeake. This woman will be waiting."

Cailin didn't understand how Sterling could see to walk, let alone run, or have any idea what direction they were traveling. There had been no time for a joyous reunion with her husband, no moment when she could relax in his arms and tell him how much she loved him. Instead, they kept moving, trying to put as much distance as possible between them and the hilltop fortress before the Iroquois found it.

She didn't know how far she and Sterling had come, but they were still close enough to hear the first volley of rifle fire echo through the valleys.

"The Mohawks!" Her belly knotted, and she swayed on her feet. "Sweet Jesus."

Sterling's only reply was to sweep her up in his arms and begin to run.

Dawn found Cailin and Sterling wading through the debris of a burned-out section of forest. The blackened trees and heaped ash seemed all too appropriate to Cailin. The landscape around her seemed as bleak as her hope of eluding the Mohawks.

"It was wrong," she argued with Sterling for the fifth time. "It was wrong to leave them, and I was wrong to take Moonfeather's dress. 'Twas done for my safety, not hers. Do ye think me stupid? She proved her power in front of the entire Mohawk village. They might be afraid to shoot her."

"That's true enough," he admitted. "But what she said about the Dutch was true, too. She'll need to look English if she wants the help of any white settlers."

"Why did she choose Kitate and Joseph to go with her? Why did Lachpi and Ake and Pukasee have to die with my father?"

"Lachpi couldn't have run much farther with that bullet in his leg. Joseph and Kitate were the strongest and best able to protect the peace woman. Besides, Kitate is her son."

Cailin stopped and looked up at him. "Isn't Forrest Wescott her son?"

"She was wed to a Shawnee warrior, years ago, before she met and married Robert Wescott, Lord Kentington. He was the Viscount Brandon when they wed; that's why she calls him Brandon. He later inherited his father's title when the old earl died. Kitate is the son of your sister's Shawnee marriage. Robert Wescott took Moonfeather away to England, and Kitate's never really forgiven Robert or the English. He's Shawnee through and through, but he's devoted to his mother. If anyone can get her home, he will."

"Kitate is Cameron's grandson then."

"And your nephew," he said.

She shook her head. "You knew all along that she was my sister, didn't ye?"

"Once I saw Cameron, I knew. Moonfeather's story is common knowledge among the Shawnee."

"You never told me about her necklace."

Sterling shrugged. "It's not the Indian way to talk about magic. Moonfeather kept it hidden. So do you, for that matter. I'd not have seen it if I hadn't bedded you."

Cailin touched her amulet. "I wish I'd had time to love him," she said. "I didn't think there was room in my heart for another father, but—"

A musket cracked from the hillside behind them. Cailin twisted to see a puff of white smoke.

"Get down, you little fool," Sterling warned. He shoved her behind a charred log and fired off a return shot at the small moving figures in the distance. After what seemed an impossible delay, one Indian toppled over and rolled down the slope.

"Looks like our ploy didn't work too long," Cailin said.

"You're still alive, aren't you?"

She felt as though she was going to be sick. If the Mohawks had followed them, that meant they knew that the two of them weren't with Cameron. Her father, Lachpi, and the others must be dead or captured.

"We can't stay here," Sterling said. "They could circle around and come at us from two sides."

"I hope Cameron's dead," she whispered dully. "Better dead than being taken back to the village and burned alive."

Sterling looked down into her eyes. "They'd not be taken," he assured her. "Lachpi would see to that." Sterling began to work his way right on his hands and knees. "There's a washout a little ways ahead. I saw it from the ridge. If we can reach that, it will give us cover to get out of this burned area. Stay close, and keep your head down."

Once Cailin and Sterling reached the gully, they got to their feet and sprinted a few hundred yards into a low place. They waded a stream and dashed into the forest beyond that.

An hour later, two Mohawks leaped from the foliage ahead of them. Both braves fired. At the same instant, Sterling threw himself on top of Cailin, knocking her flat. Before she could catch her breath, he had raised to one knee, leveled his pistol, and shot the first warrior through the heart.

The second warrior screeched an Iroquois war cry as he dashed toward them swinging a war club. Sterling flung the empty pistol into the Mohawk's face, spoiling his aim and giving himself a few seconds to pull his tomahawk from his belt. The Indian balanced on the balls of his feet and edged to the left.

Cailin spat sand and dirt from her mouth and raised her head. The forest around them was hot and still. Not a bird chirped; not a squirrel chattered. Cailin could smell the Mohawk and hear his heavy breathing. Cautiously, she dragged her pistol from her hunting bag and cocked it.

The Mohawk's sloe eyes were focused on Sterling. As soon as the brave moved far enough to the left so that Sterling was out of her line of fire, she took aim at the black circle painted in the center of the warrior's chest and squeezed the trigger.

The flintlock roared, and a neat, round hole appeared in the black circle. The Mohawk's eyes widened, he took a few steps, and then he fell with blood running from the corner of his mouth.

Sterling grinned at Cailin. "Good shooting." He grabbed the dead man's rifle and slammed it against a tree. After disposing of the first brave's gun in the same manner, he stripped them of powder and shot, and stuck an additional tomahawk in his belt. Then he removed one of the brave's moccasins and put them on his bloody bare feet. Motioning for her to follow, he started down the deer trail at a trot.

The sun was high overhead when they crossed another river and stopped to rest in a natural rock shelter. "Get some sleep," he told her. "I'll try and find us something to eat."

"Don't leave me," she begged him.

"We have to keep up our strength, Cailin. You especially." He put two fingers under her chin and tilted her face up. "I want you to know that I'm glad about the baby. I'm sorry that this is hard on you. I promised once that I'd take care of you, and I haven't done much of a job, but—"

She smiled at him. "I'm not complaining."

"No, you're not." He grinned. "Some honeymoon."

"You really want this babe?"

He nodded. His dark eyes gleamed with moisture. "We'll make it home," he said. "All three of us."

She covered his hand with hers and brought them to her flat stomach. "Our son won't be born until February or March by my reckoning. Surely, we'll be home by the time the leaves start to turn color."

He leaned his rifle against the rock wall and pulled her into his arms. For a long time, he held her and didn't speak. And then he said, "Where's home, woman? The Chesapeake or Scotland?" He pushed back Moonfeather's shawl and buried his face in her hair. "You can't expect me to walk out of hell and then let you leave me."

"I promised, Sterling. I gave my word to my family, but I can't leave you. What can I do?"

"I'm your family now. We can send for them. Hell, I'd go myself before I'd let you risk your life to go into Scotland."

She chuckled and wiggled free. "Before you'd let

me risk my life?" She looked around her. "This isn't exactly the deacon's parlor we're sitting in."

"I mean what I say. I'll not let you cross the ocean again."

She met his gaze stubbornly, then shrugged and made an attempt to lighten his mood. "Look at you," she said. "You look more Indian than white."

Sterling glanced down at the beaded Iroquois strap that held his hunting bag and powder horn, and at his scanty loincloth and moccasins. "No war paint," he commented wryly.

"You do seem more Shawnee than English out here," she said.

"And I'll look more white when we return to the settlements." He grinned again, a slightly crooked, devil-may-care smile that made her go all soft inside. "I've no wish to raise our children in a wigwam." His eyes grew serious. "But I will try and give them a respect for my mother's people and their ways. I'm only part English, Cailin. I forgot that for too long. Whatever I do with my life, I'll still have two sets of heritages to draw on."

"Does that include Indian magic?" she asked.

"When necessary."

She nodded. "I still don't understand it. I saw Moonfeather walk across those hot coals with my own eyes. I saw, but I canna believe it."

He chuckled. "She's a peace woman. Rules for normal people don't apply."

She sighed, sat down, and put her head back against the rock. "Maybe I am hungry," she admitted. "I'll have roast beef, potatoes browned with onion, and—"

He chuckled. "How does raw trout sound?"

"Awful."

"A little wild onion, and you'll never know the difference."

"Don't be gone long. I'm only brave when you're with me," she said.

"Try and sleep. I don't know how long we'll be safe here, and I can promise you, we'll walk all night."

"You be careful," she admonished him. "I want our son to have a father in residence."

"Me too."

Nothing could stop the constriction of her throat as she watched his broad back vanish through the trees. She was determined not to be childish and shame herself by crying again. She tried to ignore the rustle of branches and the other sounds of the deep forest around her.

Were there bears out there? she wondered. More wolves? She shivered. Sterling really didn't expect her to sleep, did he? She rubbed her bare arms to brush away the goose bumps and vowed to stay wide awake and alert until he got back. She was too frightened to sleep. At least, she thought she was. But her eyelids grew heavy in the still afternoon heat.

The grating sound of gravel scraping underfoot woke her. Cailin opened her eyes with a start and saw Ohneya standing over her, a sixteen-inch scalping knife in his hand and murder flickering in his black heathen eyes.

Chapter 28

~~~ ∽∾ ~~~

Cailin screamed. Ohneya's painted skull face glowed white in the shadow of the overhanging rock. Whispering harsh, guttural threats in Mohawk, he came at her. She pressed herself against the granite wall, but there was no place to run and nowhere to hide.

Ohneya grabbed her hair and yanked back, slashing down with his knife to cut her throat from ear to ear. She scooped up a handful of sand with her left hand and threw it full into his grotesque face. He howled in rage as the sand blinded his eyes.

Cailin twisted away. His steel blade missed her jugular and sliced a fiery trail of pain across the upper section of her right arm. Ohneya drew back his arm to strike again.

Then he shuddered and fell forward heavily on top of Cailin, Sterling's tomahawk buried between his shoulder blades. He convulsed twice and gave an agonized groan. Sterling seized him by the shoulders and dragged him away. The Mohawk's body sprawled across the back of the cave, his sightless eyes already glazing over.

"Are you all right?" Sterling demanded as he pulled Cailin to her feet. He saw the blood running down her arm and swore a foul oath.

Drawing his own knife, he cut a strip of cloth from

362

Ohneya's shirt and wrapped it tightly around her arm. "It's not deep," he said. "It's a good thing you yelled your head off."

Her teeth were chattering. "Next time ... next time, don't be so slow."

"That bastard." Sterling put his moccasined foot in the center of Ohneya's chest and took hold of the Mohawk's scalp lock.

"No!" Cailin cried. "Don't."

Sterling glanced back at her and sheathed his knife. "For your sake, woman," he agreed. "But he deserved to lose his soul. Without his scalp, they wouldn't let him into heaven or hell—or wherever Mohawks go when they die."

"No more blood," she begged him. "We've seen enough bloodshed."

He nodded.

"Now what?"

"Now, Highlander, we start running again, north, out of Mohawk country into Canada. We'll have to cross the St. Lawrence River and swing west around Lake Ontario. Losing their war chief on top of Bear Dancer's death will slow the Iroquois down for a week or so. But once they elect a new leader, they'll call in the Oneida, the Onondaga, the Cayuga, and the Seneca. The entire Iroquois Confederacy will be hot for our scalps."

"Couldn't we go to some French settlement and—"

He uttered a sound of derision. "Not if you want to stay alive. The French would be quick enough to trade us back to the Iroquois. They're as eager to court favor with the Five Nations as the English are." He enfolded her in his arms. "I'll get us home in one piece," he promised her softly. "It just may not be as quick as you'd hoped. I believe the Ottawa will help us. They're Algonquian-speaking and not at war with the Shawnee; at least they weren't the last time I heard. If we have to, we'll go west to the Menominee. They've been our traditional allies, and they'll welcome a sister of a Shawnee peace woman."

"So we go south to the Chesapeake by walking north and then so far west that the maps don't show anything but emptiness."

"Something like that," he admitted. "Trust me."

She sighed. "That's what got me into all this in the first place."

The first crimson and gold leaves of autumn floated down around their shoulders in an Ottawa fishing camp in Canada. As Sterling had said, the two had found refuge among the northern cousins of the Shawnee after weeks of forced marches and near starvation.

The Mohawk had hunted them fiercely. Twice, they'd nearly escaped death by ambush. Cailin had lost track of how many warriors Sterling had killed. She had shot three, and one—she was certain—she'd finished off. She'd seen his war-painted body sink in the St. Lawrence River.

The Ottawa had confirmed Sterling's suspicions that the French would betray them. One hunter had told of being offered a reward of fifty pounds for Sterling's head. She was worth thirty pounds, a detail he teased her about over and over.

An old squaw, Kills Birds With a Sling, made a dye of walnut hulls for Cailin's hair and skin, and dressed her from head to toe in an Ottawa wedding dress and moccasins Kills Birds had sewn for her granddaughter. Sterling traded his extra flintlock pistol for the clothing, and the elderly woman's son and daughter-in-law let them stay until Cailin was rested enough to resume the journey.

It had been Sterling's idea to try to follow the northern shore of Lake Ontario south and west, either crossing Lake Erie by canoe or circling it to reach the Ohio country. The Huron, or what was left of them, prevented any attempt at that option. Smallpox had broken out among the tribes, and animosity was running high toward strangers of any nationality. Instead, the two continued west, passing from village to village, guided by hunters or traveling family groups.

The pace was no longer urgent, and Cailin found inner peace in the days and nights of walking though the vast timberlands beside her husband. They were no longer Sterling and Cailin, an Englishman and a Scotswoman, but the Shawnee Warrior Heart and his Delaware Indian wife Sweet Spring. Not even the occasional glimpse of a gray furry shadow moving through the trees or the far-off howl of a wolf disturbed her.

To her delight, Sweet Spring found that she had a talent for learning languages. Soon she began to understand basic phrases in Algonquian and even to venture a few words in return. Their lives were surprisingly simple and carefree. By day, they walked. At night, they sat beside a campfire with new friends and shared food, gossip, and laughter. Each night, Sweet Spring slept in her husband's strong arms. And each morning, she became more aware of the new life she carried within her.

None of their hosts believed that Sweet Spring was really Indian, but it didn't matter. She was invariably shown a warmth and hospitality that she had rarely known, even in the bosom of her own Highlands.

Once she stopped looking at the native peoples through Scottish eyes, she became captivated by their kindness, their generosity, and the love they showed toward their families and friends.

The autumn days slipped by like beads on a string. And as Cailin became more absorbed with her coming babe, she put the end of the trip out of her mind and concentrated on living each hour to the fullest.

Sterling was a tender and passionate lover. He watched over his wife with compassion and unending patience. Sometimes, they talked late at night when the sky rang with the mournful calls of wild geese flying south. Cailin loved these times most of all, when they were alone in a blanket, sharing silly jokes and planning for the joyful arrival of their son.

In late October, Cailin woke to find the forest white with snow. The first dusting melted by mid-afternoon, but the temperature dropped day by day. Sterling exchanged a Huron knife for a woman's cape of otter skin, and an Ojibwa hunter gifted Cailin with high moccasins of fur and a pair of child's snowshoes.

Soon winter came to grip the north country in earnest. The last canoe passage was fraught with danger from chunks of floating ice and stretches of frozen water too thin to support human weight. On Christmas Day, Cailin and Sterling were welcomed into a Menominee village by the young chief, Coiled Plume, and his laughing wife, Heron.

In less than an hour, Sterling and Cailin were treated to a feast of roast duck stuffed with onions and wild rice and escorted to a spotlessly clean wigwam near the center of town.

"You must be very weary," Heron said in a mixture of English and Algonquian. "My sister and her family are away for the winter. She would insist that you care for her home and keep the crows from nesting on her hearth."

"Yes," Coiled Plume insisted. "Tomorrow, will be time enough for talk. There is much this man would ask you about the English soldiers and the price of beaver in the east. Tomorrow, we will smoke a pipe and share hunting stories. You must consider our village your own for as long as you like."

When they were alone in the wigwam beside a crackling fire, Sterling looked into Cailin's tired eyes and took her stiff fingers in his. Rubbing her chapped hands to warm them, he promised that she could rest there until the birth of the child. "Coiled Plume assures me that there is plenty of meat, and the elk are numerous this winter. We will go no farther until the spring thaw."

Cailin nodded. It was time to stop, time to wait. The wigwam was snug and cozy, and her belly was full of hot food. Curling up on a thick bearskin rug, she put her head in her husband's lap and closed her eyes. Not even the baby's vigorous kicking could prevent her from drifting off into a deep sleep. She dreamed of a hillside of purple heather and the shrill coo of infant laughter.

Cailin was watching Heron prepare a porridge of wild rice and dried berries when her first labor cramp hit. Cailin's back had been aching since the night before, but she attributed the pain to a spill she'd taken on ice the morning before. It hadn't been a bad fall, just enough to shake her up. She'd not even mentioned it to Sterling before he left to hunt deer with Heron's husband and several other Menominee braves.

Cailin clasped her swollen middle and sat down. "Oh," she gasped. She let out her breath and waited. After a minute or two, she relaxed and shrugged. "It's nothing," she said in English to her friend. "I just—"

The next cramp seized her and doubled her up.

"We make ready for little one," Heron said.

"No, it can't be," Cailin insisted. "This is late January. I didn't expect the baby for another three weeks."

Heron chuckled. "Heron birth two. Baby come when baby come." Putting a sturdy arm under Cailin's shoulder, she helped her back to her own wigwam.

"Sterling said they wouldn't be back tonight," Cailin said as she sat down on her sleeping platform. Another pain rocked her, and she felt light-headed. She had known that childbirth was uncomfortable, but she hadn't thought that labor would come on so swiftly.

"Heron go for Pine Basket. She wise. Bring many children into world. Pine Basket have . . ." She used a word that Cailin couldn't understand but suspected meant a particular herb. "Make hurt less," Heron finished. Then she smiled and squeezed Cailin's hand. "No have fear, Sweet Spring. Tomorrow, you be happy with little one in your arms and proud husband."

Minutes passed, and the contractions came harder. Her water broke, soaking her legs with birth fluid.

Old Pine Basket was pleased. She stirred a handful of powdered root into a pot containing a few cups of water, and insisted that Cailin drink the warm, bitter liquid. Then she ordered the patient up on her feet. With the aid of two other women, they kept Cailin walking back and forth. "Earth pull child," she explained. "Mother sing, dance. Tea stop pain."

Pine Basket's brew did ease the pain. The contractions continued all afternoon and into the night. When Cailin could no longer walk, they stripped off her clothes and laid her on the smooth underside of a clean bison robe.

Sometime after midnight, the contractions slowed. When dawn came, the child had moved no farther down the birth canal, and Cailin was growing frantic.

The sun was high in the cloudless heavens when the hunting party returned. When Sterling reached Cailin's side, his face was bleak with worry.

She had not screamed when Pine Basket's tea no longer blocked the pain, but she couldn't help crying out when she saw Sterling.

"Shhh, shhh," he soothed. "I'm here." Seeing Cailin like this was a shock. Her hair was soaked with sweat, her lips were swollen and bleeding from being bitten, and her strained features revealed the agony she was in. "I'm here, and everything's going to be all right," he promised her.

"Dinna leave me," she pleaded.

"I won't leave you."

"You should not stay," Heron warned.

The other women were clearly disturbed by his presence. "They say that a man at a childbed is bad luck," Pine Basket mumbled.

"That's crazy," he said. "I wish I could take this pain from you, Cailin. Since I can't, the least I can do is to give you someone to hold on to." He took her hands and held them. Something was wrong. He felt it in his bones; he'd suspected it for hours. That's why he'd hurried home instead of staying out to try to bring down a few more deer. And now that he was with Cailin, he had no intention of being hustled off by a gaggle of women.

Heron frowned and whispered something that Sterling couldn't catch. Then she tapped his arm.

"Dinna go," Cailin said.

"I'm not," he assured her.

Heron tugged at his hand.

"I'm just going outside," he said to Cailin. "I'll be right back. I need to wash the deer blood off."

"Come back," she gasped. "Please."

Outside, he glanced at Heron. "What is it?"

The Menominee woman shook her head. "Bad. Very bad. Pine Basket say baby is turned." She motioned with her hands. "Not headfirst, but back and bottom."

"A breech birth?" His pulse quickened. He was no expert in midwifery, but even he knew that a breech birth was a difficult one, often ending in death for the child.

Heron shook her head. "Baby stuck. No come. If child no turn by self, baby die, mother die."

Sterling refused to accept what she was saying. "That's crazy. Can't you turn the child like you'd do a calf?"

Heron burst into tears. "Baby caught like beaver in trap. Pine Basket want to kill baby."

"What? What did you say?"

"Kill baby. Save mother." She wiped her tear-streaked face. "Pine Basket say, no choice. Baby will die. If she kill baby now, mother have chance have another baby."

"You're telling me that you want to kill our child, and that I may lose Cailin—Sweet Spring—as well?" Hot fear spilled through him. "Not Cailin," he swore. "I won't let her die. Not for a hundred babies."

He entered the wigwam with a sinking heart. Heron whispered to the women, and they all filed

out, leaving him alone with his wife. He knelt beside
her and took her hands.

"What is it?" she demanded of him. "The baby's
not dead?"

He wanted to lie—to tell that it was so—to take the
easy way out. But he couldn't. He'd hurt Cailin too
many times. If he betrayed her now, she'd never forgive him. "The baby's alive," he said, "but the
women say that it's breech."

"I was born breech. That's nothing," she protested
weakly. "My mother birthed me and two more."

"Heron believes that Pine Basket knows about
such things. She says that this baby will die ...
and ... " A lump rose in his throat and choked him.
"They want to take the child, Cailin ... to save your
life."

"Take it?" Another contraction seized her, and she
arched her back and dug her nails into his hands.
"What do you mean, *take it?* They want to murder
my baby?"

"They say it's a matter of time ... that the babe
will die anyway."

"And ye'd let them?" Her eyes caught the reflection from the glowing hearth and blazed like fire-
brands.

"I can't lose you, Cailin."

"No! No, I tell you. I don't care if I die. This is our
child. I'll have it, or we'll die together."

Sterling put his arms around her and hugged her
to him. "Think what you're saying," he begged her
as tremors of emotion wracked his frame. "We can
make another babe."

She stiffened again. And when the pain had run its
course, she whispered to him. "No. I'll nay agree.

And if ye truly love me as your wife, you'll stand by me in this, Sassenach."

He lifted her hand to his lips and kissed the center of her palm. "I'll stand by you, Cailin, but if you die on me, I'll—"

"I won't die, damn it," she gasped. "I won't." She reached up and clutched the amulet around her neck. "This is magic, remember," she said. "Whoever possesses the Eye of Mist has one wish. You remember, don't ye?" she begged him.

"I remember, Highlander." He'd never been a man for tears, but her image wavered in front of him as his eyes filled with moisture.

"The power of life and death," she murmured. "If there is a God up there, He won't blame me." Her fingers tightened on the golden pendant until her knuckles turned as white as tallow. "I, Cailin MacGreggor Gray, call on thee," she declared with the last of her strength. "Save my baby's life."

"Magic can't work unless you believe it," he said.

"I believe," she insisted. "Damn it. I believe in the amulet—in ghost wolves and fairies too, if that's what it takes to save our baby!"

Again, the pain came, and Cailin struggled to keep from screaming. "He has to live," she whispered hoarsely. "He must."

Heron entered the wigwam and moved to Sterling's side. He glanced at the Menominee woman. "She wants to keep trying," Sterling said. "She won't give up."

The Indian woman handed him a cup of water and a cloth. He used it to moisten Cailin's lips, and she nodded gratefully.

Heron put another log on the fire. The rest of the women came in. Pine Basket conferred with her companions and went to Cailin's side. "Up," she said in Algonquian.

"No!" Cailin cried.

Heron laid a hand on Cailin's head. "She will help you," she said. "No one will hurt your little one. Let us help you."

"Sterling!"

"Pine Basket only wants to get Sweet Spring on her feet again," Heron said.

"Not them," Cailin said to Sterling. "You."

He assisted her to her feet, and they began to walk in a small circle around the wigwam. Old Pine Basket tossed a handful of leaves onto the coals and began to chant. Heron took Cailin's other arm.

After the space of an hour, Cailin suddenly dropped onto her knees and groaned. "Something— something . . ." she managed.

Heron motioned to the sleeping platform. Sterling gathered her up in his arms and laid her back on the bearskin. Pine Basket peered between her legs and began to laugh.

"Hold her hands. Now!" Heron ordered.

Sterling did as he was told.

Cailin took a deep breath, strained, and pushed with all her might. And the bloody infant slipped out, feetfirst, into the old woman's wrinkled hands. "A little warrior!" Pine Basket proclaimed. "A man child."

"Is he all right?" Cailin demanded. "Is he—"

The loud wail of an angry baby answered her plea. In seconds, Pine Basket tied and severed the pulsing cord, and placed the naked infant into Sterling's arms. "Your son," she said proudly.

"Give him to me," Cailin begged. "Let me see him."

Carefully cradling the tiny head, he laid the screaming boy against Cailin's breast. He rooted until he found his mother's nipple, then began to suck lustily. Cailin laughed through her tears. "He's got hair," she said. "Look at all that black hair."

"At least he's not a redhead," Sterling teased, stroking the infant's sturdy back with two fingers. He glanced at the old woman anxiously.

She grinned, exposing white teeth worn down nearly to the gum. "Your woman is fine," she said. "Will bear you many sons."

Sterling leaned close to Cailin's ear. "I love you," he whispered.

"And I love you," she answered. Her eyes devoured the baby. "Look at him. Isn't he the most beautiful bairn you've ever seen? What shall we name him?"

He smiled at her. "I was thinking about Cameron," he admitted.

"Aye, that makes two of us," she confided. Her joyous laughter filled the last chink in his heart and made him whole.

Chapter 29

By the light of a full Shawnee moon, wee Cameron Gray crossed the Ohio River with his mother and father in a birch-bark canoe. The baby took no notice of the brilliant May moon hanging low in the sky, or of the virgin forest stretching on either side of the river, illuminated as clearly as some fairy kingdom. Snugly laced into his Menominee cradle board and strapped to his mother's back, he slept, unaware that each mile carried him closer to the sea and his future home along the Chesapeake.

Sterling, Cailin, and the infant had set out from the Menominee village lying in the natural triangle formed by the two great lakes, Superior and Michigan, on a brisk morning in April. Not wanting to risk the health of their newborn son, Sterling and Cailin had traveled slowly, stopping at friendly villages and passing from one tribe to another until they'd reached the first Shawnee town lying between the Falls and the Great Miami River.

At the village of Chalahgawtha, Sterling's Shawnee heritage assured them hospitality, but it was Cailin's shell bead bracelet that ensured the escort of fourteen armed braves and the loan of canoes and provisions

375

to take them east to the Great Shell Fish Bay, the Chesapeake. "A sister of the peace woman does not need to ask," the Shawnee shaman had said. "We are honored to offer assistance."

Now, the same canoes that had carried them across the swift-flowing Ohio followed the twisting course of the Kentucky River south and east to a point near the junction of the Konhawa River.

Cailin felt as though she'd been traveling forever. She'd rapidly regained her strength after childbirth, and now, the long days of traveling on foot and by canoe had added to her feeling of well-being. For the first time in her life, she was truly happy. Culloden and the deaths of so many of her kin no longer shadowed her dreams. Somewhere in the peace of the great trees and endless sky, she'd forgiven Sterling for killing Johnnie MacLeod and for being part of the English military.

Laughter came easily between them and was as easily shared with their fierce companions. It was impossible for Cailin to wake without anticipation and wonder for the day ahead. Cameron's tiny face, sturdy body, and baby antics were an unending source of delight for both his parents.

And somewhere on the trail, Cailin and Sterling had come to a decision about her loved ones in Scotland. "A letter can cross the ocean from Annapolis to Glasgow in less than three months," her husband had assured her. "I'll write to friends I knew in the military and to families near your home who remained loyal to King George during the rebellion, promising a reward for information about your family. And once we make contact, I'll provide passage to Maryland for them if they want to come. If they don't, we can provide support for your young half-brother until he's of legal age. I can see that he's educated as befits a laird's son."

"And if our letters come to nothing?" she'd asked.

"Then you and Cameron will remain in Maryland while I go and hunt the rascals out. I'll find them, Cailin," he'd promised. "I swear it. If your father told the truth about the inheritance he left you, money won't be a problem. If he didn't, then I'll sell part of my land to get it."

The compromise was what she needed to satisfy the vow she'd made. Never would she risk Cameron's life by taking him on an ocean voyage, and leaving him behind was impossible to consider. He and Sterling were her world, and if Sterling said he'd find her grandfather, her sister, and Corey, then he would. She'd learned that Sterling was a man who kept his word, a rare treasure even in her native Highlands.

"Will we rebuild your plantation?" she asked him the morning they forded the Konhawa River and started walking due east.

"Not for a few years," he'd replied. "The Mohawk have a long memory. They have a new sachem and a new shaman by now, but I'm certain there's still a bounty on our scalps. I'd like to keep you and Cameron closer to the settlements until danger of war with the hostiles is over. Unless you'd consider remaining in Annapolis while I work the plantation alone."

She'd scoffed at that. "Nay likely, Sassenach."

"Why did I think that would be your reaction?"

"I couldn't say, not for the life of me," she answered sweetly. They'd both laughed at that, and little Cameron had opened his eyes, puckered up his face, and demanded to be fed in no uncertain terms.

Cailin shifted his cradle board, unlaced him, and tucked him into the curve of her arm so that he could nurse.

"If you aren't a rich heiress, times may be tough for us," Sterling warned. "I spent every coin I had on building the first time."

"Dinna fash yourself," she said, her gaze riveted on the precious bundle tugging at her breast. "This is our treasure. If we have him, what else do we need?"

It was June when they strode down the hill toward Annapolis harbor. Cailin was not oblivious to the stares and murmurs of curious townfolk. The Shawnee warriors had turned back the night before, but even without an honor guard of savages, Cailin attracted enough attention with her Indian buckskins, dark-haired infant in a cradle board, and beaded headband.

By the time they reached the market square at the water's edge, a group of gaping children and busybodies were trailing after them. A horse auction was in progress, amid a score of farmers selling produce, live chickens, fresh fish, servant indentures, and bags of wool. It had been Sterling's intention to hire a small boat and crew to carry them to Lord Kentington's plantation, but as they crossed the crowded common, Cailin stopped short—her sun-tanned face as suddenly pale as if she'd seen a ghost.

"What's wrong?" Sterling asked.

"There. That man," she whispered in shocked tones. She tried to keep her voice normal, but it was impossible. Those shoulders, that square head, and the wrinkled Scots bonnet could belong to no one else on earth.

"Which man?" he demanded.

She shook off Sterling's hand and took a few steps closer to the giant balancing a live pig on one shoulder. The pig's feet were bound and its snout was wrapped tightly with twine, but it weighed close to a hundred pounds, and it could still struggle mightily. "Big Fergus! Big Fergus, is that you?" she called, unconsciously switching to Gaelic.

The big man turned around, and a grin split his homely face from ear to ear. And Cailin saw the boy who'd been hidden by Fergus's massive bulk.

"Corey!" she screamed. "Corey MacLoed!"

The child saw her and began to run. Close on his heels ran a black and white sheepdog. "Cailin!" the boy cried above the sharp joyous barking of the dog. "Cailin!"

Forrest Wescott took them home on his sloop, not to New Westover, but to the land Cailin had inherited from Cameron Stewart, the plantation he called Scot's Haven. There, she put her infant son into her grandfather's arms and shed tears of joy as she listened to the tale of Corey's adventures as he'd struggled to find her.

"When Corey and Big Fergus came back to Glen Garth, your sister and that man of hers had already left for Canada. There was nothing else to do but bring the boy to you," James Stewart explained.

"But how?" Cailin demanded. She couldn't keep her hands off Corey or her grandfather. She kept stroking their hair and touching their faces to assure herself that they were real and not just a figment of her imagination. She'd even given Big Fergus a hug and a kiss, and she'd gotten down on her knees to hug old Lance. The sheepdog kept butting her with his head and burying his wet nose into her hand.

"Good boy, good Lance," she said. "How did you get here, Grandda?"

"'Twas easy enough, once we made our way past the English soldiers and out of Scotland," her grandfather boasted. "I may be sightless, but I'm not stupid. I kenned well enough that Cameron Stewart was your father and that he lived in America. I counted on finding someone at his London estates who would find us passage to this wilderness. His solicitor wasted no time in putting us on a ship, and we've taken our ease here waiting for ye to come home ever since. 'Tis time, too. The laddie's been running free as an Indian himself. Time he had school."

"Ye didna come as ye promised," Corey reminded her. "We thought ye might be in danger, so we decided to come and rescue ye. I would have gone into the woods looking for ye, Big Fergus and me, but Grandda pleaded his age. We stayed to watch over him."

"A good job they've done too," her grandfather said. "This house is so big that it's taken me a while to learn to find my way around it."

"Don't listen to him," Corey teased. "He pretends to be helpless so that the housekeeper, Mistress MacCarthy, will see to his every whim. I think Grandda's sweet on her."

"Be that true, Grandda?" Cailin asked him.

"None of your cheek, lass," he retorted. "A man's never too old to like a soft place to lay his head. When I stop smiling at the women is the day ye can lay me in my grave."

Cailin barely had time to walk through the halls of Scot's Haven and inspect the stables and outbuildings before Forrest's sloop returned to her dock with Moonfeather and a host of other relatives whom she didn't know.

Cailin put Cameron into his father's arms and ran down the oyster-shell path to meet her sister. Again, tears and hugs were given and received, and both women tried to talk at the same time.

"You must see our little Cameron," Cailin said. "We named him after ..."

Moonfeather wiped the tears from her smooth, honey-colored cheeks. "Father would be proud," she replied. "He died well. Quickly, without being taken by the Iroquois."

"How do ye know?" Cailin asked. "Are ye sure?"

"A wolf told me in a dream," the peace woman answered softly. "It is so."

Sterling came down the walk and handed Moonfeather the baby. "We brought home a little keepsake from Menominee country," he said. "Cameron Gray, meet your Aunt Moonfeather."

She laughed and held the infant high. He reached out with chubby hands and grabbed her dark hair. "Aunt Moonfeather is too much for him to say," the peace woman replied. "My father called me Leah. Aunt Leah will do very nicely for this young laddie."

"The amulet was real," Cailin said. "We nearly lost him, but—"

"Shhh," Moonfeather said. "Magic is best not spoken of, only cherished ... as we shall cherish this little one." She looked into Cailin's eyes. "He carries the best of two worlds in his bloodline. Indian and European. In time to come, the red man will vanish, but we will leave something in the hearts and minds of young ones like this."

"Is it true?" Sterling asked as he put a strong arm

around Cailin's shoulders. "Did Cameron Stewart leave this plantation to Cailin?"

"He did," Moonfeather assured them. She kissed little Cameron's cheeks and nuzzled his neck. "Ye have a rich wife, if that matters to ye . . . a very, very rich wife."

Sterling grinned down at Cailin. "I'll not leave her because of it," he teased.

"I should hope not," she said.

"If you can stand a few more reunions, there are some people who have been wanting to meet you," Moonfeather said with shining eyes. "Your sister Anne, your sister Fiona, my husband Brandon, Anne's husband Ross, Fiona's husband Wolf Shadow—"

"So many?" Cailin cried.

"Aye, little sister," Moonfeather answered. "And many more. There are your nieces and nephews and more wee ones than you can imagine. Many have prayed for your safe return."

Trembling, Cailin looked up at Sterling. For once, she was too full of emotion to speak.

He leaned down and kissed her mouth with slow tenderness, then found the words for her. "We'd best go and make them welcome, Cailin, Cameron, and I."

Cailin held out her arms for the baby. He crowed with excitement and put out a tiny starfish hand to seize his mother's golden amulet. Cooing happily, he popped the shiny pendant into his mouth and gummed it in utter contentment.

"Once the separate pieces of the Eye of Mist were one," Moonfeather murmured. "It may be that the Great Spirit wishes them to be one again."

"Aye," Cailin agreed. She glanced up at Sterling.

He nodded. "What your father divided, you can make whole."

Moonfeather smiled. "So. The circle is complete."

Sterling's hand tightened on Cailin's. And together, the three of them walked down the hill toward the sparkling waters of the Chesapeake and the American family that awaited them.

Chapter 30

~~~ ◦◯◦ ~~~

Scot's Haven Plantation
Maryland Colony
May 1758

Cailin allowed her footman Guy to assist her down from her coach onto the marble steps at the main entrance of the manor house. "Bring that large pigskin chest first," she instructed the slender, tow-haired servant. "That has my gifts for Sterling and the children. Tell Robert that I said he is to help ye bring in the rest of my boxes. Be especially careful with the china, and remind Edgar that the new black and white pony is to be brought around to the garden after breakfast tomorrow. It's a gift for wee Master Jasper's birthday, and I want it to be a surprise. None of the bairns are to see the pony until then."

"Yes, mistress, I'll tell him." He pursed his thin lips. "Won't be easy keeping them out of the stables. Miss Kelsie spends so much time in the barn, Edgar says—"

"This time Edgar must be firm with my inquisitive daughter. He is the head groom. I want nothing to spoil Jasper's birthday."

Guy murmured a proper reply, bowed, and hurried back to enlist the coachman's help in unloading her belongings.

Cailin paused for a moment and looked up at the house with a sudden rush of emotion. Home, she thought giddily. Her visit to Williamsburg had been exciting, with a never-ending round of parties and shopping, but after two weeks at her niece Cami's magnificent home on the James River, she was ready to return to Sterling's arms and the noisy clamor of her children.

Corey's reports from his second year at William and Mary were excellent, and despite his late start at a real education, Cami's husband, Sir Miles, had assured her that Corey had a real future as a barrister in Williamsburg. Corey had chosen not to come home this summer, but to remain behind with Fergus and assist Sir Miles's solicitor in his office near the royal governor's palace. Cami suspected that part of the attraction was a Miss Mary Randolph, but she'd met the girl and was well-pleased with her little brother's choice in lassies.

Moonfeather and Brandon's oldest daughter, Cami, had surprised everyone by marrying into one of Virginia's finest families after the death of her first husband. Despite the distance between Scot's Haven and Williamsburg, Cailin and Cami had become as close as any sisters. Cami had been among those who'd come to welcome Cailin to Scot's Haven ten years ago. The two had gotten along well at once, and they'd continued their friendship by letters and regular visits.

Cami had been sorry to miss Jasper's birthday fete on the morrow, but one of her stepdaughters was near lying-in, and Cami couldn't get away. She promised to be with them in August for her mother's birthday celebration at New Westover. Anne and Fiona would be there, as well as their husbands, children, and grandchildren, not to mention an assortment of Shawnee and Delaware Indian relations, most of whom Cailin had never been able to sort out.

Of course, both Anne and Moonfeather and their immediate families would be joining them for Jasper's party. It never failed to thrill Cailin how dear her recently acquired sisters, nieces, nephews, and in-laws had become to her, and how important they were in everyday life in the Maryland Colony. Especially Brandon and Moonfeather, she mused . . .

The double entrance doors swung open, and Hannah's exclamation ended Cailin's reverie. "Miss Cailin! What you doin' standin' out here like some poor relation? Has Guy lost his good sense, not openin' the door for you? Welcome home, miss'us. We sure missed you."

"It's not Guy's fault," Cailin said. "And I missed all of you too."

Sally, the newest maid, peered around Hannah's substantial bulk and stammered an echo of the housekeeper's warm greeting. "Welcome home, miss'us." Hannah flashed her a withering glance, and Sally blushed and dropped to an awkward curtsy. "Miss'us."

Cailin entered the spacious front hall and glanced around her. Everything seemed in place. Not like last time, when she'd come home to find Cameron's pet fox chasing a hen up the grand staircase, and the time before that, when a clan of visiting Delaware Indians had taken up residence in the east wing.

She pulled off her gloves and dropped them on the hall table. The walnut finish gleamed, free of dust and small fingerprints. Cailin smiled. Hannah had been very busy in her absence. "Where's Master Sterling? And the children?"

Sally shrugged and blinked. "Don't know, miss'us."

Cailin glanced at Hannah.

"We weren't expecting you until tomorrow, miss. Master Jasper is across the river at New Westover. He spent the night with Lady Kentington's grandsons."

Cailin removed her wide-brimmed hat and handed it to Sally. "Kelsie's nay in the house either?"

"No, miss'us," Sally replied.

"Surely Nurse and the twins are—"

"No, Miss Cailin," Hannah said. "Nurse Alice's father took a bad turn last week, and she had to go 'cross the bay to tend to him."

"Who's been looking after the bairns? Becky?"

"Becky and Jane done most of the runnin' after the big'uns," Hannah said, "but Becky can't do nothing with the twins when they get in one of them moods. The master has been takin' charge."

"Of the twins?" Cailin asked. "Sterling?" She couldn't stifle a giggle. "Wasn't he supposed to be meeting Baron Lee in Annapolis this week about the new tobacco shipments?"

"He said the baron would have to wait till you got home, miss," Hannah said. Her own amusement was obvious. "He said that without Nurse Alice here, he wouldn't set a foot offen this place until you got back."

Cailin walked into the dining room. The table was set for the evening meal; an arrangement of fresh flowers adorned the Irish hunt board. The odor of baking bread drifted from the kitchen wing. The room was immaculate, the fireplace brass shone, and new candles stood in the silver candlesticks. A yellow tabby cat dozed in a woven basket on the hearth. Not a single child's boot or discarded toy marred the chamber's perfection.

"Have my children all been kidnapped by pirates?" Cailin declared. Order was a nice change, but the house was too perfect—too quiet. "Are they all well, Hannah? No one's sick?" A pang of guilt tugged at her conscience. The twins were only fifteen months old; she'd never left them for more than a single night before. She'd only gone without the children because one of Cami's daughters had had the chicken pox, and Jasper had been so sick with the pox two years before, she hadn't wanted the littlest ones to be exposed yet.

"No, miss." Hannah beamed. "They're as full of spit and ginger as ever. Miss Kelsie put molasses in Master Cameron's riding boots, and he glued her new hat to the nursery table. Baby Leah ate half a moth yesterday morn, and the other twin—"

"Enough, Hannah!" Cailin cried in exasperation. "Not a thing happens on Scot's Haven that ye dinna know. Where is my husband? And where are my bairns?"

"I did hear some whooping coming from the far end of the orchard," Hannah admitted. "But that was a while ago."

"We'll see," Cailin replied. She went back into the hall and hurried through the house and out the back garden entrance. Down the steps she went, then followed the path past the boxwood maze and the statue walk, and through the opening in the hedge to the lane that led to the peach orchard.

Seth, the head gardener, raised his hat as she passed. "Welcome home, mistress," he called.

"Have you seen my husband?" she asked.

His plain Welsh face split in a grin, and he pointed toward the river. "I'd be careful if I was you,

ma'am," he warned. "Sounds like some mighty fierce
Injuns down there."

As she started through the peach trees, two black
and white half-grown pups and their mother, Flo,
came running up to wag their tails and demand her
affection. Cailin crouched down and rubbed heads all
around. "Someone's glad to see me at least," she
murmured.

Overhead, a mockingbird trilled its cheery song.
She looked up to catch a glimpse of it through the
new leaves. Peach blossoms were drifting down
around her, landing on her head and dress and filling
the air with a heavenly aroma. Several black-faced
sheep grazed at the base of the trees. None seemed
concerned enough about the dogs to look up from
their steady munching.

"I'm getting close," Cailin said. "Wherever the
dogs are, my bairns aren't far away." She quickened
her pace, eager for Sterling's embrace and the sweet,
sticky hugs and kisses of her babes. "Sterling!" she
called. "Kelsie? Where are ye?"

Another pup, yipping with excitement, scrambled
out of the trees to join the pack trailing after Cailin.
The smallest of the last litter, this one was pure black
with a white spot on his nose. He was Kelsie's favor-
ite. She'd named him Midnight, Silky, Lucky, and
Lancelot in turn. Cailin wondered if the pup had gotten another new name in her absence.

At the far end of the orchard was a gentle slope
and another hedge. Beyond that, ancient oak and
beech trees grew down to the river. The trees were so
big that the branches formed an intertwined canopy
overhead, leaving the moss-covered forest floor clear
of underbrush, and creating a natural park.

As Cailin stepped through the arch of hedge, she

looked around for her family. To her disappointment, the place seemed empty. "Sterling?" she called again.

Silence. Then, she heard one childish giggle.

A Shawnee war whoop screeched in her ear as a feathered and painted Sterling leaped out from behind the hedge and grabbed her. Immediately, Kelsie and Cameron popped out from behind trees and threw themselves at their mother.

"Where are my babies?" she demanded, amid the hugs and shouts. "What have you done with—"

A sheepish-looking maid backed out from behind a beech tree with a squirming toddler under each arm. Cailin took one look at Becky's war-painted face and chicken-feather headdress and burst out laughing.

"Weren't my idea, Miss Cailin," Becky protested. "Miss Kelsie—"

"Come to Mama!" Cailin cried, holding out her arms for the twins. Johnnie spied his mother and began to giggle. Little Leah squealed with delight. Becky thrust both of them into Cailin's embrace. The added weight was enough to throw the lot of them off balance, and Sterling, Cailin, and the children fell down on the thick moss carpet in a flurry of arms and legs.

As usual, confusion reigned at first, but eventually the squirming mass came to rest. Cailin lay back in the circle of Sterling's arms and rested her head against his chest. Babies and bairns surrounded them, all, Cailin noticed, streaked with yellow and blue paint and wearing various items of Shawnee apparel. The twins had circles of paint around each eye and beads woven into their dark hair. Kelsie's mass of unruly red hair was confined with a beaded headband, and she was weighed down by one of Sterling's ceremonial hunting shirts.

"Ye didna miss me at all, did ye?" Cailin teased.

"What did you bring us, Mama?" Kelsie demanded.

"Daddy said you weren't coming until tomorrow," Cameron added, pulling Johnnie onto his lap. Leah yanked at Cailin's earring, and her twin began to chew on a chicken feather. Somehow, a pup squirmed into the center of the pile and began to lick Kelsie's cheek.

"I'm here today, and I brought presents," Cailin said. "Shall I go away and come back tomorrow?"

"No!" the two oldest shouted in unison.

"Nay!" Johnnie crowed.

"Aye," little Leah cried.

"Since you're here, woman, I suppose we'll keep you," Sterling teased. He tilted Cailin's chin and kissed her lips tenderly. "We've been lost without you," he added huskily. "You are the heart and soul of this family."

She sighed, savoring the joy of having her loved ones close around her. She was sorry that Jasper wasn't home as well, but he'd be back later, and his visit to Moonfeather's would make it easier to keep his birthday pony a secret until tomorrow. He wasn't the only one who would be surprised, she thought, unconsciously touching her already thickening waist. She had something wonderful to tell Sterling as well . . . but that could wait until they were alone in bed tonight.

"I love ye all," she said happily. "I think I love ye all more each time I come home."

Sterling kissed her again.

"Daddy," Cameron admonished, "Mama brought us presents. Can't we—"

"All things in good time," Sterling answered. "Right now is time for hugging." He put both arms tightly around Cailin and clasped her tightly against him.

You're the light of my life, he thought passionately. You always were, from the first moment I laid eyes on you in my vision years ago. You're my strength and my guardian angel, and I'd never want to live a day without you. He lowered his head and whispered in her ear. "Any chance we can get away from the children for an hour?"

She laughed. "Not a chance," she answered.

"Later," he promised her, "I have something for you."

"And I have something for you," she said.

Cameron tugged anxiously at his hand. "Daddy, come on. I want to see what—"

Kelsie pulled at her mother. "We want to see what Mama brought us."

Cailin winked at him mischievously. "Later," she murmured.

"I'll hold you to that," he said.

Still laughing merrily, she rose and lifted Johnnie in her arms. Sterling scooped up baby Leah and followed Cailin and the other children back up the rise into the peach orchard and into the full light of another day.